CHRISTINA SKYE

BRIDE OF THE MIST

AVON BOOKS ◆ NEW YORK

AVON BOOKS, INC.
1350 Avenue of the Americas
New York, New York 10019

Copyright © 1996 by Roberta Helmer
Cover art by Judy Unger
Inside cover author photo by Bill Morris Studio
Published by arrangement with the author
Visit our website at http://www.AvonBooks.com
Library of Congress Catalog Card Number: 95-95179
ISBN: 0-380-78278-2

First Avon Books Printing: May 1996

AVON TRADEMARK REG. U.S. PAT. OFF. AND IN OTHER COUNTRIES, MARCA REGISTRADA, HECHO EN U.S.A.

Printed in the U.S.A.

WCD 10 9 8 7 6 5

With warmest thanks . . .

to Earl Martin, for ensuring that all the remotes, receivers, and circuits were where they should be, *when* they should be;

Helen Woolverton, for leaving no stone unturned;

Peggy Kulp, for being superwoman;

and Melinda Joy Miller, for so generously sharing her firsthand experiences with fêng-shui.

And to Lucy Morris, a shining example of all the reasons independent bookstores are here to stay; and for all the Ladies of the Club: Vickie, Ginny, Lucy, Barbara, Kim, Terri, Betsy, Oneta, Debbie, Chris, Trish, Penny, Misty, Kristy, and especially Loretta.

From the lone shieling of the misty island
Mountains divide us, and the waste of seas;
Yet still the blood is strong, the heart is Highland
And we in dreams behold the Hebrides.

—ANONYMOUS BALLAD, NINETEENTH CENTURY

Prologue ～

The rising moon hung like molten silver, scarred by the dark trees dotting the hillside. Beneath the silent walls of the weathered fourteenth-century English abbey, the swans had folded their heads and gone to rest.

Nothing moved by the Witch's Pool. Nothing crossed the cliffs by Lyon's Leap.

Only one lone figure eased from the shadows, his tall frame wrapped in black. At his wrists, cuffs of fine Belgian lace drifted in the wind. His face was hard, worn by old cares, and his mouth was tense as he studied the restless night.

Nothing shook the implacable silence.

And yet he felt something there.

His eyes moved over the patchwork of fields and ancient hedgerows, each one known and well loved. As he watched, a cloud of birds shot from the hill, scattered like inkblots over the violet sky.

Beside his foot the bushes twitched and a great gray cat eased through the soft grass, his amber eyes unblinking.

Adrian Draycott, the abbey's guardian ghost, reached down, running a practiced hand over the cat's soft gray fur. "It has begun, I fear."

The cat's tail arched. His head cocked.

"You are wrong, my old friend. There will always be danger. The world does not change. That is why our abbey has such need of us."

1

Close by, a small creature rustled through the foliage. The cat tensed. Ears back, he waited, every muscle rigid. Control finally conquered thousands of years of instinct. With a soft hiss, the cat relaxed once more.

"The hunt would be good tonight, and yet you forsake it for me, Gideon. Too much homage you do me, old friend." Adrian Draycott looked off into the darkness. "But perhaps there will be a different hunt afoot."

Down the hill came the low, sad chime of distant church bells. Before their sound had begun to fade, the abbey ghost had melted back into the shadows, black against starker black, the gray cat close at his side.

One ~

She was shaking.

It was the middle of the night, the moon a hard curve of silver above darkened New York streets, and Kara Fitzgerald was racked with tremors.

She sat up, blanket rumpled, clutched to her chest as spasms raced through her legs.

Not again, she prayed desperately. Not *now*.

The prayers didn't help, nor did the trembling fingers she dug into cool sheets of Irish linen.

Moonlight played over a leather-bound Gaelic dictionary lying open on a tartan of bold red and green. The haunting strains of a Scottish ballad drifted from her radio.

It had to be the music, she told herself wildly. Tuned low and then forgotten, it had reached out to her mind while she'd dozed in the middle of her Scottish research. Even now the clear melody rose in a poignant lament.

Kara Fitzgerald's nerves were stretched taut as she closed her eyes against cold images that brushed at her like mist. Somewhere she heard the hiss of distant voices.

Just dreams, she told herself. The quaking climbed up her knees and seized her arms. The result of one too many stirring Scottish tales, she told herself.

She huddled in a tight, miserable ball, watching shadows play over the bed.

Ignore it.

3

Her jaw began to clench. *Ignore it?* She could have laughed—at any other time than this.

Hold it back. Drown the words out with brighter sounds and truer dreams. Sweat ringed her brow in beads as cold began to inch up her fingers, a sign she had come to recognize with terrible certainty. There would be no escaping her visions now. Soon she would see a face in some distant place, hear the words of a stranger who desperately needed her help. It always began for Kara this way—first the shaking, then the cold.

Beside her bed a phone began to ring.

Let it ring.

The shrill crying continued.

Ignore it.

Barbs of fear climbed her spine. Light played behind her eyes, heavy with images and sound, sharp with meanings only she could see.

She didn't move, couldn't say the words of protection that would let her senses reach out in phantom contact with a stranger's mind.

The prickling grew to a stab. Her knees began to shake.

Danger in the touch. Danger in the seeing.

All around her the dark sense of danger rose, gray and shifting like cold mist drifting over a wild Hebridean shore. Kara bit her lip as she recognized the gathering shadows in her head.

This time death was involved. In fact, it was certain, unless she opened her mind and reached out to help.

She raised the phone receiver with trembling fingers. "Hello."

"Sorry to bother you, Kara."

She knew the voice. She knew the room it came from, a crowded police squad room on the edge of midtown Manhattan, a place filled with the raw smells of anger and the sounds of despair.

Kara had heard the police detective's voice a half dozen times over the last year, always in the cold, sharp hours before dawn. Always with news of a missing child or a battered, unrecognizable body or an anonymous threat of brutal death. "Hello, Amanda." There was resignation in Kara's voice. "You need me again?"

"I'm afraid so." In spite of fifteen years away from the rolling mountains of western North Carolina, Detective First Class Amanda Rivington's voice still held the soft trace of southern cadences. Tonight it also held an edge of shredding control, something that Kara had never heard before. "Two students from the East Seventies are missing. Both from prominent Upper East Side families with pedigrees that go back to the Mayflower. The parents are highly visible—old money, old politics. They also happen to own major real estate in upper Manhattan." Her voice tightened. "The ransom letter came in an hour ago."

"A prank? Teenagers have been known to stage their own kidnappings."

"Not these kids. No history of problems in school or at home. And there are signs of violent removal from the car where they were sitting while waiting for a friend."

Kara felt another cold stab of fear. "Why call me, Amanda?"

"Because the scene is bare. The F.B.I. is in, but none of our forensics people can find anything, not one hair or nail scraping. There are signs of smudges on the rear window, indicating that the kidnappers used gloves, but there are no usable prints. If any blood was spilled, it's been wiped clean. In short, this is a damned professional job, Kara."

Silence pressed at Kara's chest, heavy and threatening. "Are you sure no one else can help?"

"Right now I've got four angry parents and probably twenty journalists camped outside my office, and they're all screaming for answers. Meanwhile, we're getting nowhere, the FBI is being damned tight-lipped, as usual, and I've a bad feeling that our time is running out. Just give it a look, okay? Touch the ransom note. See what you can get." The police officer coughed softly. "I'd be grateful. And your involvement would be strictly off the record, of course."

"Of course."

Irritation laced Amanda Rivington's well-bred voice. Kara could almost see the detective's elegant mahogany lips fold down in a frown. "Listen, that's not *my* choice. You're the one who insists on staying anonymous. You're the one who refuses compensation or credit for your input. You know, if you'd just come back and work for us, we'd give you full credit for your work. You could do a lot of good, Kara. This time you'd have unqualified support around here, from the top on down. Not like before. In fact, the word is—"

"The word is no, Amanda." Kara made her voice hard, though the tremors were slamming her like storm waves now. "It got so I couldn't see anything but pain and fear. Dead bodies followed me down lonely streets at night. Do you know what that's like?" Kara caught a ragged breath. "I'll help you when I can, when it's absolutely essential, but I won't go back. Not ever."

The striking black detective, the first woman ever to hold full detective status in her precinct, gave a slow, irritated sigh. Kara could imagine her pinching the bridge of her nose. "I hear you, Kara. Now you listen to me. These are *kids*, barely fourteen. And they're both girls."

Jennifer, Kara thought. Amanda's daughter was fourteen.

"I'm sorry, Kara. Sometimes this job feels a long way from Asheville, North Carolina. Sometimes I think I'd be better there than in this war zone."

Kara's fingers dug into the tartan throw on her bed. The wall of gray around her was getting denser. "What do you have for me to work with?"

"The ransom request came in on white typing paper. Standard dot-matrix printer. Postmarked in Michigan on paper without any identifying marks. The envelope is clean."

"You know paper isn't my best medium."

"We've also got an earring from the car, though that's confidential information. It must have come off during the removal." Amanda's voice tightened as she added, "It's silver.".

Kara shivered.

Metal worked best. Metal sent Kara's blood humming and set up an almost palpable psychometric link that flooded her mind with an explosive rush of images.

Metal was also very dangerous. With metal, the power of the link was so strong that Kara sometimes had to fight to break psychic contact.

"Kara?"

"Give me thirty minutes."

"I'll come to your apartment." Hesitation. "Look, Kara, my daughter's fourteen. All her friends are fourteen. It might be Jennifer out there right now, terrified and hungry. Bound and gagged. Maybe worse. I can't get that thought out of my mind."

"That's what makes you such a good detective, Amanda. Even after all these years, you find a way to keep it personal." Kara sighed. "I'll . . . do what I can."

When she hung up, her body was tense with cold. She tugged on a heavy sweater of oiled wool and looked down at the magazines scattered over her bed. Peat fires and slate-roofed castles. Endless shimmering lochs wrapped in mist. From the radio a classic *piobaireachd* for solo piper teased the silence.

Kara closed her eyes. Scotland would come later, she told herself.

Right now she had two lonely, frightened girls to find.

When her doorbell rang thirty minutes later, two candles framed the old wing chair and Vivaldi soared through the room.

Amanda Rivington's face wore the look of someone who needed a vacation, but she glanced around her with approval at the bolts of muted tartan plaid. "Scottish phase?"

"I'm researching our next issue. I've found a wonderful old castle on the Scottish coast that will be perfect for *New Bride*'s annual honeymoon special."

"That magazine again." Amanda sniffed. "Instead of writing rhapsodies about bridal veils and articles about honeymoon havens, you could be saving lives."

Kara stiffened. "I *am* saving lives. Starting with mine and going from there to every woman who's ever agonized over what kind of vows will bless her union best and what kind of location will make her and her groom feel wonderful and happy and at ease for the most important ceremony of their lives. I'm touching far more people now that I ever could in that rickety desk in Midtown East."

"Okay, okay." It was an old argument, and Amanda threw up her hands in resignation. "I'm not denying that you inform and entertain or that *New Bride* magazine is a major success. It's just—well, damn it, Kara, you have a unique gift, and I hate to see you squander it." The police officer sighed. "I didn't mean that the way it sounded."

"In that case, I won't take it the way it sounded." Kara straightened her shoulders. "Can we stop arguing and begin?"

After a moment Amanda drew a plastic bag out of her pocket. "Here's the earring. I didn't touch anything. I don't need to tell you that I had to bend a few rules to get it removed from custody." She smiled just a little, suggesting she had enjoyed bending those rules. "It came bagged straight from the crime scene unit."

Kara sank down into the wing chair and let the crashing violin strains of Vivaldi sustain her. Eyes closed and breathing slowed, she held out her hand.

When the small curve of metal hit Kara's palm, her stomach twisted in a knot of pain. Her face paled, stark against the wild vitality of her deep auburn hair. As her fingers slid carefully over the cool metal earring, images raced into her mind.

Her words came low and jerky. "The girls—surprised. The men came out of nowhere. Three—three of them. Sitting in a van." The images grew, became sharper, until they filled her head. "A pungent smell. Some kind of drug, maybe. It's cold, and I think there's the sound of water nearby . . ."

Inches away, Detective Amanda Rivington clicked on a small tape recorder, pulled out a notebook, and began to scrawl rapid notes.

Kara's hair was dark with sweat when she sank back against an old chintz cushion an hour later. Her hands were limp. Dark images continued to spill through her mind like the shadows that prowled the dangerous streets of lower Manhattan twenty floors below.

Pulling free of those shadows had been even harder than Kara had expected.

But Amanda was smiling. "You did good, Kara. Now we have someplace to start, probably over by the East River. We might be able to fix a location by the timing of those ferry horns you heard." Abruptly Amanda frowned down at Kara. "Listen, you want a blanket or something? You're trembling like a schoolgirl who's just spotted Keanu Reeves."

"I don't know about Keanu, but a—a blanket would be nice." Kara's teeth chattered slightly as a tartan blanket was pulled over her legs.

The policewoman carefully rebagged the earring, then studied Kara's sweating face. "How about something to drink before I go? I make a darned good cup of tea. Or maybe you need something stronger right now."

"I'll be fine." Kara pulled the wool tartan closer about her body. "If I get anything else—about the girls—I'll let you know."

"It matters, Kara. Just remember that."

Kara didn't answer, her fingers listless and pale against the soft wool.

"I'll close up when I go."

"Thanks, Amanda. Just . . . tired. Need to rest. Close my mind."

"Sure, honey."

Behind Kara, the door closed softly. The night was quiet except for the backfire of a passing truck.

But Kara could have sworn that bagpipes echoed dimly from somewhere in the distance.

Sunlight spilled over Kara's shoulders as she stood in the chaos of a sunny studio on West Fortieth Street two days later. A felt pen was anchored in the chaos of her deep red hair, and bolts of Battenburg lace spilled over a table beside a curtainless window. The sun emphasized the pallor of Kara's face, and her eyes carried shadows that hadn't been there a week earlier.

"Megan, did those four damask bridal gowns come in from London yet?"

Kara's assistant was twenty-five, with wide green eyes and an astonishing mass of freckles that left her looking about sixteen. The guileless look was deceptive, however. She was famous for her organizational abilities, and her mind was like a computer from which no detail strayed.

Megan O'Hara smiled as she pointed to a metal rack crammed with plastic-covered garments. "The gowns are right over there."

"And the flatware for the Tiffany shoot?"

"Left bottom shelf, opposite your desk."

"What desk?" Kara squinted down at an expanse of utilitarian gray metal buried beneath fabric swatches, telexes, and watercolor sketches.

The skin around Megan's eyes crinkled with fine lines of laughter. "The sketches for the new bridal veils are in your third drawer, right beneath the filigree earrings you hate and your receipts from last month's photographic shoot in St. Bart's."

Kara raised her eyes skyward. "What would I do without her? No, don't tell me. I don't want to know." She reached for the drawer, only to stop, frowning. "Have we had any answer to the last fax we sent to that man in Scotland?"

Megan looked uncomfortable. "You mean about renting the castle? For our honeymoon issue?"

"Of course I mean that. Megan, what's wrong?"

"Nothing. I just want to be certain we're talking about the same man."

"We're talking about Lord Dunraven, of Dunraven Castle. The same man we've been faxing for a week now!"

"You never know." Megan picked at a tiny speck of lint on her sleeve. "After all, he did have a brother. At least I think he did."

"My research was curiously vague on the subject, but I gather the brother died five years ago. There was some kind of boating accident in South America." Kara laughed tightly. "After all the research I've done, I could probably quote you the whole lineage of the illustrious Dunraven clan. All except the current generation and this mysterious brother. Stop stalling and tell me the truth. We heard, didn't we? And Lord Dunraven said no again."

Kara's assistant stared fixedly at a row of prints tacked on a corkboard wall. Mist coiled over moors purple with heather, and seabirds rocked like tiny ships in a sheltered ocean cove. Her hand tightened, hidden behind her back. "Not exactly. What he actually said was—"

Kara snatched the sheet of paper from Megan's fingers, her eyes darkening with fury as she scanned the fax that had just come in from Scotland. " 'Lord Dunraven is not now, nor ever will be, willing to open his ancestral home to *New Bride* magazine. His reasons are simple. He is not interested in predatory journalists with more money than morals, nor in the idle curiosity of a nation crippled by celebrity voyeurism.' "

The felt pen in Kara's hair swayed, dipped, then catapulted to the floor. With a muttered oath, Kara crumpled the fax and flung it into a wicker hamper that served as her garbage can.

"Listen, Kara, there are other castles. We'll find another one just as good. In fact, just last week I read something about—"

"Damn him! We've been patient, haven't we? We've offered everything this man could want for a four-day shoot using the exteriors of Dunraven Castle. How does *that* make us predatory journalists?"

Megan shrugged. "I guess you'll finally have to cross Lord Dunraven off your list. There must be a dozen other Scottish lords willing to rent us a castle for a few days."

"Anyone home?" An olive-skinned man with dancing eyes strode through the door, arms filled with boxes. "Here are the new contact sheets from St. Bart's, Kara. Those scenes on the beach came out pure magic. Even Martin is going to jump for joy over these." He shoved away a pile of papers on Kara's desk and balanced the boxes, every movement filled with grace. "Don't all clap at once. Good Lord, where's the funeral?"

Megan turned away, suddenly busy straightening a lace veil draped over a chipped plaster mannequin.

Hidoshi Sato, chief photographer for *New Bride* magazine, squinted at Kara, then at her assistant. "It's the Scotsman, isn't it? He said no."

"He said no," Kara said flatly.

The tall Japanese-American rubbed his neck. "Did we try the vanity approach? You know, tell him we'll let him appear in some of the photos."

"We don't know what he looks like," Megan said tightly. "The man appears to be phobic about journalists. There isn't a single picture of him in any file that we can lay our hands on. What if he's—well, not exactly the most photogenic person in the world?"

"A dead ringer for Quasimodo?" Hidoshi bent forward and shuffled dramatically across the floor.

Megan's lips twitched. "Idiot. Aren't you ever serious?"

Some unidentifiable emotion flitted through the photographer's eyes. He stood up and reached for a box on the desk, lifting out a neat square of sushi. "So the man has a fear of journalists."

"A fear of *'predatory'* journalists,'" Kara said tightly. "'With more money than morals.'"

Hidoshi frowned. "Sounds like we're talking about a serious dislike here." He shrugged. "Still no problem. Have some sushi and we'll choose another spot."

"I don't want another castle; I want Dunraven." Kara popped a perfectly formed square of rice wrapped in paper-thin seaweed into her mouth. Hidoshi's cousin owned the finest Japanese restaurant in New York, and Hidoshi took shameless advantage of the connection. Not that it required much effort, since it was the general belief of the staff at *New Bride* magazine that the award-winning photographer could have charmed the tusks off a rogue elephant.

Right now, Kara wasn't in the mood for being charmed. She hadn't been sleeping well since she'd begun her work for Amanda Rivington. Every night her dreams were filled with angry shadows and growing dread. It wasn't surprising that the exquisite square of rice and vegetables tasted like sawdust in her mouth.

"Kara, are you all right?" Hidoshi peered at her in myopic concern, dark eyes owlishly magnified behind gold-wire glasses.

"What do you mean?"

"I mean you're pale. You're also trembling, in case you hadn't noticed."

Kara did feel a little dizzy. Suddenly she felt the prick of awareness at her spine, the vague rush of light playing behind her eyelids.

Not now. She couldn't allow contact now. There was no time for focusing, for the centering and words of protection that grounded her before she made a psychic link.

Hidoshi looked at Megan. "Get a chair. She's having one of those damned visions again."

Frowning, Megan caught Kara's arm and pulled her into a swivel chair by the window. Car horns screamed up between the narrow steel canyon running up Sixth Avenue, and old newspapers whispered as they skittered crablike down dirty alleys.

Kara felt sweat break out on her neck.

The prickling grew. Her knees began to shake.

Not now. Please, God, not here, like this.

But the visions were coming again, the way they always did when someone needed her help. When Kara was twelve, her aunt had lost a wallet with two years' savings tucked inside it. After two hours of concentration, with her aunt's watch clutched in her fingers, Kara had finally traced the green square of leather to a pile of leaves in the backyard, where it had been dropped and forgotten.

In the years that followed, Kara's skill had grown. Through bitter experience she had learned to be wary of what she touched, since a link in an unguarded moment could send unwanted images slamming into her mind with dangerous force. By trial and error she had learned to control the contact, focusing her mind and allowing the images to filter through gradually.

Except when the tremors began. When the cold crept up her legs and her sight blurred, Kara had no control.

She looked down and saw that her hands were shaking. Her feet were like ice.

She swallowed hard as a vision of a battered van filled her head. One headlight was shattered, and the front fender was crooked.

Kara had struggled to keep this part of her life hidden, carefully controlled. And it had worked.

Until times like this, when the pain of someone's need reached out and enveloped her with burning images that ate into her mind in waking or in sleep.

Just as they were doing now.

An old green van. The license number ends in 1SD. There are only two men now.

"Kara, have some tea." Hidoshi was pushing a cup into her hand. "You're looking shaky. I'll even get out my hidden bottle of Glenlivet, if it will help."

Kara struggled to smile at this ultimate sacrifice by Hidoshi. "I'll be fine. I just need to make a call. A private call."

After a moment Hidoshi nodded. "Whatever you say."

"I'll leave a cup of tea here on the desk," Megan said helpfully, setting a mug of pale green porcelain within Kara's reach. "Don't forget to drink it."

Hidoshi cleared his throat. "Look, Kara, are you sure—"

Megan caught his arm. "Let's go, Hidoshi. She needs some time alone."

Kara didn't look around when the door closed. Her fingers were unsteady as she dialed.

"Rivington here."

"Amanda, it's Kara. I've picked up something else from that ring you sent over yesterday. The van is green, and the plate ends in 1SD. It's in water, nearly covered. Maybe discarded." A wave of nausea shook her.

She swallowed, looking down at the crowds in the street. A meat truck was parked in the right lane near the corner of Fortieth Street. A cabby veered sharply, trying to pass, nearly running down a pedestrian in black biker boots and a military beret. Kara watched the man raise his fist and slam one heel into the cab's fender.

She closed her eyes, shuddering. "It's too late. You should have sent the money in two parts."

"Damn it, Kara, how did you know about—" The detective's voice ended in a curt oath. "What else?"

"The girls got free. They tried to run. It was dark, and they heard their captors behind them. A gun went off. And then . . . it was too late." Kara blinked back tears, her eyes fixed on a line of dust rimming the window sill.

Suddenly the clouds were everywhere, following her, cold as midnight, dark as despair.

Silent as death.

"They're dead, Amanda. The bodies . . . they're in the back of the van. It's near a big bridge. There's a signboard somewhere, banging in the wind." Kara rubbed her wet cheeks. "Look, I've got to go. Don't—don't call me for a while, okay?"

She put the phone down. In the street a peddler's cart jumped the curb and jolted crazily into the center lane, tying up traffic even further.

As her forehead sank against the grimy window, Kara tried not to hear the car horns and angry shouts that rose from the street.

This time she let the tears fall without bothering to shove them away.

Two

When Megan peeked through the door an hour later, Kara had regained her self-control. Cold water had removed most of the blotches beneath her eyes, and a dusting of color had concealed some of her pallor.

"Everything okay in here, boss?"

Kara swallowed. "Sure." She gave a crooked smile and pointed to the crumpled fax she had retrieved from the garbage can. "I've just been making some plans about Scotland."

"Forget Scotland. You need a vacation, Kara." Megan pointed to the cluttered desk. "All this will keep, but your state of mind won't. Remember what that doctor friend of yours said? Three weeks of doing nothing."

Kara pushed aside a Gaelic dictionary and fingered a bolt of exquisite hand-embroidered Irish linen. "I don't have time for doing nothing. We've got a honeymoon issue to plan, remember? A location to scout and gowns to choose."

"And what about the visions? They're getting more frequent, aren't they?"

Kara tried to shrug. "What visions?"

"Don't try that with me, Kara. They're coming when you least want them now," Megan snapped. "They hit you when you cross a street or in the middle of a meeting. They make your eyes dilate. Your hands start to shake."

Kara swallowed. "Don't tell me it's *that* obvious."

"Not yet. But it will be unless you take some time off and deal with them. Go back and talk with that doctor, for a start."

Kara gazed at a framed row of Hidoshi's prize-winning photographs on the far wall. The doctor in question had been interested in a personal rather than a clinical relationship, Kara suspected. And an explanation of the special sense of touch that plagued her couldn't be found in any medical text. She knew exactly what caused it and exactly what made it worse—stress, tension, and not enough sleep.

In short, the normal, hectic pace of daily, twentieth-century life. "I don't need a medical diagnosis, Megan."

"But you *do* need a vacation. Two weeks mini-mum. Somewhere with hot sun and endless sand. With turquoise water so clear you think it's a mirror. Not one of those singles circuses, either. Somewhere quiet, with children around, noisy and grubby with sand."

Kara's heart tightened cruelly at the thought of tousled hair and round faces flushed with sun. "*No.*"

"Don't worry, I'll handle Martin. I'll convince him you need some time away."

"After the issue is done," Kara said tightly. "You know that *New Bride* makes almost half its annual revenues from this one issue. If I don't produce, I'm out of a job, Megan. We both are."

"Blast it, Kara, it's not worth my job to see you like this. I don't know what that policewoman has asked you to do this time." She raised her hand sharply as Kara began to speak. "No, I don't want to know. All I know is that there's a limit to how much longer you can continue to balance on this tightrope."

Kara gave a crooked smile. "Looking to replace me already, O'Hara?"

"I couldn't. I doubt anyone could, even that jerk Geoffrey, who used to run things around here. No, all I want is to see you having fun again. Taking some time for yourself now and then."

It sounded good. Actually, it sounded fantastic. But the whole thing was impossible. Until the honeymoon issue was completed, her time was not her own.

Kara looked down at the crumpled fax in her fingers. Dunraven Castle was magical, a place her readers would never forget. The fact that it had never been photographed inside made its attraction even greater.

Kara slowly raised a photograph from the corner of her desk.

The paper seemed to throb beneath her fingers.

Outside, the blaring horns along Fortieth Street faded away to dim echoes. She didn't see the pigeons swooping outside the high windows or the taxi that lumbered over a curve and nearly crashed into a furniture-delivery van.

Her world shrank to the narrow dimensions of the grainy photograph cradled in her hands while an odd, aching sense of recognition surged through her fingers.

She closed her eyes as power bled from the glossy colors of the print her sister had snapped six months earlier in Scotland, where she had gone to research a book on the haunted homes of Europe.

Even Kara's sister, with her vast skills of persuasion, hadn't been able to talk her way inside the castle. But the photograph had been enough.

Kara took a sharp breath. The power of the stone walls and circular towers reached out, overwhelming her like nothing she'd felt before.

Conelike turrets of blue-black slate towered against a turquoise sky. Banks of windows burned golden in the afternoon sun. The walls of earthy peach, weathered the color of light malt whiskey, rose above deep green fields that ran down to distant terraces of roses and banks of enormous flowering rhododendrons brought back from China, Burma, and the Himalayas by some seafaring Dunraven ancestor.

Kara had never seen so many shades of blue before. Hard and flat and cold where the loch was streaked by fleet passing clouds. Warm and shimmering where a column of sunlight pierced shifting walls of mist. Soft and sheer where the sky mounded protectively above a dozen small islands dotting the water to the west.

Just as romantic as the castle was the rose-covered cottage in the lee of the hills overlooking a gentle cove. Legend held that two lovers who passed the first night of their honeymoon in Dunraven's Rose Cottage would never be torn asunder.

And the legend was true.

Kara could feel it. There was power here, energy born of blood oaths and old love. This castle was the perfect spot to touch the heart of every bride.

She tasted magic as she stroked the glossy paper, reading the mist-wrapped castle with the uncanny skill she'd possessed since childhood. Through her mind spilled the haunting strains of a solitary piper. Yes, Dunraven Castle's curving towers and slate-topped turrets would be absolutely perfect for the next honeymoon issue of *New Bride* magazine.

Now Kara had to convince the elusive laird of Dunraven of that fact.

"Martin?"

Seated behind a vast, marble-topped desk, the sixty-something publisher of *New Bride* magazine wore the wary look of a man who expected bad news—and usually got it. "Maybe. Good news or bad?"

"Good. At least I think so." Kara gave a crooked smile. "I've found our honeymoon house."

Martin Grant rocked his six-foot frame back in his leather chair. "I was starting to worry about that, Kara." His eyes narrowed. "I've also been thinking I've been giving you too much work. Maybe you need to—"

"Has Megan been talking to you?"

The publisher ran a hand through his black hair. "So what if she has? I have eyes of my own. You're working too hard, Kara. I've got too much invested in you to risk losing you."

Kara went very still. "Why would you lose me?"

"Damn it, you know what I mean. You've been walking around here like a ghost for the past week. You're restless and distracted. I'm not going to ask about your personal life, but I am going to tell you this. You need some time off. I'm going to call in someone else to handle the honeymoon issue."

"You can't!" Kara's pale cheeks were suddenly more stark against her vibrant red dress.

Martin pushed his reading glasses onto his forehead and frowned at her. She was the best editor he'd ever had. Since she'd joined the staff, their subscriptions had tripled and their newsstand sales had sprouted wings. Most successful of all had been Kara's annual dream-honeymoon issue. In the last five years Grant had come to rely implicitly on Kara's judgment, but now he was worried about her. She was too pale, too restless. Martin Grant was not a man to pry into his staff's personal lives, but in Kara's case he was almost ready to make an exception.

Kara tugged at a stray curl. "The place where I want to shoot is not exactly around the corner, Martin."

"The wilds of Minnesota again? Okay, take the company van and two journalism interns. Take three days. No, take five days," he said expansively.

The felt-tipped art pen wavered dangerously in Kara's hair. "Five days won't do it. I'll need eight days at the very least."

"Fine. If the material is as good as you say, it will be worth it."

"We're also talking farther than Minnesota. A lot farther."

A crease appeared between Martin's brows. "West Coast? One of those foggy coastal enclaves with enough redwood to incite an environmentalist to file papers with the EPA?" He tapped his pencil on the desk, then shrugged. "It will still be worth it. Take your assistant and that giddy photographer you swear by. The one whose name begins with the same letter as headache."

"Hidoshi?"

"Who else can waste five rolls of film trying to get the shadow of a shoelace just right?"

"Hidoshi is an artist, Martin. Someday he'll be called a genius."

"Not while he's on *my* payroll, he won't. Just keep him out of the Great Orion Nebula and bring me back a portfolio full of great photos." The skin around his eyes crinkled slightly. "The way you always do. If you're sure you're up to it . . ."

Kara squared her shoulders. "Of course I am. Only it's not the West Coast this time, either."

"*Where*, Fitzgerald?"

"It's near Mull." Kara took a little breath. "Mull as in a little island off the western shore of Scotland. In the inner Hebrides."

Grant sank back against his chair. "Several thousand miles away." His keen gray eyes narrowed. "Are you sure you're up to this, Kara?"

"This will be a winner, I know it."

"You didn't answer my question."

"Yes, I did. I'm up to this. No, I *need* this." It was true, Kara realized. Something about that misty headland overlooking the sea had gotten into her blood.

Or maybe it had wrapped itself around her heart.

Kara slid a file down in front of him. "Look for yourself."

"Castles are all the same." His keen gaze moved over the photograph. "Nice," he said finally. "Worn but not stark. Grand but not overwhelming. This cottage covered with roses is a nice touch, too. A bridal magazine can't ever have too many roses," he added sagely. He tapped one corner of the picture. "You're going to ruin me, Fitzgerald."

"You want my resignation? I still have a copy of the letter I gave you last year before Mexico."

"Resignation—are you nuts?" Grant's feet slammed to the floor and his ample frame jerked upright. "I just wish you could find your romantic hideaways without going halfway around the world. Downtown Milwaukee worked fine for Mildred and me on our honeymoon."

Kara refrained from reminding him that that had been twenty years before. "We did Milwaukee two years ago."

"What about Chicago? Great homes all over that town. They really knew how to build estates back then."

"They also knew how to build back in the twelfth century," Kara said dryly. "And you know you hate downtown Chicago."

"Okay, Fitzgerald, you've got your six days."

"Eight days," Kara corrected.

A reluctant snort. "Eight, then."

"And two days in London first."

"London? But why—" His gray eyes narrowed. "More of your consulting work?"

Kara nodded. "At a price I couldn't turn down. It will pay my airfare."

"Fair enough. But remember, I want receipts for everything. Every box of pencil leads and rubber bands, understand? If this is going to cost me an arm and a leg, at least I want to be able to deduct it."

"Are you suggesting that I've been derelict in my paper work?" Kara managed to look affronted.

"*What* paper work? Your idea of a receipt is a note scrawled on the back of a cocktail napkin."

"I'll be better."

"And keep those two dreamers you work with on a tight rein, will you? Headache—I mean, Hidoshi— will see a ruined tower and be catapulted off into a parallel universe for hours if you don't watch him." Grant frowned. "Come to think of it, when Megan gets around him, she's not much better."

"We'll stay on target, Martin, I promise."

The line buzzed on his desk, and Grant put it on the speaker. "Yes?"

Megan's voice emerged, sounding rather breathless. "Sorry to interrupt, Mr. Grant, but Hidoshi's calling from the printer's. He wants to know if Kara is planning to go visceral for the Caribbean piece or are design considerations foremost?"

"Visceral," Kara called.

Grant rolled his eyes. "The best university in the U.S. They graduate with honors, *summa cum laude*, double majors, and still the two can't speak plain English. What did they teach you kids at Princeton, anyway?"

"Chaos theory, the ethics of genetic manipulation and nonlinear geometry," Kara said. She took the phone and spoke directly to her assistant. "Megan, you can tell Hidoshi that I said he is *not* to stop at the botanical gardens on the way back here. Otherwise, he'll end up photographing cutlery for the back of the classified section for the rest of his life. What's *left* of it."

There was a chuckle at the other end of the line. "I'll tell him word for word. Meanwhile, would you tell Mr. Grant that someone representing the Pulp Manufacturers' Council is out here waiting to take him to lunch?"

The publisher of *New Bride* rolled his eyes. "Some lunch. The man wants to tell me all the reasons we *don't* need to use recycled paper."

"Go get 'em, champ."

"You sure you're up to this, Kara?" he asked once again.

"Dead certain."

Grant shook his head. "Maybe I'm getting too old for this business. Be careful, Kara. One day everything's fresh and you've got more ideas than you can possibly exhaust in one lifetime. Then suddenly you turn around and you're all used up, with nothing but an engraved silver pen and a pile of dusty parking tickets to show for it." He shoved a rumpled Phillies baseball cap onto his head and headed for the door. "It's your game now. Just be sure you get all the legal releases signed. I don't want to wake up the morning of press day and find some irate Scottish laird trying to squeeze triple fees for the use of a cover photo."

"Of course, Martin. Whatever you say," Kara murmured, her gaze already back on the photo.

"Why do I get the idea you're not listening to me?"

"Absolutely. No problem," Kara said vaguely, lost in an endless horizon of drifting mist and setting sun, power jolting through her once more. The sound of bagpipes was growing clearer now.

"Kara?"

"Absolutely, Martin. That, too," she said vaguely, hunched over the photograph on his desk. "I'll call you from Scotland."

"Sure, you will," her long-suffering boss muttered as the door closed behind him.

Kara was still studying the photo when the telephone rang. She punched the button for the speaker phone. "Mr. Grant's not here, Megan."

"I know. It's for you." Her assistant's voice hardened. "It's that policewoman again."

Something cold and hard pressed at Kara's chest. She took a slow breath. "Put her through."

"Kara, are you sure you—"

"Please, Megan."

The line filled with static, followed by Detective Rivington's soft, rounded vowels. "Kara? No, listen. I have several things I'm going to say to you."

Kara stared down at the slate turrets and the riot of roses in the photo. Cold crept up her fingers, rushed into her throat.

"I'm sorry if I pushed you. I'm sorry if it ... took too much from you this time. Sometimes I forget what this costs you."

Kara didn't answer.

"We found them, up by the Triboro. They were in a van, half hidden in mud beneath the bridge. Just the way you said."

Just the way she'd said.

"But we got the bastards who did it. That license number you gave me helped. *You* did that, Kara. And you saved the grieving parents months of torment, of wondering whether their children were dead or alive. Always wondering, always hoping . . ."

The cold hit Kara's neck, relentless and blasting.

"Kara, did you hear me? You *helped*. It's not your failure—it's not ours either. It's just the way things are."

The way things are.

"Thank you, Amanda, but somehow that doesn't help. They're gone, you see, and now I've got two more ghosts to carry around with me."

"Damn it, Kara—"

Kara punched a button, plunging the room into silence.

Only then did it hit her.

The girls were dead, their captors run to ground. The case was closed. So why were her hands still shaking? Why was her body gripped with cold?

She stared down at the photo in her hands, watching the roses blur into waves of red and pink. And then she knew.

It wasn't over.

Danger in the touch. Danger in the seeing.

It was just beginning. Sweat beaded on Kara's brow.

Death was involved.

And this time it was Dunraven Castle that called out to her.

Three ~

Belgrave Square
London

The room had the smell of money.

Faint.

Subtle.

Unforgettable.

He thought about money as he crouched in the shadows, eyes narrowed behind a black nylon mask. Bars of light slanted down from the recessed ceiling, outlining glass cases full of sixteenth-century Cellini gold, hallmarked English silver, and a stunning array of Etruscan jewelry.

Every case screamed an invitation to a thief.

The man in the darkness smiled at that, invisible in a black turtleneck and dark twills. In his pocket was the code for the second of three high-frequency silent alarms that protected Calendish and Sons, one of the finest jewelry shops in England.

Tonight he was there to subvert those alarms, elude the team of efficient armed guards, and selectively burglarize the most expensive contents of those fine glass cases.

He glanced down. His watch read 9:20. Four minutes until the second guard moved past. He had recorded the movements of the security team carefully over the last week, secure in a rented flat across the street.

Right on schedule, the broad-shouldered guard from Brighton ambled through the central pool of light.

Duncan MacKinnon eased forward. He now had exactly eight and one-half minutes to cut through a plate-glass case and steal a million pounds' worth of rare, antique jewelry.

With steady hands MacKinnon eased open the front of a small Plexiglass case near the reception desk. The first two alarms had been circumvented, and he was bending low to survey the third, a code-activated German model that the manufacturer had declared to be foolproof. He smiled when he saw the small green board that led to the device's heart.

By bypassing three chips, a half-million-dollar alarm system could be tied up in knots for hours, with no one the wiser.

Attaching an input cable to a hand-held generator, he substituted the first new chip. The green power light did not waver. Deftly he replaced a second and then a third chip, set up to activate in case the primary circuit was compromised. He looked down and smiled faintly, his hard lips outlined by shadows.

The electronic security system was now deactivated. No silent alarm would trigger the attention of the police station three blocks away.

Somewhere a police car screamed off into the London night. The tall Scotsman tensed for a moment, waiting for signs of pursuit, but the cruiser headed away until the sound of the siren fell to a dim whine.

Before him the green power light continued to flash without a break. The circuit had remained complete. The only difference now was that he could knock down the building brick by brick, and the system would take no note. When would they learn to store their backup systems in a remote location? he thought, smiling cynically. Probably after this theft.

He looked down at his watch.

Four minutes left.

Unhurriedly, MacKinnon closed the case, pocketed his tools, and made his way to a glittering case by the far wall. Inside lay a pair of burnished golden chokers, made to grace the neck of an ancient warrior's wife.

Or more likely his mistress, the Scotsman thought cynically.

He did not waste time trying to cut the heavy plate glass. Instead he slid a military-issue torch from the pack at his back and triggered a point of bright blue flame. The blast of heat was high enough to sear diamonds, and in seconds it left a curled and darkened hole in the glass.

Not a sound split the silence as the black-clad intruder reached past the melted glass and caught up half a dozen pieces of rare jewelry. With each movement, triumph spilled through him. MacKinnon ruthlessly suppressed it. Any emotion was dangerous at a time like this. Next came the final touch: replacing the stolen objects with replicas. That should buy him the time he needed to clear out safely.

The substitutions made, he closed the velvet-lined bag, eased it into a zippered pocket, then scanned his watch.

Two minutes until the second guard returned. Just enough time to make his way back to the foyer and climb back out to the roof, with the help of a rope secured just out of sight.

Suddenly footsteps approached from the neighboring room. He froze, crouched next to the plundered case with its gaping side. What was the guard doing here two minutes early?

But it wasn't the guard. It was a woman with auburn hair and a distracted air who started toward him, a notebook clutched beneath her arm. One step more and she was bound to spot him.

MacKinnon raged a silent Gaelic curse. He looked at his watch, feeling the tiny hairs lift at the back of his neck. *No time.* At any second the guard would appear at the far door.

He reacted instantly, moving shadowlike until he was right behind her. With one hand over her mouth, the other at her waist, he wrenched her into a storage closet at the far side of the room.

She didn't go easily. Struggling angrily, she tried to bite through the leather gloves at her mouth. Strong, the Scotsman noted distantly. Good muscle tone, too. But she was no match for a man nearly twice her weight.

Thirty seconds later, a guard in a black-and-gray Calendish uniform padded through the room. MacKinnon tensed. His fingers tightened on the woman's throat. Any sound now would destroy all his meticulous plans.

The officer, a taciturn Yorkshireman named Farrell, halted beneath a column of light. His gaze swept the glass cases, persuading MacKinnon that he'd been right to use replicas. Not that the masquerade would hold up for long. Any closer and that hole in the glass was going to be all too obvious.

Without warning his captive twisted. Her teeth sank with painful accuracy in the soft leather folds near MacKinnon's thumb. Pain jolted through his fingers, and he bit back a curse.

The little fool was going to pay for that.

Seconds crawled past. MacKinnon's left ankle began to ache as he watched the guard make a final survey of the room. Finally satisfied, the officer tugged a pair of headphones up over his ears and ambled off.

Which left MacKinnon alone with a throbbing ankle, an angry captive, and four and a half minutes to escape down two corridors and over ten feet of barbed wire fence.

"One scream and you're a corpse, understand?" His fingers loosened fractionally.

No answer.

"Did you hear me?" His captive shivered, then nodded jerkily.

"Good. Now, who in bloody hell sent you? Giovanni? Or was it one of the Hong Fat people?"

His fingers eased open, encouraging her to speak. Her breath slammed hot and damp against his hands, but no words came.

"Answer, damn it."

"Not—them."

Her eyes were wide, the color of fine old amber, he thought. She was terrified and trying hard not to show it. Only what she deserved, he told himself cynically.

She was having trouble breathing.

"Answer the questions and I won't harm you," he hissed.

She shivered, and her notebook slid to the ground.

MacKinnon scooped it up, all too aware of the passing seconds that brought him closer and closer to discovery. He frowned down at page after page of neat pencil sketches.

Alarm plans? Guard-movement patterns? Damn it, what was the woman up to?

"What *is* this?" He jabbed at a page crisscrossed by lines.

"It's—energy. P-patterns of electricity. Flow charts. I'm—I'm supposed to trace them." Her voice was stronger now, and her eyes were filled with anger. "And who in the hell are *you?*"

Duncan scanned her jacket and silk slacks. Nice, he thought. No frills. Everything sleek and understated. Obviously, someone was paying her very well to pirate Calendish's security designs.

Clever idea, he conceded reluctantly. No one would think to search her for her notebook. She didn't look the type of woman who would be involved in theft.

"Who's paying you?"

"None of your damned business. Who's paying *you* to rob this place, you—"

His hand clamped over her mouth. "I'll do the talking. In three minutes that guard is going to be back. Since I don't particularly fancy spending the next ten years in prison, I'm getting out of here. The only question is whether you're coming with me."

Her lips tightened, silenced by his gloved hands. He winced as she aimed another bite at his palm.

Stubborn, was she? MacKinnon could appreciate such determination, but it wouldn't do her any good. She'd never make it out on her own. And if she triggered an alarm, she would get them both caught.

Damn the woman.

Steps echoed outside the corridor. No choice now. They'd have to brave the two alarms that ran to the storerooms.

His hand clenched on her waist. "We're getting out of here," he said tightly. "Together. If you stay quiet, I'll let you go when we're outside." It was a lie, but he wasn't risking the truth with a guard mere seconds behind them. "Do you see that doorway?"

After a moment she nodded.

"It's protected by a laser-controlled optical grid twenty-four inches from the floor. Just keep quiet and do what I tell you."

The fear had left her eyes. All MacKinnon saw there was anger.

Fine. Things would go more smoothly if he let her think she would soon be safe.

"Understand?"

Her nod was curt.

"Good." MacKinnon shoved her notebook into her pocket, pulled her backward, and pointed silently across the room, where shadows blanketed a narrow doorway. He shoved her through only seconds before another guard appeared at the arched door leading from the front foyer.

The officer stood quietly, his gray uniform blending into the shadows as he scanned the far wall. Silently he moved to check a row of electrical boxes flanking the door.

Only a few feet from his arm a green light flashed intermittently, illuminating a small metal receptacle.

In the room beyond, an invisible beam cut through the shadows, exactly twenty-four inches above the floor.

MacKinnon felt the woman's tension. His hands

tightened, holding her still. He glanced at his glowing watch dial and frowned. They had seventy-two seconds before the next laser sweep. There was no hope of going back the way he'd come, through the showroom, across the foyer, and up the rope that still hung from a skylight outside the ladies' coatroom.

Not with an unwilling captive as dead weight.

The woman began to struggle in his arms, and he answered her with a jab of his finger at her side, a motion she clearly mistook as indicating that he held a weapon. Just as he had intended.

Behind them came the low squish of rubber soles as the guard moved into the adjoining showroom. Seventy seconds had passed.

Now or never. Grimly MacKinnon swept his hostage before him into the shadows.

Kara Fitzgerald swallowed hard and clenched her fists to keep from shuddering.

She'd expected two quiet days, doing a few room sketches for a very tidy fee. And now she was aiding and abetting a jewel thief involved in stealing one of the greatest collections of Roman and Etruscan art found anywhere outside Italy or the Vatican.

She glanced sideways at the hard features shrouded by a nylon mask. Why hadn't she waited until morning to make her last sketch, instead of dashing back across town and signing in with the friendly Yorkshire guard whom she had come to know well in the last two days?

Stupid, Fitzgerald. Very stupid. But there was no time to think now. At her slightest delay, her captor's fingers dug into her wrist, dragging her forward. With a gun shoved against her ribs, she didn't dare risk a shout to the guards.

Fear settled in her throat, and danger clung to her. For an instant her shoulder pressed against the thief's chest, and she was swept with waves of dizziness. *Danger in the seeing.*

Her notebook slipped from her pocket onto the

floor. She shoved wildly at the rigid fingers clamped at her waist.

"My notebook. I have to have it," she hissed. All her diagrams for the last two days were inside. She didn't have time to start all over.

She bent forward, searching blindly in the darkness, and heard a hard curse. Smoke rose from a freshly lit cigarette in her captor's hand.

The next moment the slam of his body knocked her breath free. Terror built as she was flattened to the cold marble floor with a pistol wedged between her ribs.

Kara decided that fighting wasn't such a good idea. But why was he smoking?

Her breath came fast and raspy as she watched blue light streak in a horizontal path straight to the far wall. A second burst followed, this one scattering into dozens of beams that shimmered like a grid above the floor.

Then there was only darkness.

In an instant her captor was up, pulling her to her feet. Kara followed blindly, feeling hysterical laughter burn her throat. *Don't worry; all he wants is a million pounds' worth of rare jewels.*

And then what?

She had seen him, after all. She could identify his voice, even though his face was hidden behind that mask.

They lurched through the door just as another beam swept the floor. Now she was beyond help. Before her a door led into shadows, the perfect place for a robber to dispense with an unwanted hostage.

Kara froze.

"Come on, damn it." The man shoved her forward.

Suddenly wind played at her hair, and Kara smelled air rich with the tang of rain. They were in some sort of glassed area at the rear of the shops, she realized. Probably a work area with the natural light crucial to accurate design work.

"I—I won't talk." Instantly Kara regretted the words. One weak promise wasn't about to divert a cold-blooded professional like this man. She'd seen his eyes, hard and unblinking. If she hadn't been so upset, she would have tried to probe the touch that would reveal his emotions.

Something made Kara flinch from the thought. Jewels, then freedom—those were the only things on this man's mind. His eyes were unreadable.

"That's right, you won't talk," he said.

Oh, God, he *was* going to kill her. He didn't even bother to hide his intention.

"Wait, I—" She caught a raw breath. "It's, well, I have to . . ."

"To what?" he hissed. His gaze flickered to the ornate wrought-iron door and the high fence beyond it.

"To go," Kara said raggedly. She feigned jumping from foot to foot.

He shook his head in exasperation. "Hold it."

They were through the gate now. Kara caught a deep breath. She wasn't going to give in without a fight. Time for plan number two. She grabbed his arm, swaying wildly.

"What *now*, damn it?"

"I'm going to—" She swallowed loudly, clutching at her stomach as an unpleasant rumbling noise came from her throat.

He cursed, looking down at his watch. "Five seconds, that's all you have, understand?" He gave her a shove. "Right over there, and don't try anything clever. Don't touch the fence, either. It packs a whole lot of volts."

Kara nodded desperately, fingers locked on her mouth.

Don't overplay it, idiot. He'll be watching every step you make.

But at that moment her nausea was very real. She turned awkwardly, searching the terraced backyard. The floor plans that Calendish had sent her had shown a small storage shed down a set of narrow stone steps to her left.

She charged behind a row of bushes and manufactured some descriptive noises, the sort he would be expecting. Then she crept down the first of six steps, stopping once to rattle the bushes above with a branch she'd found by the stairs.

She located the shed and eased past it, her fingers cold and tense, feeling as if they belonged to someone else. *Almost there.*

The fence was inches away now, iron bars narrow and threatening. Electrified, she reminded herself. Funny, no one had mentioned *that* in the letters from London.

She eased forward through the shadows, careful to avoid the fence, thankful she had covered every inch of those blueprints in advance.

It was funny, really. Her surly captor had done the same thing in preparation for his robbery.

She found the shed. Beyond it rose the dim outline of a metal box.

"Time's up. Come out or I haul you out." There was a foreign cadence to his words, the trace of a language Kara couldn't quite recognize. She saw a shadow rise over the row of bushes. *Empty* bushes.

She heard his low curse, then the slam of feet.

Too late. The game's over, and you've lost. Now, let's see how you like this little surprise.

Kara's fingers hit the front of the metal box and felt blindly in the darkness. With a clang a metal plate slammed home against a row of switches.

Behind her, lights exploded to life all over the building and sirens began to wail. With all hell breaking loose behind her, Kara ran for the side courtyard.

She didn't look back.

Four ⁓

Sunlight streamed through the damask curtains. Forty stories down, freighters steamed like toys along the scudding swells of the gray Thames.

Silent and uncomfortable, Kara studied the man behind the mahogany desk that looked twenty feet long. At his right hand two Baccarat crystal vases framed an arrangement of perfect white tulips.

Suddenly Kara was intensely aware of the pain at her elbow and the cuts on her knee. With the alarm bells screaming behind her she had made her way safely back to her hotel, purseless and with one heel broken. Before dawn she had left three urgent messages for the owner of Calendish's showrooms, relating the night's events. But for some reason Andrew Calendish had seemed reluctant to see her.

Now his frown implied that she was more than a little deranged. "So you are telling me that someone tried to kidnap you last night in the middle of my Belgrave Square showroom, where you were working. Long after hours, I may point out." His voice was cool, almost—but not quite—at the edge of insolence.

It wasn't *her* fault, Kara reminded herself. He should have been growling at that brute in the black nylon number. This was all *his* doing! "I told you, Mr. Calendish. I had just finished my notes on the orientation of your entrance foyer and was moving

into the display area when I stumbled onto a burglary in progress."

"So you say. All I know is that you triggered a
control panel in the backyard that sent five police
cars screaming to my showroom, followed by a
horde of journalists."

Kara pushed angrily to her feet. "Are you implying
that *I* was to blame for what happened last night?"

"I'm saying nothing of the sort, Ms. Fitzgerald. I
simply want to know exactly what you saw, as well
as exactly what you know about last night's events."

It struck Kara that he had used an odd choice of
words. "What do you mean?"

"Just tell me what you saw, please."

"I saw a man. He was wearing a mask. He tried
to *kidnap* me!"

"You are understandably upset, Ms. Fitzgerald. All
your nerves are on edge. But try to remain calm. Did
you get a glimpse of this man's face?"

"No. I told you, he was wearing some kind of
mask."

Andrew Calendish toyed idly with one of the Baccarat vases. "I see. And did you hear him speak?"

"Only a few sentences. There was something rough
about his voice—some kind of accent."

The man at the desk sat forward, his fingers going
still. "I see. Well, Ms. Fitzgerald, I want to thank you
for your cooperation. I'm certain the police will want
to take a statement from you in due time." He came
smoothly to his feet. "But for now why don't you go
back to your hotel and rest." He moved to the door,
signaling that their meeting was finished. A moment
later Kara found herself in the broad reception area.
A woman in impeccable tweeds gave her a curious
look, then turned back to a pile of telexes.

That was all? Good-bye Ms. Fitzgerald. Go back
and rest, Ms. Fitzgerald.

Kara's eyes narrowed as she spun around and
shoved Andrew Calendish's door open without
knocking. "Now, just one minute—"

Her voice fell. Andrew Calendish was no longer

alone. A man in a dark suit stood by the broad windows, his back to Kara.

He turned, and the moment froze.

Bottomless eyes of blue gray. An angular jaw below a face too strong to be handsome in any usual sense.

The result was a sense of utter calm coupled with arresting power.

Gradually other details worked their way into Kara's consciousness: his thousand-dollar Savile Row suit and perfectly knotted tie. His skin, tanned to mahogany.

She took a deep breath and forced her gaze back to Andrew Calendish. "You can't just sweep this under the rug. I can identify the man who tried to kidnap me. I insist that you phone the police and have them take my testimony. Tomorrow will be too late."

"Indeed." Calendish's eyes narrowed. "And why is that?"

"Because I have urgent business in Scotland."

"Ah, yes, *New Bride* magazine. I enjoyed your last piece on Old World diamonds."

The man by the window stiffened. "*New Bride* magazine?" His voice held a hint of roughness. A hint of an accent.

Kara paled. "*You!*"

Andrew Calendish shot a look at his frowning visitor, then came quickly to his feet. "My dear girl, what you are suggesting is impossible. This man is on the board of at least six international merchant banks. In addition, he is descended from one of the oldest families in Scotland."

Scottish. So that accounted for the faint burr Kara had heard in his voice last night. "He's still a thief," Kara said tightly.

"Nonsense. In fact, Lord—"

The man by the window made a sharp gesture with one hand. "There's no need for formality. My name is Duncan MacLeod, and you must forgive my stupidity, but I thought I just heard you accuse me of trying to kidnap you."

His smile was cool arrogance itself. The sight of his composure made Kara's blood boil. "That's exactly what I'm saying, and I'll be only too glad to testify to that effect. Go on," she said grimly to the slightly balding Calendish. "You'd better phone the police. After all, he might still be carrying that pistol he used on me last night."

Calendish blinked. "Pistol? He used a *weapon* on you?"

"Jabbed right into my ribs. I'll have the bruises for a week, I expect." She glared at Duncan MacLeod. "Mr. Calendish, aren't you going to do anything?"

Calendish cleared his throat.

"This man is a dangerous thief! Haven't you heard a word I've said?"

Kara's stare moved from one man to the other, anger dark in her clear amber eyes. She wasn't about to back down. This man MacLeod had tried to kidnap her, and he was going to pay.

"Mr. Calendish," she said tightly, "I don't think you understand—"

"Oh, but I do, Ms. Fitzgerald. Far more than you imagine." The Englishman sank down into the chair behind his desk and steepled his fingers. "Duncan?" he said finally.

"You're asking *him*?" Kara's voice was tight with disbelief. "You think I'm making this up?" She waved her wrist, mottled and purple from an angry bruise. "What about this?" She raised her leg, revealing a long red welt along one calf. "Maybe I should show you the bruises he left on my ribs. Then you can say I made those up as well!"

"Come, Ms. Fitzgerald, I hardly think that we need to be hysterical about this."

At that moment the Scotsman pushed away from the window. "She's right, Andrew. This is a serious matter." A pair of the bluest eyes Kara had ever seen locked with hers. She had a blurred impression of irritation and the probing of a powerful, focused mind. His gaze moved over her flushed cheeks and down to the blouse half tugged from her silk skirt. "So you recognize my voice, you say."

That unmistakable burr she had heard the night before was there again. "I'm not likely to forget, considering that you left me flattened to the floor beneath you while those lasers swept the room." Her voice tightened. "How is your arm doing today?"

"My arm?" He fingered the sleeve of his navy wool suit, tailored to perfection.

Old money, Kara thought resentfully. An old title and *very* old manners. There were centuries of confident charm in his practiced smile.

But last night he'd been hard and dangerous, and Kara wasn't about to forget that. "That's right, your arm. You hit the floor hard. I felt you wince. As I recall, you had a pistol in my side at the time."

His long leg was perched on the edge of the conference table. Sunlight poured through the window behind him, picking out flecks of gold and auburn in the deep mahogany of his hair. "Burglary? Kidnapping?" He looked questioningly at Calendish. "Andrew, this is some sort of joke, surely."

The balding man at the desk cleared his throat. "Er, no, Duncan. That is, yes. Yes, it is," he said nervously. "My American friend, Ms. Fitzgerald, was just—"

"It's *not* a joke." Kara slammed down her portfolio. "I want some answers, and I'm not going to wait much longer to get them. I'm perfectly willing to go to the police myself if I have to." She shoved a notebook under the Scotsman's nose. "I suppose you don't recognize this either."

His brow rose. "Should I?"

Kara muttered a pithy phrase consigning all Englishmen to the nether regions of a very hot and humid place.

"I'm not English ... Ms. Fitzgerald, was it?" His eyes were suddenly intent.

"My name is hardly your concern. And I know

exactly what you are, which is a thief." She glared
at Calendish. "Was anything missing today?"

"I could scarcely mention private details of company security to an outsider, Ms. Fitzgerald, much
as I value your input regarding the layout of the
building."

The tall Scotsman picked up a letter opener of
carved lapis. "A decorator?" He frowned at Calendish. "You didn't mention you were redesigning the
shop, Andrew."

"I'm not." He shrugged. "Ms. Fitzgerald has a different kind of design expertise."

"And that is?"

Calendish didn't answer, wriggling in his chair like
a schoolboy caught up in a lie. Kara had seen the
response often enough to recognize it perfectly.

She sniffed. "I'm not a decorator. I was hired to
do a fêng-shui consultation," she said gravely.

And then she waited.

For the usual sniggers. For the quick, low chuckle
and the knowing nod. After all, most people ranked
the Oriental art of energy flow right up there with
voodoo, mesmerism, and necromancy.

But the man opposite her neither sniggered nor
chuckled. His left brow rose fractionally as he twirled
the lapis letter opener, his eyes assessing. "Geo-
mancy? That's Chinese, isn't it? Something to do with
room placement and energy-flow patterns."

Not bad, Mr. MacLeod, Kara conceded silently. *For
someone who practices armed robbery for a living, you're
very well informed.* "That's right. I was working on my
proposal for redesigning the showroom last night. As
I suspected, the building has some serious anomalies
in its areas relating to wealth and business. There are
also strong indications of difficulty with robberies,"
she added tightly. "Not that *that* should surprise
anyone."

The Scotsman uncurled his long body with sleek
grace. "I applaud your foresight, Andrew. Anything
that helps the bottom line is always useful."

"No advice in the world will help if there's a thief

working on the inside," Kara challenged. "Especially the kind of insider who has access to security codes and surveillance equipment."

The blue-gray eyes roamed over her face. Kara felt as if she were being measured, tested. She wondered for a moment what it would be like to forge a link with this man, feeling the sharp probe of that restless mind without any barriers or protection.

The thought made her shiver.

"So I'm the insider with the security codes. What do you suggest Andrew do about that?"

"Contact the police," Kara said curtly, feeling an odd tension as those probing eyes went on exploring every inch of her face. "And then see that the thief is arrested."

"And you say that thief is me?"

"Exactly."

There was a faint tightening of his lips. "And there is no way I could convince you to change your mind? Money, perhaps? Maybe even an offer of one of Calendish's magnificent jewels?"

"I'm not interested," Kara said coldly. "Now, I have a great deal of work to finish before I leave tomorrow, so I—"

"Ah, yes, your work for *New Bride* magazine. So you're a journalist? A member of that noble profession whose speciality is hounding innocent people until they say exactly what you want them to say."

Kara shook her head in amazement. "What planet did you teleport down from? After last night, I'd say that *you* were the specialist in hounding innocent people. What makes you hate journalists so much?"

The lips tightened. "I have my reasons."

"So did Al Capone."

"This is getting us nowhere."

"I quite agree."

"In that case we have a problem. A most unfortunate problem," MacLeod said coldly. "So let's speak a language that journalists understand." His long fingers slid into the pocket of his perfectly tailored jacket.

Kara's throat tightened. A gun, that's what it would come to. Two bullets in swift succession and blood all over the mahogany desk. Not even time to finish her next issue.

She flinched, waiting for the sharp report of a weapon.

Finally she realized she was listening to silence.

The Scotsman was studying her curiously. "I mean money, Ms. Fitzgerald. A great deal of money." His fingers opened slowly.

Sunlight blazed off a heavy golden necklace encrusted with pearls and emeralds. Kara was no expert on gems, but she knew the piece had to be worth a fortune.

She gasped. "That was one of the pieces in the showroom!"

"Very observant of you." Her abductor held up the heavy necklace, his eyes appreciative. "Early Etruscan. Worth in the neighborhood of six hundred thousand pounds, I should think. Am I right, Andrew?"

"Rather more in today's market. But Duncan, are you quite sure you should be—"

The Scotsman cut him off. "You can see for yourself that she's not going to give up, Andrew." He crossed the room, his eyes locked with Kara's every step of the way.

Cold metal filled her palm, anchored in place by a calloused hand. The unexpected contact was like opening an angry electric circuit. Kara had a sudden sharp impression of pounding seas. A mist-veiled cliff.

Danger in the touch.

Something blocked her throat. Cold lapped at her chest.

Danger in the seeing.

"Well, Ms. Fitzgerald, is it a trade? Your silence in exchange for this Etruscan trinket?"

Kara shivered, letting the necklace slide back into his hand. The ancient gold gleamed in soft squares, each link caught with delicate filigree wires worked in the shape of lions. "It's beautiful," she whispered.

"Not half as beautiful as your eyes." The words were a rough whisper, given almost unwillingly. "And it can be yours."

"*No.*" Kara sank into a chair, feeling tremors lash her arms. She looked in confusion at Andrew Calendish. Why would he be involved in burglarizing his own family's generation-old jewelry enterprise? "I don't understand. Not any of this."

Calendish gave a long sigh. "It appears that Ms. Fitzgerald will not be bought. What happens now, Duncan?"

Kara felt the full force of those probing eyes on her face. "I expect that unless I explain, I may soon find myself memorizing the inside of a jail cell." MacLeod's mouth flattened. "But nothing said here must go beyond the confines of this room. That means forever, Ms. Fitzgerald."

"As long as there is no illegality, I suppose. But why the secrecy?"

"Because I am indeed a thief." MacLeod studied the priceless necklace in his palm. "But after I steal things, I return them. My skill lies in probing the weaknesses of corporate security systems and offering concrete proof of penetration. All of which I was about to do quite nicely last night," he said dryly, "when a distracted young woman with a notebook burst in on me as I was preparing to leave, purloined necklace in hand."

"You're an industrial spy of some sort?"

"A reverse spy. I steal to protect against anyone else doing so."

"So you were just pretending to rob that building?"

"Oh, the exercise was real enough, Ms. Fitzgerald. If anyone had gotten in my way, I fully was prepared to immobilize him," he said grimly. "If you're not deadly serious, you don't last long in my particular line of work."

"Immobilize temporarily," Andrew corrected.

"There was nothing temporary about that pistol I felt jammed into my ribs."

The Scotsman's lips twitched. His hand rose, thumb and forefinger making a right angle. "A grrrrreat deadly weapon, to be sharrrrre," he said, his voice taking on a heavy Scottish burr. He frowned at Calendish. "What in the devil was she doing there at that time of night? Your guard was supposed to be certain the building was secure."

"Ms. Fitzgerald made rather a hit with the fellow, and he let her inside. I'm sorry, Duncan. I've made a bloody mull of this whole business, I'm afraid. Now we'll never know about that new system."

The Scotsman's smile was cocky. "Nonsense, Andrew. Your complex is outdated, understaffed, and a lure to every professional thief in Europe. Once a system is breached, word soon leaks out, no matter how hard you try to keep it quiet." He slid a computer disk from his pocket and tossed it onto Calendish's desk. "All the details are in there, along with my recommendations for the customized security system you should install."

"I'm impressed, Duncan."

The Scotsman shrugged. "The only problem now is what to do with Ms. Fitzgerald. My identity has to remain a secret or I lose all my usefulness." His lips pursed as he stared at Kara. "I regret that things became rough last night. My first suspicion, I confess, was that you were engaged in a burglary of your own. I meant to turn you in to Andrew as soon as we were outside, but you vanished. Just one question: how did you know there was an alarm box by the shed?"

"It was in the floor plan Mr. Calendish sent me. I always insist on full blueprints before I begin."

His brow rose. "Just why is that?"

"A good deal of my work involves electrical patterns, and those can splinter the proper flow of energy."

Andrew Calendish bounced out from behind his desk. "She's bloody good, Duncan. She's done fantastic things for our shop in Georgetown, improving both sales and general staff morale. She has recommendations from both private and public sectors. In fact, I think you're both too valuable to lose."

The Scotsman frowned. "I don't follow you, Andrew."

"Your expertise is identifying and sealing security gaps. Ms. Fitzgerald does the same thing—with energy, of course. I'm simply proposing a partnership." The head of Calendish and Sons rubbed his jaw thoughtfully. "I'd like to see your talents combined in these new designs." He tapped the computer disk. "That combination could mean all the difference in next quarter's balance sheet. You're a stockholder, Duncan. You must know we can't afford another year of problems like we've just had."

"You're circling, Andrew. Get to the point."

"Very well. I want you two to go over the new designs as a team and see that everything meshes." Calendish steepled his fingers. "Any more thefts and our reputation will be in shreds, Duncan. You've seen the books."

Duncan laughed sharply. "Let me get this straight. You're asking me to provide *my* designs to a ... a geomancer? I can't wait to hear what the board members think about *this*."

Kara pushed herself to her feet. "I'm afraid this discussion is pointless, since I won't be staying."

"Please, you two. Think of how much good you will be doing. That bottom line is going to affect you personally, Duncan." A cunning look entered Calendish's brown eyes. "In addition, I am prepared to triple your fee in return for this collaboration. Of course, if you refuse, I shall be forced to consider our contract severed due to noncompliance."

"The hell you will!"

"You failed, Duncan, old man. The terms were clear: you were to enter and exit without detection. By that definition, you failed entirely."

"Only because *she* was there."

"There were no conditions, by your own request.

You never fail and you never leave tracks, so you assured me."

The Scotsman shoved his fists into his pockets, muttering something graphic beneath his breath.

"As for you, Ms. Fitzgerald, your report was intriguing, but far from complete. You can hardly expect me to pay for a few sketches."

"But it's not *my* fault that this—this *thief*—"

Calendish smiled hugely, fingers steepled. "Two days, shall we say? I'll have the designs for our new security systems sent on to you, along with the relevant architectural plans. You can use the corporate yacht in Brighton. I've already spoken to the captain."

"Now, wait just one bloody minute!" Duncan growled.

Chuckling, Calendish leaned back and thumbed a button on his phone. "See that the Daimler is brought around, will you, Susan?" His smile grew as he took in Duncan's black look. "Anything else?"

"I can think of quite a few things," the Scotsman said savagely. "Unfortunately, double-edged claymores are considered illegal weapons."

"If you think I'm going anywhere with this man, you're mistaken!" Kara glared at one man, then the other. "I've got work to finish, people to track down."

"Tell Ms. Fitzgerald that I have no interest in going anywhere with her either. The sooner this hellish weekend is over, the better I'll like it."

"Lovely." Calendish rubbed his hands with great relish. "I'm sure you'll have two very productive days."

The Scotsman muttered something in a low voice.

Gaelic, probably. Not that it needed translating, since the message was clear enough. Kara rubbed a knot of pain at one temple and balanced her portfolio on an Italian leather sofa that had probably cost the equivalent of her whole annual salary. "This is *entirely* unacceptable, gentlemen. I have no more time to spend here. I'm far behind in my schedule, and unless I get to Scotland tomorrow ..."

Her voice trailed away.

A beam of light slanted through the window and played over the priceless old necklace on the desk. Without conscious thought, Kara found her gaze pulled to one of the fine, patterned squares where a golden hawk soared, wings outswept. From its beak dangled a lush rose.

A humming filled her ears, low at first, then higher, until the sound formed a haunting melody.

Bagpipes. The same sound she'd been hearing for a week now.

Kara took a jerky breath. "I—I have to go. Now, before—" She tried to turn, but her legs were shaking, cold rising through her in waves. Not now, she thought. "Please ..." Dimly she realized that the Scotsman had moved. She could feel the heat of his body just behind her.

"Ms. Fitzgerald?"

Kara barely heard. The cold was climbing, her body sliding into a numbness beyond her control. When the paralysis was complete, her mind would jerk free, triggering a psychic link with a place she had never seen and a person she had never met.

Danger in the touch. Danger in the seeing.

"Maybe you'd better get her some sherry, Andrew." There was an edge of command in MacLeod's voice. "And then you'd better sit down, Ms. Fitzgerald."

Kara's hands were trembling as she leaned against the soft leather couch. *Have to go. Have to break free of the link.*

The shaking grew. The skirl of the bagpipes pounded at her in restless, haunting waves. *So cold. Hatred here, and an old hunger for revenge.*

Her knees refused to hold her weight, and she slid back against the couch. "Danger. Must warn—" Her eyes found haven in a tanned face that wore wariness in every hard angle. "Dunraven," she said desperately, her hands still shaking. "Do you—know it?"

"I know it." Grim. His cynicism like a shield. "What kind of danger?"

"He must be warned. Lord Dunraven." Kara blinked as images churned through her mind like hordes of bright, eager fish. "There is fire before him, fire behind him. A man—cradling a bow. The piper . . ."

It was close now. So little time left. And then the cold was absolute as the last of her energy bled free. For one blinding instant she felt calloused hands circle her wrist, heard a voice whisper her name.

Danger in the touch.

"What about Dunraven?"

Kara felt a body slant against hers. She gasped at the shock of the contact.

Danger in the seeing.

Bright, jagged images rode the touch of those calloused fingers, and a wild chorus of voices rose above the drone of crashing waves.

"Danger . . . so close. There in the mist."

But her words echoed, slow and hollow like a voice through a tunnel. *Cold, so cold. Have to get away. Can't let them guess . . .*

Shuddering, she gripped the soft leather beneath her, and then she closed her eyes, swallowed up by the gray fury of the link.

Five ～

Duncan Douglas Wynters MacLeod MacKinnon, Lord of Dunraven, stared down at the woman in his arms and scowled. The shaking had stopped, but she was still cold, bone-chill to the touch. His fingers were drawn to her cheek, where a strand of her unruly red hair fanned out in disarray.

She was wild one minute and silent the next. Too pale. Too still. Too . . . strange.

She disturbed him, and Duncan MacKinnon wasn't used to being disturbed by women.

"What's wrong with her?" Calendish's voice was shaky.

"Damned if I know."

"It looked like . . ." Calendish cleared his throat. "Well, like some kind of trance."

Duncan gave a cynical snort. "I've seen quite a few journalistic tricks, but never one that involved predicting my impending death."

"I don't know, Duncan. She looked sincere—and most upset. Besides, you heard her. She doesn't know *who* you are. Why didn't you tell her your real name?"

"MacLeod *is* my real name—part of it, at least. For the moment I prefer to keep my connection with Dunraven a secret."

"Good Lord, man, you can't really suspect her of trying to steal information! She represents a thriving and well-respected bridal magazine."

Frowning, MacKinnon eased away from Kara's immobile form. "A magazine that has tried to contact me seven times in the last week, offering a vast amount of money to photograph some sort of honeymoon issue at Dunraven." He laughed sharply. "And it will be a very cold day in hell before that happens."

"Not all journalists are snakes, Duncan." Andrew's eyes took on a speculative gleam. "And just how much money are we talking about here?"

"You'd sell your firstborn for the right fee, Calendish. The money is immaterial. Dunraven will never be open to carrion who want to watch another victim bleed out a lifetime of secrets for the titillation of several million bored readers. I've learned my lessons well. There will be *no* journalists at Dunraven. Not ever."

"You think this is some sort of ploy to poke into your past? I mean, everything that happened with your brother, Kyle."

Duncan stiffened.

Kyle again. Always Kyle.

His twin brother's secrets were dead and buried, and they were bloody well going to *stay* dead and buried. "If Ms. Fitzgerald is interested in my brother, she is going to be in for a very long wait."

Calendish shook his head. "I meant what I said about your input on those designs, Duncan. I need both of you in top form. We can't bear any more losses around here."

"Don't worry, you'll get your designs, Andrew. I'll see to that. But until I know what kind of game Ms. Fitzgerald is playing, my name will remain MacLeod." His eyes hardened. "By the end of our two days, I'll know all there is to know about Kara Fitzgerald, including her *real* purpose in trying to contact the laird of Dunraven Castle with this nonsense about danger." He stiffened. "No more for now, Andrew. She's coming around."

The icy layers receded slowly. With the gradual return of heat the images in Kara's mind grew dimmer.

She remembered.

A bow. A falcon and a rose. The haunting strains of a bagpipe rising in a final lament.

She felt a lurch, a jolting impact, and shuddered beneath an oppressive weight as sensation returned to her body.

And then the link was broken. Her body slumped, exhausted, the flood of phantom images now no more than a dream, while the real world, the world of heat and sound and solid dimensions, returned in a rush.

But the sense of danger remained.

Dear God, what had she said?

Duncan's body tensed as he watched her wake— from whatever supposed trance she was in, he thought bitterly.

Oh, she was good. Her face was the color of the white roses that grew up Dunraven's weathered walls, and her body seemed immensely fragile, though from their scuffle in Calendish's showroom he knew she was strong.

All in all, it added up to an act. A masterful one, well conceived and well rehearsed, but an act just the same.

Her eyes opened, amber streaked with gray and green. They reminded him of an old family brooch his mother had worn. How many times he had watched her touch that brooch while she looked out over the sea, her face shuttered and bleak.

Cursing, Duncan pushed himself to his feet. "Who are you, Ms. Fitzgerald? Or perhaps I should say, *what* are you?"

She tensed. He saw the movement clearly through the flimsy silk blouse that matched the color of her hair. He wondered if the strands would feel as warm as they looked, if each one would spring tightly around his fingers.

Desire, like a dull blade. Like a vast, aching wound. So much loneliness, never touched, never healed.

Seldom even admitted.

He cleared his throat angrily, watching her struggle to sit up. Even then, every movement looked natural, utterly persuasive. "Well, Ms. Fitzgerald?"

Slowly her gaze focused on his face. "I frighten you, Mr. MacLeod. I wonder why. Perhaps it's because there's something you're trying to hide." She brushed the hair from her cheek. "It's Lord Dunraven, isn't it? You know him."

"You tell me," MacKinnon said coldly.

For a moment anger roiled over her face. With a tight smile she reached for the Etruscan necklace lying in a velvet box at the edge of the desk.

When Andrew started to pull it away, Duncan stopped him. "Let's hear what she has to say." He crossed his arms. "No doubt it will be an inspired performance."

Kara's chin rose. Gently, so gently, she touched the priceless metal links. "You've been somewhere in water. Murky. Thick with mud." Her fingers traced slow patterns over a magnificent emerald. "You're cursing to yourself as you try to put in some kind of metal plate—a seal of some sort." Her voice tightened. "One man has already died."

Damn her, how did she know about that last project? He'd lumbered around in the mud for four weeks, trying to install an interlocking seal on a new oil pipeline under construction. No one had told him about the sharks until it was nearly too late. That had made news, all right.

His eyes hardened. News. Of course. The death at the pipeline had caused a work stoppage that had made the international papers. She must have read all the details. "Brava, Ms. Fitzgerald. What happens next? Am I supposed to offer a generous donation in return for your predicting my future?"

Kara's eyes flashed. "I'm not interested in your money, and this is no game. If you know Lord Dunraven, you must contact him. Tell him there is danger all around him. Fire." She blinked. "Fire—in the mist."

The necklace slipped from her limp fingers.

Duncan had to fight not to reach out and steady her as she slumped against the sofa. She was trembling again, and she looked exhausted. Her act was perfect.

"I know Dunraven. If you give me something halfway concrete, I might be persuaded to contact him. Tell me a name. Quote me a place and a weapon." His eyebrow rose when Kara didn't answer. "Or was that not part of the script?"

Face flushed now, Kara shoved to her feet, swaying for a moment, then steadying herself. "Damn it, I don't know when or where it will happen. The images don't always—" Her voice broke. She spun around, reaching blindly for her portfolio. "Now I can see why your brother said you have all the imagination of a flea!"

Duncan bit back a raw curse. He seized her wrist and jerked her around to face him. "Who told you that?"

Her body was rigid. "No one told me. Now let me go. You're hurting me."

Duncan barely heard, caught up in anger and suspicion. The mention of his brother always had the same effect, even now. "Did *he* tell you that? Was this some sick plan of Kyle's?" His fingers tightened. "Tell me, damn it!"

She didn't answer, her gaze locked on the throbbing skin where his fingers gripped her wrist. "That has—always bothered you, hasn't it?" She shivered, her eyes unfocused. She seemed to be trying to listen to something. "When he called you names, it made you feel small and silly and lost. You hated him for that. You still hate him."

Duncan shoved her hand away, pale with fury. "Whoever taught you did an extraordinary job, Ms. Fitzgerald. My congratulations. But if you expect my assistance with Lord Dunraven, you'll have to be a great deal more convincing than that. And for your sake, I suggest you leave me and my family out of your parlor tricks."

"With pleasure," Kara snapped. "Now, if you

don't mind, I'd like to go back to my hotel and pack for this enchanting two-day torture session I've just been blackmailed into.''

Duncan's eyes were hard. "Blackmail. An interesting choice of words. A very dangerous one, too.''

"Is that a threat, Mr. MacLeod?'' She frowned, fingering her wrist.

"Not at all.'' Duncan smiled faintly. "That was most definitely a promise.'' He was still smiling when Kara Fitzgerald stormed out of the room a few seconds later.

He glared out at the clouds gathering over the river. "I only hope you don't regret engineering this project, Andrew.''

The man at the desk wiped a fine sheen of sweat from his pale forehead. "So do I.''

After MacKinnon had gone, Andrew Calendish sat for a long time in silence. His soft fingers caught a crystal vase, turning it around and around in slow, precise circles. Twice the intercom on his desk chirped and twice he ignored it.

Finally he straightened and picked up the telephone. "Susan, I'm going out. Cancel my calls. That's right, all of them.''

A sea gull swept past the window, long gray wings brushing the glass in an angry hiss of feathers. Shocked, Calendish spun about, and in the process his sleeve snagged the priceless old vase and swept it to the floor. He watched in a kind of tortured fascination as the fragile crystal shattered into a thousand glinting pieces.

There was fresh sweat on his forehead and fear in his eyes when he snapped shut the velvet case containing the necklace and shoved it into his pocket.

Six ~

Twenty minutes later, the clouds opened and a fine, sharp London drizzle spattered mud on the daffodils in Hyde Park. Clouds darkened the dome of St. Paul's and huddled oppressively over the leaden Thames.

"Damned insufferable man."

Kara muttered as she slung garment after garment into a large leather bag scarred from years of travel. In went a battered pair of blue jeans, followed by another oath. In went cotton leggings, T-shirts, and a worn flannel nightgown, each addition punctuated by another imprecation.

But most of her anger was for herself. Why had she allowed herself to be baited? Why had she wasted her words on a man whose mind was obviously closed? She had dealt with skeptics before without feeling any need to prove herself, yet today, faced by a pair of bitter blue-gray eyes, she had responded without care or caution, opening herself to ridicule.

She slammed another sweater into her case. What had possessed her to hold the necklace and search the faint energy trails of his touch, probing for a detail that would convince him she was telling the truth? What did *she* care for the opinion of a stranger? Trying to convince other people always turned out to be a mistake.

Clearly, Mr. MacLeod was going to be trouble. If she let him, that is.

Kara's hand brushed a clinging damask sheath with a low neckline and a tulip hem. Frowning, she discarded the dress in favor of an oversize sweater, soft leather boots, and roughly two weeks of paper work.

The final addition to her bag was a portable tape player.

That was to tune out the arrogant jerk who made his money by pretending to steal things.

Rain spit at Duncan MacKinnon's hotel windows as he scowled down at the meager supply of clothing jumbled in his drawers. He tossed a worn cashmere sweater into his canvas duffel bag, along with a pair of battered corduroys. There wasn't very much else to choose from. He'd been on two assignments back to back, and he'd planned to return to Dunraven over a week before.

Somehow that was what happened to most of his plans.

A dark gleam lit his eyes, and he fingered a pair of silk pajamas. With an oath he sent them flying back into the drawer. He didn't believe in the sacrilege of wearing clothes to bed, and if the wretched female didn't like it, too bad. Not that she would have an opportunity to notice his sleeping habits.

He tugged on a pair of faded denim jeans and sprawled on the bed. His chest was burned copper by the Greek sun, and muscles rose in tight ridges as he crossed his arms behind his head.

Little as he liked it, he would have to cancel this weekend's invitation from his cousin, Nicholas Draycott. The bond between the MacKinnons and the Draycotts stretched back for many generations, the blood ties strengthened by a bond of deep affection between the two men. Duncan had been bloody well looking forward to spending several days at Draycott Abbey. Damn Andrew Calendish anyway!

He dialed Nicholas's number from memory and smiled when a very formal voice answered.

"You have reached Lord Draycott's residence. How may I assist you?"

"Marston, don't tell me Nicholas still has you corraled there at the abbey."

There was a pause, then a low chuckle. "Indeed so," Lord Draycott's butler said crisply. "Better the abbey than that cliff on the edge of nowhere you MacKinnons call home."

Duncan smiled at this old sparring. "That cliff on the edge of nowhere builds moral fiber, develops spiritual character—"

"And gives a man acute rheumatism," Marston said coolly. "And now I shall fetch his lordship. He will no doubt be happy to argue with you."

The Scotsman was still smiling when his cousin came on the line.

"Duncan, welcome back! How was Crete?"

"Don't ask."

"Like that, was it? Ah, well, that's the price of being the young genius that no corporate security can do without. Let's face it, you're just too successful for your own good, cousin."

Duncan said something low and curt in Gaelic.

"Don't toss ancient curses at me, Duncan. And don't tell me you're crying off again. Kacey has been driving me mad arranging things for this weekend." Both men knew that meant a well-screened female friend invited for a casual luncheon, in hopes that Duncan's interest would be piqued.

Duncan had found that he greatly enjoyed those quiet weekends at Draycott Abbey, sitting by the moat and watching the swans cut restful arcs in the silver water. It made him feel . . . comfortable. Satisfied.

Almost as if he had a real family again.

"Blast it, Duncan, if you bow out now, she'll likely strangle you, and me along with you."

"Sorry, Nicky, it can't be helped. Something's come up." His voice tightened as he spoke.

A pause. "Anything I can help out with?"

"Afraid not."

"You're not flying back to Crete already, are you? Can't those people manage anything by themselves?"

Duncan thought of the four exhausting visits he had made to Greece and Crete in the last year. Several shipping complexes had been plagued by robbery and vandalism, and Duncan had been called in to update what had turned out to be medieval security systems. "No, this is much closer to home."

"You'll still be down *next* weekend, I hope."

"I wouldn't miss it for the world, Nicky."

"You'd better not, or Kacey would never forgive you. Come to think of it, neither would I."

There was a discreet tap at the hotel door. "Your car is waiting, Lord Dunraven."

MacKinnon frowned, thinking about the weekend to come. For the hundredth time he wondered exactly what Kara Fitzgerald's game was. Playing cat and mouse was hardly what he had planned to do on his first free night back in England after nearly two months of working abroad.

He fingered the heavy gold Roman coin that hung on a chain around his neck. First should have come a superb meal at White's with an old and very intimate friend. After several hours of laughter and seductive talk over two bottles of very good Taittinger Blanc de Blancs, they would have returned to the Ritz for a long night of explosive sex.

And then a clear-eyed parting the next morning after a late breakfast, with no emotions and no regrets. Daniella preferred things that way, since her husband had left her for a dewy-eyed fitness teacher half his age.

Instead, Duncan was going to discuss energy anomalies with a scheming journalist.

"Duncan, are you still there?"

"Right here, Nicky. Just a bad connection." Duncan frowned as he fingered the old coin at his neck. "Listen, could you call on some of those platinum

connections of yours and run a trace on someone
for me?"

"How deep?"

"All the way. Business, family background, personal life, politics—all of it. I want to know what she
eats, where she eats, when she eats."

"And with whom?" There was a note of specula-
tion in Nicholas Draycott's voice.

"Don't get your hopes up. I'd sooner go to bed
with a Howitzer." He snorted. "Her name is Fitzgerald. Kara Fitzgerald."

"Irish?"

"American. A resident of New York City."

"I'll see what I can dig up, Duncan. Will tomorrow
evening do?"

"Fine."

Rain streaked the windows, and for an instant
Duncan was back in the Mediterranean mud, fighting
twenty-foot waves as he tried to free a clogged, oil-
intake plate.

Anger filled his eyes. How had the bloody woman
known about that?

He tried not to think about water that rose in horizontal sheets. He tried to forget the feeling of being
perpetually cold, body caked with mud and oil in
every pore.

Some glamour job, MacKinnon.

There was another tap at the door. "Look, Nicky,
I'm afraid I have to go. Give my love to Kacey and
assure her that nothing could possibly keep me away
from Draycott Abbey next weekend."

Except, the Scotsman thought grimly, the strait-
jacket he would probably need after two days spent
in Kara Fitzgerald's presence.

Two counties away, in a room bright with sunlight,
good prints and blood-red roses, Nicholas Draycott
stood frowning at the telephone in his hand. There
was a sprinkling of gray at his temples, and his
face had lines carved by both laughter and grave
responsibility.

And nightmares.

But those were nearly gone now, thank heaven.

"Nicky, have you seen Genevieve's other shoe?" A woman with laughing eyes padded into the study, four-year-old daughter at her side. "What's wrong, love?"

"That was Duncan. He can't make it this weekend after all." Nicholas frowned at his American wife of five years. "Sorry, I know how much you were looking forward to pairing him off with that friend of yours from Vermont."

Kacey Mallory Draycott said a very rude word under her breath and settled her wriggling daughter on the fine old Tientsin carpet. "The following weekend he'd better be free. Everyone is expecting to see him."

"And Duncan will be there, so he assured me. It must be one of his security projects tying him up today."

"You look worried." Kacey's eyes narrowed. No detail of her husband's expression ever escaped her notice.

"Nonsense. My only worry at the moment is that my lovely and very intractable daughter is going to carve a hole through that two-hundred-year-old carpet."

Genevieve, blond curls flying, looked up in rosy innocence. "Do you mean *me*, Daddy?"

"No, of course not," the viscount said, scooping his giggling bundle up into his arms. "You were just checking for moths, I expect."

Kacey Draycott wasn't fooled for a second. Her husband was definitely worried. When Duncan MacKinnon showed up on their doorstep next week, she vowed, she would find out why.

Out beside the moat, roses spilled in wild, colorful profusion over the abbey's weathered walls. Here and there a bee rumbled through the glorious red blooms, and swans eased through the shimmering waters.

On the parapets above, shadows pooled in the corners of the roof, and in one of those pools of darkness a gray cat sat sleeping.

Abruptly the great amber eyes opened. Keen and bright, they surveyed the abbey's empty roof. And as they watched, a lone figure took shape, half sunlight and half shadow. The sculpted features that looked out over the abbey's green lawns and shimmering water were as hard and weathered as the granite walls below.

There was pride in those guardian eyes—and challenge as well, for the abbey was his domain, a responsibility blood-borne for centuries.

In death as well as life.

Adrian Draycott, the eighth viscount Draycott, studied the green quilt of fields and frowned. Something played at his senses, something that drifted as light and subtle as the mist that even now clung to the distant river beyond the cliff known as Lyon's Leap.

"Do you sense that faint touch as I do, old friend?"

At Adrian's feet the great cat stirred, tail aloft.

"Something subtle, yes. But probing just the same." After a moment he shrugged. The day was too fine to worry about nebulous threats. Guests were expected at the abbey, and Adrian found himself relishing the arrival of their unpredictable Gaelic visitor. "Yes, it will be good to see the clansman again. The ties of MacKinnon and Draycott go back to a braver age." His eyes narrowed as he reached out with senses unseen and immeasurable. "I can feel the Draycott capstone, still standing at the great Dunraven Castle by the loch. All is well, if one can overlook the execrable dampness and the mist that climbs up the valley." He turned slightly, tension spreading over his hard features. "And the MacKinnon stone likewise bides well here, set into the foot of the south wall below me, exactly where the cantankerous old laird saw it laid all those centuries ago."

With that exchange of stones had come a responsibility. Now Adrian's duties included not only this beautiful old abbey, but also the distant Highland castle that held one of the abbey's stones.

He had not accepted the responsibility lightly—or well. He still chafed at any contact with Dunraven Castle. A cold, unhealthy place, he called it.

At his feet the cat's back arched.

"Yes, I quite understand your liking for the fat salmon that spawn just beyond the loch, but the dampness disturbs my bones." His lips curved, granting his face a look of rare warmth. "What bones that are left to me."

With a soft hiss, the cat jumped to the edge of the parapet and pushed against Adrian's lace-clad wrist.

"Do you sense it too? Something as fragile as the rose fragrance that drifts on the wind." The guardian ghost of Draycott Abbey nodded. "There is skill here, Gideon. Very great skill, I think."

The cat meowed.

"You think it a warning?" He frowned as his long fingers moved over the cat's soft fur, warm in the bright June sunlight. "It is too faint to say. The touch is no one familiar to me. A woman, perhaps." His eyes glinted for a moment. "And isn't a woman always at the heart of our turmoil? Our worst friends and our best enemies, I sometimes think."

The cat's amber eyes blinked.

"You are right, of course. All except for *her*." Adrian stared out over the granite walls, caught, as he had been twice before, by the sense that someone was trying to reach him—or his abbey.

Beneath his hand, the great cat purred, settling back on the narrow rim of the stone parapet.

"Reckless as always, I see. No more than I was in my time." Adrian's fingers stilled, and for a moment sadness seemed to trail around him. "I am glad for your company through these long years of duty, my old friend. And tonight we shall watch together, feeling ... whatever it is we might feel."

As Adrian's strong fingers stroked the warm fur, wariness gathered in his singular, granite-gray eyes.

Seven ～

A driver with bored eyes was waiting for Kara outside the hotel. Without a word he deposited her bag in the trunk of a black Daimler buffed to a mirrorlike sheen, and then swept open the rear door.

She frowned as she slid into butter-soft leather seats. *Nice try, Andrew, but even this car isn't going to make me any happier about this weekend fiasco.*

She shoved back a strand of copper hair and peered into the gloom, making out a small refrigerator, a cellular telephone, and a laptop computer. A fax machine was wedged beside the arm of a seat, just as Calendish's secretary had promised.

Things were definitely looking up, Kara decided.

Then she saw the long legs jutting from the far seat.

"Glad to see you could finally join us," the Scotsman muttered, looking pointedly at his watch.

"I had to finish a telephone call. Some of us have to do serious *work* for a living. Work as in gainful and legal employment involving more than sneaking past security alarms."

"You call drawing diagrams of energy flow work?" MacLeod said coolly. He was wearing a soft denim shirt and dark gray flannels. A strange match, but somehow it worked on him.

Not that she cared whether it worked or *not.*

Kara shrugged off her suede jacket, swung it down beside her, and reached toward the refrigerator.

Deftly she fished out two cold Perriers, tossed one to her companion, then found two packets of pretzels.

One of these she sent flying toward MacLeod, who caught it without an inch of wasted motion.

Kara barely noticed, busy squeezing a slice of lime over her spring water. She smiled as the fax machine began to beep and spit out paper. She shoved a pencil into her disordered auburn curls and tore open the bag of pretzels. "Lunch is served, MacLeod." Then she scooped up the incoming papers and curled up on the seat, kicking off her shoes and tucking her feet beneath her.

Already her thoughts were a thousand miles away.

When Kara looked up from her paper work, quiet green fields flanked the road. She knew the way to Brighton, and this was not it. "We're not going south?"

"Brilliant deduction, Ms. Fitzgerald."

"Why didn't you tell me?"

"I tried. You wouldn't have heard a cannon fired beside you. We stopped about five miles ago, after Andrew phoned the driver to say something was wrong with the stabilizers on the yacht."

"So the weekend's off?" Kara's eyes brightened.

"No. We'll just be staying elsewhere."

Kara sighed. "Whatever," she mumbled, her gaze sliding back to an incoming fax.

He bent close and managed to make out a row of sketches. "Some sort of dresses?"

"Back off." Kara shoved at his hand.

"Of course, how foolish. I suppose those are energy grids for Windsor Castle, and national security is at stake."

Kara smiled faintly. "You might just be surprised, Mr. MacLeod."

The Scotsman frowned. "Don't tell me you've actually been called to the castle to—"

"I won't. Tell you, that is. But believe me, that place has an energy imbalance in the area of family

relations that could swallow the whole state of Texas."
Still smiling, she turned back to her work.

Duncan scowled at her down-turned head. It just
wasn't possible. The British government simply did
not invite foreign nationals into the royal household
to advise Her Majesty the Queen on blocked energy
and inauspicious furniture alignments.

Then again, considering some of the rumors he had
heard lately, maybe they *did*.

MacKinnon studied the unruly hair glinting a hundred shades of red in the sunlight. Here and there
the light seemed to catch, settling in little pools of
gold. His eyes slid lower, and he frowned at the welt
slanting across her knee. He hadn't meant to push
her down so hard the night before, but he'd had no
choice. The woman had shown every sign of being
an intruder in a business plagued by thefts.

He hadn't trusted her then and he wasn't about to
trust her now, no matter how good her references
were.

Neat villages rushed past in a blur of green as
they glided east. The rain had gone, and now the sky
stretched, cloudless, in a blinding arc of turquoise.
Somewhere a kestrel called from a hedgerow, but
Kara hardly noticed, nose deep in a pile of faxes.

As he watched paper pile up on her side of the
seat, Duncan frowned, reminded of his own responsibilities after six weeks abroad. The factory in Scotland had a new prototype dive computer he needed
to inspect. Three malfunctions in one month was entirely unacceptable, and the next accident might well
prove fatal. Duncan knew he would have to take the
models down and personally oversee the tests.

Then there was the problem with the oil rigs up
at Magnus. The most northern of the North Sea oil
platforms, Magnus stood in some of the world's
roughest water. The head of maintenance was an old
friend of Duncan's, and he had called twice, re-
questing help on problems with the dive apparatus.

That meant another two weeks away from home while he worked at the rig.

A pile of papers slid to the floor, and Duncan reached for them at the same moment Kara did. Their heads met with an audible crack.

"Watch where you're going!"

"Stay on your side of the seat and I wouldn't have to." Muttering, Duncan eased closer to the papers scattered over the floor. He could just make out a row of sketches of things that looked like scarves.

"Stay away. I have those in order."

Duncan ignored her, rubbing his forehead while he scooped up the top sheet. "Wedding gowns and veils. Is *this* what you do for a living, Ms. Fitzgerald?"

"You mean studying arcane energy flow isn't good enough?"

MacKinnon tapped the top sheet. "Not half bad. Are you some sort of dress designer?"

"No." Kara dove unsuccessfully for the paper.

"Don't tell me: you write about celebrity weddings for that magazine of yours." His tone was mocking. He eased back against the seat, the papers well out of her reach.

"Give me those designs."

"Not until I have an answer."

"What I do is none of your business."

Duncan was about to launch into another inquisition when the telephone on the wall beeped.

Kara beat him to it. "Who? Oh, just a minute." She covered the phone. "For you." Her brow rose. "Nice voice."

Duncan's lips curved as he heard a sultry voice purr his name. Leave it to his friend Daniella to track him down in record time. The sound reminded him that he should have been embarking on a quiet weekend of three-star relaxation, four-star cuisine, and five-star sex with Daniella in a luxurious suite at the Ritz just then.

Blast Andrew Calendish.

"I'm sorry too, Daniella. No, something came up. Yes, something very important. Of course not. No, never." He frowned, fielding the questions laced with irritation. "Yes, I'd like that too. But not next week. I'll have to phone you back with a date."

Daniella was clearly not pleased. "I'm afraid so. Yes, I'm due back up north on Monday. I'll ring you next week and we'll discuss it. Of course. Yes, I remember that you're leaving for Ibiza. After you return, in that case."

Irritation grew like a hard knot in Duncan's throat. Everything had been perfectly arranged, with nothing left to chance. Blast Andrew Calendish for ruining those careful plans. And blast this damned American journalist with her hidden agenda.

He slammed down the phone, glaring at the neat stone wall running beside the road. He liked schedules to be set, people to be orderly, and his time to be well planned. Now everything was in turmoil.

And after six weeks away, six weeks of hard physical labor and uninterrupted celibacy, Duncan MacKinnon was finding himself uncomfortably sensitive to female proximity.

Any female proximity. Even the disturbing creature glaring at him from the opposite seat.

What *was* that fragrance she wore? Violets or something with lavender? He turned away, wishing she wouldn't bend over so that the light played through her hair, streaking it all the colors of a highland sunset. He especially wished that every movement wouldn't make her sweater cling to her full breasts, hinting at lush, high nipples.

He turned away, furious to feel the jolt of desire.

Kara slanted him an appraising look. "Sorry if this has broken up your big plans for the weekend."

She didn't look sorry, Duncan thought angrily. In fact, she looked as if she was thoroughly enjoying herself. "It was nothing special."

"No? Your friend didn't sound so cool. It was going to be an intimate little weekend. Somewhere very elegant like the Dorchester, wasn't it? Or maybe the Ritz."

"Way off, Ms. Fitzgerald. Daniella is just a friend."

"Funny, she didn't sound like a friend. As a matter of fact, she sounded furious that the rendezvous was off."

"Daniella always sounds that way. Her mother is Greek and her father is Irish." He turned away, signaling the end of the discussion.

"I bet she's great in bed. Greek and Irish blood must make a volatile mix."

She didn't know the half of it, Duncan thought grimly. Three prior encounters had left both parties tottering on the edge of exhaustion and supremely well satisfied. "I wouldn't know. As I said, we're just good friends."

"Right, MacLeod. And I was born yesterday."

His eyes darkened. "What about you, Ms. Fitzgerald? How are *you* in bed?" He watched in fascination as a faint flush began at her neck and worked up over her cheeks. Somehow the damned thing only made Kara Fitzgerald's face more fragile, her eyes more startling.

"That's another thing you're never going to know, isn't it?"

Duncan saw her stiffen and rub her forehead. "What is it?" he asked.

"Nothing."

"More visions? More danger lurking nearby? Maybe there's a terrorist army camped out in that field with those sheep. In fact, maybe those aren't *sheep* at all, but armed insurgents in clever costumes."

Her voice was very cold, very steady. "Stop it."

"I will if you tell me what those papers are for."

"They're magazine layouts," Kara said after a brief hesitation.

"Ah. For your bridal magazine." He looked at her hand. "I don't see any ring." He reached for her fingers, but she pulled away before he could touch her. "Don't."

Duncan's jaw hardened. "I can control myself, Ms. Fitzgerald. Don't worry about my touching your hand. Nothing's going to happen in the back of this Daimler."

"I—I'd just prefer that you didn't touch me."

He wasn't going to ask, Duncan told himself. Hell, he didn't care if she went stiff whenever he reached anywhere near her. He certainly didn't wonder what had put those shadows in her eyes. "Why no ring?"

"Because I'm not married. That's none of your business either."

"No? Things are going to get very private this weekend. I don't want to wake up and find the loaded barrel of an irate husband's pistol waving in my face."

"You won't." Kara's eyes darkened. "Except maybe one that belongs to Daniella's husband."

"Oh, she's not married. Husband number three had the good grace to expire suddenly and painlessly during a photographic safari in Kenya. Husband number four recently ran off with a fitness trainer half his age." Angling his broad shoulders against the far wall, Duncan probed Kara's face. "So you write for *New Bride*. Somehow I don't see you drafting fluff pieces about naughty lingerie and package deals to trendy honeymoon resorts."

"I *don't*." Glaring, she shoved her pencil deeper into her riotous hair. "For your information, *New Bride* is about believing—about learning how to make wonderful dreams come true out of practical strategies that begin in the present. I do pieces on aromatherapy, on sound financial planning for newlyweds, as well as the pros and cons of prenuptial contracts. We even do bridal unplugged."

"I beg your pardon?"

"Unplugged. As in MTV."

Duncan's face was blank. "MTV?"

"You know how they showcase musicians in simple acoustic performances. We do a behind-the-scenes look at the real work that goes into making a wedding gown or a floral arrangement. The unvarnished truth—without the fluff, as you put it."

He nodded. "Unplugged. I'll have to remember that."

Kara balanced her pencil against the chiseled point

of her chin. "Where have you been, MacLeod, Borneo or the moon?"

"Borneo and Crete, actually."

The pencil wavered slightly. "You're kidding."

"Not in the least."

Her eyes narrowed. "Borneo. I could probably use that."

Duncan watched, fascinated, as she flipped open her portfolio and began to write. He was beginning to see that Kara Fitzgerald always measured facts, events, and people to see if they could be of use in her precious magazine.

She shot forward, chin on one palm. "Borneo still has headhunters, doesn't it?" She gnawed one lip, tapping the pencil against her knee. "Yes, headhunters would be good. Okay, do they have any strange customs? You know, bride price—visiting and clothing taboos for the weeks before the wedding ceremony, things like that."

Duncan felt a sudden pang of regret. He couldn't answer her. The truth was, he had spent most of his time in Borneo's coastal waters, checking oil pipelines and evaluating security systems for a billion-dollar petrochemical facility going up there.

Then again, *she* didn't know that.

A slow, outrageous smile began to play over his lips. "Well, they did have some rather unusual customs. . . ." He let the words trail away, deliberately hesitating.

"Go on, you don't have to gloss over the details. This will make a wonderful piece for our next issue. We can learn a lot from the sexuality of other cultures." Her voice was ardent.

Duncan watched her dig into a leather bag, retrieve a new notebook, then wait expectantly, her pencil poised.

She was eager, intent, just waiting for him to start regaling her with stories of the jungle. Hell, he hadn't even made it to the jungle. He had barely made it out of the water.

Still, it wouldn't hurt to humor her.

He frowned. Her cheeks were streaked with glorious color. Her breasts rose and fell eagerly, high and lush where they pressed against the soft cashmere of her sweater.

Two days with her like this, in his unsatisfied condition? God help him.

God help them both.

"You really can tell me, Mr. MacLeod. I grew up with four brothers. Very little shocks me."

Duncan sat back slowly. "Nothing at all?"

She shrugged. "Not much. So spill, MacLeod. Firsthand detail makes for intriguing stories. Our readers are up-scale and well educated, but Borneo is not exactly a typical tourist haunt."

As she spoke, she sat forward, unconscious of the way her hair spilled over her flushed cheeks, unconscious of how her sweater molded her nipples. Duncan only wished *he* were equally unaware.

Because in spite of all his caution, at that moment, with her whole attention focused on him, he felt like the most important man in the world. And that, no doubt, was what she wanted him to feel.

"Forget it." He was speaking to himself as much as to her.

"Come on, MacLeod, you don't look like the kind of man who has scruples over plain speaking with women."

"How do you know *what* kind of man I am?" There was unexpected bitterness in the question. Duncan found her quick assumptions annoying. Even more annoying was the fact that he couldn't seem to pull his eyes away from the little shadow beneath her bottom lip.

"Oh, I know your type." Her amber eyes narrowed. "You play by the rules—as long as they're your rules. No clinging, no whining, and everything organized in advance. Most of all, no questions asked." Her head slanted back. "Am I close?"

"Way off target," he lied flatly. "Besides, we weren't discussing my private life. I thought you wanted to know about those obscure jungle rituals."

Her pencil snapped to attention. "I'm all ears."

He cleared his throat experimentally. "The natives I met had several unusual prenuptial customs. One involves rubbing the bride-to-be with fragrant oil." He paused. "And then removing it."

This was a lie, of course, but it might shut her up.

"Removing it? I don't understand."

Duncan's eyes locked on her face. "Slowly. Carefully. With the groom's tongue." He paused again. "Everywhere."

Color slammed through her cheeks. "Oh." She cleared her throat, frowned at her pencil. "You wouldn't happen to know what kind of oil, would you?"

So much for shutting her up. "Oh, the usual edible varieties. Wild neroli. Ylang-ylang." Duncan hadn't a clue whether they were edible or not. He hoped she didn't either.

Kara looked down, cutting off his view of her face. "Any . . . er, others?"

"You really want to hear this?"

"Of course." The words were muffled. He noticed she didn't raise her eyes. Good.

"Another custom involved flowers. Rare jungle orchids, to be exact." Duncan steepled his hands and settled into his role. He let the fantasies from weeks of pent-up sexual drive form heated images. "In the central mountains they scatter orchid petals over woven grass mats where the couple spend their first nights after the wedding. And then . . ."

"Yes?" This time her voice was a croak.

Duncan smiled in wolfish pleasure. "The bride takes the leftover petals and weaves a wreath. She uses that wreath to circle the most prominent feature of the groom's anatomy."

Another croak. The pencil jerked, then crept back into motion.

Duncan hid a smile. How was she going to put *that* in words suitable for a general family audience?

"Is there . . . more?"

The woman just didn't give up, did she? "Oh, yes, there's more. Are you sure you want to hear it?"

Her pencil sketched slow circles for a moment. "Of course."

"Then I'll tell you about those orchid petals, Ms. Fitzgerald. They have an unusual oil in their biochemical makeup. This particular oil enhances the biochemical activity of nerve receptors. Especially those in the human erogenous zones."

He waited.

The pencil lurched, then began to circle. Slowly. Thoughtfully.

And Duncan was suddenly on fire, victim of his own lustful images. Feeling the heat of a jungle night. Seeing Kara Fitzgerald, all creamy skin and wide, haunting eyes.

Beneath him while he scattered orchid petals over every silken inch of her bare skin.

He cleared his throat. "Any *more* questions?"

"About those oils—you mean they act as aphrodisiacs?"

Her voice was steady, blast her. He found he had to clear *his* throat. "Only if properly used."

That brought her face up. Damn it, her eyes were even more beautiful than he'd imagined they could be, all smoky and golden. Her lips were parted, and he found himself imagining how they'd feel pressed against his chest, his palms, his naked—

"I just asked you a question."

"Yes, they do." He hadn't even heard it. *Take hold, MacKinnon.*

"They do?"

"Of course." Be confident when all else fails. His father, the late laird, had taught him that. Duncan wondered if his father had ever faced a woman like Kara Fitzgerald.

"Fascinating. Then what?" Her eyes were wide with curiosity.

"The groom makes his own chain of orchid petals. Slowly, carefully, he places it ..." His eyes fell, scouring her creamy cheeks, imagining every erotic moment of the scene he was describing.

With a jolt he realized his hands were trembling. Damn Andrew Calendish for getting him into this. "Inside the woman he loves," he said fiercely. "Then he removes them, inch by inch. By the time he's done, his new bride is wild with passion. So is he. Now the fragrance is everywhere, enveloping them in a cloud of desire as hot as the jungle night. There is very little prudery among this tribe. Whatever did exist in the bride or groom has vanished by dawn, I assure you."

Her pencil was no longer moving. Her eyes were averted. "I ... I see."

Duncan sent the note pad flying with a curse. "No, I don't quite think you do. For your own sake, Ms. Fitzgerald, I am going to make several things very clear to you. I have been out of the country, part of that time in the tropics, doing backbreaking work for nearly two straight months. All that time I ate, drank, and slept my work. I had very little human companionship—and none of it was female. I was just about to remedy that lack when Andrew Calendish drafted me for this ridiculous collaboration with you." His hands were tense. He had to fight to keep them from drifting over the sleek curve of her lower lip and tugging her toward him.

Damn him. He couldn't pull his gaze from her lips. They were the color of crushed raspberries. Probably they would have the same musky, rich taste if he kissed them.

Which he bloody well *wasn't* going to do.

"So?" Her eyes were riveted to his.

"So unless you want more than you bargained for, you'll keep out of my way. I'm not proud of the fact, but I'm not apologizing either. It's just the way things are." His eyes hardened. "Since you're the very experienced sister of four brothers, I'm sure *you* understand all about that."

She frowned. "Urges, you mean."

"Urges."

"Hormone things."

"Exactly."

Her eyes slanted downward. MacKinnon cursed silently when he saw where her unconscious look was focused.

Instantly the unruly inches of male muscle tightened in a passionate, unmistakable response to her glance.

She swallowed.

Audibly.

"I'll try to remember that. I certainly wouldn't want to cause you—to cause anyone, that is—discomfort."

Discomfort was far too feeble a word for the pain he was feeling at that moment.

Her face rose. Her eyes were wide, intent.

Filled with concern, Duncan realized, shocked. The woman was concerned for *him!*

"Is there, er, anything I can do? To help you?"

Sweet God, strike him down right now! Anything to release him from this unfathomable woman and the pain he was feeling. "To help? Me?" he croaked. He couldn't seem to think straight, not while her bare legs were sliding over the butter-soft leather in their eagerness.

All he could think of was how she'd feel pressed beneath him, their bodies slick with sweat as he slid off her sweater and took her against all that soft leather.

Belatedly, he realized she had spoken again. "What?"

"I said, maybe you should phone Daniella. You could have her meet you in—" She frowned, snagging a full lip between white teeth. New pain slammed into Duncan's groin. "In whatever city we're going to."

It was then that Duncan realized he didn't want Daniella. Not ever again. What he wanted was clear amber eyes, focused intently on him. What he wanted was cool white hands that trembled slightly when she slid open his shirt and eased off his belt.

And after that he wanted her soft lips melting over

the whole length of his body, as passionate and intense as she was in everything.

A stream of silent Gaelic curses raced through his mind. "I will. Phone Daniella. Just as soon as we arrive." *Wonderful, MacKinnon. Try to manage six words in a row, can't you? Next the woman will have you groveling at her feet.*

"I'll disappear discreetly, I promise. She won't even know I'm there."

But Duncan would know. He'd feel this woman if she was anywhere within two counties. He would smell that soft, woodsy perfume that drifted from the skin behind her ear. He'd hear the soft hiss of silk against warm skin when she walked.

"Duncan?" Her long legs moved restlessly over the leather seat. Until that moment, he hadn't realized how erotic noise could be, how many images a sound could invoke.

Or how much lust a man could endure while trying to stay in control of his senses. "Wonderful. Great idea. I'll call her."

"You could even try to find some orchid petals to—"

Those words drove the last shred of sanity from his mind. It was not going to work. Absolutely *not* going to work.

Duncan finally accepted the fact. Maybe in a normal state he'd be able to steel himself to remain unaffected, but in this sensitized state, with every nerve screaming for release, he'd be lucky to get through one night without losing control and trying out some of those techniques he'd just described.

It was no good. Andrew would have to find someone else for his dirty work.

Duncan was reaching for the phone to call Andrew when a siren screamed behind them. He saw Kara stiffen, her eyes going dark with fear. "Kara, what is it?"

"It's—wrong. Something—" She shook her head.

An electronic voice cracked to life out of a burst of static.

"Slow your automobile," it said. "Then pull over."

Eight ~

A police car raced past, nudging the Daimler onto the shoulder. Two uniformed figures stepped out, their features hidden behind mirrored sunglasses.

Kara looked across at Duncan, who shrugged. "Don't worry, it's just some formality or other. These country officers are so bored they'll do anything to break up their day."

Kara didn't believe it. A pulse was hammering at the side of her neck, and every beat told her this was no ordinary procedure.

One of the officers tapped at the window, and Duncan eased down the glass. "Yes, officer?"

"I'll need you both out of the automobile."

"Is there some sort of problem?"

The man ignored the question. "I'll need you to step out right now."

The throb in Kara's neck turned into a wild hammering. She couldn't move, her eyes narrowed on the expressionless face outside.

Something was very wrong. She sensed shadows, anger—cold that brushed at her neck. "May I see your badge?"

Did the man hesitate or had she only imagined it?

"Of course." He leveled a laminated identification card complete with photograph and official stamp. Impressive, all right.

Kara bent forward and took a deep breath. It was

risky, worse than risky, but she had learned long ago never to ignore the stab of her intuition.

Slowly she reached out and brushed the cold plastic sheet. Somewhere in the distance a car backfired. Two bluebirds argued angrily from a hedge beside the road. Kara listened, her senses reaching out for the source of her uneasiness. And then the fear grabbed her, starting in her fingers, which curled as if pressed down by a great weight. For blinding moments she could not move, could not pull her fingers from the cold plastic.

Her breath caught in a gasp. She looked up, plummeting into the dark expanse of the officer's sunglasses.

She knew then that her instinct was correct. There was danger all around them. "Thank you, that will be fine." She passed back the badge, managing a smile.

No answer.

Duncan frowned. "Perhaps if you would tell us what this is all about—"

The officer's voice did not rise, but this time the muzzle of a pistol pointed at the window. "Step outside. Keep your hands in clear sight."

The Scotsman's face hardened as he complied, and with every second Kara felt her foreboding grow. Through the window she saw their driver being escorted across the road by the second officer. Then Duncan was outside, hands pressed to the roof of the car.

Kara shook her head at him and saw his eyes widen.

"We've received information that this automobile has been stolen," the officer said while he ran his hands over Duncan's back and shoulders.

Stolen . . .

Kara shook her head wildly. Another lie. She would have picked up the images from the ID card if it were true. No, there was a deeper goal, something that felt heavy—like buried secrets.

"May I ask who made this report?"

"You'll find out all you need to know in due order." The veiled eyes turned, fixed on Kara. "Now you. Out of the car."

Warnings growled through Kara's head. "Of course. I just need to find my shoes." She held up one bare foot by way of explanation.

"Leave the shoes."

"Damn it, the woman can't go barefoot. She needs her—"

The officer jerked Duncan around and slammed the pistol into his jaw. Kara watched in horror as blood trickled down his cheek.

"Shut up. Both of you will do exactly as I tell you from now on. Any complaints or questions can be handled later. Down at the station."

Down at the station.

Another lie. They would be taken somewhere lonely. Somewhere hidden. There would be questions and then—pain. The certainty of their danger made Kara gag, and she knew if they didn't act fast there would be no hope of escape.

"Now you. Outside." The muzzle turned, a cold staring eye.

Kara saw that Duncan's gaze was focused on the shelf just beneath the window. She looked down, wondering what he had been trying to tell her. Half out of sight lay a pile of papers clipped to a plastic file.

Owner's documents. Registration. "We have papers, if that's what you want. The car is registered by Andrew Calendish of Calendish and Sons in London. I'm sure if you take a look at these, you'll see that—"

Her hand was only partway to the shelf when it was twisted in a painful grip. "Forget the documents. You're coming with us."

Anger surged over her. She felt the cunning, the cold force of lies practiced over weeks.

If they went, they would die.

She dived for the back of the car.

It was just what Duncan had been waiting for.

Without a sound he spun sideways and slammed the ball of his foot against the officer's back. Another kick struck home before Duncan was flung sideways against the Daimler. The pistol barked.

Kara shot out of the car. "Duncan, are you—"

The officer slid limply to the ground at her feet. "Is he—"

"No," MacKinnon growled, wiping blood from his cheek. "Not yet, at least." He looked across the road. The other officer had shoved the driver aside and was running for his car. A moment later he hurtled off in a hail of gravel. "If *that* was an official representative of the Sussex Police Force, then I'm bloody Prince Charles."

"But *why?* What did they want?"

"Hell if I know. But I'm going to find out." After a last grim glance at the motionless officer, Duncan slid into the car and stabbed out a number on the cellular phone. "Andrew Calendish, please. Yes, right now." He waited tensely, his fingers curled over the receiver. "He's gone? Listen, Susan, we've just come out of a little tussle with some officers near Alfriston. They say they received a report that the Daimler was stolen." There was a moment of silence, followed by Duncan's low curse. "I see. That's exactly what I thought. But if you didn't send them, who did?"

Kara could just make out a muffled voice on the line as Duncan nodded. "That's what I mean to do. In the event that they were *not* the police officers they appeared to be, I want to know who they were." He slammed down the phone, his eyes on Kara's face. He pointed to the seat opposite him. "Sit."

"Why?"

"So you can tell me how you knew those two weren't what they said they were."

Kara felt heat skid through her cheeks. "What do you mean?"

"I'm referring to the way you went chalk white when you touched that character's phony badge. I'm referring to the way your hand began to shake when he started giving orders. And don't tell me it was some burst of psychic inspiration."

"I'm not going to tell you anything." Dear God, how could things get any worse? Now he thought she was part of some deadly conspiracy, and the only way she could convince him of her innocence was by opening herself to more of his mockery and questioning.

"I'm waiting, Ms. Fitzgerald."

"And you can go on waiting. I don't have to tell you a single thing. What's more, I am not going to sit here and—"

"You're going to sit right here and answer every question I put to you. In case it has escaped your notice, we're in this bloody business together. I have just shot what appears to be a duly licensed officer of Her Majesty's Sussex Police Force, and your presence makes you complicit in that crime. Now tell me what made you suspect something was wrong."

Kara cleared her throat. "His uniform."

"What in bloody hell has the uniform got to do with anything?"

"The color was wrong. So was the design on his hat." She lied wildly, improvising as she went. "*New Bride* did a story two years ago about honeymooners protecting themselves in foreign countries. Of course, we were talking mainly about politically unstable third world nations, but the article included a list of suspicious details. We included representatives of the police." She looked down at the man lying motionless on the ground. "His uniform was wrong. Also his gun wasn't standard issue."

"You're expecting me to believe that you're familiar with standard police-issue firearms?"

Kara crossed her arms defiantly. "You, Mr. Mac-Leod, can believe whatever you like. As for me, I'm heading for the nearest town. From there I intend to take a comfortable, quiet, and entirely solitary seat on the next train back to London." She grabbed her bag from the car, then spun about, shoes in hand,

and was starting up the hill when an arm slid around her waist and yanked her to a halt.

She felt his fury and his uncertainty. He was far more frightened than he was showing. For a moment Kara saw a name—something that clung to the shadows in his mind.

"You're not going anywhere except with me." Scowling, the Scotsman began to tow her over the open fields.

"With *you*? I'd rather eat cobra meat. Poisonous cobra meat," she added.

His grip tightened. She tried to see beyond the anger but found her senses blocked. "What about the limousine driver?"

"He'll be fine. Until I know what happened, I don't intend to stay around and wait for another visit from Her Majesty's police. Fortunately, our destination is no more than a few miles through those woods."

"If you think I'm going one more step with you, you're crazy. I have a magazine to finish. As exhilarating as I find your company, MacLeod, I'm going to have to forgo that pleasure."

He kept on walking. "If we don't stop, we'll be there by sunset."

She caught an image of warmth, of roses thick on a weathered gray wall. Answers there—and safety.

Behind them came the hiss of gravel. Another police car slammed to a halt just in front of the Daimler.

"Then again, maybe you prefer to stay here and have a polite discussion with an armed officer or two."

Kara shoved his fingers from her wrist, sighing in relief when the touch was broken. She caught a jerky breath and saw him looking at her. "Well, what are you waiting for? Let's *go*."

Hidden deep in the forest, a figure stood watching. The scent of their fear drummed in his blood, heady as wine. He savored their shock and fury, smiling when he saw the man being flung against the side of the Daimler.

The woman was the unexpected factor. How could he use her best? And what was her interest in Duncan MacKinnon? Two calls would give him the answers. Soon he would find the best way to draw out the fear and sharpen it.

His fists curled as he realized something had gone wrong. They were free, running through the fields toward the woods. Cursing, he jerked the binoculars to his eyes and saw one officer on the ground and the police car swerving away to the north.

He raised his rifle until the fine crosshairs marked Duncan MacKinnon's back. His forefinger trembled, the taste of death was like the thick heat of sex.

Slowly, slowly, he lowered the gun.

There would be time. The fear would come first, then the pain. They would soon feel all the things he had felt.

And next time there would be no more mistakes.

Nine ～

"Where are you dragging me, MacLeod?" .

"Over the hill."

"I gathered that." Exasperated. "*Where* over the hill?"

"You'll see."

"Damn it, MacLeod—"

"Look, call me Duncan, will you? Then *move*. It's not going to take those officers long to realize we've headed this way."

Kara caught his arm and jerked him to a halt. "*Where?*"

"To see my cousin. Nicholas Draycott is a major stockholder in Calendish and Sons, and his estate is just over that hill—more or less."

As if that would shut her up.

"I've heard of Lord Draycott. A man with an interesting past, as I recall. But why are we going there now?"

The Scotsman scowled. This bloody masquerade as Duncan MacLeod was wearing thin, and so were all her questions. Didn't the woman realize they were in real danger? "Because, among other things, I trust the man."

"And you don't trust many people, do you?"

"Do *you* right now?" He heard her quick intake of breath and hated the way her eyes filled with uncertainty.

Exasperated, he watched her struggle to haul her

heavy bag over her shoulder. Even now her scent tormented his senses, and the smooth way she walked left him no doubt that she was in perfect physical shape.

Trim calves. Powerful legs that would straddle him and clench when she—

Duncan caught her bag and tossed it over his arm. "Listen, Ms. Fitzgerald, the sooner we get to Draycott Abbey the better. If we save our breath for the trail, we'll get there a whole lot faster."

No doubt about it, the man was infuriating. He was arrogant and peremptory and far too good at hiding his feelings. He scorned every idea that she believed in, and he wouldn't have known an energy anomaly if it had held open his door and taken him to tea.

Then again, his confidence was unshakable and his talents were impressive. He had the moves of an experienced fighter and seemed to be good at guessing what people would do next. All in all, that left Kara feeling amazingly safe in his company.

Except when she wanted to murder him.

But the warning was still there, drumming through her blood like a mantra gone bad. She had sensed danger before, often as a cold, colorless cloud that clung to objects impregnated by anger and intense fear.

But what she'd felt in that quiet Sussex road had been different. Crushingly heavy. Cold and blank. And with it had come the keen sense that they were being watched.

Touching the badge had been risky, of course. Even with preparation, Kara knew she could easily be swept over the edge, her own reality snapped as she was flung out into the chaos of a stranger's emotions. The more intense those emotions, the greater the threat to her.

As it was, she'd had to pull back before she traced the angry threads of emotion back to their source. She'd been close enough to sense the face and hands of the man who'd made that badge. She could still feel the pressure and darkness of that mind. One more second and she'd have known.

But the price would have been too high. And without that contact, she was left with nothing useful or tangible.

A riot of wild roses swayed in bright pink clumps. Kara frowned as she stepped around them. "What happened down there, MacLeod?"

No answer. Thorns dug at her feet.

Kara frowned. "I asked you what—"

"I heard. Do you want the soothing lie or the nasty truth?"

"I think you just answered my question."

"I'll know more when we reach Draycott Abbey. Until then, it would be a waste of your time and my breath to speculate."

Speculate! Heaven forbid! "How much longer until we reach this place?"

"A few minutes."

"That's what you said ten minutes ago, MacLeod. And about an hour before that."

The Scotsman cursed as a vine slapped his face. He swung her bag to the ground. "We'll stop here for a while."

"Here?" Down the hill, a ring of weathered stones towered beside the ruins of an ancient castle. The worn stones were half hidden by a berry thicket and rose hedges. Kara found the sight ineffably beautiful, but she wasn't about to stop until they were safe. "I can keep up with you just fine, MacLeod."

The keen eyes twinkled faintly. "Maybe the stop is for me, Fitzgerald. That bag of yours weighs a ton."

After a moment Kara sank back against a warm stone mottled with sunlight. Overhead, bright wings cut through the turquoise sky, and somewhere over the hill a stream gurgled softly. Closing her eyes, Kara felt the warmth seep into her aching muscles.

And then she realized there was something odd about this place of soft grass and dark woods, something that crept close in veiled silence.

Watching them.

She froze, expecting menace. Expecting the first dark slivers of danger. Instead she found a silence that went on forever like a cool, shimmering pool. And in the middle of that unbroken silver silence, Kara found something else.

Peace. It seemed to stand alone, beyond the ceaseless turn of time, beyond the reach of petty mortal destiny. Untouched by wars and famine and the centuries-old chaos of armies, rebels, and kings, it waited. And it watched.

Without conscious thought, her fingers opened, brushing the sun-warmed stone beneath vines of wild roses. Her hand tensed. She reached out, searching.

There came an answering wisp of contact, sentient and fragile, like a single shard of silver.

A kestrel cried shrilly. Dimly Kara heard the clang of church bells carried on the still air. In that instant her touch-probe was caught, examined, and thrown back at her, until it burned through her head.

She fell to her knees as a blinding light filled her mind, stormy with pride and shock and anger. And then, as fast as it had come, the touch was gone.

"What's wrong?" Duncan crouched beside her, frowning.

Kara felt her arms tremble. A rose was clutched between her fingers, and new blood dotted her palm. "I don't know. The blood ..."

"You've cut yourself." Duncan eased away the thorn, then brought her palm to his mouth and sucked gently.

The contact slammed at her while she was most vulnerable. Like lightning it crackled. She couldn't move, couldn't breathe.

So many memories ...

"Kara ..." Duncan's fingers tightened.

In that moment the link was complete. Like a silver rope, it trembled between them, throbbing with a life all its own. As if through drifting mist, Kara saw into another time, when a dark-haired boy cut his hand while hiking past streams dark with peat. She felt the squish of wet sand as the same boy, bigger now, gritted his teeth and lowered his trembling body into cold waters beside a sunny cove. She felt his boyish fury as he watched a kilted figure—his twin brother, Kara realized—pass him in a race through cheering villagers.

As the mist drifted, she saw the years unfold. The boy became a man and tasted his first passion in the soft shadows of a highland peak. The young woman's eyes had been green and her hair a wild red. The pleasure had been shocking and very fine.

Kara gasped and jerked away. "Don't! Don't t-touch me." She stumbled backward, her cheeks on fire, her body throbbing with the memories of his passion.

She gritted her teeth as new visions engulfed her. She felt his pain from a scar at his left knee. There had been mist and water and handfuls of mud. His brother had been there, calling hoarsely.

Kara shivered, reliving the Scotsman's pain as he slipped from a cliff and was tossed into rocky seas.

Fifteen years before.

Why couldn't she break free? Why was the link suddenly so strong?

Hard fingers shook her. "Damn it, what's wrong?"

He wouldn't believe it if she told him. *I'm simply reliving your boyhood, right up to the giddy creature who taught you everything there is to know about sex.*

Sex was the right word, Kara decided. There had been animal attraction between the two, but nothing more. She saw their stolen moments race past, first in a warm mound of hay in a highland twilight, then in the back of a battered Range Rover. The Scotsman's body became hers, his feelings spread naked for her to read.

They left Kara shaken and filled with unspeakable loneliness.

Beyond the treetops came the low throb of motors. "What's going on? Why are you shaking?"

"I'm frightened, okay? I'm not used to being kidnapped by rogue police officers, having pistols pointed at me, and being chased through the English countryside.''

Duncan looked up, cursing as light flashed off distant metal. ''Let's go.''

''What are you doing now?''

''The same thing any intelligent, courageous man would do at a time like this.'' He pulled Kara to her feet, tugging her toward the thickly wooded valley to the north. ''First we run. Then, Ms. Fitzgerald, we're going to hide.''

Ten ~

They ran through thickets bright with bluebells and wild roses, over blankets of green grass stretching down to a gray river. Twice Kara tripped over hidden stones, and twice Duncan pulled her back up to safety in time.

Behind them the motors droned closer. Kara heard the crack of breaking tree branches.

She turned and caught a glimpse of silver fuselage before Duncan yanked her down behind a tangle of bushes. Her body flattened, anchored beneath his on the cool, damp earth.

"Don't move or he'll spot us."

The helicopter thundered overhead, banked north, and circled back for another view, this time hovering close above the trees.

Kara's muttering stopped. Atop her, Duncan lay perfectly still as the beating of the great blades sent dried leaves hissing upward in a whirlwind spiral. Like a bright noisy insect, the helicopter made one more slow, tight circuit of the valley. Kara felt her heart slam in time to the rhythm of the blades. Duncan stiffened, one elbow shoved against her ribs. Then the silver body rose in a malignant roar and thundered north.

In the sudden quiet, Kara's breath came thick and noisy in her throat. As she looked up, the sky seemed to flash into night.

"I've got their call numbers." Duncan pushed to his feet, wiping twigs and leaves from his clothes.

Kara didn't answer. Didn't move. She saw another flash of darkness and heard the chant of angry voices.

"Let's get going. I'll check out their ownership and registration when we get to Draycott. That will give us somewhere to start."

Kara barely heard. Again came the black night, the shouts of angry voices, the drum of hoofbeats.

Coming. Just over the hill.

Cold raced through Kara, cold that was not of this time, but of some distant past. She shuddered, hands to the loamy earth and weathered pebbles, where old memories still lay locked.

Dogs this time. No more hope of escape. Kara twisted, pain biting through her side. She looked down, was surprised that no blood covered her fingers.

And still she felt it, warm and thick, oozing from a wound that throbbed with every breath.

An ancient wound, delivered centuries before. To a woman whose body had long since fallen away to dust.

Duncan caught her shoulders. "Kara, what in bloody hell is *wrong* with you?"

Blank words. Blank face. A stranger scowling down at her. Her fingers dug into the dirt. Behind her, over the hill, came the sharp bray of hunting dogs.

The helicopter droned away, and Kara's logical mind had to fight to recognize the sound. For the woman she had become, the woman born long centuries before, did not know the meaning of a vehicle that could hang in the air.

"*Hurry.*" Hard fingers dragged her forward over a ragged ridge of stone. As she ran the memories began. She saw a kingdom without peace, a country without its king. There, in that time, night stretched over a frightened land where she was alone, chased down like a rabbit in a cold, cruel hunt. . . .

*   *   *

The winter had been long and hard. In the hedgerows brittle leaves rustled like the bellies of hungry peasants, while inside the royal forest, dark glades were speckled with anemones, violets, and sorrel.

And blood lay heavy, streaked across the hungry earth.

Across that earth she ran, driven by fear, hunted like a poor beast before a cruel pack. Her long hair flew in her face, and she yanked it back, knowing she left her own life blood behind with every step.

Behind her came low pounding. She looked up and saw a bloodied fox head flung over the back of a horse. She stumbled forward, away from the grasping hands, away from the jeering voices.

"Let her run. I'll have some speech out of her, or her body will bear the mark of my whip." Crude laughter shattered the silence of the woods as she darted forward, nimble as a rabbit and just as familiar with every turning of the forest's dark paths.

It was that familiarity she called on now, vanishing past a tangle of berries into a hidden glade. Behind her curses filled the air, but she made her way with silent skill through the woods that had long been her shelter, her safety, and her only home.

No, better not to think about the old days, when the Great Hall had rung with laughter and the gentle plucking of the troubadour's lyre. Dangerous, too, the memory of gowns of velvet and tissue silk in hampers scented with precious myrrh from the Holy Lands to the east.

Tears streamed down her face. She fought the vines that slapped at her cheeks, less cruel than the memories that haunted her now. Memories of the endless horror she had suffered in a land plunged into chaos and cold-blooded savagery. Memories so terrible that they had stolen her ability to speak.

The dogs were close. The horses strained forward beneath cruel spurs. Only three more turnings and she would be at the hill overlooking the abbey. One hundred steps and she would be safe in the nave of the church.

A mounted rider burst through the foliage. His rope

lashed at her shoulders and sent her reeling. "Talk, wench! I grow tired of waiting to hear your answers."

Horses ringed the glade, their manes flecked white with sweat. She stumbled forward, a rope hissing about her ankles, wrenching her to the ground.

Too late. All too late . . .

Now no words could explain, even if she could utter them.

A wild, unnatural sound escaped her lips. High-pitched and keening, it made her pursuers stiffen and sketch the sign of the cross in fear.

A rider spurred forward and shoved at her with a stick. "Where's your tongue, wench?" The point drove between her shoulders and sent her tumbling, pain at her cheeks, pain at her shoulder and side. Blood spilled over the snow-white anemones.

In a blur of movement she dove beneath the horse and into the foliage beyond, green shadows flashing past in a blur. She did not know how long she had run, when hard fingers caught her waist and yanked her to a stop. Desperate, she swung at her captor.

Then she froze.

A jagged scar ran down his cheek, setting off a perfect, cruel face. He wore the mail of a warrior, and his heavy, two-edged sword clanged as he caught her shoulders and shoved her behind him. "Who are you that you draw men like a pack of hungry dogs?"

She fought him without answer, her violet eyes searching for escape.

He laughed darkly. "There is no escape, not from the royal woods. Nor from those riders, if they are William of Blois's men."

She stood tall, hiding her fear even when the first of the dogs crashed through the underbrush and came snarling at her skirts.

Her captor kicked the beasts away. "Talk, damn it. Tell me why they hunt you. Are you held for theft?"

She could tell him naught. Surely he knew that. She recognized his scarred face from the months he'd spent at the abbey. Surely this warrior must have heard the stories about the mute woman who drifted through the hills, *glimpsed only in the light of the waning moon or the mist that wreathed the abbey's hills at dawn.*

The villagers gave her many names, and none of them were nice, but she minded her world and they minded theirs. So it had been until William of Blois had come to hold the post of sheriff. Once he had cast eyes on her creamy cheeks and windblown hair, she became his preferred form of sport. His men were given orders to crisscross the royal woods in search of her, with promises that whoever bore her into William's Great Hall would receive ten pounds of silver.

All had failed. She knew the woods too well, using uncanny skills to save her from their traps. The villagers crossed themselves in fear, whispering of sorcery and dark magic. Sometimes even she feared that her visions came from the devil's hand.

And now she was taken. William would show her no mercy.

Her captor's fingers tightened. "If you do not talk, then I must talk for both of us."

The first rider galloped forward, a heavy man with ruddy cheeks that spoke a love for ale. "So you've found our little hare, have you? William will be glad of it." He jumped to the ground, a cold smile on his lips as a heavy leather thong snapped between his huge fingers. "I'll take her now. My lord has promised ten full pounds of silver when this one is delivered to his hands."

The warrior raised one gauntleted arm. A moment later his sword sang through the air and the leather thong was slashed cleanly in two. "She is not yours to bind. She has run onto abbey lands, and I claim her, as is my right."

The bailiff blustered, his eyes dark with fury. " 'Tis not Draycotte land for another furlough!"

The sword rose, sunlight splintering off its inlaid hilt, where a huge sapphire blazed. "The top of this hill marks the edge of Draycotte. Bailiff as you are, you should know that, Rufus. Now, be gone, and take your ill-bred hunting dogs with you."

"You are not the lord at Draycotte! He is gone to the Holy Lands and his lands given over to the church."

"I am Draycotte's man until his return, the order marked by his own seal. These lands are mine to secure."

"What about the church?"

The knight scowled. "The church may tend to souls. I will tend to the people of these lands." His sword rose. "Unless you choose to offer contest."

The bailiff shifted angrily from leg to heavy leg. "What am I to tell William?"

"That you lost his prey. That the devil himself appeared from the shadows in the glade and swept her up, just as the villagers whisper." Hursh laughter rumbled from his throat. "That may not be so far from the truth."

The man slapped the broken thongs in impotent fury. "He'll see your head sheared from your shoulders, so he will. And I'll be there to laugh while he does it."

"Save your laughter until the deed is done, bailiff. Far better men than yourself have tried, Saracen and Norman alike, and as you see, my head remains my own. It is your blood that may soon be staining this holy ground."

The bailiff spat, his pig eyes dark with anger. Only when he was safe on horseback did he turn, snarling. "You go too far, crusader. This time William will have your neck in his noose. Then your blood will darken my own blade when I—"

Out of the dark woods behind them a falcon circled, plummeted in a swoop, and sank his claws into the bailiff's horse. The beast neighed in pain and plunged wildly.

The bailiff was thrown. Around him the other riders jerked back in fear, their horses barely kept from bolting.

Amid the chaos, the knight stood laughing, the sound echoing through the forest. "I will be here waiting for you, bailiff. Come and seek me at your leisure. But beware. If you cannot even counter my falcon, it is your blood that will stain the rocks when next we meet."

The horde was gone as swiftly as it had come, dead leaves swirling beneath the horses' hooves as they thundered out of the forest. Only then did the woman with the violet eyes unclench her fists and turn to face the silent warrior beside her. There was confusion in her face, and a warning.

"You think me foolish, do you?"

After a moment she nodded sharply.

Overhead a pigeon cooed, darting through a willow tree. The knight seized the bow that lay behind him and with one arrow caught the bird in flight, pierced through the breast. Head over feet it plunged, caught on the sharp point. It fell at her feet, fresh blood staining the green earth.

She knelt and pressed gentle fingers to its still-warm breast. When she looked up, eyes were accusing.

"What kind of beast am I to shoot down such a poor creature? Better that small bird than you."

And so it could have been. Shooting a bird should have been a small thing to her, who had seen so much cruelty in the long months of winter.

"Everything has its place, and that pigeon will serve to dress our table tonight. Some are meant to eat and others are meant to be eaten." He frowned. "Why do you stare at me like that?"

He fingered his cheek. "The scar, I suppose." When she did not speak, he scowled. "Answer me, curse you."

But she did not answer.

She could not answer, nor had she been able to voice a single word for long years now. Beneath the knight's angry gaze she stood straighter, her long hair shimmering in the sunlight. And her pride answered for her, gaze for angry gaze.

He stiffened. "You do not speak. You cannot speak."

She nodded.

"I have heard of such a woman." He reached out and fingered the fine, soft linen of her gown. "You are no common villein. Your garments are finely woven and your bearing is too proud. A mystery, I think. A mystery I would give a whole suit of mail to understand."

Because he was staring at her, with her hair like a cloud about her shoulders, he did not see the rider who bolted from the greenwood. He did not hear the angry hooves or see the blade rise toward his neck.

But she did.

Her face white, she seized his arm and wrenched him doggedly to one side.

His hand gripped the heavy pommel of his sword.

"What's amiss, you little fool? Why are you—" The bailiff's sword was already flashing down when the knight's eyes hardened in understanding. In one swift leap he was out of range, twisting with the skill earned through a hundred battles.

Dust rose in the little clearing. Sunlight flashed off steel. The bailiff plunged to the ground, unseated, and the warrior's heel ground down against his throat.

"I could have your life for this. By God, and so I should." The knight's eyes narrowed. "But perhaps to play the messenger is a better role for you. Aye, hie yourself back to your master and tell him he has failed again. Tell him, too, that his little hare has escaped his clutches and is now in my keeping." His heel bit into his enemy's throat. "And do not think to return to Draycotte again or you will rue the decision with your very last breath." Slowly, he raised his foot, and his enemy scrambled to his feet, his cheeks red with fury.

When the bailiff was once more mounted, sword in hand, he hurled back a challenge. "I'll deliver your message to my master. Then I'll be back with two hundred horsemen and archers. Enjoy your sport while you may, crusader. Even the pleasures of her ripe body will not blot out the knowledge that your days are nearly done."

The wind tossed the willow trees. The same wind tossed the woman's hair in a shimmering veil as she watched the retreating rider.

"Come." The warrior seized her hand, but she shook her head, trying to pull away. She looked back over the hill, knowing it would be only hours until the prediction was fulfilled.

He shoved up the skirt of her kirtle and saw the dark bruises mottling her ankle. "You will come with me. There is no place of haven for you now, not in forest or village. Not with William on your track."

She shook her head wildly, pulling at his hard fingers, pointing back toward the cool green shadows.

He shook his head. "There is no running possible. He'll find you wherever you go. It will be sweet sport for him, in truth." His eyes glinted at the fair strands of hair that danced about his hard fingers. "Your only refuge now is *at the abbey, and the only one to ensure that refuge is me."* Emotion played over his face, a blend of anger, desire, and self-mockery. *"A woman without words is fair match for a knight without honor. Aye, you will suit me well."* His fingers slid through the rippling tresses that gleamed like golden silk.

Her eyes were a storm of color. She shook her head violently, wrenching at his fingers, refusal screaming from every taut muscle.

Her resistance brought a curl to his lips. *"You have more courage than wit, I fear. I could break you in a second, little fool. I could have you beneath me right here, in any way that suits my pleasure."* Suddenly his jaw hardened. *"But perhaps the great William has already had you. Is that why you fear him so?"*

The surge of angry pride that snapped in her eyes was answer enough.

He laughed softly. *"A clever little hare indeed. You've led him a merry chase."* His eyes narrowed as the wind drove the soft linen kirtle against her body. For a moment his fingers sank into her hair, and he stood inhaling the heat of her skin, wondering at the faint hint of herbs that teased his senses.

Aye, she goaded a man's lust with her great violet eyes and her angry pride. But was she innocent or temptress, her lack of speech a tragic loss or clever ruse?

No matter. He would have his answers before another day had passed. Meanwhile, he would savor the thought of William's fury.

Ignoring her struggles, he swept her to his chest and carried her toward the granite walls rising in the distance. As they approached, the high, clear pealing of church bells filled the valley.

"Aye, well met are we this day. You shall be the means of my pleasure. And then you shall be the source of my sweetest revenge."

Not one of the holy brothers looked up as the knight carried his bleeding burden over the abbey's smooth grass. Past the herb gardens he strode, past the neat rows of foxglove and vervain used for the abbey's infirmary or *beyond where his own cottage stood, walls thick with primrose and Damascus roses. The woman did not fight him, but her violet eyes were hard, intent on a revenge of her own.*

"Slay me you may, but not until I've tended your wound." He frowned as he brushed back a gleaming strand of hair.

Such softness.

For years he'd known nothing but war, unceasing travel beneath a blinding sun.

And now such softness. He wondered if he had ever felt its equal.

His smile faded. Fresh blood oozed over his fingers at her side. With a fierce slam of his boot he kicked open the cottage door. Inside, the floor was covered with pine needles and fresh herbs, the air rich with rosemary and lavender. He carried her to a pallet of clean straw and turned to a leather case standing against the far wall.

He had barely pulled out a pack of herbs when he heard a scuffling at the door. "My Lord, you cannot! You must be mad!"

A stooped monk, his bald head shining, bustled through the doorway.

The knight shot him a warning look. "Not 'my lord.' Neither title nor honor is mine, as well you know. Bear the thought in your head or you will taste my wrath, holy brother though you are."

The monk bowed quickly, then shook his head as the woman struggled to sit up. "She is wounded." There was reproach in his voice.

"Of course she is wounded. That is why I brought her here."

"You did this to her?"

The knight laughed darkly. "Such ideas you have of me, Brother Peter."

"Forgive me." The monk frowned. "But if not you, then who?" Comprehension filled his eyes. "It was William's men. That mule's arse of a bailiff, no doubt."

"Such talk, Brother Peter." Chuckling, the knight turned away, sorting through neat piles of herbs, which he laid out on top of the leather case. "Much as I would *love to dispute my morality with you further, holy brother, I must fetch water from the stream. She will pass a bad night otherwise."*

"The iron cauldron in the infirmary is well scoured with sand. I will fetch it."

The knight frowned. "She does not speak?"

"Nor ever has. We found her some months past, huddled in fear against the statue of St. Thomas near the nave. The abbot called her Tamsyn—for Thomasina, you understand. She seemed to have no other name."

"Tamsyn." The knight considered the name, then shrugged. "It is as good as any other, I suppose."

"But she cannot stay here, you must know this. Not with William's men about." A deep line creased the monk's brow. "Oh, dear, whatever will the abbot say?"

A shadow fell through the bar of sunlight. "The abbot will say much the same thing."

The abbot of Draycotte Abbey moved into the cottage. His face wore the lines of many winters, marks of disease and famine and even, perhaps, the horrors of war.

The knight nodded curtly. "Holy father."

"Brother Peter is right. The woman cannot stay." The abbot's voice was deep and rich, but he spoke awkwardly, as if unaccustomed to its use. The vows of his order were severe, in truth, and the brothers were forbidden speech for most hours of the day.

"She stays." The knight's words carried cold conviction.

"Her presence endangers us all. You of all people must know that, my lord."

"Not 'my lord,' " the knight growled. "I am knight without honor or name. Remember this well."

The abbot bowed his head in grudging assent. "I try. But I am an old man and grow tired of the ways of the world." There was reproach in his voice, reproach in the rich words of a man who might once have been minstrel, bard, or poet.

Brother Peter watched uneasily. "What about William? The bailiff has surely ridden to inform him of what has passed this day. He will bring a score of men." He rubbed his tonsured head. "If only the lord of Draycotte had not gone off to the Crusade."

"We all must fight our wars," the abbot said. *"Some fight across the sea. Some,"* he continued softly, *"fight hardest in their own minds."*

The knight snorted. *"Let William come. We shall be ready."* Triumph filled his voice. *"Indeed, it is a moment I have waited long to see."*

The abbot spoke slowly. *"It would be best for you to remember that revenge is a blade that cuts two ways, crusader. William has wronged many, us among them, for he has refused us lands that Draycotte meant for us to hold in his absence. But revenge remains the Lord's."*

"The Lord will have his turn," the knight said darkly, *"but only after I have had mine."*

"Blasphemy," the monk said softly, crossing himself.

Outside came the snarl of dogs and the angry clamor of voices.

The knight's eyes locked with the abbot's. *"It is time, my friend. At last our enemy comes."*

Kara shuddered.

She smelled drying herbs and the pine of cooking fires. She heard the bray of hounds and the drum of horses' hooves. And in the same moment she knew she heard none of those things.

"Kara, we're almost at the abbey. Can you make it?"

A man. A stranger. She knew she ought to recognize him, but she did not. In the sea-dark eyes and hard features she saw something that reminded her of a cottage bright with Damascus roses. And his hair—

It had been longer then, wild and faintly streaked with gray. There had been a cruel scar down one cheek.

Knight and crusader. A man with no name and no honor.

"You stare as if you don't know me."

Kara's breath caught, her blood charging madly through her veins. She didn't, not in this place and time. But well she knew him in another, and the link of that knowing throbbed through her still, leaving her knees weak and her head dizzy. Longing assaulted her, carrying a regret that had swept unchanging through the empty centuries.

Kara fought a rush of images, away from the herbs and the column of sunlight slanting into a cottage that had fallen away to dust centuries ago. But the fear did not leave her; nor did the terrible intuition that an old danger had followed her here through those dusty corridors of time.

"Are they coming?" She had trouble shaping the words.

"The men in the helicopter?"

She had been thinking of dogs and horses and angry men. "Of course."

"Kara, are you sure that you—"

"I'm fine," she lied grimly. Her hands were trembling only a little now, and she would learn to ignore these images that were more than images. "Let's find this abbey you keep talking about. I'm freezing, in case you haven't noticed. On top of that, my side is aching."

She realized her mistake the instant the words were said.

"Freezing? It's the middle of June. And as for your side—" Duncan indicated her skin with a sweep of his palm. "That looks fine to me."

Kara closed her eyes, shivering with a cold that was centuries old. There should be no link now, since she was touching nothing. But the pattern was changing. Touching or not, thoughts flooded over her with no order or predictability.

Thoughts—or were they memories?

"Can't we go?" she asked.

"Not until I have the truth. Something's happened to you, and I want to know what."

"I—I don't know what you're talking about."

"No? Why did your face go totally blank? Why did you say you were freezing, when it has to be nearly ninety degrees right now?"

"All this fresh air and exercise must have gone to my head."

"Something's gone to your head, that's for certain."

The air was hot and still. The first hint of twilight was gathering in the valleys.

"I'm ... upset, that's all." Kara tried to keep her mind off the throbbing in her ankle. "That shouldn't be hard to understand."

"*Everything* about you is hard to understand," the Scotsman muttered as he climbed the hill behind her.

And then, as they came out of the trees, the abbey burst upon them, all weathered gray stone and climbing roses. At its foot, silver waters shimmered and danced, crisscrossed by silent white swans.

Her breath caught. "Beautiful. So this is Draycott Abbey."

He nodded. "Even now I feel an odd kind of jolt whenever I see it. I played here as a boy, you know, chasing Nicholas all over these woods. And even now I get that same old shiver. There's a kind of magic about this place, strange as that may sound."

No, it didn't sound strange to Kara.

"You sure you can manage?" he asked.

"Perfectly." Her ankle did feel better. In fact the odd visions had begun to recede like sand lost before a wind.

"Better not look behind you. Nicholas swears that Draycott land is haunted."

Kara felt her flesh tighten. Haunted. Oh, yes, Nicholas Draycott was certainly right about that.

"We'd better move." Duncan half pulled, half shoved her toward the moat just as a distant growl split the silence.

"They're coming back."

A car engine droned from the hill. Cursing, Duncan shoved Kara before him, running over narrow paths cast in shade while the roar of motors grew louder.

And then the last stretch was before them, where the woods gave way to five hundred yards of open lawn flanking the moat.

Heavy tires clawed up the earth behind them, and Duncan cursed softly.

They weren't going to make it.

Eleven ~

Duncan ran, keeping his body low, knowing that would add to his speed. But it wasn't going to be enough. The vehicle—a Land Rover—rumbled closer.

He had thrashed through icy waters in gale-force winds off the northern tip of Scotland. He had faced down sharks in treacherous undersea canyons off the Australian coast. Now it appeared that his life was going to end within shooting distance of Draycott Abbey's familiar gray walls.

"My lord!" Gears grated behind them. "I must beg that you stop!" A door crashed. "My lord, you really must—" The voice broke off in hoarse coughing.

Duncan turned. "Marston?"

The figure standing just outside a battered gray Land Rover wore black trousers, a black coat, and a crisp white shirt that bespoke his position as a respected majordomo, but it was the neon green running shoes that assured Duncan his eyesight was not failing.

Marston, Nicholas Draycott's butler, was notorious for his unflappable demeanor and exuberant footwear. The neon shoes flashed as he hailed Duncan. "I'm afraid I'm not used to this kind of mad dash. I tried calling, but you wouldn't stop."

"We weren't exactly expecting friends," Duncan said grimly. "How did you know we were coming?"

"Lord Draycott phoned after receiving a call from someone at Calendish and Company. I had better

take you and the young lady around to the stable
entrance immediately, since Lord Draycott said we
should expect visitors."

A look passed between the two men. "I see,"
MacKinnon said harshly.

"Well, I don't." Kara's cheeks were flushed, her
auburn hair a tangle around her shoulders. "I don't
understand any of this. Who *is* this man?"

Marston bowed with perfect civility. "I am Lord
Draycott's manservant," he said. "I am most pleased
to welcome you to Draycott Abbey."

"The welcome will have to wait." MacKinnon gestured to the north. "Unless this is a very bad nightmare, those are engines I hear."

Marston's head cocked. "You're quite right. I think
we had better be going."

Duncan made his way to the other side of the car,
hauled Kara into the seat next to him, then nodded.
Behind them the motors grew louder. "Get down,"
he ordered, pushing Kara out of sight as Marston put
the car into gear.

A look of unholy glee filled the butler's face, and
he gunned the motor, sending the sturdy old vehicle
bucking over the rough terrain. "Forgive me if I'm a
trifle rusty. I don't get to drive this thing much anymore, but I'll get you to the abbey in good time.
Then I know one or two spots where no outsider
would ever dream of looking."

Kara frowned at the gray walls that loomed up
before her. They were more weathered up close, each
face showing the lines of age beneath the tangle of
overhanging roses. Every stone looked expressly
carved for a television commercial promoting England's glorious heritage. But it was the energy shimmering over the moat and drifting about the
battlements that made Kara's breath catch in wonder.

It might have been a dream, except that Kara knew
she wasn't dreaming. The dreams had come before
while she crouched in the middle of that sunny field

and felt herself being flung back to a world long gone.

They jerked to a halt at the abbey's back entrance, just off the stables. Kara looked around curiously, half expecting riders in hunting pinks to sail over the low stone wall.

But all was silent as Marston shoved open the rear door and led them through an immaculate kitchen, with copper pots hung on high beams. Sunlight spilled through the windows and pooled golden on the polished wooden floor.

Kara frowned. The prickling at her neck told her that the *ch'i* energy was high here—and maybe the energy of other forces as well. She had time for only a quick glance as they moved on—fragile Chinese porcelain, old English silver, roses everywhere—and then Duncan came to a broad oak staircase that rose up through the heart of the house.

Hammering filled the front courtyard.

Marston said a very uncivilized word and looked at Duncan. "I would very much prefer that you were not about when I answered that door."

"I agree. Any suggestions?"

Marston frowned. "There is a priest hole behind the staircase. I doubt you would be discovered in there."

Kara raised tentative fingers and brushed the paneled wall at her side. The energy felt wrong here, funneled downward instead of flowing upward.

Behind them the hammering grew louder.

"I think you had better hurry."

With deft fingers Marston probed the polished wainscoting at the rear of the staircase and slid his thumb into a gap beneath two carved cherubs.

There was a soft click. The base of the wall slid open.

"Well, I'll be damned. Nicholas always said this was a house with too many secrets, but he never told me about this one." Duncan gestured to Kara. "After you."

The priest's hole smelled of dust and great age,

and dated back to the uncertain times when every great English estate required hidden nooks and secret avenues of escape. Kara squeezed inside, her right arm pressed against a wall of rough stone. Unfortunately, the space was less than two feet across, and a moment later Duncan's shoulder was wedged against her back.

She stiffened, trying to move away.

"There's no more room, blast it, so you can stop wriggling. And if you don't mind, I'd appreciate your taking your hand off my thigh."

Kara uttered a strangled cough. "I was doing no such thing!"

"You certainly were. Not that I might not enjoy it under other circumstances, but right now we have the minor problem of being hunted by most of the Sussex police force."

Marston's voice drifted toward them from the other side of the wall, coldly formal as he responded to a series of sharp questions. No, the viscount was not at home. No, he had no guests currently at the abbey. Yes, the two officers were quite welcome to search the house if they liked.

Footsteps. Something swished against the door. Kara held her breath.

Long minutes passed. Fabric shifted, and she felt Duncan's body tense. A moment later he bent down beside her. "They might still be upstairs with Marston."

"What do they *want*?"

"I wish I knew. Marston will deal with them."

"Something tells me the man is capable of getting rid of a few police officers."

Duncan chuckled softly in the darkness. "He's a paragon, all right. Nicholas's friends have been trying to poach him away for years, but the man is cursedly loyal. Even I've tried my hand at getting him to come work for me."

"And where would that be, MacLeod? The south of France or somewhere in Tuscany surrounded by miles of olive fields?"

"Nothing half so elegant. Just an old house on a cliff overlooking the inner Hebrides, and there's not a single olive grove in sight."

Kara frowned. "Is that how you know Lord Dunraven? Is he a neighbor?"

Hesitation. "We're close."

"How long have you known him?"

His arm moved restlessly. "A very long time."

"Have you seen him lately? Did he mention any problems?"

"Lord Dunraven is not the sort of person to talk about his problems, so you can stop trying to pump me for information," he said flatly.

"What would it take to get you to contact him?"

"You just don't give up, do you?"

"Damn it, this is important, MacLeod!"

"So is what's going on outside that door."

Kara stiffened. "Do you still think I'm making all this up? Do you think this is some kind of joke?"

"You tell me." His voice was icy. "After all, you're the one with the vision."

"Damn it, Dunraven's *life* is at stake."

"Maybe. Or maybe it's money that's at stake."

Kara jammed her elbow into his chest. "Move. I'm getting out of here."

"Not yet, you aren't. You asked what it would take for my help, so I'll tell you. Answers, Ms. Fitzgerald. Just give me a single concrete reason why I should trust you."

"Dunraven Castle is in danger. I know that without question."

"Prove it."

She couldn't. Not in the way he meant. The warning came as pure images, without tangible clues of dates or place. All Kara knew was the sickening lurch of danger—and the death that waited. "I can't."

"Give me something. If you are what you say, there must be some fact, some detail—" His voice broke off in a curse.

Kara knew then that he was hiding something. "Why are you blocking me like that?"

"That's not a block, that's lust, pure and simple."

The lust *was* there. Kara could taste its fire spilling into her veins. But there was something else. . . .

His body shifted restlessly. Each jolt of contact made her breath catch with sensual intensity. Muttering, she tried vainly to put some distance between them in the cramped alcove. "Do you mind? Your knee is wedged up against my hip."

"That's not my knee." There was a low, hard challenge in his voice.

"It's not? Then what—"

Kara's question ended abruptly. Face flaming, she tried to flatten herself against the cold stone at her back.

"Forget it, Fitzgerald. Wiggling is only going to make things worse. It's nothing personal, just bad timing. Any female would make my body react right now."

Kara kicked him. Not that it did much damage, jammed together as they were, but it made her feel infinitely better.

"Ow." He shifted, facing her, and she felt the sudden tension in his body. "So you'd like it to be personal?" His voice came low at her ear. "You want it to be more than simple animal attraction? That might be arranged." One hand slid around her neck.

Kara gave a strangled cough. She felt the drum of his pulse, the heat of his hard body. Suddenly she was drowning in his touch, awakened by an electric sense of vitality. "You mean—"

"You're bloody right I do." His breath played over her cheek, stirring her hair. She was intensely aware of his fists nudging her sides, of the knee braced against the damp wall, of his thigh against her hip.

Aware. So aware she wanted to scream.

He wanted her. Fiercely. Blatantly. The images in his mind were sharp and graphic as they spilled into her through the link. But beneath his hunger Kara sensed what perhaps even he did not recognize: the ache of loneliness and a hidden need for sharing that began at wrist and lip and went much deeper, working between the checked breaths and broken sighs until it found the quiet, aching spaces of the heart.

Kara knew because she had felt that same kind of ache. It came most often in the still hours before dawn when unwanted visions left her shivering and afraid, cursing the unnatural sight that forever set her apart from other people.

But she did not feel it now.

Now she tasted the thick currents of his desire, and it became her own desire. Her muscles quivered, her body clenching in the sudden shock of arousal.

Her knees began to shake as images poured over her. Connected by the intimate press of their skin, some part of her *became* him, and she found herself looking back into long years of loneliness and anger.

And there in the shadows Kara saw a name. A name he tried hard to block.

"What are you hiding, Mr. MacLeod?"

"Everyone has secrets, Ms. Fitzgerald. Even you."

"You're wrong. All I want is to talk to Dunraven, to tell him what I've seen." She rubbed furtively at her brow, where pain was digging at her eyelids. "I have to do that much. Maybe then . . ."

He muttered a harsh oath and pressed her back against the cold stone. "Then what? Is someone forcing you to do this?"

Kara stiffened. How could he be so wrong?

Suddenly a new certainty grew, filling her mind. "It's a word. A name." She frowned, crushed between hard muscle and cold stone, overwhelmed by the force of this stranger's raw emotion.

The certainty grew. "Who is Kyle?"

"Congratulations," Duncan said harshly. "Did you enjoy your research? Did you laugh at the thought of pulling me in, detail by detail, so you could sink your bloody little claws into me?" His hands were at her cheeks, hard and angry. "Damn it, I warned you. I told you what would happen if you kept pushing."

His breath was loud in the silence. His body

shifted. Then heat. Angry contact. Awareness that screamed through her body, making her gasp.

The kiss was angry, the intent to punish.

Or it would have been, had Kara not tasted the haunting loneliness that drove him.

"Duncan." The word slid out in a whisper. Her hands clutched at his shirt as she tried to keep her head while her lips parted beneath his mouth.

Her breath caught in a rush of pleasure.

With a curse, he angled her face, and his mouth softened against her, searing now instead of punishing.

"This is crazy," he said hoarsely. "I'm crazy." When his hands opened on her tight, aching nipples, Kara didn't pull away. She shared his fire, plunged eagerly inside it, her tongue tangling with his in a blind search for deeper contact.

His knee drove between her thighs, and he molded her against his erection. "God, I want to touch you." His fingers shoved at her sweater as Kara explored the hard lines of his jaw. Desire was a scream in her blood. She wanted him naked. She wanted his body against hers. She wanted—

The name came between heartbeats, carried by the link that pulsed between their bodies. "My God, you lied." She tried to turn, tried to shove free, her body shaking with the chill of his betrayal.

His hands went still. "Kara?"

"What you said—it was all a l-lie." She fought backward inch by inch until the dangerous contact was finally broken. "Not MacLeod." Her fists were clenched. "*MacKinnon.*"

Though his breath came in jerky bursts, he did not try to hold her. "Kara, listen to me. This—what just happened—it's not what I planned. Damn it, I never expected to—"

She caught a ragged breath, feeling tears spill onto her cheeks. "To what? To want me? To care when you lied to me?" She shoved blindly at his chest. "That name—Kyle—it was the start. The other images were tied up inside it." She laughed bitterly.

"When were you going to tell me your real name, *Lord Dunraven*? After you had me in your bed?"

His body was rigid. "Kara, stop."

"Why?" She pushed open the door, blinking in the sudden light. "Does the truth hurt?"

"You can't go out there. Those men—"

"They can't be any worse than you." She shook her head. "Just tell me why. I only wanted to help. I actually thought I could make a difference. But to you it was all a joke."

"Not a joke. You were a serious threat. At least I thought so. Now"—he stood stiffly, fists clenched—"I don't know what I believe."

She saw the shadow that wouldn't leave his eyes. "Go on, ask it."

"How, Kara? How did you know Kyle's name?" The words were hoarse.

"The same way I knew everything else. From . . . the visions."

"How can you expect me to believe that?"

"I don't care *what* you believe. I learned a long time ago not to apologize for what I am," Kara said bitterly. She pushed into the hall, her body trembling with shock and anger.

Duncan caught her hand. "Kara, listen to me."

"Don't *touch* me."

After a moment he released her, but only to move forward, blocking her way. "None of this was meant to happen. I had heard we were receiving faxes at Dunraven. Then when I saw you at Calendish's and connected your name with the faxes, I was certain . . ." He drove a hand through his hair. "I was certain of the worst. I don't much like journalists."

"Very prettily said, Lord Dunraven. Now move the hell out of my way." Kara's hands were shaking. Mist seemed to drift at the edge of her vision, and she could have sworn she heard the faint lilt of bagpipes.

Danger in the touch.

"I have to go." Desperation filled her voice.

"Not yet. Wait until we have some answers. You're

tired. Hell, we both are, after what's happened today. Neither of us is thinking straight right now."

Danger in the seeing. "No. I—I have to go."

"Marston will show you upstairs. You can rest while I make some calls. Then we'll try to sort this out."

Cold at her chest. Cold behind her.

"Kara?"

No time. Danger—like a wall of shadows. "You've got t-two hours, Lord Dunraven. Now what about that room?"

Marston strode purposefully through the Great Hall just then, his face thunderous. "A more sour-faced set of officers I have never met. He was asking if we had any guests here at the abbey or anyone who had arrived in the last hour." Marston smiled faintly. "I told him we had not, but that he was welcome to take it up with Lord Draycott and the two members of parliament who were due to arrive at that moment." The butler's smile grew. "Of course *that* sent the fellow packing soon enough. Now I can welcome you properly. Would you care for your usual souchong tea, my lord?"

"Not now, Marston. Ms. Fitzgerald is exhausted and needs to rest. I believe the moat house would be better just in case those two officers return."

The butler nodded. "What shall I say if they do?"

"Let me handle that. By the way, where is Lord Draycott?"

"In Brighton with the viscountess. He said for you to stay out of sight until he can make some inquiries. He should be back later tonight."

"I see. And there have been no calls for me from Dunraven?"

Marston shook his head.

"And nothing from Andrew Calendish in London?"

"I'm afraid not."

"Damn." Duncan turned. "Kara? You're pale."

"I'm . . . fine. Just tired."

"The Rose Room is right this way, Ms. Fitzgerald. I think you will enjoy the view over the moat."

Kara knew that in ten minutes she wouldn't be enjoying any views at all. The cold was inching through her, and with it came the press of sound and color, growing stronger by the second. "It sounds . . . lovely." She moved through the Great Hall with the slow, awkward motions of a swimmer fighting against deep currents.

Standing before the open French doors, Duncan watched twilight settle over the abbey. Once he thought he saw a light flicker far down in the forest, but almost instantly it vanished.

Another one of the abbey's odd tricks.

He tossed back a glass of excellent whiskey, frowning. None of his phone calls had turned up anything. Andrew Calendish was still unavailable, and his secretary had no idea when he would return. Nor did she know anything about the Daimler's being reported stolen.

It had to be a misunderstanding, Duncan told himself. As soon as Andrew returned, he would straighten things out with a single phone call.

And as for Ms. Fitzgerald . . .

MacKinnon frowned. Was her story sincere? Had she truly sensed some threat to himself and Dunraven? Or was it all part of a clever scheme to squeeze money out of him by using her access to data on his brother? If so, how was he to explain the terror he had seen in her eyes out in the woods?

There were no answers. He only prayed that Nicholas could supply some. He was swirling his drink when he heard a sound at the door.

"Drinking my whiskey again, are you?"

Duncan spun around as the abbey's owner strode into the room. "Afraid so, Nicholas. You've still got the best selection south of the Tweed."

"Not for long, if you keep putting it away." Viscount Draycott's black hair was flecked with gray, and his handsome features could have graced the society page of any newspaper. As the viscount poured himself a glass of Glenlivet, Duncan noticed the lines of worry at the edges of his mouth and the corners of his eyes.

"Sorry it took me so long to get back. I left Kacey and Genevieve in Brighton. I thought it would be ... better."

"Thank heaven Marston was able to track you down. This is turning into one bloody fine mess."

"The door." Nicholas's face was grim. "Close it."

Duncan pulled the glass doors shut. "You think the abbey might be watched?"

"I'd prefer not to take any chances."

"What have you found out?"

"Damned little. Calendish is gone, and his office doesn't know when he'll return."

"I heard the same thing. What about the police report?"

"I checked with a friend in Hastings, and no one locally has heard anything about a Daimler reported missing."

Duncan's jaw hardened. "So she was right."

"I beg your pardon?"

"Nothing." Duncan's eyes narrowed. "Go on, Nicky."

The viscount ran a hand over his jaw, then finished his drink, as if searching for words. The silence stretched out, and Duncan had the odd sense that the room was alive with memories, fragments of bygone emotion and the ghosts of all those who had lived and loved in this splendid old house.

"There's something else, isn't there?"

Nicholas steepled his fingers, studying his cousin's face. "You're not going to like it. I'm afraid ... it has to do with Kyle."

Duncan remembered how Kara had stiffened as they hid in the priest's hole. Dear God, was it possible that she had actually picked up some impression about his brother?

He didn't believe it. He *couldn't* believe it.

The last inch of whiskey swirled in the glass beneath his fingers, its pungent, smoky aroma bringing memories of peat fires, of returning cold and tired from a day's salmon fishing on the loch. There had been happiness then, long, lazy afternoons tramping on sandy beaches, and dozens of innocent boyish escapades.

But he could never go back. He had reason to know that better than most. "My brother is dead, Nicky."

"Maybe the men were looking for something—possibly something Kyle had taken. After all, his last set of friends don't play by any rules except their own."

"I have nothing of Kyle's. Besides, they didn't even check the car." Duncan shook his head. "No, they didn't want things; they wanted me."

"Perhaps they wanted the woman."

"Kara? But why? It doesn't make sense."

"Sometimes the right answer doesn't make sense. Not until you have all the clues."

"Don't talk to me in riddles, Nicky. I'm not in the mood for it."

"There are ... other possibilities."

Duncan waited. "Back to Kyle, are we?"

After a moment Nicholas nodded.

"Kyle is dead. We both know that."

Nicholas didn't answer, his gray eyes filled with regret.

Duncan's glass slammed down onto the mahogany mantel. "Damn it, Nicky, are you telling me that my brother is *alive*?"

Twelve ～

The silence was strained. Shadows seemed to fill the corners of the room.

"You're saying those men on the road were some of Kyle's ex-friends?

"It seems the most logical possibility."

Duncan frowned. "A chopper was running passes over the woods when we came in. More of Kyle's friends?"

Nicholas shrugged. "For now, all I have is theories. When I hear from London, I'll know more."

"Damn it, why are they looking *here*?"

"Possibly because your brother was holding a great deal of money that wasn't his. Ten million pounds was the figure I heard mentioned in London."

"That sounds just like Kyle. But there's one small problem. He's *dead*, Nicky. I saw his body."

"Maybe that's what you and everyone else were supposed to think."

Duncan looked out into the darkness, remembering the sight of his brother's bloated body after it had been fished from Honduran waters. The face had been unrecognizable, battered by rocks along the coast.

The fingerprints had matched. So had the dental fillings, determined by state-of-the-art X rays.

Or had they? The verification had come to London authorities via a Honduran official. Maybe that, too, had been part of Kyle's plan. Dead, he was no threat to anyone, and the case had been closed. But somehow Duncan's memories of Kyle were always simmering just below the surface. So were the scars.

And where did the truth begin? Where had everything gone sour? As boys they had been inseparable, fishing the loch with handmade poles and stealing out for moonlight swims in the icy waters.

But it had gradually become clear to Duncan that his charming, moody twin brother had a darker side. The first time had been when the boys were barely ten, and their groom had insisted that Kyle ride a horse the boy considered too docile. In an instant Kyle's smile had hardened to a sneer. "Take him away and fetch me Rob Roy," he had ordered curtly. "Otherwise I'll see you sacked within the hour."

Duncan had listened, horrified, for the groom was an amiable Perthshire lad who had turned a blind eye to their boyish escapades. Because of that very loyalty, the groom had stood firm, refusing to fetch a horse that might endanger one of his young charges.

Livid, Kyle had stormed off to see their father and with chilling sincerity recounted seeing the groom stealing whiskey from the Dunraven wine cellars. And not for the first time, he had added.

The old laird had been furious. Just as Kyle had threatened, the groom was sacked and gone within the hour, despite Duncan's attempts to intervene. Over the years there had been more and more such incidents, whenever Kyle's will was thwarted.

Duncan's fingers clenched as he stared down at the blood red roses on the abbey's antique carpet. "You're saying that Kyle faked his death in Honduras—that he's alive?"

"I'm saying it's possible." Nicholas had had his own experiences with Kyle MacKinnon's fury at Draycott Abbey. Whenever possible, during the annual family reunions, Kyle had delighted in tormenting the abbey staff. Invariably small items had disappeared, keys were stolen or valuable antiques misplaced. Kyle was always too clever to give away his involvement, but those fortnightly visits to the abbey soon turned into silent battles, Nicholas grim and vigilant, Kyle smiling and dangerously confident.

And caught between the two boys had been Duncan, torn by anger and love for the stranger who was his twin.

Their father had remained oblivious, caught up in hog-breeding techniques, land reclamation, and a dozen different investment schemes—the riskier the better.

As the years passed, Kyle had smiled and schemed his way into a charmed circle that included the restless young aristocrats of most of Europe. Over the years he had learned to mask his temper, but never to control it. There were always too many women charmed by Kyle's reckless energy and unending quest for excitement. They learned too late that with Kyle the chase was everything.

Money had been harder to come by, and for Kyle there had never been enough. The two brothers had worked together for a while, using the electronics skills they'd learned from their brilliant but icily undemonstrative father. In the Philippines, Mexico, and Australia they had developed a reputation for providing the finest security systems at the lowest price, and their business had flourished. Then Duncan had discovered why: Kyle was targeting his clients with the help of a team of thugs who threatened the company if it did not use their services, then terrorized its staff and vandalized its equipment if company officers were unwise enough to refuse.

The memory of their fight that day still made Duncan curse beneath his breath. Their work together had ended that very moment—so had any personal contact.

Frowning, he downed the last of his whiskey. "If he's alive, Nicky, let me see proof."

The viscount's hand rested on his shoulder for a moment. "I don't have it. All I have is a feeling. The same cold feeling I had when we were boys."

Duncan stared at the floor, remembering that feeling all too well. He had finally decided that Kyle hated him because he could never be charmed and manipulated like all the others. His voice hardened. "What kind of game has he set us playing now?"

"A dangerous one. And I'm afraid he hasn't left us very much time."

"Tell me what he's done, Nicky."

Nicholas Draycott stared out at hills that rose black against the blue sky. "Kyle—or someone using his name—has hidden a small, self-contained explosive device somewhere in the showroom. Calendish and Sons received a telephone call an hour ago in London. If four million pounds is not paid into an account in Zurich by noon tomorrow . . ." His eyes met Duncan's.

"Go on."

"Then the bomb will be detonated precisely on the stroke of six tomorrow evening, just as the streets are filled with commuters." Nicholas's voice tightened. "The authorities now realize that he's . . . done this before. Belfast, Paris, and Mexico City in the last two months. A busy boy, your brother. After he separated from you, he took advantage of all the training he could get."

"In hostile countries, I take it?"

"I'm afraid so. It began after the Philippines."

Duncan heard the wind rustle the roses on the abbey's stone walls. As he listened, he thought of another wind on another evening, far away on a mist-covered Scottish hill. "I always wondered if I could have known—and changed him somehow."

"Damn it, Duncan, you're not to blame. What Kyle did was by his own choice."

Duncan's boyhood had ended cruelly on a night twenty years before, when he was barely ten. It had been a lazy summer evening, and there had been laughter and talking by the loch, even a sip of whiskey between bites of fresh salmon cooked on an outdoor fire. When Kyle had suggested taking a rowboat out onto the loch, it had seemed the perfect adventure.

But the adventure had become a nightmare when a gale blew in without warning. One moment they were bobbing in gentle swells, and the next moment the boys were fighting to stay upright in nine-foot waves.

And *she* had been with them, the mother whom they both adored, her copper hair blown in damp tangles as she fought to hold the boat steady.

The storm had howled over the loch, smashing them at the trough of every fierce wave. Duncan had been exhausted by the time the first shouts echoed from shore and rescue boats headed out for them.

By then it was too late.

He could still remember the giant wall of water that had exploded over the hull, slamming him overboard. Choking and frozen, he had fought to reach the surface while wave after wave broke over him. He'd finally clawed his way to the air, his energy nearly spent from trying to swim, his right arm weighed down by a heavy cast.

Perhaps Kyle had planned that part too.

Duncan's face was a hard mask as he remembered how he'd lunged for his mother's hand. Each time he had missed, unable to pull himself high enough because of the weight of his cast. Finally she had come overboard herself, her hair matted about her face. She had held him upright, shoving him toward the boat.

Through the blinding waves, Duncan had blinked to see a wooden oar shoved past his face. Grimly he'd caught hold, then turned to his mother.

Only she hadn't been there. Again and again he had searched the dark surface while Kyle gasped and cursed and sobbed. With the last bit of energy in his young body, Duncan had dived deep in one last desperate attempt to find her. Her body was cold when he pulled her up into the gusting wind.

Duncan had no clear memory of the nightmare moments that had followed. He only knew that his numb fingers had had to be pried away from his mother's cold arms.

She had lived only thirty minutes more. Her cheeks had been bright and feverish at the end, and wildness burned in her eyes. "Guide them well, Geordie," she had rasped to the laird standing stony-faced at her bedside. Every scrap of emotion had been locked inside him, good Scotsman that he was. Never once had he shed a single tear, even when her voice broke with her final, husky apology: "I tried so hard to keep them safe. Forgive me, Geordie. And forgive them."

But he hadn't. Duncan had seen the anger in his father's eyes when she sighed her last breath.

Never again had they spoken of that night; in that failure the poison had grown. Duncan had always felt the damning suspicion of guilt. Kyle had stayed in the boat. Kyle had thrust out the oar, and it was Duncan's fault that their mother was dead.

No one had ever breathed a word of reproach, but the long, cold years of silence had been worse than any accusation.

Now, as Duncan looked up at Nicholas, he wondered how much of the truth his cousin knew. "Maybe I could have rescued him from that jail in South America."

"No one could have rescued Kyle. He was in too deep with the wrong people and had betrayed them once too often. It wasn't money they wanted, but to teach a lesson, stark and clear, to anyone else who might consider betraying them. He escaped with the help of a new set of friends, who were even more monstrous than the old ones," Nicholas went on grimly. "They taught him new skills and gave him a new identity. There's reason to believe he's been all over Asia and South America for them."

"All these years he's been alive." Duncan rubbed his forehead, feeling as if all the air had suddenly been sucked out of the room. "What else did the message say?"

"If there's any sign of government or military interference of any sort, he'll detonate the bomb instantly." Grimly, Nicholas held out a sheet of paper.

Duncan stared at it, filled with revulsion. How stupid of him to think that it could have ended so easily with Kyle.

"He was most precise in his instructions. You're the only one who's allowed to go in. At the same time that the money is wired into the Zurich account, you're to enter the showroom. You'll be given six hours to find the bomb.

"*Damn him.*" Duncan slammed his hand against the paneled wall. How could he outmaneuver Kyle, an expert in every contraband explosive device used in the Third World? Duncan's skill lay in protection, not destruction. "Have you been in touch with the authorities in London?"

Nicholas nodded. "They'll try to cooperate as much as possible, but only because they're desperate to get their hands on Kyle."

"They'd better not count on it. Even as a boy, Kyle always kept to the shadows." Duncan shoved Kyle's message into Nicholas's hand and began to pace the room, fists shoved deep in his pockets. "Does Andrew know?"

"Andrew appears to have disappeared," Nicholas said grimly.

"Kyle's doing?"

"Who can say? The building has been covertly cleared, and monitoring facilities have been set up discreetly in the basement next door. James Sinclair, the officer in charge, is a good man, but I have to warn you, the prospects aren't good. There's a good chance that Kyle is using techniques that are unfamiliar to us."

"You can't find what you aren't looking for, is that it?"

Nicholas nodded. "Given time, the people in London could take the place apart brick by brick, but time is what they don't have."

"Which leaves it up to me."

"There *is* one other possibility."

Duncan turned, his back to the doorway. "What possibility?"

Nicholas didn't answer.

"Something I've overlooked?"

"Not something." Nicholas stared at the doorway. "Someone."

"I don't understand." Duncan followed Nicholas's gaze, feeling a sudden rush of premonition.

She was standing in the doorway, the light a golden nimbus around her. There was a question in her eyes.

Duncan ignored it. "No."

"She has a special skill, Duncan. She's used it before in difficult circumstances."

"You call encountering an explosive device at close quarters *difficult?*"

Kara hadn't moved.

"She can help, Duncan. There are ways."

"You read Kyle's letter: no one goes in but me. We'll play this by Kyle's rules, Nicholas, understand me?"

Kara looked from one man to the other. "Maybe he does, but I don't."

"Don't get involved, Fitzgerald. This one is way over your head."

"This is important, isn't it? You need me for something?" Kara looked at the viscount, who nodded and held out the message from Kyle.

"Stop, damn it."

"Let her try, Duncan. How can it hurt?"

Ever afterward Duncan would remember her quick, soft breath and the way her eyes went wide and unfocused on his face when she touched the paper. It was almost as if he was the only thing that could bring her back—from wherever it was she was going.

Her fingers opened on the heavy paper. Her breath slowed. "A man."

Duncan watched her fingers trace invisible patterns over the unlined sheet.

"Kara?" Nicholas said tentatively. "Can you pick anything up?"

She seemed to slide deeply inward, her whole being focused on the paper cradled in her hand.

"Mist. Clinging." Kara stiffened. "Maybe it's anger." She shook her head, shuddering. "Anger— yes, so much of that. Turning outward, gnawing at everything. His face—twisting now. He's tugging at his ear. It's his habit when he's worried."

Duncan told himself that many people had seen Kyle rub his ear as a boy. Her statement proved nothing.

"Pain. In the right knee."

Kyle had fallen from the castle's north tower as a boy, onto his right knee.

Only about four other people in the world knew that.

"He's waiting," she said jerkily. "He's planning everything right now, down to the final detail. There are traps, obstacles. He . . . he takes great pleasure in his game."

Marston tapped softly on the door. "Forgive me, my lord, but a Lieutenant Sinclair just rang to say that the time has been changed. He said you would understand. You're to go in at four P.M., not noon. And the deadline is still six."

Two hours to find the bomb.

Duncan stared at Kara. She was shivering, oblivious to the sunlight pouring over her hair and shoulders.

Good God, he thought. *Her gift is real. Somehow she knows.*

He strode forward, his fingers cupping her shoulder. "Can you see anything else? Anything at all?"

He felt her pulse race beneath his fingers. He wanted to tell her to stop, to throw away the paper that carried the taint of Kyle's evil.

"A clock. Ticking, I think. Shining tables. Glass. Everything is in the open, just where it should be." Suddenly her eyes blinked open and Duncan felt her look into him and beyond.

The paper crinkled in her fingers, the sound like

dried leaves in an old stone courtyard. "K. Maybe . . . Kent."

He had always wanted to be named Kent. He had insisted that the name be sewed into all his clothes.

"No, it's different." The paper rustled again, her fingers tense. "Konrad, I think. It's . . . blurry, as if the letters have been erased. Strange, they're not really there, except I can feel them."

Not really there.

Konrad had been Kyle's imaginary companion as a boy. Only Duncan knew that.

Something cold and bleak tightened around Duncan's heart. Kara Fitzgerald was good. And he didn't want her involved. "You're wrong." His voice was curt. "None of this makes any sense."

She swung about slowly. Her balance was off, her usual grace gone. She seemed groggy, only half awake. "Then try another word that begins with K. Try . . . Kyle." Her face was very pale and she held the paper with fierce concentration.

Duncan knew at that moment that they would be lovers, that one day she would touch him with the same concentration with which she touched the paper. Her eyes would be the color of smoke and amber when he sank inside her and brought her to moaning pleasure.

Her eyes narrowed slightly. He wondered if she had sensed that image too.

"Let it go," Duncan ordered, tugging the sheet from her fingers. "You've seen enough. His name is Kyle, and his home used to be at Dunraven. He is a monster and a madman—as well as my brother. And for those reasons neither of you will have anything more to do with him."

Thirteen ～

"The answer is *no*, Nicholas."

"She can do things you never could, Duncan—see things none of your fancy equipment can see."

"Forget it, Nicky."

"She was right about those names. She's bloody good, and she's worked on police cases before."

"*No!*"

Nicholas glared at his cousin. "We need all the help we can get, Duncan. In case you hadn't noticed, Kyle is holding all the cards right now."

"This is my problem, Nicky. I have no intention of dragging anyone else into it."

"Be quiet, both of you." Kara's voice was tight. She slipped the sheet of paper from Duncan's fingers. "He's going to hurt someone, isn't he? Your brother, Kyle."

Kara's soft question pulled Duncan from his angry thoughts. "A good deal of London, I'm afraid."

"Let me help you." Each word was deliberate, as if she knew exactly what she was offering.

"*No.* I don't know how you did what you just did, Ms. Fitzgerald. I'm not sure I want to know. But this is not your battle."

"Maybe it is. Maybe that's why I've been having these . . . visions of Dunraven Castle."

"I don't believe in visions, and I don't believe in letting strangers fight my battles for me."

"He planned on your saying that." Frowning, Kara

129

looked past him, into a world of images Duncan could not see.

"Enough! You've convinced me that your skill is real. You can stop now."

"He wants you to be alone." Kara's voice was strained. "He wants you to be like he was, in that dark place. A prison of some kind."

Cursing, Duncan gripped her shoulders. "Break it, Kara. Now." It was the first time he had used her name. The sound shocked both of them. "This ... link ... can't be good for you."

"It's not. Then again, it's never been so deep before. When I touch this paper, it's like having all the heat pulled out of my hand. Like a cold so intense it swallows everything it touches."

"That's a remarkably good descriptior of Kyle," Nicholas said grimly.

"Good or not, you're out of this," Duncan growled. "I'll take on my brother alone. It's me he wants—not the money."

Kara looked at him. "He wants both. But it doesn't end there. He wants ... pain." There was sadness in her eyes. "This time he'll hurt as many people as possible. There's a hole inside him, eating its way outward. Something very old to do with a boat and a death. I—I can't see more, because it's blocked."

Duncan stared at her. He was frightened. Awed. Wondering how he could keep her safe from contact with his brother's madness. "Where is he?"

"Now?" She shook her head. "I can't say. But that letter was written in the south of France." She gave him a strange smile, half wistful. "There's a tiny *auberge* high in the hills above Nice, with lavender growing everywhere."

"Give me something I can use now, Kara."

"There's nothing else—only anger. Maybe I can pick up more if I touch something else of his. Let me go with you to this place, Duncan. I can help."

Duncan trapped her hand, his eyes very hard. "I believe you could, Kara. But I won't let you be part of anything to do with Kyle." He looked at his cousin. "Nor you, Nicholas. You know what he's like."

"I'm not likely to forget. But you can't beat him, Duncan. Even with all the police backup that can be mustered, it will be you in that room alone against the clock. Kyle's had days to plan this and the help of very dangerous friends."

"But I know things about Kyle that no one else knows."

Kara ran her hand along the mantel, then turned, frowning. "Something's wrong." She studied the room. "The energy—it's changed."

"What do you mean?"

"There is something different all of a sudden."

Nicholas looked at Duncan, then put one finger to his ear. Without another word he searched a drawer on his desk, then pulled out a black metal box the size of a large camera. Duncan watched him snap in a probe and turn to sweep the room for signs of low-frequency carrier currents.

For bugs.

Over the outlet by the outer door, a red light began to blink as a silent alarm was triggered. Nicholas's mouth hardened. "It's nothing. This is an old house. There are false panels, rebuilt floors, and all kinds of plastered-over doors. A smuggler's delight, my mother used to call it." As he spoke, Nicholas brushed his mouth, warning Kara to guard her words.

"I see," she said slowly. "Of course, that would explain it."

"Good. And now since there's nothing more any of us can do tonight, why don't we get some rest. I'll have Marston wake you at six." Nicholas pointed to Duncan, then motioned to the box, where the red light indicating a listening device still glowed.

Duncan nodded and pointed outside. "Very well. But first I'm going to check the other rooms. I've put down a book somewhere and I want to find it before I go to sleep."

After a moment Kara moved across the room and

held out her hand to Duncan. "I hope you find it, Lord Dunraven, that and whatever else you're looking for. And now good-bye. I would have enjoyed using your castle in my article, but we'll survive. There must be more than one beautiful, slightly haunted castle in Scotland."

Her smile wobbled, and Duncan caught her fingers. With slow deliberation he raised them to his lips. "At any other time, I'd be delighted to discuss it with you, Ms. Fitzgerald. Maybe—later, when all this is settled . . ."

Kara looked at their touching hands and shook her head. "I don't stay where I'm not wanted." She pulled her hand away, and their eyes locked, energy churning between them. "No, this is good-bye, Lord Dunraven."

The kitchen was silent. Nicholas finished making a circuit, watching the small electric monitor in his hands. Finally he pulled off his earphones and nodded. "All clear."

But Duncan touched his arm and shook his head. From the bag on his arm he removed a three-tiered device with a tuner dial and half a dozen frequency bands. With a slender metal probe, he swept the perimeter of the room. Over a jar of roses beside the back window he stopped, frowning, and pointed silently.

Nicholas nodded. Together they made their way outside in the darkness, to the edge of the stone bridge that crossed the moat, where they could speak in private.

"A pulsed transmitter," Duncan said tightly. "That box is something I modified myself. I never expected to be using it here at the abbey."

"Damn the man! Three taps on my telephone, a high-frequency transmitter on my computer, and now *that*. What was it, by the way?"

"Wall-plug transmitter. Perfectly designed to look like a working plug. Average range of reception about ten yards."

"The bastard," Nicholas growled. "He's been in my bloody house. When?"

"Those roses on the windowsill probably came from a local florist. A gift?"

Nicholas nodded.

"Easy enough to slip a little transmitter among them. Setting the phone taps would have taken only minutes. You weren't *expecting* anyone to be eavesdropping, remember?"

"But how can we be sure he isn't somewhere out there right now, listening to us?"

Duncan patted the pocket of his suede jacket. "Radio-frequency detector with a silent vibration alarm. I designed it myself. If there's a transmitter activated within a thousand feet, I'll know it."

Nicholas gave a hard laugh. "Now I see why you're in such demand."

"Safety is largely a question of attitude, Nicky. None of us was expecting this."

Nicholas watched a bar of moonlight sway and splinter on the still water. "Ms. Fitzgerald knew. Maybe at the exact moment when those devices were activated."

"It seems very possible." Duncan sighed. "Who the hell *is* she, Nicky?"

"A woman with an amazing gift." Nicholas tossed a pebble into the moat and watched it break the surface into sparks of moonlight. "I finished that trace you wanted, by the way."

"Forget it. I trust her now. There's no need for that."

"Maybe you should hear it anyway. I spoke to her office in New York. It seems that her magazine is under a tight schedule to finish a photo shoot somewhere in Scotland."

"At Dunraven," Duncan said tonelessly. "Except I refused permission."

Nicholas gave a soundless whistle. "Now I see why the air gets tense when you two are together." He gave Duncan a sidelong glance. "Or is that for other reasons?"

"The timing's wrong, Nicky."

"The timing is *always* wrong, don't you know that?" Nicholas toyed with another pebble. "I also spoke to a police officer in New York, a woman named Rivington, who told me she worked with Ms. Fitzgerald on a recent case. Kara picked up details no one else could have found."

"What kind of case was it?"

"Kidnapping—then a homicide. The ransom transfer was bungled and two girls were killed."

"Good God." Duncan cursed softly. "What about Kara?"

"The officer gave me the impression that Kara took it very personally. She also said Kara has been under a great deal of strain lately."

"Enough strain to cause visions—hallucinations?"

"Who knows?" Nicholas sent a pebble skimming toward the far bank of the moat. "Meanwhile, we've got Kyle to deal with. What do we do about those transmitters?"

"Keep them in place until I leave tomorrow. We'll feed Kyle something to throw him off. In the meantime, I'll contact your man in London on a secure line and have him start tracing those transmissions."

"Can that be done?"

"With enough time and enough money, *any* signal can be traced anywhere. Kyle knows that, too. I expect he'll pull out long before the location is traced. Still, it's worth a shot." Duncan's jaw hardened. "Meanwhile, I'm going to contact Mctavish up at Dunraven and tell him to be on the lookout. Kyle might be trying some tricks up there." Duncan looked down at the luminous dial of his watch. "It's nearly midnight. I think I'll go over a few contingencies before I turn in. By the way, I'm sleeping in the moat house tonight."

"What will the moat house's other occupant have to say about that?"

"Nothing. I expect Ms. Fitzgerald will be fast asleep by the time I bivouac on her sofa."

"Wouldn't both of you be safer in the house?"

"Maybe, but I checked the moat house, and there are no bugs. I need to ask Kara a few more questions, and I don't want Kyle listening in. Meanwhile, I'll see that no one—or nothing—gets through to the moat house tonight."

Fourteen ～

$\mathbf{M}$idnight.

Silence filled the abbey, and lightning stabbed at the horizon.

Standing at the open French doors, Kara watched a storm move in, sending blue-white bolts along the far hills. The air seemed heavy, supercharged by the coming storm.

She rubbed her neck, feeling the sheer curtains drift around her in the wind. Though she was exhausted, she knew that sleep would not come easily.

Lightning flashed and twisted against the darkness, and she thought about what she had said to the laird of Dunraven. She had meant what she said. The visions did not come by her choice or understanding. Whether gift or curse, they could not be ignored.

She had tried to warn him, tried beyond reasonable bounds. Her obligation had been fulfilled.

But Kara knew the visions would not end until the danger vanished—or Duncan MacKinnon was dead.

Outside, a shadow moved against the sudden flare of lightning. Her fingers tightened on the curtains.

He came over the iron railing with a smooth, silent curl of legs. "You'd better close the doors and stay inside. It's going to rain any minute."

You're not worried about the rain, Kara wanted to say. *You're worried about a man with dead eyes somewhere out in the darkness.*

Instead she lifted the curtain and watched the horizon. "I like the rain."

He eased one shoulder against the granite wall. He was wearing all black. He looked cool, efficient, and thoroughly professional. "This isn't about rain, and we both know it."

"What is it about, Lord Dunraven? You tell me."

Duncan's features were lit briefly as another bolt of lightning twisted blue-white through the sky. "It's about hatred, old hatred. It's about knowing you can't do one damned thing to change it." His fingers slid around the rail. "Have you ever felt like that?"

Only every time I have a vision, Kara thought. *Each time I think something will be different, that I can make things better, but each time I'm wrong. Just the way I was wrong with those two girls locked in a wrecked van under twenty feet of dirty water.*

Kara took a long breath. "Sometimes."

"And what do you do about it?"

"Mostly I feel bad. My head aches a lot and usually I throw up." Why was she telling him this? He wanted her gone, out of his life; he'd made that very clear.

So why was he standing in the darkness gripping the cold iron rail as if he were a drowning swimmer and it was a rope?

"Does that help?" he asked.

"Not much."

He said something in Gaelic beneath his breath. "I'm sorry you got dragged into this mess. Tomorrow you'll be gone and this will all be behind you."

"Will it?"

Duncan didn't speak, turned toward the distant thunder. "I appreciate what you tried to do. You cared enough to warn me, and that makes you an exceptional person."

"I didn't come here for your thanks." Kara pulled her cashmere sweater closer about her shoulders as the wind whipped across the moat. "I came here to help. It's not too late, you know."

"Yes, it is. Maybe it was too late years ago. No

matter what happens, you stay here, out of Kyle's reach."

Staying wouldn't stop the visions, Kara knew. And if a bomb tore through the London streets, wiping Duncan MacKinnon from the face of the earth, she'd know the exact instant it happened. She would *feel* it, churning and twisting through her with sickening force.

"You don't want my help? Fine. Absolutely fine."

"It's best this way."

"I couldn't agree more."

"And where does that leave us?"

"Nowhere." Kara's voice was hard. She had to make him believe that. Maybe then *she* could believe it, too.

He turned, his eyes dark with anger. "All done. Just like that?"

"Just like that."

"What about Dunraven and your plans for the magazine?"

"Forget them. I already have."

"Maybe I don't want to forget them. Maybe I can't. I don't think *you* can either."

"Did anyone ever tell you that you've got a million-dollar imagination?"

"Only once. On a night in the wind, a night I'll never forget." His eyes didn't leave her face as he reached into his pocket and pulled out a burnished gold coin.

He didn't move as the old coin dangled before her face, casting fine sparks of light onto her pale cheeks. "Put this in your hands. Hold it the way you touched that piece of stationery and say it's over."

Kara didn't move. She could sense the sharp energy of the coin, saturated with his life force. If she actually touched it, opening her mind to its power . . .

Danger in the touch.

"Count me out of your parlor games, MacKinnon. Take your medallion and find someone else to bother."

"Am I bothering you, Kara Fitzgerald? Does the

thought of touching this coin upset you? Knowing that it's part of me, lying right against my chest in the heat of the jungle and in the cool water—does that upset you? I hope so, because you're doing the same to me. Ever since I saw you in that damned jewelry shop, you've done nothing else." He moved closer. Kara felt the energy of his body engulf her. Caress her.

Seduce her.

"Go on, Kara. If I'm wrong, it won't matter. So take it. Touch it. Prove to me that there's no reason for you to stay—or for me to want you to."

The old Roman coin dangled between them. Kara felt an ache gather in her throat. "I've already made my offer, MacKinnon. You turned it down, remember?"

"It was too dangerous. My business with Kyle has nothing to do with us."

"Not even if I can help you?"

"My decision stands."

Kara shrugged and turned away. As she did, the medallion slid onto her shoulder. At its touch, her body went rigid. Her senses blurred with a rush of churning images.

Silver waters beside a jungle beach.

The drone of jackhammers slamming into steel pipeline.

Bad water. Bad food. Bad luck.

His last job site . . .

The medallion slid to the floor with a hollow ring, and Duncan's fingers closed over her hand. "I'm sorry, Kara. I'm just trying to understand—"

"You can't understand," she said raggedly. "Sometimes even I don't understand it."

"Then *make* me understand. Make me see what you see. Tell me what in bloody hell is going on here."

Kara looked down at the old coin glittering against the flagstone terrace. "Be careful with that thing. There's a lot more of you invested in it than you imagine."

The Scotsman picked up the heavy old coin without taking his eyes from Kara's face. In one smooth movement he opened his shirt and slid the simple gold chain over his head.

And Kara felt the medallion slide home, felt each cool link shimmer and sink as if over her own skin. Once again he trapped her, overwhelmed her, possessed her.

But she would not be possessed. Not by him or any other man. She had learned that danger too well once already. "Go away, MacKinnon. You made the right decision. Now we both have to live with it."

For a moment it looked as if he would protest. His hand rose. He touched the rim of her mouth slowly.

And then with a curse he turned away.

At the opened French door, he stood for a moment, framed against the darkness. He did not turn, his body rigid. "You make me wish I could forget about hard choices, Fitzgerald. You make me wish that for one night, just one sweet night, there were no reasons to say no."

Lightning glowed behind him. The first fat drops of rain beat down against the flagstones as he stepped back into the night.

He watched, a line of shadow amid the heavy darkness that clutched at the weathered stone parapet. Gray as the abbey walls, his eyes narrowed on the patchwork of fields and woods, touching every leaf and branch with intimate knowledge.

His land.

His legacy.

His abbey.

But another mind had ranged over those fields, a mind whose keenness had for a moment locked with his.

He frowned, angry at the thought of any outsider here at the heart of his beloved acres. Near his feet came the rustle of ferns, pushed apart by a great gray cat.

"Do not tell me it was my imagination," he thundered. The cat made a low sound of complaint, somewhere between a hiss and snarl. "No, it was there, just as I told you. It has been a long, long time since I have felt another psychic power at work in my abbey."

The cat ghosted to the edge of the parapet and stood, tail flicking as it surveyed the stormy night.

"Yes, I feel it." The man in the black waistcoat nodded. "Danger. Cold and sharp at the edge of my lands."

The cat meowed.

"Nicholas Draycott does well enough, but he needs my interference now and then. Not that he would recognize it." The tall figure laughed grimly. "And I mean to continue interfering. This abbey shall stay safe from all attack, thanks to our vigilance."

The cat's head was cocked, a question in his keen amber eyes.

"Of course I enjoy it, Gideon. Interfering is one of the few pleasures left to us, after all." Those dark features grew hooded. "And now let our night's work begin."

The cat's tail flicked sharply. Somewhere in the dark woods behind the abbey a bird cried shrilly.

Fifteen ✑

Streaks of rain carved ridges into the moat, and the wind growled around the stone walls. Restless and tense, Kara did not move, one hand locked on the cool windowsill.

Something was out there.

Out there watching *her*.

She jerked the damask drapes closed, her hands trembling. *Just your imagination*, she told herself grimly, turning toward the big four-poster bed. But the tall portrait on the wall caught her eye. The sad, keen eyes of some early Draycott ancestor were entirely arresting. And for a moment those same eyes seemed to move, following her. Almost as if they were trying to tell her something.

Kara flung back the damask quilt and crawled in, curling up tightly, trying to ignore the rain lashing the tall French doors. But she couldn't ignore the danger she felt gathering somewhere in the night.

On the wall, the dark face glowed in a flare of lighting, and the keen eyes seemed to burn.

He wanted her.

The knight's face locked in stern lines as he looked across the fields of oats and barley toward the abbey. Even now he could not shake himself free of the memory of her.

He wanted her long hair spilling through his fingers. He wanted to remove her coarse gown and explore her silken skin. He wanted to watch her eyes when they filled with pleasure.

Cursing, he turned away, feeling his body harden with desire. But he ignored that desire, as he had so often before. He had planned too long to lose now, out of lust.

His scarred hands were tense as they fanned through a set of heavy, painted cards. The heavy parchment slid through his fingers, each card bearing a different prophecy. Swiftly he selected four cards and spread them before him on the table.

On top, body secured by a leather thong, hung the upside-down figure of a man.

The hanged man, who sacrificed his interests to a higher calling. Frowning, the knight swept the cards onto the floor. He would not be thwarted in his goal. He was a fool for letting hope inch into his hardened heart. For a man such as he, there could be no home, no soft arms, no quiet laughter.

And certainly no love.

She called herself a fool, a thousand times a fool, as she stood in the doorway of the knight's wooden hut. Outside, the monks bustled about performing their evening devotions. In the garden two brothers gathered herbs for a line of ragged villagers with hopeless complaints.

Wariness, fear, and a dozen other emotions burned through her thoughts.

And desire. She had never known such yearning before. She had believed it beyond her after the horrors she had endured. But like a sweet heat, it buffeted her, making her hungry to feel his hands tremble on her as they had in the cottage.

There would be no concealing her emotions from the knight. He saw everything.

He would understand her desire, and use it mercilessly for his own ends.

Her ankle was stronger now. Better that she run before she betrayed herself.

Gathering her threadbare shawl about her shoulders, she made her way through the busy courtyard, keeping to the shadows. He would not bother to look for her. It was her *own weakness she feared, the weakness of a woman who had never been admired, protected, or cherished.*

Better to leave now, with her heart still resisting, before she tasted a paradise that must be denied her. She tugged her shawl over her head, hiding her fine features and long, plaited hair. No one stopped her. No one called out as she moved through the noisy crowds.

And in her eagerness to be gone, she did not see the flat black eyes that watched her disappear into the forest.

"She is gone, my lord!"

"When? How, by all that's holy?"

The little friar shook his head anxiously, his fingers clutching his rough robe. "It must have been just after I left. I do not understand it. She seemed so content to rest here beside the fire. Then she sent me out for thread for her sewing, and when I returned she was gone."

"She tricked you," the knight said softly. "She has tricked us all, I think."

"You judge her too harshly."

"I judge all women harshly. They are fickle always, devious usually, and they command far more of a man's time than they are worth."

"But this one ..." The friar shook his head. "She seemed different. She is an artist with her needle, and she has helped us before with our mending. Just last week, the abbot asked her help with a torn altar cloth. Why would she trick me in such a way?"

"All women are capable of treachery, my poor, ignorant friend." The knight was already buckling on his long sword. It slapped against his thigh as he strode toward the door.

"What will you do when you find her?"

The hard eyes locked on the distant hills, where the sun was fading in a blood-red pool. "I shall teach her the price of betrayal," he said harshly.

She made her way deep into the woods, melting back into the silence and the shadows, far away from the sneering gazes of the village folk.

A branch slapped at her face, and she rubbed the fragile

skin where a welt had already begun to rise. She was in
the depths of the royal forest now. Were she caught here,
she could be branded or blinded or worse.

The silence of the thick woods stretched around her,
unbroken except for the whisper of leaves in the canopy
high above. The stillness suited her own silence, which
went back nearly as far as she could remember. Sometimes
she had vague memories of a different time, when cascades
of words and even the ripple of laughter had tumbled from
her lips.

But no more. Now she stayed to the forest, a shadow
among other shadows, a small, hunted creature wary of
men. At least here her silence would not be noticed.

Before her the path widened slightly. Moonlight lit a
small clearing, bright with woodbine and primroses. She
tugged at the cloth bundle on her back, filled with torn
vestments and an altar cloth from the abbey. Mending
them was the least she could do to thank the brothers for
their hospitality. Though she would never venture back to
those grounds herself, somehow she would see that the
mended items were returned.

With her needle she was happy. With her needle she
could shape soft sleeves and flowing skirts. They spoke, her
gowns, carrying all the golden laughter now denied her.

"So the rabbit dares to venture back into darkness."
Callous fingers gripped her throat. She turned wildly, but
the hard hands tightened. In a blinding flash all her nightmares came true.

His eyes were harsh, the color of mud flung on stone.
His mouth was thin, a blood-red line twisted with cruelty.
"Did he tire of you so soon?" William hissed.

She shoved against his hands, cursing her carelessness.
She should have scented this trap.

"Come, my love, do not fight me. Not here in the darkness." William scowled as she swung furiously at his
chest, planting blow after blow on his unyielding flesh.
With a curse he jerked the bundle from her shoulder. The
costly silks spilled into his fingers.

His laughter came in a harsh bray. "A thief, are you,
now? My men will hang you for stealing these from the
abbey. Unless I choose to intercede, that is." He fingered

her kirtle roughly. "And for that favor, you must repay me well."

She jerked her head in fury.

"What a pity to see these priceless fabrics muddied." Laughing, he dropped the silks and ground them into the dirt, while his captive struggled to pull free. *"Easy, my little rabbit. You shall wear clothes more beautiful than this in my hall. When you do, you shall belong to me, and none else."* He pushed her to the ground, his hands at her thighs. *"Did you cry out when he took your maidenhood? Damn you, did you moan when he left his seed within you?"* His breath played over her cheeks, dank with ale and venison. His tongue filled her mouth, hard and searching, as his fingers wrenched at her kirtle.

Even then she could not scream, and she railed at her weakness. She kicked wildly, clawing at his face, but William merely laughed. In truth her struggles inflamed him. *"I'll have you here, my sweet witch. Here on the ferns, where no one can interfere. I've waited too cursed long as it is."*

This time he would succeed. This time there would be no escaping his fingers and the pain of his angry entrance. Always before there had been a nearby alley, a hidden door, or a villager who owed her a favor.

But no more. Here in the depths of the forest, Tamsyn was friendless, powerless.

His knee was between her legs. Her skirts rode up, caught between their twisting bodies, offering him ever more access to her flesh. She bit his hands, his shoulder, his arm.

A twig snapped. Something hissed past her cheek and slammed into the trunk of the elm tree. *"Leave your hunting, William. These woods grow dangerous by night."* A figure stood in shadow, his face silvered by the moonlight spilling through the dark canopy. Yet he commanded all, touched all in that quiet glade, as if he were the very spirit of the forest itself.

William struggled to his feet. *"Be gone, wanderer. You have no power in the royal forest. Tonight my men will trap you like the animal you are."*

"I see no other men here. Only you, William."

"They are close at hand," the sheriff blustered. "They do but rest across the hill, awaiting my word to summon them."

"Indeed? How strange, for 'tis a fact that I have crossed that hill myself, and the only creatures sleeping there were a pair of deer, full with grass." The knight's voice rose in mockery. "Mayhap I should summon them to serve you, my lord sheriff."

"Damn you!" William's fingers tightened as he searched clumsily for his sword. Too late he realized that, frantic in his lust, he had cast his weapon down in the long ferns beside him.

"Let her go, William."

"I think not." The sheriff's hands tightened cruelly on Tamsyn's neck. "My partner is flushed and filled with lust. Are you not, my love?" he sneered.

"To my eyes, the woman wants nothing to do with you."

"You always did see only what you wanted to see, brother dearest."

Tamsyn looked from brother to brother, her eyes wide at this revelation of their blood tie.

Laughing, the sheriff jerked her back toward the edge of the glade. "So now you've returned from the Holy Lands. But where are your prizes of silk and gold? Where is your glory and high rank, tell me that?"

The knight did not move. "Stand away from her, William. These arguments of ours will be left for some other time and place."

"No, here. Now. You've harried me too long with your mysterious comings and goings. My father is gone, our mother long dead. Now even the Lord of Draycotte is far away. You have no rights here, and no more land to hold. In this valley all answer to me. So shall you, Rowan de Beauclair."

Moonlight outlined a smooth curve of polished wood. "Stand away from the woman. I tell you this for the last time." The crusader's longbow drew level before his chest, an arrow nocked against the taut bowstring.

"So it's a mute you want, brother?" William laughed

harshly. "A weak creature who makes no protest when you push between her legs."

"My pleasures can hold no interest for you, William. Release her. She has no place in the old anger between us."

"Is that what you think?" The sheriff laughed, his hands moving intimately over his captive's breasts. "Then you are wrong, in this as in so much else. Everything holds a place in the anger between us. It always has and it always will. There is not room enough for both of us in England."

"Then one of us must leave." There was a glitter in Rowan de Beauclair's gray eyes. The bow pointed at William did not waver.

"Shoot, then. Let us see your skill, archer." With a harsh laugh, William wrenched his captive as a shield before him.

The words were barely from his lips when an arrow hissed through the darkness. The feathers singed the sheriff's wrists, making him leap sideways with a curse. "There's your warning, William. The next one will be fatal."

Cursing, William stumbled backward, his captive clutched before him. "Do you dare to test your skill in the darkness, where one slip may mean your whore's life?"

Another arrow sang out. This one nailed the end of William's tunic to the trunk of a towering oak. Muttering, the sheriff ripped free and stumbled backward, his arm locked about Tamsyn's throat. Dimly she heard the neighing of a horse before she was thrown across the animal's back. As air returned to her lungs, she fought to escape with every scrap of will she possessed.

William clambered onto the saddle behind her, his mount dancing skittishly. They had gone no more than three strides when a dark creature charged across the clearing, black wings unfurled like a messenger from hell itself.

Around and around the creature danced, while the horse tossed its head, neighing in terror, and threw its riders to the ground.

Rolling sideways to a row of bramble brushes, Tamsyn squeezed to safety, leaving her pursuer to face a wall of sharp thorns.

"The devil's very handmaid you are! You'll pay for that, woman."

Another arrow hissed through the air, followed by still another. William looked up to find himself pinned right and left against a broad yew tree.

Rowan de Beauclair shouldered his bow and, striding forward, held a small, curved dagger to his brother's throat. "End it now, William. I claim the land you stole from me and the restoration of all Draycotte's lands and revenues to the abbey until his return."

The sheriff's face was mottled with fury. "The abbey land will stay mine. As for the lands our mother marked for you, those will stay mine also. And why not, for those are the best fields between here and Alfriston. You have the same cold cunning and clever tongue of your father, but this time you're too late. For I carry your father's seal and contracts now, and they show that the land is mine, granted by his hand."

"You lie! They were to be shared. He swore that on his dying bed, with our mother as his witness."

William laughed coldly. "Prove it, brother. Bring her back from the dead. Let her show that I lie."

Somewhere overhead a night bird screamed shrilly. "Did we ever do anything but fight, William? Was there ever one kind word between us?" the knight asked harshly.

"I gave as I got, brother. It was my father's way. Blood parent or not, he molded you in the same hard way. Have the long years away made you forget?"

Rowan de Beauclair laughed. "You know exactly what the years have done to me, for you have had your spies close about me every day since I left this valley."

His half-brother shrugged. "There is power in knowledge. My father knew this well. In your absence, I made it my business to know everything about you." His eyes glittered coldly. "They told me how you turned coward and betrayed your band—and how later you denied it."

"We were all betrayed that day. Now I return home to find my lord gone, my lands confiscated, and my home turned into a pigsty. Meanwhile, the abbey is in turmoil, its coffers raided, and every article of value removed to my dear brother's house."

The sheriff's lips twisted. "So you say. But where is your proof?"

"You may be certain I shall have it, William. Until then stay out of my path, and stay away from my woman."

"So you have had her. I suppose it amuses you to lie with a clumsy mute."

De Beauclair's voice cracked like a whip. "You will not be so brave after a night spent alone in the woods. Come," he ordered Tamsyn, who was watching wide-eyed at the edge of the glade. A moment later he scooped her up onto the back of William's mount.

"You will die strung up like a wild pig!" William cried. "I'll parade you through the streets, brother dear, with all the villagers to watch, do you hear? You will die slowly, crying out for mercy. But there shall be none. I only wish our mother could see you scream in torment. She would not have thought her favorite son so grand then!"

"You're mad, William. I think you have always been mad."

The sheriff's angry curses continued long after the two riders vanished back into the forest.

"I should whip you for leaving the abbey."

The woman sitting before de Beauclair did not answer. She could not answer; he knew that now. And yet her silence goaded him. "I should do far more than whip you, in fact."

She had shed no tears or shown any other sign of emotion since they had galloped from the glade. For the hundredth time de Beauclair found himself wondering why she could not speak. He felt her long hair drift over his shoulder. Like fine silk, it covered his fingers. Every movement sent more of the fragrant strands spilling against him.

For some reason this woman made him think of the past, and all he should have been. He had gone off to fight in the Crusades, swearing all honor to his king and country and church.

Now, ten years later, he had come back—an older man, eyes hardened by too much killing, the laughter long gone from his lips. There was no king to greet him, for the king *himself was gone to some far battlefield, and in his absence England was suffering.*

As for his God, de Beauclair could not say. In the blazing sun, even his faith had left him.

Tamsyn turned and tugged at his shoulder, pointing back toward the abbey.

"Not there," Rowan said tightly. "It is no longer safe."

He did not tell her the truth, for the truth was that he desired her beyond all controlling. That desire made him weak, distracted, vulnerable to William's endless tricks. It also put the abbey and village at risk, for they would become the battlefield for William's old hatred.

Suddenly Rowan de Beauclair had discovered he was tired of fighting. He would leave William his land. No more blood would be shed because of him.

He pointed north, where dense forest ran in unbroken waves. "That is our direction now. I know a place where you will be safe."

He felt her instant stiffening. She shook her head fiercely, stabbing her hand again toward the valley behind them.

"No." His face was hard. "Not there. We will never see the abbey and its valley again."

Kara tossed frantically, captive in a world of smoke and shadow and anger. And in that dream she felt another woman's fear, another woman's passion, exactly like her own.

It held her fast, this dream, locking her to a past that seemed but moments gone. Every surge of her blood drove her deeper into the vision, carried her another step away from the world she ought to know, into a world she could not forget. . . .

Yew branches creaked in the wind as they made their way, weary and dirty, into a small valley at the edge of a swift river. Only as the horse came to rest did Tamsyn notice a figure following on a small black pony.

"He is one of mine," the knight said, "small but with a brave heart, as you saw in his attack on William in the glade. But he has been marked like too many others, his

hand cut off for the crime of theft. Do not show surprise, for any notice pains him."

As he spoke a small boy in flapping black sleeves trotted his pony up to them. "No one following, my lord. All is clear." Grinning, the boy swung down from his small mount and moved to hold the knight's horse.

"After you, my lady." The knight swept a hand gallantly toward the firelight that danced in the clearing.

Tamsyn slid down, feeling de Beauclair's hands steady her fall. As she watched in amazement, he carried away boughs of foliage to reveal the gaping outline of a cave.

"Well hidden, is it not?" De Beauclair laughed softly. "It keeps us safe, far from William's reach." They were surrounded by a ragtag band of boys. Some were mending torn tunics, some stirred huge caldrons set on iron frames, while others groomed the half dozen ponies tethered just beyond the firelight.

Tamsyn's amazement grew.

"They are outlaws," the knight explained softly. "Boys, true, none of them old enough to grow a beard, yet outlaws still. Young Allan is wanted for poaching a rabbit from the Royal Forest. Our young scout you have already met. Over there at the fire is Old Tim." The boy in question looked scarcely more than five, and delicious smells drifted through the air as he tended the boiling caldron. "You like it? 'Tis my own recipe, brought back from my travels," he called.

A breathless figure ran toward them from the fire, doublet all awry. "You're back, my lord! But with a—a woman?" The boy caught himself in a cough. "No rudeness meant, m'lady. Only come, for the stew is nearly done." He looked up at the knight with adoring eyes. "I stirred it just as you said. The others kept trying to taste it, but I held them off," the boy said proudly.

The knight bent and rustled the young cook's hair. As he did, firelight danced over the left side of the boy's face. The eye socket, Tamsyn saw, was bare, marred by a huge scar.

She swallowed a gasp.

"Come, my lady," de Beauclair ordered grandly. "It is time to eat."

Tamsyn took the arm that he held out in exquisite courtesy, aware of the curious eyes of the boys gathered around them. Then the tense mood was broken. The boys tumbled forward, laughing with the abandon of childhood, slapping de Beauclair on the back, jabbing him in the ribs, and offering him bread and ale.

Tamsyn took a steaming bowl, her eyes closing with pleasure as the rich scent of game and herbs filled her lungs. When her stomach growled loudly, the boys burst into delighted laughter.

"It tastes even better than it smells, I assure you," the knight said, smiling. "I am a fine cook, in truth."

"So he is," one of the taller boys echoed. "Except when he brews berry wine. 'Tis vile enough to make your very tongue fall out."

The knight gave a good-natured oath and watched appreciatively as Tamsyn emptied her bowl. "There is more, you know. We shall all eat well and sleep soundly tonight."

Now that she knew there would be enough for all the younger ones, Tamsyn held out her bowl for more. A chunk of bread, still warm from the fire, was thrust into her fingers, and with it a tankard of wine.

She took a sip—and instantly broke into bitter coughing.

It was clearly a long-standing joke, for the boys brayed with laughter, slapping their sides loudly.

"My apologies." De Beauclair rubbed his jaw, chuckling. "It is their way of welcoming new visitors to our camp." One dark brow rose in question. "You do not like my wine?"

Like it? She could like it as much as she could like swallowing fire! To show her answer, Tamsyn dipped her palm into the tankard and poured a handful of wine over the knight's grinning head. His face was bronze and silver, half in moonlight, half in fire. He caught her hand, grinning, and pulled her to him.

And the world stood still.

At that moment Tamsyn's life truly began. Suddenly there was sound where there had been only silence; suddenly there were words and songs dancing in her blood, racing through her heart. Heat invaded her body with the stealth of a thief.

Was this what the bards meant by love, the thing that blinded men and set women to tears?

Tamsyn did not know. She had never felt such heat before. In truth, it was not one feeling but many all at once. It was running barefoot through a field of lilies at dawn. It was the throbbing in the chest that came after swimming a long, cold river. It was other things too, like the emptiness that came when she had had nothing to eat.

Suddenly reckless, she traced the scar at Rowan's cheek.

His fingers closed tightly on hers. She could feel him tremble.

"Bewitched, in truth." It was but a whisper. "You'll regret this, my lady. We both will, I fear." His body was stiff, as if he fought to keep from moving. "You had best go on before me. I will have two of the younger ones bring you a blanket. I shall stay here, for there are things to discuss—plans to be made—" He cleared his throat, torment in his eyes.

He tried to step away.

She was quicker. Her fingers twined with his.

They stood so for an eternity, measuring all the dark pathways where their future would take them, pondering all the choices they could make at that moment.

And knowing that there was only one choice.

An ember hissed in the flames. De Beauclair's fingers tightened. "It's wrong," he murmured, almost to himself. "There's too much you don't understand."

He pulled away then. His face was masked, as he offered her a bow, harsh with self-mockery. "Sleep well, my lady."

The pallets were soft straw, clean and fragrant with herbs, but Tamsyn chose the cold stone floor instead, for it kept her from thinking of the man who paced stubbornly, his shadow dancing just beyond the firelight.

She watched, unblinking. She watched, not understanding. And then finally the dreams came.

There was smoke, as always. There were fire and shouts and fear at the back of her throat.

She sat up, heart slamming at her ribs, nails clutching

*her torn and muddy skirts. She felt him before she saw
him, her nerves screaming with awareness.*

He stood at the mouth of the cave. There was no movement behind him in the little camp, where dark figures lay
tumbled in sleep. Behind him the fire had gone out, and
the embers were but a bright memory.

Her heart filled until it seemed to burst.

"Tamsyn?"
Rowan spoke the words again, peering into the darkness.
He heard a rustle on stone, to his alert senses as loud as
a scream. When a twig snapped in the cave, he plunged
forward in fear.

Then he froze. What comfort could he offer her? He had
meant to treat her as a tool for his revenge. Yet with his
control so weak, her danger grew.

How could he kneel beside her? How could he brush
the curve of her cheek and not want much, much more?
One look and he would be lost. One touch and his desire
would be beyond all subduing. He would take her there,
thighs spread beneath him, her violet eyes huge and dazed
as he drove himself inside her.

He cursed darkly. What difference between him and
William, in truth?

But he could not leave her, not without the certainty
that she was well. He made his way forward, blind in
the darkness, steered by the small rustling sounds at the
cave's edge.

She was not on the pallet. She lay instead on the cold
stone, her body nudged into a ball and her hands locked
around her skirts. The harsh pace of her breathing told
him that she slept—and that her dreams were as dark as
his own.

And then the choice was made. In truth there had never
been a choice.

His fingers settled over her brow, easing a strand of
golden hair away from her eyes. " 'Tis but a dream, my
Tamsyn. Only shadows, and they cannot harm us." He
felt her tense, felt her breathing still, and knew she was
experiencing that moment of vulnerability when sleep
gives way to waking. His fingers buried themselves in the

warm flow of her hair. He bent low and touched his lips to her cheek. It was a kiss without lust, he told himself, meant only as reassurance.

But Rowan de Beauclair knew instantly that he lied. With that one touch, fire burst within him, a thousand raging desert suns. The warrior became the conquered, a willing captive of her beauty.

And of her courage. He had seen that she was stronger than most men. Possibly stronger than he.

The memory made him smile. "You are safe," he whispered. "No one comes. There are watches posted in the trees. You need not fear William will follow here."

She did not move. His fingers, brushing her cheek, met moisture.

Tears that even now slid in hot, awful silence.

"Don't," he ordered desperately, knowing tears would break him when nothing else could. He had had enough of them in the hot Saracen dawns, in the smoke and turmoil where a thousand warriors fought and fell upon the restless sands. "I'm leaving. You are safe here. There is no need to cry, I swear this."

He sensed a movement. His hand rose. He gasped as he found only the hot satin of naked skin.

Her hand rose to cup his neck.

"Why?" It was a ragged, desperate sound. He hadn't the right to ask and she hadn't the ability to answer, but Rowan had to ask nonetheless.

Her fingers gripped his wrist. Her hand locked as she brought him closer. She carried his palm to her heart, which raced within her chest, wild as a pigeon trapped inside a cage.

"Because of this? Is this your way of answering?"

He felt her nod, and it awed him, this giving of hers. "You don't understand." He tried to ignore the softness that welcomed his fingers, her bravery and all she offered him, but it was like turning away from blue water after months of sand. It was more than his strength permitted.

Her homespun linen fell away. "He will track us both now." Rowan spoke harshly, compelled to warn her. "He will never rest until his madness and pride are satisfied."

But Tamsyn had no interest in anything except the man

before her. Her body was as supple as the birch trees be-
yond the cave, silver in the light of the moon rising above
the hills.

"So beautiful," he whispered, half-mad himself, beset
with hunger for a way of life long gone, for peace and joy
and family. Why must she summon up the past for him
this way, in painful fragments that bit into his heart?

There was danger, too. She made him soft and useless
for revenge. There was irony in that, since she was meant
to be the pawn, his weapon with which to weaken his
greatest enemy.

"Too late," he said. To himself. To her. He was trapped
and must have her, now in this place of silence and stone.

Her hair rustled, pale in the slanting light, but not as
pale as her skin. Even then Rowan made one last try to
save her. "You choose with your heart, my lady, but mark
me well. I have no heart left. It lies hard and dry in the
shifting sands of the Holy Lands. Because of that, I will
take and take, and for you there will be only loss. Know
now that I will hurt you. No amount of your giving can
satisfy this hunger inside me. In the end there will only
be loss for us both."

Light shimmered, bent and broken from a polished blade.
With a hiss his dagger slid free. In her hands now, it
pressed against Rowan's neck.

With his cold blade she spoke the words so long denied
her, issued the proud command, and claimed his warrior's
body. Moonlight pooled around her, and the air churned
with a dangerous energy.

You are claimed, my knight, *so the blade sang.* You
are mine, slave to do my bidding through one night's
darkness. This is mine to command.

The hard-eyed warrior was no match for her woman's
magic, for her woman's courage. He fell, though he did
not move. His heart of stone shattered, though no muscle
betrayed him.

The dagger stayed. Her body curved to his, singing the
world to life with its warmth. He sighed, a small, still
sound that began in his chest, worked through his throat
and in the end screamed from every pore in knowledge of

his defeat. "Woman," he whispered. "Temptress. Forest elf or angel, I shall betray you."

Her hand brushed the long, misshapen scar at his cheek. "I'll hurt you. I'll try to stay away and I'll fail. . . ."

Her body was pressed to hard muscle now. She freed his tunic with trembling fingers.

"And God forgive me, I'll love you. That most of all."

The dagger slid from her fingers and clattered over the cold stone floor as he pulled her fiercely against him.

"Damn it, where is she?"

Firelight shifted harshly over the frightened faces of the men assembled in William's hall. None answered. None dared. The strange, silent woman with hair like dawn was gone, and each man knew the sheriff's rage would be great that night.

"Speak now, or I'll have all your tongues ripped from you!"

A man with hard eyes and dirty teeth inched forward. "My lord sheriff, she is gone. Gone from the abbey and from the village."

"Of course she's gone from the abbey, you fool! I myself saw her leave. I sent you to find her, and you come back white-faced, like a pack of old women, moaning about strange lights and evil sounds."

"My lord, no traveler moves safely through those woods at night. You cannot expect us to track the woman there."

The sheriff's dagger slid to the man's throat. "I expect, my dearest Gilbert, for you to do exactly what I tell you to do."

The man caught back a curse as the blade nicked his skin. "Of course, my lord. We shall ride back tonight."

A ripple of fear sped through the little group, drowned by the harsh ring of the sheriff's laughter. "So you shall, Gilbert. You shall take these men and twice as many more and ride through the forest until you track the woman down like the puny rabbit that she is. There is something about her—something familiar. I shall have the story of her birth from her." He cut himself off, aware of the curious looks of his men. "Ride, damn you, and on the way, you'll make one stop."

Gilbert frowned. "My lord?"

"In the cottage outside the abbey walls, you will find the unknown knight." The sheriff laughed shrilly. From his pocket he withdrew a leather bag, which he tossed up and down until the bright jangle of coins filled the hall. "Fifty gold crowns for his head resting on this platter in my hall. Nay, I must not be chary. One hundred crowns. Two hundred if he is brought to me before nightfall," the sheriff said recklessly.

"But my lord, surely you cannot—" The blade slid back to Gilbert's neck. Blood blossomed over his throat.

"I do exactly as I wish," the sheriff hissed. "Do not forget this, Gilbert. Otherwise, your head will be the next to fall."

Drifting smoke and the sizzle of frying dough wafted through the mouth of the cave, waking de Beauclair from his dreams.

Ah, but what dreams they were, with rose petals thick and pink upon the soft earth; dreams of fine satin and rare fragrance that filled his senses with an intoxicating beauty.

Dreams of . . .

His eyes blinked open. His fingers met skin of warmest satin.

He sat up with a start and saw that his vision had been no dream. Against his chest lay hair like silk and skin like the softest petals. Tamsyn lay lost in sleep. Outside, dawn glittered above the silhouette of trees, showing him the truth of all that had happened in the long night.

De Beauclair caught a handful of silken hair and let it slide between his fingers. If only he knew her real name. If only he knew the mystery of her past.

Her breasts were high and full, her body lush enough to satisfy a man's most potent dreams. His eyes darkened, a smile playing around his lips as he remembered how her body had sought his in the night. The smile made his face younger. So great was the change that he might have been a different man.

He might have been the young and idealistic knight who had ridden from Draycotte Abbey ten years before, bright *mail agleam in the sunlight and banners snapping proudly before him.*

But ten years of bloodshed, ten years of horror and betrayal in the sands of the East, had destroyed that young knight forever. Now it was time to trap his old enemy. Tamsyn would be safe in the north, but he would never be content until he saw his half brother crushed beneath his heel.

So why did he dally here like a lovesick youth? Why did he dream of lazy afternoons with nothing more urgent to do than let his fingers slide through hair that gleamed like silk?

She moved. One violet eye eased open.

"My lady," he said huskily. "A welcome to the morning outside."

Color suffused her glorious cheeks. Something warm and hazy filled her startling eyes.

The knight knew it was the same emotion that filled his. But before he could speak, her fingers slid to his chest. In the light of dawn the old scars were clearly visible, and her forefinger gently measured each one. Slowly, she eased against him and bent her head to plant her lips where her fingers had been.

Instantly there was heat. Instantly there was slamming lust and a blind need to possess.

But de Beauclair did not move. Her touch was too rare. When her head finally lifted, her hair a wild fall of gold and copper in the sunlight, he gave her a lopsided smile. "The wounds do not pain me, my lady. They are long healed."

She just looked at him. And in her look, de Beauclair felt a strange intensity, as if she could part the long years and find the idealistic knight he had used to be.

Perhaps in this quiet cave, in this ridge of forest far from prying eyes, such dreams might live again. From a leather pouch beside their pallet, he drew a length of bright-colored cloth and a gleaming brooch of pounded silver in the shape of a falcon. "For you. For what you gave me. Last night," he began haltingly, his hands cupping her cheeks. "I must . . . explain." There were words to be said, the past to be explained.

*But Tamsyn shook her head. Pushing forward, she cap-
tured him beneath her.*

*He was resolute in his honor. There had not been
enough words last night. Now, in the clear warmth of
dawn, the words must be said. "I have nothing to offer
you, my sweet Tamsyn, nothing to share with you but
bitterness and dusty roads. And always there will be William, my half brother, baying at the moon like a dog,
desperate to have his spoils."*

*Her thighs eased against him, supple and searching. He
felt the fire of her touch leap from vein to vein, until he
was ablaze. "You must listen before it is too late. Now,
while there is still time to turn back."*

Her fingers rose and blocked the movement of his lips.

"I must speak," he said hoarsely.

*But as she slid down against him, it was already too
late for words. It was too late for anything but the golden,
impossible dreams she brought him when her body opened
and welcomed him inside her.*

*They rode out of the sunset, dust rising in sullen clouds
beneath their horses' hooves. Young Allan had first
brought warning of the riders' approach, glimpsed from a
tree at the crest of the hill. Now de Beauclair stood frowning down at three score riders thundering toward the
forest.*

Toward the forest that was no longer safe.

*He turned, his decision made. "Mount up," he cried.
"We ride north, away from the sheriff's men. I know a
place of silver waters and pure beaches, and there we will
be safe."*

*One of the boys tugged at his arm, frowning. "But what
of William and your chances here, my lord? He is your
half brother. You told us you would fight to have your
lands back."*

*De Beauclair's face was hard. So he had vowed, to re-
claim all that William had stolen from him.*

*But that was before the woman. That was before he
found there was something more precious than land or
title or rank.*

"We ride north," he repeated harshly. *"Do not question me further."*

He found Tamsyn before the cave, holding a piece of white linen caught fast within a frame of wood. The bright woolen shawl lay around her shoulders, secured by his brooch. He smiled at the sight of her, head bent as her needle raced in and out of the cloth.

His shadow fell. She looked up, startled.

"We ride, my lady."

Her fingers tightened. He looked down, touching the exquisite stitches. Then he stiffened, again the warrior, again his face a mask. *"We cannot stay. William will have set prices on our heads—ten full pounds on yours alone. No village or vale will be safe to us now."*

She gave him a questioning look, her fingers touching the silver brooch pinned at her shoulder.

"There is no time for questions. We ride. I order it."

She came to her feet, her shoulders square and proud. She did not move.

"Now. You will come now, because I order it."

Her thumb slipped. The needle drove deep into her palm.

Blood welled onto the white fabric and covered the stag she'd so carefully sewn there.

A shudder ran through Tamsyn. It was an omen, a clear sign of the danger before them. This was her doing. Now William would stop at nothing to secure de Beauclair's death.

The warrior brought her palm to his mouth and licked away the blood. *"And I order it, my dearest love, because I am blind with desire for you."* His shadow fell as he bent his face to hers. *"You entrance me, seduce me, infuriate me,"* he muttered.

Their fingers locked. Their lips touched, light, tentative. And then with reckless hunger.

But even the thunder of their hearts could not block out the shouts that drifted up the hillside. *" 'Tis the sheriff's men! God help us, we'll be taken for sure!"*

The memories were all around her, locked in every stone, sealed in every branch. They were part of the abbey itself, part of the shimmering web of love and loss that was wrapped around this ancient, beautiful place. And Kara could not pull away from sights so keen and a past that loomed so near.

She twisted in her dreams, terrified. Obsessed.

Afraid. Running from a man who had died six centuries before.

"Kara, are you in there?" Duncan slammed his fist against the door. "Answer me, damn it!"

There was no sound from the darkness beyond the heavy moat-house door, and Duncan felt the first brush of fear. Was she asleep or had she fallen into another of those cursed visions?

He slammed at the outer door, but it held firm, solid English oak. Cursing, he ran to the rear, where a stone bridge spanned the moat. Beyond him French doors lay open onto the balcony, white curtains billowing in the wind.

As he stumbled up the bank, a scream split the rainy night.

Kara stood on the wet bank, her eyes blind. She was rigid, shaking. The slightest movement would send her toppling down onto the rocks beside the moat.

Sixteen ⁓

Smoke. Hammering hooves. The wind through a black sea of trees. Riders coming fast, and no place to escape . . .

Kara stumbled backward, away from the dreams, her knees trembling.

We ride, my lady. Because I order it.

A shadow fell over her face. She felt the brush of lips, light and tentative. And then with blinding hunger.

The hammer of her heart, which turned into distant shouting.

The cry that swept up the hillside.

The vision was beyond controlling, fueled by the power of centuries of memory and emotion locked in this strange old house.

"Kara, stop! Don't move."

She looked down, blinking. She stood at the edge of the wet bank. Below her, the moat shimmered restlessly, and banks of roses trembled in the evening breeze. She closed her eyes, struggling for control.

And then she felt her body sway.

Duncan sprinted up the hill and angled his shoulder seconds before Kara slammed against his chest.

Her eyes were hazy. "I was sleeping. A dream . . ."

MacKinnon scowled. "Do you scream in your sleep, too?" His fingers tightened as part of the bank gave way beneath their weight.

"I'm fine now. You can let me go." Dressed in a

164

man's Oxford shirt three sizes too large, Kara pushed awkwardly at his chest.

Duncan ignored her attempts to pull free. "What happened?"

"It was just a dream. Don't *you* ever dream, MacKinnon?"

"Oh, I dream, all right. Not necessarily about pleasant things. But when I do, I never open a double set of French doors, climb over a balcony, and totter along the edge of a rock-lined moat."

"It was stuffy inside, and I . . . I must have opened the doors."

"And then I suppose you decided to take a midnight swim," Duncan said acidly.

Her fist hit his chest. "I don't have to answer to you or anyone else. I'm done with this ridiculous project for Andrew Calendish and I'm done with this bizarre old abbey. I'm leaving, do you hear?"

"Not just yet, you aren't." His fingers tightened. Slowly, he lowered her to the ground. Every inch of the way her trembling body was locked against his. "I heard you scream, Fitzgerald. After that I heard you pound on the French doors. Something terrified you in there, and I want to know what it was."

"I told you, it was just . . . dreams."

He muttered a curse, edging up the bank to the moat-house wall. "It was one of your visions, wasn't it? Like what happened out in the field today?"

Kara stiffened.

She tried to look away. She tried to deny that she was feeling anything, and she failed dismally. Because at that moment, with the roses whispering around her and the moat shining at her feet, with Duncan's hard chest pressed against her, Kara was utterly awash in sensation. His every movement aroused her with aching clarity.

Anger. Confusion. Alarm.

Between them she felt the cold metal of his Roman coin. From it, sharp visions poured into Kara's mind.

A deserted beach in spring. A castle of warm pink stone, topped with fairy-tale turrets and gables. Bright tartans draped on polished oak. The faint, haunting skirl of bag-pipes . . .

Dunraven Castle. Kara recognized it from the photograph. Even without the photo, she would have pulled the name from Duncan's mind, because at that moment the link between them was deep.

Kara trembled as she saw a boy running through fields of heather, a woman with red hair close behind him. She saw the same boy, older now, standing proudly before the battered Range Rover that was his first car. She saw him again, full grown, face hard, after he returned from work in pounding seas. Day after day he had gone down into the mud and darkness, his fingers numb with cold as he checked and rechecked pipes and meters and underwater scaffolding. And all the time someone had wanted him gone. That someone had rigged a little surprise for Duncan on his second week of work.

The bomb had been half concealed inside a fiberglass rail twenty feet below the surface. It had torn apart most of a steel girder and claimed over a dozen lives. Had Duncan been where he was scheduled to be, rather than in the control room taking a call from London, his body would have been among those floating in the wreckage.

Kara shuddered, paralyzed by the dark memories of oily smoke, raging flame, and broken bodies amid twisted metal. She touched Duncan's raw despair and his fury at failure. There had been a woman that night, followed by other women in the nights to come. In his mind they had blended together, their bodies all the same. Nothing had taken away the throb of failure.

It hurt to be so close to him, to feel his memories bleeding into hers, but Kara couldn't shield herself from their link.

"I—I want to go inside." Her shirt was bunched up between them. Only one fine layer of fabric separated their tense bodies.

Duncan's coin pressed against her chest, smooth and cold, fueling the link.

Kara felt him stiffen. His hand anchored her thigh. She saw other images from his mind then—shadows of what would be between them. It would be slow and hot. His hands would open and clench. He would bend her to his passion, leave her moaning, twisting, hungry . . .

"Let me *go!*"

Duncan's eyes were unreadable. "If you want to go inside, I'll take you."

The coin lay locked against her. Kara knew she had to escape it. "No! I can walk myself."

"It's because of the coin, isn't it?" He looked down at the gold disk glinting in the moonlight. "This metal is a link, focusing those visions of yours."

"Let me go." This time there was desperation in Kara's voice.

"If we were linked, then you saw what I saw. You felt what I felt—and everything that I want to feel." Slowly Duncan slid a strand of copper hair away from her cheek.

Kara felt the touch to the very bottom of her toes. "I don't know what you mean."

"I mean what happens when I touch you." Frowning, he stepped away.

Kara shuddered as the contact was broken. Her knees wobbled, but now she would be fine. The flood of images would finally ebb.

Only it didn't happen. Even with Duncan a foot away, the air between them shimmered with power. And with each breath, each look, Kara felt the link pulse anew.

An azure sea in the middle of the South Pacific. Swimming underwater, something heavy and metallic strapped on his back. A storm coming. Waves that slam him against underwater rocks.

It wasn't fair! It had never happened to Kara this way before. With their physical contact broken, she should have been free.

But she wasn't. Like a bright cord, the link held.

"What's happening, Kara? Damn it, I can't help you if you don't talk to me."

She gave a ragged laugh. "What makes you think you can help me, anyway?"

"Somebody's got to," Duncan said harshly. "You're shivering. You can barely stand up. There must be something I can do."

But Kara knew no one could help. She was meant to be here, drawn to this beautiful abbey, linked with this brooding Scotsman. There was something unfinished between them, something that had waited for centuries.

She shoved at her hair. "Just ... just let me go back inside. I'll feel better when I'm warm. All I need is to—"

She looked at the abbey, and suddenly the image blurred.

She saw cold halls, filled with hoarse laughter. Rush lights glittered in golden bowls set on a table of hand-hewn pine.

And against the light stood a man, his eyes filled with madness and hate.

Hard fingers bit into her shoulders. "Kara, break it! Break free of whatever is holding you!"

She tried. Dear God, how she tried. But the vision was stronger than anything she had ever felt.

Kara had been so careful to protect against this loss of control. Few close friends, a quiet and solitary life, and sacrificing physical intimacy had been a painful part of that choice. So had the aching decision never to pursue having a family of her own. Kara had believed that her careful control would protect her, allowing her to lead at least a seminormal life. But she had been wrong.

Energy pounded over her in waves. Her whole body reeled beneath the force of her visions.

"Kara, talk to me." Dimly, she felt the tension of Duncan's hand at her waist. Somewhere metal clinked against stone. He had dropped the coin, she thought. How clumsy.

Then Kara realized he had done it purposely, hoping to save her.

The ground swayed. She felt the sharp outline of

Duncan's elbow at her side. She was too dizzy to protest when he lifted her in his arms and carried her inside.

"Kara."

Water. Cold water.

"Kara."

More water drizzled down her neck and cheeks. The sensation made her angry. She wanted to shout for it to stop, but her mouth didn't seem to work.

"Open your eyes."

She couldn't. She just wanted the sound to go away. She was so tired. Or maybe she was dead. Kara couldn't seem to remember. . . .

Something soft brushed against her foot and made a low meowing sound. A cat?

Her eyes opened to find a gray cat perched on a damask pillow beside her, amber eyes burning into hers. They made her think of endless orange dawns. She opened her mouth, swallowing. "Thirsty," she managed to squeak.

She heard footsteps. Duncan's face loomed up, stark with worry. "Kara? Can you hear me?"

"The cat . . . he woke me."

MacKinnon's eyes narrowed. "Cat? There was no cat in here."

Carefully he slid one hand beneath her neck and raised her head. "Drink this."

A bottle of very good sherry touched her mouth, and Kara savored the taste. Her memories seemed to blur like paint poured into moving water. "There *was* a cat. I saw him. He brushed against my foot." But it was hard to remember. She was exhausted, her body like melting wax.

"It was the medallion, wasn't it? It—connected us somehow."

Kara didn't answer.

Duncan scowled.

She was propped up against white pillows. Her faded shirt was askew and her hair was tangled.

"You look like hell, Fitzgerald," Duncan said gruffly. She should have, but she didn't.

Her head cocked. "I might say the same for you, MacKinnon. Don't you believe in razors?" Her hand brushed the stubble on his cheek.

At her touch, Duncan felt his insides turn to mush. "Sometimes even I take a vacation." His eyes narrowed. "You had me damned worried out there."

"I . . . feel fine."

"You weren't fine when I heard you screaming."

Kara looked away, toward the portrait whose eyes seemed to follow her. "Just give it a rest, will you?"

"I can't. I've got to face my bastard of a brother in a few hours and I need to know if what you saw has something to do with him. If there's even a hint of a chance that it does, I need to know exactly what you saw."

Duncan saw her fingers lock. He hated having to push her this way, but Kyle's threats had left him no choice. "It's not my call, Kara. There are too many lives at stake."

Kara shrugged. "It was just a dream."

"Tell me about it."

"A dream, MacKinnon. Even *you* have to sleep sometime."

Duncan frowned. That night when he slept his dreams had been full of Kara, their bodies caught in blinding passion. "When I dream, I don't scream as if I'm being hunted by a mob."

A tear slipped down her cheeks. Duncan took her hands gently in his. "One way or another I'll find out. I know about the work you did in New York with Detective Rivington. She swears you're the very best. That's why I need your honesty now, Kara. Tell me about the dream."

"You were in it, only it wasn't you. It wasn't even *now*."

"You're not exactly making sense, Fitzgerald."

"It gets worse. I saw the abbey, only it was probably six hundred years ago. There were fires and men in long brown cassocks. I saw a vast royal forest and a man who wanted to see us both dead." Her eyes locked with Duncan. "He was your brother *then*, too."

Duncan felt as if he had been kicked in the stomach. "You saw the abbey in the past, when it was a place of worship?"

She nodded.

"And you saw us there, together, along with someone who was my brother?"

Another nod.

Duncan wanted to laugh, except that he'd been having some equally strange dreams of his own. "What happened? In the dreams, that is."

"We went to the forest. He sent men after us." Kara shuddered.

"And then?"

She sighed. "I don't know. That's when I woke up—or you woke me up. I would have fallen, wouldn't I? You saved my life out there."

"Call it lucky timing."

"You're not wearing your medallion. Why?"

A shrug. "The chain broke."

"You're lying," Kara whispered. "And you're doing it to protect me." When he started to speak, she covered his lips with her fingers. "No, listen. I'm not used to trusting people, Duncan. I've been careful to keep this . . . touch of mine from going beyond my control. But now it has. I'm seeing things—all kinds of things."

"And it's tearing you to pieces."

"I didn't say that."

"You didn't have to say it." Duncan muttered harshly in Gaelic. "It's written all over your face right now. Let me help somehow, even if it's just as someone to talk to."

Kara blinked. "It doesn't . . . frighten you? Shock you?"

"Why should it? My own mother had some powerful visions on occasion. She was known as a *frithir*."

"*Frithir?*"

"That's Gaelic for a seer. I have a clear memory

of her worrying about my father while he was off in the jungles of Brazil searching out new coffee cultivars. Finally, after three days of fasting she rose before dawn and walked with closed eyes to the front door. Bareheaded and shoeless, she asked God to let her see why the laird had not answered any of her messages."

"Did she receive an answer?"

"She did. The guide had stolen all my father's money and left him to rot on an island in the middle of the Amazon. My mother flew down herself and found him just as the local villagers were deciding his head might make an interesting ornament for their longhouse." Duncan chuckled. "My mother gave them hell."

"She sounds very brave—and quite wonderful."

"She was." Duncan's voice fell. "She would have liked you vastly. One *frithir* to another."

"It didn't ... bother you when she saw such things?"

Duncan shrugged. "Not particularly. There's a long tradition of the sight in the Highlands, you know." His eyes darkened. "What I hated was how the bloody London journalists had a field day when they heard of it. By the time they were done with my mother, she sounded like a gnarled old crone tending her stew of newt and salamander."

Kara touched his stubbled cheek. "I'm sorry. Now I understand why you hate journalists so much."

"Some things don't change," he said harshly. "They still come sniffing around Dunraven every month or so, hoping to find something they can make into front-page news. Now that Kyle is back, it looks as if they might find something. It would have broken her heart to see what he became."

Kara's fingers moved gently over his jaw. "Maybe it's just as well she never knew. She must have been very beautiful with that wild red hair of hers."

Duncan's hand locked over hers. "How did you know that?"

"She was in your mind as you described her. I think she loved you very much."

Duncan's fingers intwined with hers. "You're damned good, Kara Fitzgerald."

"Do I frighten you?"

"Why should you? I'm not exactly known for my tact. Like any good Scotsman, I generally say exactly what I'm thinking, so I'm not much afraid of someone reading my thoughts." His hand moved to trace her lips. "Can you sense what I'm thinking now, Kara Fitzgerald?"

She could. Color filled her cheeks. Her pulse quickened.

"It's going to happen. I'm going to have you in my bed very soon. Even when I was telling you those stories about Borneo, I was already fantasizing about how you would feel against me, restless and hot and very naked."

"Duncan, I haven't—" Her breath caught. "Because of this touch of mine, I haven't had much practice at—"

He brushed her mouth gently with his thumb. "At loving a man?" he asked softly.

She nodded, cheeks aflame.

"You will soon," he said thickly.

The phone began to ring. Neither moved.

"The phone." Kara's voice was ragged.

"I heard it."

"Maybe . . . it's important."

"Let it ring," Duncan said harshly. There was no mistaking the thick desire in his voice.

After five more rings, they knew it wasn't going to stop.

Duncan yanked up the receiver. "MacKinnon here."

Silence. Then the line went dead.

He looked at the telephone for a long time, then shrugged. "A wrong number."

There was something dark gathering in his head when he felt Kara move behind him and rest her hand on his shoulder. "We can do this, Duncan. Together we can fight this man."

"You don't know Kyle or what he's capable of. You're not going anywhere near Belgrave Square."

The phone began to ring again, and this time Kara lifted the receiver. "Yes?"

Duncan heard a low, curt laugh.

"How very interesting. But I must not be rude. It is Lord Dunraven I am seeking."

Kara held out the telephone. "For you."

A roaring filled Duncan's ears as he took the cold receiver in his hands. "Dunraven here."

"Ah, Duncan." There was a low hiss of breath. "My dear, sweet Duncan."

MacKinnon stood without moving, feeling the hairs rise on his neck. *Careful*, he told himself. *You could be wrong.* "Who is this?"

"I think you already know."

Again there was a faint silence. Duncan heard the sound of waves and the dim cry of sea gulls. "What do you want?"

"What do I want? I want you, of course, and anything that will hurt you."

"Kyle." The name exploded from Duncan's throat.

"That's right, it's your loving brother. And the game you thought was over is about to begin again."

"What game?" He had to keep Kyle talking. "Where are you calling from, Kyle? What happened to you?"

"Not now. It's far too late for questions. Now is for the game, the last game we'll ever play."

"I don't understand, Kyle. What do you mean by—"

"Forget these silly attempts to stall me, Duncan, and listen, because I'm only going to tell you once. Tomorrow at Calendish Jewelers, Belgrave Square. You remember, that's where you were nearly caught by the police when your break-in attempt failed." There was a burst of harsh laughter. "She must be good, brother dear. Very good. I hope she's just as good in bed, so you can enjoy the last hours of your life."

"Damn it, Kyle—"

"I've left enough explosives to level that building and the two adjoining, along with anyone wandering past in the street. At six P.M. I suppose there should be quite a few people. And you're to go in at five, not four. Oh, one last thing: the girl comes too, Duncan. It amuses me to think of you there sweating, knowing that if you make one false move she'll go up too."

"She's out of this, Kyle. This is between the two of us, remember?"

"No good. Either she's with you when you enter the building or the bomb goes off by my hand. With her, you'll have one hour precisely. I'm most curious to see just how good you are, brother dear. Just remember that I'll be watching every move you make."

Duncan's fingers fisted around the telephone. "Damn it, Kyle, face me one on one. Skye or Lewis or Barra, name your island. Or are you too much of a bloody coward?"

"Excellent try." A slow hiss. "*Lord Dunraven.*" Pause. "But our little game will be played out in a very public way from now on. No more secret negotiations or hidden tricks. From now on every mistake you make is going to *kill* someone."

"Kyle, you filthy maggot, talk to me. *Talk* to me, damn you!"

There was a soft laugh. Then the line went dead.

Seventeen ~

Kara pulled the receiver from Duncan's fingers and replaced it quietly in its cradle.

Duncan didn't speak, his face hard with anger and pain.

"I'm going with you."

"Forget it, Fitzgerald."

"Kyle will be watching to be sure I'm there. I heard exactly what he said."

"We'll use a policewoman in a wig, someone who's trained for demolition work. Someone who knows what she's getting into. He'll be using video camera relays, and videos can be fooled."

Kara pulled him around to face her. "I can *help* you, Duncan. I'll know where he's been—what he's touched."

"What about me? Don't you know if you're there my nerves will be shot to hell? I won't be able to think about anything except what happens if I fail and take you up with me. And I'll be thinking of this," Duncan said hoarsely. He drove her back against the wall, and his thighs parted hers. His calloused hands gripped her waist while his eyes filled with fury and despair.

Kara's head slanted back. "Then that will make two of us." It was Kara who closed the inches between them, Kara whose shaken, heated body rose to meet his. Her lips traced his jaw and found his mouth.

176

The kiss was slow and hot and blatantly exploratory, and Duncan was sweating by the time it was done.

His lips curved in a ragged grin. "You don't bother to lie, do you?"

"I was never very good at it."

"I'm glad." Duncan cupped her cheeks, his hands very gentle. "What a bloody mess," he whispered.

"Messes happen to be my speciality, MacKinnon."

"I don't want you in there, Kara. I don't want you anywhere *near* the place."

"It's not your choice. Your brother saw to that." She shivered suddenly, looking around the room. "Duncan, what I felt in the study, that electric device—"

"We're fine out here, I've already checked, and everything is clean."

"Kyle bugged the abbey?"

Duncan nodded grimly. "Yes. Isn't it always him?"

Kara rested her head against his chest. "It was the same way then—in my dreams. He has always hated you beyond reason."

"But this time it's going to end." He took her hand. "Nothing I can say will change your mind?"

"Afraid not, Scotsman."

Duncan's fingers tightened. "Then we work together, and it starts now. Outside this room we have to assume Kyle will hear anything we say."

Kara nodded.

"And you're going to have to do exactly what I tell you, even when it makes no sense." He stared into Kara's eyes. "If that's a problem, I need to know now."

"What if I sense something? Something you don't understand?"

"Then I'll listen to you. The same rules apply."

Kara took a slow breath. "It's a deal, Scotsman."

Duncan brought her palm to his mouth. "When this is done, I'll take you to Dunraven myself. Maybe I'll think of a way to arrange your bloody shoot without destroying every bit of my privacy."

Kara covered his mouth with her finger. "Later, MacKinnon. After we walk out of Belgrave Square with a job well done and the world at our feet."

If we walk out.

Neither said the words. Neither had to.

Kacey Mallory Draycott had just arrived from Brighton. She joined her husband on the abbey's steps while the car with Kara and Duncan disappeared over the hill. "I wish there was something I could do to help," Nicholas said grimly.

"You can't," his wife answered. "From what I understand, only one person can help Duncan, and that's the woman sitting next to him."

"Do you think he believes that?"

"Heaven only knows what that man believes." Kacey sighed. "Much as I love Duncan, getting past his defenses is like sneaking inside the Tower of London." She frowned at her husband. "Can we talk freely now?"

Nicholas nodded. "I deactivated those bloody bugs just before you arrived." He shook his head. "I think Kyle always blamed Duncan for their mother's death. Maybe that's what unhinged him. Or maybe some people are just meant to be criminals. Over the years I've watched Duncan use up every possible excuse trying to explain Kyle's exploits."

"Now what happens?"

The viscount's face hardened. "Duncan and I have gone over the plans of the showroom to pinpoint possible targets. There will be a full explosive team awaiting him in London. Meanwhile, the building has been cleared."

"But not the area?"

"As much as possible. The problem is that no one knows how much explosive power there is in Kyle's bomb. One street? Four? After all, that whole part of London can't be cleared."

"What about Andrew Calendish?"

Nicholas put his arm around her shoulder, his fingers tense. "His body was pulled out of the

Thames a little after three o'clock this morning. He had two bullets in his head."

"Oh, God, Nicholas. Does Duncan know?"

"Not yet, my love. Duncan has too many other things to worry about, but I'm sure he'll be hearing soon enough."

Overhead a gust of wind rushed through the oak trees, churning tiny ripples over the moat. Somewhere, carried over the distant hills, came the faint, lingering peal of church bells.

In a far corner of the abbey's rooftop, in a place where the sunlight did not reach, a figure stepped from the shadows, clad in black silk.

He scowled down at the gray cat at his feet. "It's damnable! I won't have it!"

The cat gave a low meow.

"He has brought his stench of danger here to my abbey! There must be something I can do. It worked for me once before, after all."

Adrian Draycott closed his eyes, his features stark as he struggled to bring his shimmering shape into a more tangible form.

And he failed. Just as he had always failed before, save for once, when a woman had touched his heart and brought him a miracle through her love.

The cat's head arched, his eyes intent.

"Wait? How in the name of heaven can I just *wait*?"

With a sharp cry, the cat jumped up to the edge of the parapet. There he stood, like a figure carved from stone, while dry leaves hissed in a spiral around him.

"You are reckless, my old friend. Perhaps we are both reckless." The abbey ghost bent down and ran his hand over the warm fur. "Very well, we shall send our touch over those devices left here. If we are lucky we may discover a clue to this monster's plans. If so, we can warn the American, for the sight is strong in her."

Beneath his hand the cat arched, his tail flicking irritably.

"Send *you?*" Adrian Draycott bit back an oath. "Outside the walls of the abbey? You know what will happen to you there, and the consequences we would both be made to pay."

The cat's eyes were unblinking, his great gray body stiff with pride.

"You shame me, as always, my friend. Very well, we shall consider it, but only when there are no other choices left."

Privately, Adrian Draycott wondered if that time had not already come.

Inside the plain black car registered to the Metropolitan Police Force Duncan was opening a sealed envelope. He scanned the top sheets, then passed them to Kara. "Here is a layout of the showroom, along with the placement of our backup teams. Video cameras are located here, here, and here." His fingers tapped the page. "Once we get inside, we'll have to assume that Kyle can see and hear everything we do."

"How do we know he won't just trigger the bomb once we're there?"

"Because if I know Kyle, he wants to see me sweat for as long as possible. And while he's watching us, our people will be tracing those video relays out of the showroom. No doubt he'll have them transmitted from several locations, so it's going to take some time to trace him."

Duncan looked at Kara's pale face. "Are you sure you don't want to change your mind? There's a policewoman standing by in London."

"My visions come to me for a reason, Duncan. I have to see this through to the end."

"Kara, I—"

The phone on the central console began to beep.

"Dunraven here." After a moment Duncan nodded. "Yes, I remember you, Lieutenant Sinclair. It was during that problem at the embassy in Hong

Kong. I'm glad to hear you'll be working with us on this. I trust you'll be able to find out who those two thugs in police uniform were, too. The blueprints? Yes, we've just been going over them." Duncan looked at Kara. "She's doing well, under the circumstances." Duncan paused. "By the way, Sinclair, have you picked up anything that my brother might have dropped or left behind? Papers, tape, coins—anything like that?" He frowned. "I see. Well, keep a lookout, will you? It could be important. Why?" Duncan looked at Kara and pulled her hand against his. "I'll explain when we get to London."

They stopped in front of an abandoned warehouse with broken windows and peeling paint three blocks from the Calendish showrooms.

"Why are we stopping here?" Kara asked. "Why don't we go inside and get started?"

"Because Kyle said five, and that's when we go in, not a second before. He wasn't joking when he said he'd detonate that bomb if we didn't follow every detail." Duncan eased the car into the recess of a grimy loading dock. "Besides, I have some people to talk to, and while I do, you are going to rest."

"Rest? What gives you the idea that—"

"Rest," Duncan said firmly. "You're going to need every bit of concentration when we get inside. It's going to hit you like a truck, and I want you ready."

Kara shook her head. "Are you *always* right, MacKinnon?"

"Not often enough, I'm afraid," he said grimly.

4:48 P.M.
Kara looked at her watch, fighting cold fingers of fear. Less than fifteen minutes to go. What happened if Duncan failed? What happened if her own senses, always so unpredictable, chose this moment to shut down?

She dragged a hand through her hair, shoving the curls off her face and frowning down at the black latex suit that clung to her slender frame. She was struggling to snap on a heavy, protective Kevlar vest when a door opened from the loading deck.

Duncan gave a soundless whistle. "Nice, Fitzgerald. Great lines. Maybe you'll show these in *New Bride* next year."

"Not a chance," Kara said dryly. The vest was heavier than it looked and cut into her shoulders. Duncan had been right, the next hour was going to require every bit of her stamina. That nap had been a good idea.

If only she'd been able to sleep deeply. If only the dreams hadn't come back to haunt her . . .

His hand brushed her cheek. "Sleep well?"

"Wonderfully," she lied.

"It's not too late to change your mind. We've got an officer inside who is just your height and weight. Even your mother couldn't tell you apart at close quarters."

"Forget it, MacKinnon. I'm going with you. And you're going to treat me to dinner when I find that bomb and come walking back out into the sunshine."

4:59.51
.52
.53

Kara looked at Duncan. She felt his focus, his total control and concentration. There was no reading him at all now.

.54
.55

He snapped the last closing on her vest. "Remember what we discussed. Watch for any kind of wires that could make a circuit, and don't touch *anything* that I haven't touched first. Remember, pressure, heat, or even light can trigger a blast primer, and the slightest movement of a trigger vessel could send us all off."

Kara nodded. Her voice had disappeared.

Duncan's eyes told her he understood exactly what she was feeling. "When we're done, we're going to celebrate, Fitzgerald. *Really* celebrate."

Kara managed a smile. "Does that include orchid petals, Lord Dunraven?"

"You're damned right." His eyes glittered. "And *everything* else." He held open the door. "Let's go."

Eighteen ～

Two brass lamps shaped like gargoyles threw down pools of light as Kara and Duncan moved up the marble steps at the front of the Calendish showroom. Duncan ran a quick eye over walls and floor, watching for a barely visible wire that would open a circuit with one false tug and take out them along with the whole building.

But there wasn't any. Duncan hadn't really expected one. Kyle was too smart for obvious clues. That was why he was so dangerous.

Duncan turned to look at Kara, fighting down helpless fury at the sight of her pale face. "How are you doing, Fitzgerald?"

"Great, MacKinnon." Her voice was raspy. "I'm expecting one major pizza when we get out of here," she said uneasily.

"Pizza? I think we can manage something better than that." His fingers locked with hers for a moment.

You're doing fine, his eyes said. *Keep your balance. Keep your focus. That way we'll get out of here together.*

"We'll try the showrooms first, then the storeroom. Kyle is probably too clever to use an audible trigger, but I packed an extrasensitive contact microphone. You can use it with this headphone, which will pick up any sounds transmitted through solid material. If the blast is activated by a mechanical timer, this microphone will be strong enough to pick it up."

"A piece of cake," Kara said unsteadily, as she settled the headphones over her ears.

Duncan was tightening the ear strap for her when a phone began to ring at the large, semicircular marble desk in the center of the entrance hall. Their eyes met for a moment, and then Duncan moved cautiously toward the telephone. He scanned it carefully. No visible wires and no suspicious additions.

He lifted the base, careful to keep the unit level. No uneven weight and no unusual smell. Duncan slid open the end caps of the receiver and scanned the inside circuitry.

Satisfied, he reassembled the telephone and raised the receiver.

"Dunraven."

"Remember how she died, Duncan." His brother's voice filled his ears, low and hoarse. "'You caused it. It's *your* fault she was lost that day. Now you're going to pay for that, along with everything else. Too bad you're a man of honor. Honor can be dangerous."

"You're not as good as you think, Kyle. I was always one step ahead of you, even as a boy." As he spoke, Duncan pointed to the base of the desk and motioned for Kara to sweep it for sound. After a moment, she shook her head.

"Very clever, Duncan. But your microphone won't pick up anything." Laughter filled the telephone line. "Oh yes, I'm watching everything you do. I'm wired into the security system."

Duncan glanced at the wall, at the video camera angled down from the corner of the ceiling. There was one in every room, he knew.

That had been *his* idea.

"What did you use, Kyle? A photosensitive cell that triggers an ignition in the presence of light? Or is it some sort of pressure-sensitive plate?"

"Oh, I promise you something inventive, brother dear. No remotes today. That would hardly be fair. Not quite a simple time fuse either. Something very elegant, if I do say so myself. By the way, don't think about sending the woman outside. I'm enjoying the sight of you two working together. Rather charming, really. If you do try to move her out, I'll use my backup remote. I never travel without one, you know."

Duncan's fingers tightened on the phone. "Damn it, Kyle, you're mad! Let her go. She has nothing to do with this."

"She does now. She got involved with you, didn't she? By the way, I want to speak with her, so put her on."

"Forget it, Kyle."

"*Now*, Duncan. Otherwise the whole building goes."

Duncan held out the phone. "He wants to talk to you. Keep it short."

Kara cleared her throat. "Hello."

"Enjoying yourself, my dear?"

"Wonderfully," Kara said tightly. "About as much as you enjoyed that stinking cell in the jungle."

Kyle's voice caught. "Duncan told you about that?"

"You figure it out."

He gave a low laugh. "I only wish I could, but my time is rather limited right now. I am going to be taking a long trip very soon, you see." He paused, and somewhere in the distance Kara heard the cry of sea gulls. "Tell my brother that I left a few surprises to keep you both on your toes. Speaking of surprises, did he tell you anything else after you finished making love out in the moat house? Did he tell you about how he left me rotting in that Colombian prison? Did he tell you about how he let our mother die?"

Kara looked at Duncan, her eyes wide.

Cursing, Duncan grabbed the phone. "Enough, Kyle. Tell us where it is now or get off the line."

"Happy hunting, brother dear." The line clicked off into static.

"He said he left some surprises for you. He said . . ." Kara's voice broke.

"I know what he said. Come here, Fitzgerald. Neither one of us is going to die today." He caught her to him with savage power, pressing her body to his.

And then his cheek moved next to hers while he whispered into her ear. "This is the only way we can talk safely. He's wired into the security cameras and can pick up everything else."

Kara's fingers tightened on his shoulders, signaling her understanding.

"A policewoman was set to take your place in twenty minutes. Now we can't chance it, not with Kyle watching every move we make." He touched her cheek. "Can you make it?"

"I'll make it. But you're going to owe me extra pizzas for this, MacKinnon. Let's get on with it."

Duncan slid his fingers into her hair and bent close to her other ear. "Whatever you can pick up, Fitzgerald. Anything at all. He said it was a time fuse, and I think he's telling the truth. Do what you can, but be careful how you signal me if you find something. I don't want him to guess that you're *my* ace in the hole."

Kara nodded, her face tense. "The display cases?"

"That's where we head next."

In the adjoining room recessed bulbs gleamed softly over flat cases filled with precious jewelry from a dozen countries. Even a cursory inspection would take hours.

Duncan ran experienced eyes across the room, recalling the night they had been there last and desperately searching for any differences. When he looked at Kara, her narrowed eyes told him she was involved in her own search. Then she sighed and shook her head. She came close, running one arm around his neck.

"There's something that wasn't here before," she whispered. "It seems to be coming from two different places. The room's energy flow is split, completely scattered. I'm trying to focus on the area, but so far . . ." Her voice caught.

Duncan squeezed her hand. "You're doing fine,

Fitzgerald." He aimed a quick glance at the wall. A camera was scanning this room as well. "Just keep it up."

Fifteen minutes later, they were bathed in sweat, hunched over the third of twelve glass cases. Kara had scanned each for sound, and Duncan had followed with a visual check. So far they had found nothing.

Kara's back was aching, and her stomach twisted in painful knots as she tried to focus on the energy patterns in the room. Something had split the energy, triggering pools of disharmony, but she couldn't yet trace the source. Having to concentrate on the microphone wasn't helping.

"Take a break." Duncan rose to his feet and stretched cramped muscles. "We're still on schedule. You're doing fine, Fitzgerald."

"Just grand," Kara said hoarsely. Why couldn't she pick up anything useful? Why were her senses so jumbled?

Duncan finished his survey of the drawer. "Maybe one of those gold necklaces in there will raise your spirits. When we get out of here, you can have your pick. Maybe this one." He gave her a smile that was only slightly unsteady, then eased back a heavy choker at his left hand.

Beneath it lay a grainy black-and-white photo.

"Damn him." Duncan glared at the photograph of two boys standing ill at ease before a blurred wall of stone.

Dunraven Castle. Kara knew it instantly. There was no mistaking the weathered walls and the hint of gleaming loch in the background. Silently she reached out for the photograph.

At the instant of contact, her throat clinched in pain. Anger billowed around her like oily smoke. She cried out, feeling the photograph burn her fingers.

Duncan knelt beside her. "Careful, Kara. He's listening, remember?" His hands smoothed her hair.

"God, I never knew you were so sensitive. This must be torment for you."

The pain still slammed through her, but Kara gave Duncan a ragged smile. "Don't think you're going to talk your way out of that dinner, MacKinnon."

"Anywhere you want. Anything you want." Duncan's lips slid over her cheek. "Did you get anything else?" he whispered. "Anything about Kyle?"

"Pain. Betrayal." Kara's voice was a hoarse whisper. "Hate. S-sorry. I'm getting a little shaky, I guess."

"Just keep thinking about that dinner we're going to have when we're done."

"Grilled lobster at the Connaught? Veuve Clicquot on ice."

Duncan traced the rim of Kara's ear. "A deal."

She swallowed. "I'll hold you to that."

Duncan's fingers tightened for a moment. Then he went back to work inside a showcase filled with two dozen pieces of rare jewelry and gold artifacts. With precise movements he inspected the sides and feet of the case, searching for suspicious wires or unusual additions to the frame.

There were none. He pointed to the headphones. Kara swept the probe over the paneled case, then stiffened.

She heard a faint ticking, tinny in the headphones.

Her face paled. She pointed, unable to speak.

Frowning, Duncan eased down beside her and took the headphones. As he listened, his frown grew. He nudged one of the dials, then cursed and eased off the outer panel of the case.

Instantly ticking filled the room. Duncan played a small flashlight over the shadowed interior. In the beam Kara saw the outline of a black-and-white photograph propped against a five-inch metal box with a white face.

"It looks like an—"

"It is. An alarm clock. My bloody brother's idea of a joke." Duncan glanced at the photo. "So is this." He lifted the sheet carefully, then turned away from

Kara's view. But she moved faster and had one brief glimpse of an awkward young boy with haunted eyes. Then Kara saw that the blotch across his chest wasn't part of the photo. A later addition, it lay dark and thick, the color of dirty rust.

Blood.

Kara reached out, but Duncan blocked her hand. "Don't."

"But I could—"

"*Don't*. Not this time. You wouldn't enjoy what you felt." His jaw was hard. "It's just another diversion to shake us up. Keep working."

Out in the marble foyer a telephone rang. Grimly Duncan went to the phone and lifted the receiver.

"Dunraven."

"Remember that bomb last year on the oil platform? That was mine. I meant it for you."

Duncan's eyes hardened. "It didn't work, Kyle. I'm still here. And from what I gather, your ex-friends are on your track. Maybe you'd better go hide somewhere in the mud, and hope they have short memories."

"I'm good at hiding, Duncan. Remember all those times in the hills above Dunraven?" He laughed coldly. "Just ask Lieutenant Sinclair how good I am at hiding."

"Sinclair?"

"Don't bother pretending you don't know who he is. I expect you've talked to him half a dozen times in the last few hours. But he won't get any closer to me than anyone else has. As for you and your attractive friend, the schedule has just been moved up."

"Let her go, Kyle."

A pause. "Is she good in bed beneath you, Duncan? Good enough for you to beg me to let her walk out of there?"

Anger filled Duncan's eyes, then he nodded. "I'll beg." He looked at the camera in the corner. "I'll do whatever you ask. Just let her go. Please, Kyle."

Cold laughter filled the line. "Too late, brother dear. I've changed my mind. You now have six minutes before Belgrave Square becomes a nasty head-line on the evening news."

"Damn you, Kyle—"

"Good-bye, Duncan. It was lovely knowing you."

Duncan put down the receiver. Kara was standing beside the desk.

"We've got six minutes." He swept a glance over the room. "Something tells me it's in that showroom. How about you?"

Kara knew he was choosing his words carefully, aware that Kyle would be listening. She put her hand on his arm and moved close. "Maybe in the case. Things have been shifted around inside. I feel the same heaviness I felt when I touched that phony badge."

What she didn't say was that she had come to recognize Kyle MacKinnon's emotional signature. Like a cold, oily skin, it clung to whatever he had touched.

Kara felt that tug now as she moved beside Duncan into the showroom and looked down at the display case. It was there somewhere. She sensed that Kyle had worn gloves as he bent at his monstrous work, and there had been a thin smile on his lips. She touched the clear rim of the case, careful to make contact only with the section that Duncan had already pronounced safe. Images swirled through her head.

Silence. Darkness. Fear.

Frowning, Kara watched Duncan probe the velvet base of the showcase. What had Kyle said on the telephone when he'd called earlier?

Remember how she died.

A boat. A boat had caused their mother's death.

Kara looked down at two necklaces of unfaceted sapphires. Beside them lay a six-inch Roman galley, oars raised.

A boat.

Kara moved to Duncan, trembling. "It's there. The boat," she whispered raggedly.

Duncan went still.

He bent lower. Listening carefully, he ran his fingers around the right side of the case, where a small metal box housed a thermometer and meter registering levels of humidity.

Duncan cursed softly. "It's the bloody mercury. That's the trigger. That's why there was no mechanical timer audible." Slowly he eased the screw out of the metal face. "Any sharp motion will cause the mercury to shift into the base. See those two wires? When the mercury makes contact, that closes an electric circuit. And good-bye Belgrave Square."

Duncan continued to speak quietly as he eased the thermometer upward. Two bare wires were inserted inside the glass tube. Duncan separated them gently and then snipped the red one in two.

Breath hissed from his throat. "Done. Thank God." He rubbed sweat from his forehead.

Kara felt the room begin to spin. *So close to death.* "Duncan, I think I'm going to . . ."

"Easy, Kara. It's all over." He caught her in his arms and carried her through the shadows to the ladies' room. With one arm at her head, he braced her against the sink. "Let it go. It happens to everyone."

Relief finally came in wrenching waves of pain that burned out of her stomach. Then Kara sagged limply against Duncan.

"The first time is the worst, believe me." He eased her into a gilt armchair and handed her a wet towel.

"I'm a mess."

"You're beautiful. I couldn't have managed without you. But I don't think I understood before exactly how much this must cost you."

His hands tightened. Hunger filled his eyes. "I meant what I said about repaying you. La Gavroche or anywhere else you want. Then champagne in a dark room where we won't be disturbed. I want to be the one who makes you forget all this. I want to see your face when you cry out in pleasure, Kara. And I just might start with that little trick from the Borneo jungle."

Heat filled Kara's cheeks. With it came a bitter-sweet ache that grew until it filled every inch of her body. Her hand touched his mouth. "Yes, Duncan. *Now.*"

"Let's get out of here," he said hoarsely.

They were halfway down the hall when a tele-phone echoed through the silence.

Duncan smiled grimly as he lifted the receiver. "I'm still here, Kyle. And you've lost."

Low laughter filled the line. "So you're as good as they say, Duncan. So was the woman you have with you. Just remember that honor can be dangerous."

The phone clicked back into silence. Duncan stood motionless, staring down at the receiver.

"Duncan?"

"I want you to head out now. I'll finish up here."

Kara frowned. Her hands were trembling. She knew that he was lying. "I'm not leaving until you do."

"That's not a question; it's an order, Fitzgerald."

Kara felt a lurch in her stomach. "I'll be in the ladies' room." At the door, she stopped, sensing a heaviness in the air that had not been there before. It was coming from the curtained room beyond the door. "Go on, I'll be a few minutes." Enough time to verify her intuition that something was wrong.

Duncan watched her disappear inside. He heard her walk across the floor. A chair squeaked in the ante-room. She was probably picking up the phone. Calling a friend to reassure her everything was fine. And he was supposed to leave her alone. To give her some privacy.

Honor . . .

He frowned as Kyle's words drifted through his mind.

Just remember that honor can be dangerous.

Duncan felt the fine hairs prickle at the back of his neck. And then he *knew.*

He hit the door at a run, elbows braced. "Stay

away from the phone!" he shouted. "Something's wrong. It's all been too easy."

Kara's fingers were just touching the receiver.

"Steady, now. Don't jostle the phone or add any extra weight. Just release it slowly and then walk over here."

She didn't question him. She looked at the phone for a moment, horror in her eyes, then moved carefully over the thick carpet toward Duncan. "You mean . . ."

"It would be just his style to leave a second surprise." Duncan knelt before the telephone and checked for visible wires, then bent to study the receiver.

One end seemed slightly longer than the other. Careful tapping revealed that one side was hollow. The other produced a deep ring. "Go downstairs, Kara."

"I'm not going anywhere."

"*Now.*"

"Duncan, listen to me." Kara caught his arm.

"Damn it, if you're here I'll be thinking of *you*, of what will happen if I make a mistake." His voice hardened. "Go. Let me finish this."

Kara straightened, and her hand fell. Finally she moved toward the door.

Duncan bent back to the heavy base of the telephone. There was no audible noise of a timing device. Neither heat nor light would be the trigger this time.

With slow, precise movements he unscrewed the casing of the telephone. His body went very still.

It was a simple device, a pack of C-4 plastic explosive worked around the heart of the unit. The first twist of the dialing mechanism would have closed an electric circuit. Whoever made the call would have caught the full, explosive force of the charge.

Every step of the way, Kyle had planned each detail.

Duncan's jaw locked as he carefully clipped the wires and stripped away the bag of plastic explosive.

He only hoped that Lieutenant Sinclair had been able to trace Kyle via the video relay in the showroom camera.

Kara was waiting for him when he walked into the front foyer. "Damn it, I told you to leave."

"So sue me. I had an investment to protect—after all, it's not often I get invited out for Veuve Clicquot at La Gavroche." She brushed a strand of hair from his forehead. "Especially not by a handsome Scotsman." Her smile faded. "I had to stay. It was up to me to help you, to pick up the clues, and I gave you nothing."

"I doubt your senses were working at peak form. You had a few other things on your mind, remember?"

"What if there are more of those things?" Kara studied the room, frowning.

"Even Kyle can only do so much in the course of several days. No, I'd wager that this is the last of my brother's tricks. He's on the run now, or we would have had another call."

As he spoke, the rear doors opened. A tall man, clad head to toe in Kevlar protective gear strode up the stairs.

He studied Kara with unconcealed suspicion before turning to Duncan. "Well done, Dunraven. The video relay has been found, and we're working on pinpointing your brother's location right now. Somewhere near Kensington, I'm told." From his pocket came the harsh static of a shortwave radio.

He listened, then looked at Duncan.

"He's in Kensington, less than five miles away. And this time, we've got him."

"Excuse me, miss, but His Lordship thought you might want some coffee."

Kara shook her head at the awkward young police officer holding out a white plastic cup. She glanced past the police and military specialists crowding the showroom until she finally found Duncan. He was frowning as he spoke to a man in a well-tailored military uniform.

It seemed that they would never be alone. In the past hour Duncan had been pulled from one officer to the next.

"Some tea, miss? Perhaps a scone to go with it?" This time the offer came from an attractive young policewoman whose green eyes were filled with curiosity. "I'm Officer McGill. I just want to tell you—well, how super you were. We all thought so. Since things are dragging on here, Lord Dunraven thought you might like something to eat."

Kara shook her head. She hadn't a hope of eating. She didn't feel up to anything beyond sitting motionless while the noise and bustle in the room swept over her. Her senses were shut down, and she was numb after the stress of the last twenty-four hours.

What she needed was peace and quiet.

What she *needed* was Duncan.

But Kara knew she needed time to sort out her tangled feelings. They *both* did.

"Kara?"

She looked up to find Duncan kneeling beside her. "It's going to take a bit longer here," he said slowly. "There are some new leads that have to be checked out. Lieutenant Sinclair insisted on speaking with you, but I told him I'd fill him in for now.

Kara saw something in Duncan's eyes, a weariness that hadn't been there before. "What is it, Duncan?"

He plunged his hands through his hair. "It's Kyle. Sinclair's men have surrounded a house in Kensington. They're going in to close the net."

"When?"

Duncan avoided her eyes. "They haven't told me. Unfortunately, it looks as if it may be awhile." As Kara anxiously studied his face, he pushed to his feet. "Meanwhile the bloody press have camped out on the front steps. That's going to make it damn hard for you to leave."

"Do you want me to leave, Duncan?" Kara's voice was very quiet.

He rubbed his neck tensely. "I don't want you here in the middle of *this* chaos. I want to go off somewhere quiet and make love to you all night." His voice hardened. "But I can't. I can't even kiss you the way I want, and take the shadows from your eyes."

"Excuse me, my lord." A young military officer stood at rigid attention beside Duncan. "Lieutenant Sinclair has just received a call from the Prime Minister. He asks if you would please join him."

"I'll be there," Duncan said irritably. "Kara, I—"

"Go on," she said softly. She was far too sensitive to his moods to miss the relief that filled his eyes.

"I'll come and find you," he promised.

"Of course you will."

The officer cleared his throat. "He said as soon as possible, Lord Dunraven."

Duncan smothered a curse and turned away.

"Uncomfortable, miss?" A young police officer with sandy hair gestured at his own protective gear. "Damned heavy, these can be. You'll be wishing to change, I suspect. The ladies' room is through there." His fair face flushed. "But I guess you know that already, seeing as how that was where ..." He cut himself off with a cough. "Journalists are gathered out front like flies. Somehow they heard Lord Dunraven was in here. The rumor is that he was kidnapped." He cleared his throat. "By an American woman with red hair. You'd better go out the rear exit when you leave. They're hungry for blood, all right. Seems as if they *always* are when there's a MacKinnon involved. Well, I'd better get back to duty. I'll be over by the video cameras if you need anything. You can leave that gear outside the door when you're done."

"Thank you," Kara whispered, her shoulders very straight. Maybe if she kept them straight enough, maybe if she moved very carefully, one foot in front of the other, not quite breathing, she wouldn't feel the pain in her chest or the suffocating regret in her head.

It was a useless hope, of course. There had been no mistaking Duncan's uneasiness or his relief at her offer to leave. She saw him now, frowning over a ream of computer printouts, with two officers beside him. He was tall, strong, immensely confident. *He* would never have to wonder why he had been born different, forever set apart from normal people.

But Kara would have to struggle with the special psychic gift that made her different. That kept her apart and alone.

She would struggle with it every day for the rest of her life.

It was better to face the pain now, rather than later. She would never be like other people. All the dreaming in the world wouldn't change that.

"Ma'am? Is something wrong?"

Kara realized the young officer was looking at her curiously. "I'd appreciate your seeing that everything gets returned. I'm a little tired now, so I might lie down on the couch inside and rest."

He nodded, happy to comply with such an easy request.

He didn't notice Kara slide open the door five minutes later. Now dressed in street clothes, her hair well concealed beneath a scarf, she made her way down the rear passage toward the street.

The knowledge came to Duncan lightly, like a leaf brushing against his shoulder. One minute he had felt Kara's presence, and the next minute the sense of warmth was gone.

Duncan was studying the crowd when he heard a low cough beside him.

"Er, she's having a lie-down in the ladies' room, my lord." The sandy-haired officer was eager to be helpful. "She wasn't looking very well. Said she wanted to have a rest inside. I thought it was a little odd, seeing as that's where, well, the bomb was set."

Duncan frowned. As he expected, when he shoved open the door to the ladies' room, he found it empty.

"Your lordship?" Two men were waiting for him

outside. "There's still the question of your brother's location to be discussed. Then there's the autopsy report on Andrew Calendish. Lieutenant Sinclair's just coming over now, and—"

Duncan gave a low, graphic curse. "Tell the lieutenant he'll have to wait," he growled, sprinting down the hall toward the rear door.

Lieutenant James Sinclair's steely eyes followed Duncan as he laid a restraining hand on his junior officer's arm. "No, let him go, Tompkins. He's done more than most men could. Besides, he's no good for anything right now, with his mind on the American woman."

"But, sir, there are security issues at stake. Kyle MacKinnon has threatened retaliation against the Royal Family if he is pursued further. This American has no security clearance. For all *we* know, she might be involved. After all, her appearance on the same night as Lord Dunraven's arrival sounds like a bit of a coincidence to me."

Lieutenant Sinclair rolled his eyes. "She's done work of a confidential sort for the NYPD, Tompkins. I doubt she's on any terrorist payrolls."

"Perhaps the IRA, sir. After all, with a name like Fitzgerald—"

Lieutenant Sinclair cleared his throat curtly. "Let's give Lord Dunraven his head for a bit, shall we? He's earned a break right now." His eyes narrowed. "Meanwhile, I want you to follow Ms. Fitzgerald. Keep an eye out for—complications. If she's going to make a move, it will be in the next few hours. Understood?"

"Yes, sir. Complications. Quite understood."

"Good. And stay well out of Dunraven's range. There will be hell to pay if he knows we're having the woman followed."

Nineteen ~

Listlessly Kara slid off her raincoat and tugged open the curtains in her hotel room. Street lights twinkled in Hyde Park and blazed along Park Lane. But the night's beauty did nothing to penetrate her gloom.

It was better this way, she told herself. There was no room for shadows in a relationship, and she had seen those shadows in Duncan's eyes today. She had sensed his uneasiness—and his efforts to block something from her.

Of course he did, Fitzgerald. He's been under unbelievable strain. After all, how often does a person find out his dead brother is really alive and is currently engaged in trying to incinerate a substantial corner of London?

But the answers weren't convincing. Kara knew from hard experience that her gift was part of her life. If she tried to deny it or ignore its warnings, she would risk her own sanity.

As she had once before.

No, secrets and mistrust were not an option for her. She had learned to guard her privacy and keep her emotions under tight control for a very good reason.

Now she would have to start doing it again, forgetting about Duncan MacKinnon and that heart-stopping smile of his.

Blindly, Kara shuffled through several files, then

sank into a chair. Fatigue and the numbing aftermath of intense stress hit her. What now?

Work, Fitzgerald.

She took a deep breath. Dunraven Castle was out. Seeing Duncan, feeling his powerful emotional energy in every room, would be more than she could bear. That left her with what choices?

There was Draycott Abbey, of course. She could do a magnificent series of shots along the moat, with the roses a dizzy profusion of color in the background.

No, Draycott Abbey was out, too. She couldn't risk any chance encounters with Duncan.

Which left only an obsequious Belgian prince with a spectacular home on the cliffs at Portofino. For something more rugged, they could head off to the hills of Telluride. The outspoken airline king who had built his western lodge right next to a gold mine that was said to be haunted would provide the kind of colorful story her readers loved.

Slowly, Kara moved to the window, her eyes bleak.

Neither would capture half the beauty and power of Dunraven Castle. She could almost hear the distant waters of the loch lapping against the sandy beach and smell the faint sweetness of heather.

Whatever the choice, it had to be soon. She had an issue to complete. She owed that to Martin and her readers.

But twenty minutes later Kara was still sitting on the bed, her raincoat cradled protectively to her chest.

"Here it is, sir. Room 682, just as you asked." The slender housemaid shoved back a strand of dark hair and gave Duncan MacKinnon a rather nervous smile. "I hope you find your lady friend, Lord Dunraven. It seems a shame for you to come all the way to London, then forget to write down which hotel she's staying at."

"An oversight I shall never repeat, I assure you," Duncan said smoothly.

A call to Kara's office had produced the name of her hotel, giving him the element of surprise. He meant to have a clear look at Kara's face when he walked into her room.

"You know, I could lose my job for letting you in like this."

"Don't worry. Just check with Adam Harper if there's any trouble."

"You know Mr. Harper?"

"We're very old friends. Tell him you did a favor for the Scotsman he knows from Macao."

The young housemaid nodded. "Shall I knock for you, sir? Maybe you'd like me to—"

"No, don't knock. I want to surprise her." *He definitely wanted to surprise her.*

"Very well, sir. If you're sure." The housemaid turned, still somewhat anxious, but Duncan wasn't about to have any spectators when he made his grand entrance to Kara's room.

"She's probably sleeping. She's had a rough time of it these last few months. She's been sick, you see. It's been . . . very hard on her."

The housemaid shook her head sympathetically. "Well, in that case, I'll be leaving now. Best of luck to you, sir. And I hope you two have a lovely stay here in London."

Duncan stood at the door until her footsteps moved away. Shock. Betrayal. They churned through him again, as they had since he'd discovered her disappearance.

He drew a special card from his pocket and slid it into the electronic lock. A few deft movements were enough to trigger the green light. Criminal, really, the way even a good hotel room could be broken into. Duncan had already done a security evaluation for two hotels that used this particular security system and new locks had been at the top of his list of recommendations.

He put his ear to the wall, heard only silence, and eased open the door. Inside, the room lay in shadows, lit only by one lamp near the door. Duncan had a quick impression of good chintz, ornate golden frames, and a marble fireplace.

Beyond, an open door led to the bedroom.

He eased the door shut behind him and crossed the carpet in silence.

Kara was seated on the bed. There were papers spread around her and a briefcase at her feet on the floor, but she sat unmoving, staring out the window.

"Why did you leave?"

The curt words made her turn sharply, hands locked to her chest. Duncan saw surprise rush through her face. So she had not expected him to find her. Did she think she could leave without any explanations?

"How ... how did you—"

"Find you?" Grimly Duncan strode across the room. His fingers itched to reach out and shake her. To rip off that ugly gray dress she had on and shove her back onto the bed beneath him. To kiss the strain from her face and make her breath catch in passion.

"Finding you was the easy part. If this were one of the hotels I've done security assessments for, I never would have made it inside."

"I see," Kara said wanly.

"Do you? I don't bloody think so. I promised you what would happen after we found that bomb. I wanted to begin all over again, Kara, to find out everything about you—what makes you laugh, what frightens you, what gives you pleasure. God, *especially* what gives you pleasure." His voice hardened. "I thought *you* wanted that too, but I can see now that I was wrong. All I want to know is why?"

"Don't, Duncan. I'm not ... up to this. Not now."

"And you think I am, Fitzgerald? Do you think my own nerves don't feel as if they've been worked over with sandpaper?"

"Maybe you handle it better than I do." Kara turned away. "Maybe ... I don't care."

"You cared back in that showroom. What we felt was real, damn it!"

Kara dragged a hand through her tangled hair and

straightened her shoulders. "If you'll excuse me, I'm rather busy." She gestured at the paper work scattered around her. "I've played spy long enough, Lord Dunraven. Now I've got a magazine to get out."

"A magazine issue that includes a shoot at my castle."

"I—I've changed my mind about that."

"Like hell you have."

Kara swallowed. "I've decided Dunraven Castle is not suitable for our needs."

"You've decided the castle's *owner* isn't suitable, you mean." Duncan's fingers locked around her waist. "I want *answers*, Kara, not a performance."

"Do you?" Kara's hands tightened into fists. "Be careful, then. To get answers you have to give them."

"You're angry. It had something to do with what happened in the showroom."

"You were hiding something. You nearly sighed with relief when I said I would go. Did you think I wouldn't know?"

Duncan sank down in front of her. "Kara, there are some things I can't tell you. Things that you are safer *not* knowing."

"That's just it. You can't hide, Duncan. Not from me. I'll know. If I touch you or the things you have touched, I'll *know*. With this gift that I have, dishonesty is impossible. I'm not surprised you can't accept that. Few people could. So let's forget everything, okay? I don't think I could bear the pain again." She caught a ragged breath and turned away, but Duncan captured her fist between his open palms.

"Wait a minute, lady. Maybe I didn't make myself clear. I *want* you. Everything about you. The fear. The trembling. Even the visions. If there have to be boundaries, we'll work those out as we go along."

Kara tried to pull her hand free. "You still don't see, do you? It means no secrets, Duncan. Nothing hidden. Can you live without secrets, with every thought on display? I wouldn't, not if I had the choice," she said bitterly.

The air churned between them, electric and intense. "I'm willing to try. But it takes two, Kara. You felt the same desire I did. You wanted the contact just as much as I did. So what in the hell is going on?"

Kara studied him in silence, then reached out to his chest.

Carefully she pulled the gold coin from beneath his shirt and rested it against her open palm. Duncan watched her eyes darken, and knew by the shudder that raced through her slender frame that she had opened herself to a deep link.

Her fingers moved restlessly over the old coin. "I'm talking about hidden feelings, about the secret thoughts you think you keep locked inside you. Except you don't, MacKinnon. You *can't*. When I touch you, it's like I'm touching me. Your emotions are all there, flooding over me. I pick up on the anger. I pick up on the desire. Then I pick up on the fear and the fact that you're trying hard to block something from me. I can't live with that kind of wall." Her fingers tightened. Duncan felt the chain dig at the back of his neck. "You're afraid of me, Duncan. Maybe you should be."

"This isn't about fear, Kara. It's about trust—or what you see as my lack of it."

Kara's fingers trembled against the fragile gold chain. "I don't want to feel shadows when we kiss. I don't want to experience the pain of your withdrawal when you wonder just how far inside your head I can reach." With a raw cry, she spun away. "No, Duncan. Not again. Not *ever* again."

"Who was it, Kara?"

"He's not important. But the lesson he taught me is. This gift is part of me. If I deny it or try to ignore it, then I cease to be whole, which is not only painful but also very dangerous."

Duncan didn't move. There had been another man, someone who had hurt her badly.

His eyes hard, Duncan watched the coin spin from her fingers. Maybe she had a reason to be afraid. And maybe *he* had a reason to change that. "I'm asking for a new start, Kara. Give me three days. Let's hold hands and walk up Park Lane in the rain. Let's watch the sun rise over the Green Park." His voice dropped. "Let me take you against me and make your body sing, again and again."

"Duncan, I—"

"Three days, Kara. That's all I ask. At the end of that time, Dunraven is yours for your shoot, free and clear, without any conditions." A crooked smile touched his lips. "I'll even leave if my presence is too disturbing to you."

Kara turned away. Though her body was trembling, Duncan didn't try to hold her. The decision was hers now. Both of them would have to live with it.

"Duncan, I . . . I'm afraid. Sick-in-the-chest, weak-at-the-knees afraid. Once, a long time ago, I settled for less. I tried to deny who and what I was." She brushed a tear from her cheek. "Never again. You see, I *can't*, because it nearly tore me apart."

Duncan eased the coin from his neck and rolled it within his fingers. "I'm not going to touch you, though I want like hell to touch you. I'm not going to try to convince you, though I want like hell to do that too. I'll be back tomorrow morning at nine for your answer. Meanwhile, take this coin of mine. Hold it in your hands and listen to what it tells you. I'm there for you to read, Kara. All of me." He pressed the coin into Kara's hand. "Is three days really so much to ask?"

He walked to the door and did not once look back.

Down in the park, walkers strolled hand in hand and lights glinted like jewels against green shadows.

Kara saw none of it.

Who did he think he was, to interrogate her? To tease and seduce her? How could he understand how much the link cost her?

With trembling fingers Kara looked at the golden coin he had left in her hand. Just as he had promised, visions slammed through her, each one an image of hot, naked intimacy.

Their bodies, skin to skin, breath to breath, while passion raced between them.

Kara shuddered. She tasted it, smelled it, wanted it, just as Duncan had known she would.

Hold it in your hands and listen to what it tells you.

With shaking fingers she dropped the coin onto the bed. But even then the hot, sweet images would not stop.

Twenty ～

At precisely three minutes before nine, Duncan MacKinnon strode through the elegant front doors of Kara's hotel. He stopped briefly at a mirror to straighten his collar and scowled at the nervousness he was feeling.

Halfway across the lobby he heard heels click behind him. "I do hope everything worked out well, Lord Dunraven." The housemaid who had directed him to Kara's room was studying him expectantly.

"Perfectly, thank you."

"Today I'm going in your direction. I have some boxes to be delivered to that particular room." The woman gestured to a table holding four cartons with express shipping labels.

"Let me save you a trip."

"But I couldn't. It's against *all* hotel policy."

Duncan gave her a conspiratorial smile. "But the hotel won't know, will it? Besides, it's a small thing, considering your help yesterday."

As Duncan shouldered the packages, he frowned. "One thing. My collar—is it, well, straight? It feels tight. Scratchy, somehow."

The woman smiled benignly. "Your collar is fine. Your shirt is fine." Her lips curved. "In fact, she'll think you're gorgeous."

A man was steering a rack full of dresses out of Kara's room as Duncan stepped off the elevator. Two male messengers, wearing jackets discreetly identifying one of London's finest department stores, stood nearby, holding a stack of parcels.

Laughter spilled from the open door as Duncan got in line behind the others.

From his spot he watched in amazement as a perfectly coiffed woman wearing a hotel badge left Kara's room, shaking her head. "I just can't believe it, Ms. Fitzgerald. It's perfect. I know my daughter is going to love it, and here I've been at wit's end for days." The woman cradled a box in her arms, and Duncan saw it held a lace bridal veil with a single tier of pearl beading. "She wanted something different. Something simple but modern. That's my daughter all over, of course. She knows exactly what she wants and is stubborn enough to wait until she finds it."

"As soon as you described her, I knew this one would be perfect." Kara was smiling, her amber eyes luminous.

She appeared to have gotten a whole lot more sleep than *he* had the night before, Duncan thought irritably. He ran one finger under his collar.

"You're certain I can't pay you, Ms. Fitzgerald? She's still a student, but her father and I have been putting a little bit aside for the last few years in expectation of the day she married. I feel most uncomfortable about accepting this."

"Nonsense, that particular company has several other veils featured prominently in our next issue. They won't notice the loss of this one, I assure you. Take it to your daughter with my very best wishes. *That*, Mrs. Marchand, will be the best way you can repay me."

The woman moved away, rubbing the soft lace reverently. She was so preoccupied that she nearly stumbled over Duncan.

He looked up the line and frowned. The department-store delivery men were next.

"Just put them on the bed, won't you, please?" Kara's laugh was low. "Yes, it is rather crowded.

Just slide those papers over to make room. That will be fine."

The two men emerged a moment later, looking rather dazed.

Duncan was starting to see that Kara Fitzgerald had that effect on *most* men.

He, however, had been forewarned. Yes, he was more than able to deal with one courageous, stubborn, and entirely exceptional American.

And if she said no, he would find a way to change her mind—even if it involved kissing her into insensibility. He strode into the room, smiling.

And froze. The smile locked on his face.

There were boxes on the bed, flower decorations spilling from the armoire, and at least half a dozen wedding gowns hanging in every corner of the room. The floor was covered with computer printouts stacked beside rough ink sketches colored with markers.

"You can put the parcels beside the table. Thank you again for being so prompt." Kara's voice was distracted, her head turned away.

Half hidden behind boxes, Duncan placed them as directed, then moved beside Kara. "Don't I get a tip, miss?"

Kara spun about. "Duncan!" She cleared her throat, a delicate flush covering her cheeks. "Is it nine o'clock already?"

"Ten minutes past, but who am I to complain? I'm simply another miserable hireling called in to carry up your mail." He looked around him. "What *is* all this, by the way?"

"A few things for our initial layouts."

"I see." Duncan saw his coin on her pillow. He picked it up slowly. "I want to hear your answer, Kara." His jaw was tense as he laid the coin against her hand. "But first I want to know if you touched this."

"I—I did." The flush in her cheeks deepened.

"What's it going to be, then? Three days in which to start over? Three days for me to get to know you?"

He moved closer and slid his hands along her neck until they were buried in the warm, silken cloud of her hair. "Three days for me to thank you in a very special way?"

He felt her stiffen beneath his touch and gently eased her against his chest. He smiled wryly. There was no way she could ignore the effect she was having on him now. He wasn't going to play fair anymore.

"I want you, Kara. I want *us*. Let me give you that—for three days, at least."

Her breath wasn't quite steady.

Duncan's smile grew.

Her body swayed; her hands slid to his shoulders.

Duncan's smile blazed.

"Under . . . two conditions."

Duncan's smile twisted to a scowl. "I'm listening."

Kara stroked the curve of his ear. Her fragrance was teasing; this soft movement was driving him out of his mind.

"Two days, not three. I just can't, not after the time I've already lost."

The smile raced back. Duncan felt a strange and utterly unfamiliar lightness in his chest. *Hold the dancing, MacKinnon. You haven't heard the rest*, he reminded himself.

His gaze clung to her lips. "Tine, we'll make it two. After all, we don't have to sleep."

He heard the little catch in her breath. He watched the flush spread to her neck as he ran his thumb over her upper lip. "The other condition?"

She blinked. "Other?" She blinked again. "Oh, yes. The second condition. That I take my work. You say you want to know about me—about us." Her voice was tentative.

"I do."

"Then work is part of me. It's what I do best. That's not going to change."

There was something fragile and anxious and intensely vulnerable in her eyes. Duncan cursed whoever had put it there. "I think I can stand the competition of two dozen wedding gowns and six boxes of paper work." His fingers traced her spine, clearly outlined in the soft angora sweater she was wearing. He cupped the swell of her hip and pulled her against his hard thighs. "Maybe we can come up with something strange and outrageous for your article on Borneo."

Her hands dug into his shoulders. He felt her tremble.

The effect was like a blowtorch on him.

"What have you done to me, Scotsman?" she said huskily.

"Not *half* the things I plan to do, *mo cridhe*."

It was true, Duncan realized. He wanted to kiss every inch of her, to hear her cry his name in the peak of her passion.

He also wanted to hold her when her visions tore her from sleep and left her shaking.

And he would.

Two days wasn't a long time, but a MacKinnon had always liked a challenge. He smiled, thinking about how she would look curled up in his bed. And about the very inventive ways he would wake her.

At that moment his very steamy fantasy was broken by the ringing of a telephone.

"The phone . . ." Kara's voice was husky with desire.

"I suppose you'd better answer it."

Her lips curved. "I notice you're making no move to let me go."

"A Scotsman always holds his claim. It's part of our culture."

"Just like a love for whiskey, I suppose."

Behind them the phone kept ringing.

"I'd better . . ."

"I suppose you should."

With a soft curse, Duncan swept her hard against his chest. His mouth opened over hers, and he caught her cry of pleasure.

He shoved up her sweater and covered her breasts with his palms.

She was hot. She was trembling. He could feel her budded nipples thrusting against his hands.

And the damned phone went on ringing.

Cursing, Duncan pulled away. He jerked the phone to his ear. "What do you want?" The words were hoarse, as if he'd just been interrupted in the middle of wildly uninhibited sex.

Come to think of it, he had been fairly close to it, Duncan thought.

"Kara Fitzgerald. I thought this was her room," an American voice said.

Duncan held out the phone. "For you."

Her eyes were dark with passion. Her lips were moist, swollen from his kiss. Duncan sighed and slid a swift, light kiss on that silken mouth. "Answer it," he whispered.

Kara cleared her throat and frowned at the phone. "Hello?"

There was a click. A moment later Martin Grant's deep boom filled the line. "Kara, is that you?"

"Right here, Martin."

"How's the work?"

"Work? Oh—fine."

"How about the sketches?"

"Interesting." Duncan leaned closer and bit gently on Kara's ear. She shivered. "Very interesting."

"What's your timetable for the castle?"

"Soon, Martin." Duncan's tongue eased inside the inner curve of her ear. "I—I can hardly wait."

There was a moment of silence. "Why do I have the feeling you're not listening to me, Fitzgerald?"

Duncan's hands slid over her waist, drawing her back against his chest. "Er—Martin, I'm a little busy right now. It's been hectic here. There have been a few ... distractions." Duncan's palm covered her breast, and her breath caught. "But the sketches are fine, and I'll have the travel arrangements for Scotland very soon."

"What kind of distractions?" Kara's boss said suspiciously.

"Nothing important." Kara blinked. "Everything's

straightened out now. I'll be on the road for a few days, but I should be able to give you the final details within twenty-four hours."

"You'd better. We have to finish preliminary layouts next week and immediately start targeting our advertisers."

Duncan smiled as he felt her move restlessly against his chest. "Don't worry, Martin. Everything will be . . . incredible."

Again there was silence.

"Something's wrong, Fitzgerald. Usually you would be ripping into me by now for checking up on you. This makes me think you're having problems over there."

"No problems."

Duncan smiled as he kissed the hollow beneath her ear. "No problems at all," he whispered.

"Kara, something's wrong. You haven't sounded so distracted for ages." He cleared his throat. "Since Geoffrey."

Duncan's stiffened. *Geoffrey?*

"Stop looking for trouble, Martin. The issue is going to be phenomenal. I'll express-mail my tentative bridal-gown layouts tomorrow."

"There's something else, Kara. I'm afraid it's— well, Geoffrey."

Duncan felt the tension that suddenly gripped her shoulders.

"What about him?"

"You know he always seems to turn up when you're on the trail of a great story. Well, Megan heard from a friend of hers that he'll be in London this week while he tries to swing an interview with the Queen Mother. He . . . called Megan asking about your schedule."

Duncan frowned and tugged the telephone from her hand. "Hello, Martin. You'll forgive me for being informal, but after all Kara has told me about you, I feel as if we're old friends. Of course I have agreed to your use of my estate for your upcoming shoot. I believe you can expect some extraordinary results."

"Your estate?"

"Dunraven Castle. I am Lord Dunraven."

Another long silence. "I see. And everything is still on schedule over there?"

"Quite. But perhaps you'll tell me who this Geoffrey person is whom Kara needs to be careful about."

Martin Grant snorted loudly. "A man whose ego could fill the Houston Astrodome, for starters. He and Kara . . . have a little history between them."

Duncan's eyes narrowed. *"How* little?" He ignored Kara's attempt to capture the phone, turning smoothly to elude her.

"Enough." Martin's voice was grim. "Anything else you'd better hear from her, Lord Dunraven."

"You can be certain that I will. Unfortunately, we're a little pressed for time right now, Martin. Are there any final messages you'd like me to give Kara?"

"No. Just tell her to take care of herself. And to express me those layouts tomorrow."

Duncan hung up. Kara was frowning at him.

"You had no right."

"I had every right. I'm not about to have our two days spoiled by bad news." He glanced around the room. "What is to be done with all of this?"

"This goes to Dunraven."

"All of it?"

"This and a lot more."

Duncan rubbed his jaw. "It will take an oil tanker to get everything up there." He saw Kara's frown. "Of course, a promise *is* a promise." He fingered a gown of exquisite antique lace hanging by the window. Tiny rosettes of satin outlined the low scalloped neck and full sleeves.

It was a dress for a fairy-tale princess. It was a dress to live a dream that would last forever.

A dress such as his mother might have worn.

"Something wrong, MacKinnon?"

Duncan released the lace. "We'd better get going," he said gruffly. "It's getting late."

"I can't leave yet. I'm expecting one more person before I can—"

There was a light knock at the door. "Miss Fitzgerald? You mentioned I might come by, but if it's a bad time I wouldn't dream of disturbing you."

Duncan looked up in amazement to see one of the police officers who had been at the Calendish showroom. What was she doing *here?* "No more problems, I trust," he said.

The policewoman gave him a shy smile. "None at all. This is a personal matter." She toyed with her belt. "But maybe I should come back later. I can see you're busy."

"Your timing is perfect, Officer McGill." Quickly Kara shoved aside a pile of gloves and two jewelry boxes, then emerged triumphantly with a bright cardboard box.

Personal matter? The two women had only met the day before, Duncan thought. What in heaven's name was going on?

When the box slid open, Officer McGill shook her head. "Oh, I couldn't. It's absolutely exquisite, but I can't afford it, Ms. Fitzgerald. Not on my salary. My Jim and I are saving up to get our own house in Essex. Nothing grand, you understand, but it will be quiet, and we'll have our own garden out back." She locked her hands at her waist, as if afraid she would reach for the lovely satin gown nestled in folds of tissue paper.

"It's yours, Officer McGill. That's an order. We've already chosen the gowns that will be used in our next issue, so this one is absolutely without any use." Kara made a move toward the large brass garbage can near the desk.

"Throw it away, that beautiful, beautiful gown? You *wouldn't!*"

Kara gave a dramatic sigh. "I'm afraid I don't have much choice. This one is lovely, but I can hardly waste money sending it back. It's an exact duplicate of a gown we used last year, so there's no way we could consider using it. In fact, you'd be doing us a favor by taking it off our hands."

The young officer stood awestruck, her fingers moving reverently over the billowing skirt of fine Alençon lace. "You would *really* discard it?"

Kara nodded.

"Well. In that case . . ."

"Good. Now that that's settled," Kara continued briskly, "let's have a look at that set of earrings you were telling me about."

The young policewoman looked faintly dazed.

Duncan understood the emotion exactly.

"They were a present from my future mother-in-law. I wouldn't dream of hurting her feelings by not wearing them for the ceremony, but the thing is, I'm allergic to gold. If I put these on, I'll be covered in red spots in minutes."

"I have just the thing." Kara disappeared into the bathroom and reappeared a moment later carrying a small plastic bottle. "One or two dabs should do the trick." She brushed the ornate gold earrings, blew quickly on them, and held them up with a flourish. "Presto, one coat of clear nail polish and even sensitive skin is protected. It won't work for long, mind you, and you have to be certain to coat all the metal that will touch your skin. But this should get you through the ceremony unscathed."

"I don't know what to say," the young woman said unsteadily. "You—well, you're a miracle worker. But Lord Dunraven looks like he has something important to say to you, so I'd better be off." She bit her lip. "Unless you change your mind and want the gown back."

"She won't," Duncan said firmly, ushering her out and then shoving the door closed to keep out any new arrivals. He crossed the room and took Kara's cheeks between his hard palms. "I had no idea I was getting involved with a miracle worker."

Kara focused blindly on his chest. "I'm no miracle worker."

"Those two very nice ladies think you are."

Kara shrugged. "It's just ... helping people. We get all sorts of promotional items, and most are things that the models can't wear. I'm only seeing that they go to a good home."

Duncan's fingers moved lightly over her flushed cheeks, over her soft lips. "Nice try," he said huskily.

Their eyes locked, Kara's dark and vulnerable, Duncan's intent and assessing.

Desire shot through his groin. Suddenly he was conscious of the bed, only inches away.

He cleared his throat and stepped back. He had plans, all sorts of plans, but they weren't going to begin in an anonymous hotel room. "Which of these goes with you?"

"Everything." Kara took a slow breath and shoved the hair back from her face. "This is only the start. Most of the clothes will be sent directly from the States."

"In that case, I'd better go rent that oil tanker. The vehicle I had in mind to take us to Draycott is not quite up to the task."

"Draycott?"

"Nicholas wants to give you a proper welcome." Duncan's lips curved. "I believe he also has some matchmaking planned."

"Oh." Kara blinked.

Duncan traced the color washing her cheeks. "And then you're going to tell me about this man called Geoffrey."

Kara turned away as a fax machine began to beep in one corner. "I have a few loose ends to tie up here before I can leave."

"Before you can tell me about Geoffrey, you mean."

Her shoulders were very stiff. "He's old news, Duncan."

"I still want to hear. Maybe you need a knight to fight a battle every now and then."

"There are no knights left," Kara said softly.

We'll see about that, Fitzgerald.

*　　*　　*

As the door closed behind Duncan, a faint smile curved Kara's lips. Duncan MacKinnon was irritating, all right. He was pushy and disturbing, a throwback to some medieval warriors she had read about.

And right now she was probably the closest she had ever come to falling in love. *Real* love this time, not the temporary insanity that had seized her several years ago with Geoffrey.

Not that Kara believed real love was possible for her. Her gift meant she had to guard her privacy and stay in control at all times. She had learned with Geoffrey the price of letting down her defenses.

Still, they *were* two grown adults. What if just for one night the two of them could . . .

Something clicked behind her. MacKinnon again, up to more of his breaking and entering tricks, no doubt. Kara made a mock smile of disapproval as she watched the door open.

Her frown turned real. Something angry and tight settled in her chest, blocking her throat.

"There you are, Kara, my love." The man in the doorway had good teeth, good hair, and the kind of casual blond good looks that made heads turn. Part of his charm had always been the fact that he seemed unaware of his effect on people. Especially women.

The truth was that Geoffrey Hampton was aware of every move he made. His pale green eyes probed Kara's slender body with the proprietary air of someone who had once known those curves intimately. "How delightful that I was finally able to track you down. With your little adventures in bomb detection, you've been a difficult person to find." His eyes hardened as he strode toward her. "And I'm damn well fed up with it, do you understand? You might not mind making an utter fool of yourself over here, but I do." His hands locked with painful force on Kara's arms. "I have a reputation to protect, even if you don't care about yours. Sometimes I think you delight in flaunting these bizarre ideas of yours. I'm on the track of a very big interview right now, and I don't intend to see it scrapped because you're involved in your usual revolting New Age drivel. Why in hell that magazine continues to employ you is beyond me."

"*Most* things are beyond you, Geoffrey." Kara caught a ragged breath. Anger, fury, and pain pounded through her, the relic of long months of confusion and self-doubt.

Self-doubt that Geoffrey Hampton had worked hard to fuel.

"What do you want this time, Geoffrey?"

"Want?" The fingers tightened, twisting cruelly. "I want you to stop making a fool out of me. I want you to try acting faintly normal, for a change."

"It seems to me that the only one who can make a fool out of you is *you*." When Kara tried to jerk her hands away, Geoffrey's fingers tightened.

"Only you could do that, Kara, and you did it brilliantly. But I've had enough. I've got some important meetings lined up over here, and I'm tired of hearing the sniggers behind my back."

"Ever stop to think they might be coming from something *you* did?"

"I know better."

Pain gripped Kara's forehead. She could feel his anger now, the same anger that, long ago, she had tried to ignore for months. After all, people in love weren't supposed to be angry or jealous or manipulative. "Go away, Geoffrey. You have no say in my life, and I have no influence in yours."

He gave a bitter laugh. "I only wish. But people remember, Kara, dear. You always made a flamboyant impression wherever you went. Now that you've built that trivial little magazine into something, there seems to be no escaping your influence." His eyes glittered. "Do you do it only to annoy me?"

Kara stared at him. He hadn't changed a bit. He still saw everything in terms of his own self-importance. *Her* mistake had been in thinking it was the self-absorption of a genius.

How stupid she had been at twenty-two. And how damned *young*. Of course, she had had next to no experience with men. She had been a perfect target for Geoffrey's clever manipulation. Even now it hurt Kara to think how easy it had been for him to make her doubt herself.

She looked down at her arm, where red welts were beginning to rise. "Let go of me, Geoffrey."

"And what if I don't? Do you plan to run me through with those corsage pins? Suffocate me with bridal veils?"

"You might be surprised what I could do to you, Geoffrey."

"Behold me trembling, Kara, my love."

"I was *never* your love, Geoffrey. All you wanted from me was to pick my brains clean and take the credit for yourself."

"Credit? You're doing that all by yourself, shouting to the world that you've snared the exacting and reclusive Lord Dunraven for your honeymoon issue. Oh, yes, it's all over London," Geoffrey hissed. "But this time the ace bridal expert has gotten herself in too deep, my sweet. No one has ever managed to do any public photography at Dunraven Castle, and I truly doubt that *you'll* be the first. It's not as if you have the body to entrap a man like Dunraven. He's been linked with some of the most beautiful women in the world."

Hurting her again. Any way he knew how. It was what this man did best.

"You never change, do you?" Kara's eyes darkened as she picked up a bowl of fruit in an intricate gilt basket and dumped it over his head. "That's for making love to my best friend a week before we were to be married."

Geoffrey ground his teeth in a mix of anger and pain. "Not a week—two days. And if I did, it was only because *you* weren't woman enough to hold my interest."

The old pain slid in, right above Kara's heart. "I used to believe that, Geoffrey. You worked hard to make me believe it. But no more."

Geoffrey's face mottled with anger. "I wonder if

MacKinnon knows the truth about you. Did you tell him there would be no secrets? That you'll always be prying in his head? Did you tell him about the nightmares?"

A hard voice cut through the tight silence. "I know as much as I need to know. I also know that you're going to be leaving here in two seconds, on your feet or on your face." Duncan MacKinnon stalked toward Hampton. "Take your pick."

Geoffrey's pale eyes narrowed. "So you've finally agreed to throw open your ancestral home to those journalists you call 'ill-smelling ruffians who would have been hung in an earlier age.' "

"As it happens, I am. And I am doing it in proper style. But first, Kara and I are going to take some time off together."

"How very romantic," Geoffrey said with a sneer.

"Yes, isn't it." Duncan slid his hands around Kara's shoulders. "And that's just for starters. After we reach Scotland, we have something even better planned."

"And what is that?"

Duncan took Kara's hand. "Ms. Fitzgerald has done me the very great honor of agreeing to become my wife."

Twenty-one ~

Silence.

Kara didn't speak.

Geoffrey didn't speak.

The two delivery men in the hall carrying a variety of cardboard boxes and mailing tubes didn't speak. After a few moments of surprised silence, however, they broke into applause.

Geoffrey was not so easily impressed. "And just when is this blessed event supposed to occur? Or is it in fact a hypothetical ceremony to take place at an indeterminate date?" He laughed coldly. "She's *famous* for that."

Duncan put a stiff hand on Hampton's lapel. "Maybe it's time you found out exactly what *I'm* famous for."

"A threat, MacKinnon?"

"You're bloody right, it is." The Scotsman's fingers tightened.

"If Kara has actually agreed to marry you, then I'll be the first to wish you luck. You're going to need it."

Duncan's eyes hardened. A moment later he scooped up the gilt basket from the floor and crammed it onto Hampton's head. "I love the fruit, but you definitely need the hat to go with it." With one swift thrust Duncan tossed the American outside.

The click of the bolt sounded explosive in the still room. "So." More silence. "You were . . . involved."

223

Kara avoided Duncan's gaze.

"When did you intend to tell me about it, Fitzgerald?"

Kara's fingers played restlessly with a bridal veil, but she managed a faint smile. "Sometime around the year 2055."

"Damn it, Kara. Talk to me."

"There's nothing to say. I've worked hard to put Geoffrey behind me and I've succeeded—except when he's decided the magazine world is too small for the two of us."

"And that happens often?"

"It's *my* battle, not yours, Duncan."

"I'm involved, whether you like it or not."

"Why?"

"Because I owe you. Also, because I want to be involved."

"Is that why you told him that lie about us getting married?"

"I saw at once it was the one thing that would bother him most. He's the sort of person who can't stand to lose. Not ever."

"He'll make sure half of London knows by nightfall." Kara gave a bitter laugh. "After all, he is the most influential senior editor of the most influential celebrity profile magazine in the United States."

"Slime, I knew it."

"But very influential slime. What are we going to do? We can't let people think it's true."

"I'll think of something," Duncan said abruptly. "Meanwhile, let's pack up these things before somebody else barges in here. I'd like to get to the abbey before midnight."

"I don't know, Duncan." Kara's body was still tense.

"You're not backing out now, Kara. You promised me two days, and I mean to collect. All you'll have to do is sit back and relax."

"At least I can work on the way."

A muscle flashed in Duncan's jaw, but he said nothing.

The fact was, paper work was the very *last* thing he had in mind for Kara.

"That's *no* limousine."

Taxis fumed and growled along Park Lane as Kara stood on the sidewalk, stunned.

"I know."

Three German tourists moved past, studying them curiously.

Kara shoved her hands on her hips. "That's not even a *car*."

"Beautiful, isn't it?"

It was low and sleek and mainly silver. There was silver on the body, silver on the two tires, even some silver on the leather bags that hung from either side of the seat. "It's a *motorcycle!*" Kara said shrilly.

"Good eyes, Fitzgerald."

She crossed her arms. "I'm not going anywhere on that thing."

"Why not?"

"Because—because of all the packages in my room, for one."

"Already taken care of. The driver just left."

Kara's eyes widened. "But how—"

"I think you're entitled to one free day, Fitzgerald. Yesterday you saved a sizable part of downtown London from destruction, remember? Relax and enjoy it."

"My clothes," she said triumphantly, pointing down at her slim skirt of navy crepe. "I can't exactly mount up wearing *this*."

A paper bag came flying through the air. Kara caught it by reflex.

"Blue jeans. A sweater. Canvas shoes. Go put them on," Duncan ordered.

"How do you know my size?"

His eyes darkened. For a moment they slid over her body. "I've always been fairly good at that sort of thing. Now get moving, Fitzgerald."

Kara didn't budge. "Why, Duncan? Why like this? What's the point?"

"Stubborn, always stubborn." Duncan shook his head, oblivious to the passing crowds. Sunlight turned his hair a rich mahogany as he put his forefinger under Kara's chin, studying her features. "Because, you stubborn Yankee, you need to relax. Today I'm going to teach you how. Isn't that good enough?"

Something hot and sweet invaded Kara's chest. "Relax when I'm perched on the back of that thing, clutching at *you* for dear life? News flash, MacKinnon—that's about as relaxing as falling off the Empire State Building."

But Kara was lying. The prospect of speeding into a soft English sunset wedged up against Duncan's back was beginning to sound distinctly seductive. Maybe as she rode she would think of a way out of this wedding business.

Duncan ran a hand through his hair, leaving it a wild tangle. In his brown suede jacket, with one hip braced against the motorcycle, he looked reckless, untameable, and incredibly attractive.

Kara told herself she was immune to that charm. She kept telling herself that right up until her lips slid into a smile. "You like to live dangerously, I see."

"Of course. It's part of being a MacKinnon."

Duncan laughed softly as two attractive blondes passed before him, their admiration obvious. But his eyes were only for Kara. He looked at her legs and smiled darkly. "Then again, maybe you ought to wear that skirt. Just . . . ease it up a bit."

"Very dangerous, MacKinnon."

His eyes glinted. "You haven't seen anything yet."

The jeans fit.

Like a second skin, they fit.

Kara looked down in shock, studying the way the soft denim clung to her hips. How had the wretched man known her size so perfectly?

Geoffrey's hissed comments came to mind. *It's not as if you have the body to entrap a man like Dunraven.*

He's been linked with some of the most beautiful women in the world.

But Kara wasn't going to let Geoffrey or anything else spoil her mood. Just as Duncan had said, today was for relaxing. They were both entitled.

Kara ran gentle fingers over the sweater, a beautiful hand-knit design of muted green and blue, exactly the sort of thing she would have chosen for herself.

It fit her just as snugly as the jeans, and the warm gleam in Duncan's eyes was unmistakable. "Perfect fit," she said.

She swept him a slow pirouette.

"So it seems. I think we'll be a perfect fit too."

Kara swallowed as heated images filled her head. She cleared her throat. "You mean on the motorcycle?"

"It's a Bentley. Great performance. Perfect control. And no, I mean in my bed."

Kara ignored his last whispered comment. "I thought Bentleys were cars."

"Not all of them." He pulled her chin up and slanted a slow, searching kiss over her lips. "A *perfect* fit." Abruptly he stood back. "Sit down and get prepared for the ride of your life, Fitzgerald."

"See the motorcycle," Kara muttered. "See Kara Fitzgerald break into a cold sweat as she contemplates riding the motorcycle."

Something hard and polished was shoved into her hand. Kara blinked down at the helmet. Was this *really* her? How long had it been since she'd taken an afternoon off?

"Put on the helmet, Fitzgerald."

Her fingers fumbled with the strap. "I don't know, MacKinnon. I've never—"

"Ridden a motorcycle before?" Duncan's slow smile was all hot male. "I'm only too glad to show you how. In fact, you're in the hands of a master."

Kara listened to the smooth throb of the motor. She looked at the shining silver body and the expanse of leather she was meant to fill.

Her thighs to Duncan's. Her chest to his back. Her

fingers locked to his waist, while the motor's power throbbed through their locked bodies.

Closing her eyes, Kara settled onto the seat. Her finger slid around Duncan's chest. She shivered, taking in the heat and power of him, feeling his excitement. Beneath his jacket he wore a blue denim shirt. She could feel the ripple of his muscles. "I don't know, Duncan . . ."

Laughter rumbled through his chest. "If you break your neck, Fitzgerald, I give you permission to come back and haunt me forever."

Kara's fingers tightened. Death wasn't a thing to joke about. Neither was haunting. As if he had read her thoughts, Duncan turned.

Their eyes met. His hand gripped hers, where it rode at his waist. "I'll take care of you, Kara. Today I'm going to see that everything is perfect."

Then he gunned the motor, slid out the clutch, and they were on their way.

Kara's face was turned to the wind, and her hair billowed out behind her. Against her chest, Duncan's body was an anchor, a source of stability, as the earth flashed magically past her.

Not bad. Not bad at all, Kara thought.

They were out of London now, flying past neat homes with flower gardens running along tidy streets. An elderly man holding a garden hose looked up and smiled in approval as they hummed past.

"Well, what do you think?"

Kara eased closer and spoke against Duncan's ear. "Tolerable, MacKinnon."

"Liar. This is one stupendous way to travel, and you know it."

So it was, Kara decided. Definitely addictive. She eased closer. "So sue me for lying."

She felt swift laughter rumble through his chest.

Thirty minutes later, Duncan downshifted and wound through scattered houses of old brick and weathered granite.

"What's wrong?"

"We're taking a break. You can stretch your legs at the inn up ahead and we'll have something to eat." Duncan eased over a narrow stone bridge and skirted a broad pond, coming to a halt in front of an old mill overhung with ivy.

Kara read the worn shop sign. "The Perfect Bride?"

"The owner and I are old friends. This mill is close to six hundred years old."

"I'm impressed, MacKinnon."

A brawny man with improbably carrot-colored hair emerged from behind the inn's broad oak door. "Is that you, MacKinnon? It's been so long, I forget what your ugly face looks like." He gave a loud thump to Duncan's shoulders. "Still on that bike of yours, living dangerously?" He turned, extending a broad, worn hand to Kara. "Snow Sedgwick, proprietor of the Perfect Bride. Delighted to welcome you, miss."

Kara couldn't resist an answering smile as her hand was pumped warmly and she introduced herself. Her journalist's eyes were already measuring the thatched roof and ivy-colored walls as a possible site for some future issue. "This is an extraordinary place. Part half-timber construction and part good Norman granite, isn't it?"

The mill's owner nodded, delighted. "A fine eye you have, Miss Fitzgerald. Our mill predates most of the other buildings in this part of the area. Full of spy holes and secret hiding places, it is. We lie on the smuggler's route inland from the coast. A great deal of history took place here at this old mill. It's even said that Robin Hood swam in our pond."

"No history yet, Sedge." Duncan draped his arm over Kara's shoulders. "We need something bracing to drink before we stand up to your stories."

Kara shook her head. "No, it sounds fascinating. Do you think I could see some of those hiding places?"

"I believe that could be arranged," her host said with a wink. "But first, I'll show you inside, in case you'd like to freshen up. I've saved Lord Dunraven's usual table overlooking the water, and with it a Roederer Cristal '62. Grilled salmon and asparagus in Dijon sauce. Fresh strawberries and scones." Sedgwick smiled. "And to top it off, two cups of very strong espresso." He looked at Kara. "You must be one special woman, Ms. Fitzgerald. Duncan has never brought anyone else here on that motorcycle in all the years I've been here."

Duncan cleared his throat. "Sedge, do you mind?"

"Well, it's God's own truth, isn't it? Not one."

Kara felt heat fill her cheeks. "Where did you two meet?"

"The Philippines. I was still doing oil work then." Sedge fingered his apron. "Burned out and fed up, I was. A man with a chip on my shoulder the size of Brazil. But when it came to security I was the best, and no one was going to tell *me* how to do my business." He shook his head, looking out to the calm pond bordered by willows. "We'd been having some supply and security problems, and Duncan was called in to track down the source—over my protests. The bloody Scotsman did it, too, in less than two days. When he told me what he'd found, I decked him. It turned out to be the woman I was involved with, you see."

"You must have been very upset."

Duncan bit back a laugh. "You should have seen his face. It was the same color as his red hair."

"Duncan's right. Upset is not the word for it." Sedgwick shook his head, smiling broadly. "When MacKinnon got to his feet, he told me calmly that we had two choices. I could either accept the facts and get on with handling the problem, or he was going to rearrange my face."

Kara smiled. "Your face looks in fine shape to me."

"After making an ass of myself for several hours, I faced the facts. The woman—and her unsavory friends—were shown off the site and told never to return. Within one day all the problems stopped."

He chuckled. "We went on a bloody great drunk to celebrate, didn't we, MacKinnon?"

"I have no recollection," Duncan said innocently.

"Bloody liar." Sedge shook his head. "Oh, I can laugh about it now. I couldn't laugh then, I assure you."

"And you stayed friends?"

"The best. Through some hellish years for both of us." He reached down and tapped his leg, which made an odd, hollow sound. "I lost this seven years ago in a well fire off the China coast, and MacKinnon kept me from losing a lot more than my leg that day. After that I got out altogether. I only wish he would," Sedgwick added tightly. Duncan made a noise of protest, which Sedge ignored. "I've been after him for months now to quit, but pinning down a Scotsman is like trying to pin down the wind."

He wiped his hands on his apron. "So there it is. I'd best get back to my kitchen now." He looked Duncan squarely in the face. "I've a lovely chintz-filled room under the eaves ready for you, and the champagne is chilled. No, don't say anything." Snow Sedgwick looked at Kara. "Just make yourself at home. Duncan is family here, and that makes you family too, Ms. Fitzgerald."

He gave the pair one final assessing look, then made his way along the flagstone path to the kitchen, whistling off key.

They sat at a glass-and-wrought-iron table over-looking the pond. Kara watched Duncan finger the condensation on his water glass. "He seems like a very good friend."

Duncan nodded. "It was hard for him to make the break from his old career. I'm glad things have worked out so well. And now I want to hear about you. Tell me about this magazine of yours."

"Me?" Kara watched a pair of swans glide over the quiet pond. "Art major. Liked fashion. Loved ritual. Add it up and you get weddings. I worked for a while as a bridal consultant. I liked the young couples but found their parents impossible to satisfy." She frowned. "And I suppose I got tired of doing the same themes again and gain. When there was an opening at *New Bride*, I leaped at the chance to try something different. I've been leaping ever since."

Duncan brushed a curl from her cheek. "Where does the fêng shui fit in?"

"I've been doing that for years. My family lived in the Orient, and our neighbor taught me everything she knew. I spent some time touring Asia on a low budget. I studied in Hong Kong, Singapore, Taipei. My first client was an international hotel chain that wanted to upgrade its image." Kara chuckled. "I was scared silly."

"But you managed it."

"I was twenty years old and was paid the exorbitant sum of five hundred dollars for my work. I suggested miniature waterfalls and an indoor fern garden. Lots of goldfish *and* a string quartet. Their occupancy rate soared. Now I have a standing invitation to stay at any of their hotels whenever I'm in Asia."

"I know."

Kara turned slowly. "You know?"

"I snitched your résumé from Andrew Calendish after our encounter at the showroom. After that, I called several of your prior employers. They all spoke of you in glowing terms."

"You thought I was a thief!"

Duncan caught her hand, suddenly serious. "I'm *trained* to suspect people, Kara. Your appearance that night seemed to go well beyond coincidence. For what it's worth, I'm sorry."

"And you . . . believe me now? About the fêng shui and all the rest?"

"I believe you have a very special skill, that you see and feel things other people can't. As for your warnings about Dunraven, I'm not convinced. You could have been picking up Kyle's reappearance. But that's not what really matters." He took her hand and entwined their fingers.

"What does matter?" Kara's voice was unsteady.

"What matters is us. I want you in my life, Kara. You've touched places inside me that I'd forgotten even existed. There hasn't been much laughter in my life for a long time." His fingers tightened. "I'm counting on you to bring some laughter to Dunraven."

Kara stiffened. "That's a tall order for two days."

"Two days, six days, or a month. Whatever you'll give me."

"But the issue—my work—"

"I meant what I said, Kara. I'll take what you give me."

Kara looked down at their hands. Silently she opened her mind to him. Just as before, beyond the passion and the laughter she sensed a grayness. A finality.

He doesn't think he has much longer to live.

"Duncan, I—"

He shook his head. " 'No' doesn't exist. Not today. Today I'm twenty and you're eighteen, and when we finish Sedge's champagne we're going to ride until we see a hill where we feel like stopping." He cradled her cheeks. "We'll count clouds and trade secrets—and I'll kiss you. Like this." His head bent slowly. He gave her time to flinch or move or protest.

She didn't. His eyes were too vulnerable, his smile too lopsided.

A brush of skin. A lurch of her heart. Gentle heat in sharp contrast to the rigid tension of his jaw beneath her fingers. He wanted more, but he would accept what she gave him. All of this she sensed in his touch. It didn't require Kara's special sight to know it.

But as Kara leaned into the kiss, into his welcoming desire, she saw the shadow image she had only glimpsed before.

Death. His death. In the cold, dark hours before dawn or in the mist that clung to a Highland cliff. It was death that haunted Duncan MacKinnon, a death he fully expected to come at the hands of his own brother.

"No."

Duncan pulled away. "You want me to stop?"

Kara made a low, tight sound of anger and despair. She couldn't lose him, not the way she'd lost the two young girls in the muddy waters of the East River. This time her vision had to be *wrong*. Maybe if she kept him from Dunraven and the danger that haunted that gray, creeping mist ...

"Don't stop," Kara said breathlessly. And realized she meant every word. She wanted his hands buried reckless and searching in her hair while his lips worked a dark, burning magic.

Maybe that way she could keep him safe.

She closed her eyes, rocked against him, her mouth trembling, her hands shaking.

Now, his mind said, and Kara read his need. *Now, before another dawn brings its danger.*

But he would never say the words, never stoop to admitting how close he felt his own death bearing down on him. His eyes were unreadable as he pulled away. "Maybe we'd both better stop. Otherwise we'll never get that ride I promised you." He chose a strawberry from a Wedgwood plate and held it out to her. "Try it. Sedge grows his own."

Kara bit down. Her eyes closed in delight as sweet pulp squirted into her mouth. "If this isn't heaven, don't wake me until I'm finished." Her tongue brushed his fingers, and she heard him curse softly.

Something dribbled down Kara's cheek. She was about to catch the bit of pulp with her tongue when she opened her eyes.

Duncan was staring at her. There was a lifetime of need in his eyes. A thousand questions that he was too proud to ask. Neither spoke. Neither moved.

And then, very slowly, Duncan's fingers rose to her lips.

Kara took the red fruit, her lips closing around his fingers. Heat oozed through her. "Umm, MacKinnon?"

Duncan's thumb eased over the arch of her lip. "Yes?"

"What are we doing here?"

"I'm thinking how you'd taste right now, *mo cridhe*." He mouthed another rough Gaelic phrase. "Your mouth would be warm, sweet with strawberries." His finger teased the line of her lips. "Would you let me inside, Kara? Would you let me taste you?"

Kara felt her body tremble at his words.

"I've never felt this way. Not about anyone." Duncan looked down at the table and caught her hand. "Do you know what I'm thinking about right now?"

Kara knew. Her face burned with the heat of her knowing.

Duncan's eyes darkened. "If I had my way, we'd be upstairs right now. I'd be taking off your clothes inch by agonizing inch. I'd make you laugh, Fitzgerald. And I'd make you say my name when you cried out beneath me. We wouldn't be out of that bed for days."

Kara knew. She felt it, flooding through their locked fingers, pounding through his pulse. "It's—just the stress. The tension of looking for the bomb."

The lie sprang easily to her lips. Maybe a lie was easier to believe than the truth, which was that she was perilously close to being in love with this man who was still so much a stranger.

"Tell me about Hampton." Duncan's fingers tightened. "Tell me how it ended."

Another lifetime ago, Kara thought. The wounds had healed now. Most of the time Geoffrey Hampton was just a bad dream. Except when their paths crossed and the memories flooded back.

She shrugged. "Classic story. I was young and naive, in love with life. Geoffrey was older and experienced—and in love with himself. It took me a while to realize that."

"What did he do to make you realize it?"

Kara stiffened at the memory. Geoffrey Hampton had made a career out of sizing people up and using their weaknesses against them. He had been quick to tap into Kara's enthusiasm. He had taken her fresh ideas and hard-won interviews and presented them as a collaboration. Kara, with stars in her eyes, had been too blind to care.

Her successful stories had put *New Bride* magazine on the map, and in three months Geoffrey had been promoted to associate publisher. Dizzy with joy, she had accepted his offer of marriage.

Then things had started to unravel.

His criticism of her stories had grown sharper. He had changed the access code on his computer and neglected to give it to her.

Then she'd found phone messages from another woman.

Geoffrey had coolly denied that anything was wrong. Instead he had suggested—very carefully, of course—that Kara was cracking under the stress of her work. Then her nightmares had begun.

First a nameless old man, then two angry, cursing boys. Kara had seen them all in dreams, felt their fear, and watched them die.

And she could do nothing about it.

As her suspicions about Geoffrey grew, so did her nightmares, until she was wrenched from sleep every night, shaking and sweating.

Geoffrey had turned her weakness against her. Stress, he had said very calmly. After a week off she would feel better. Kara had reluctantly agreed.

But the nightmares hadn't stopped. A robbery had left two people dead. After that had come a kidnapped child.

Geoffrey had shaken his head and looked grave. Maybe a few more days. Kara had believed because she wanted to believe.

With time on her hands, she'd begun sorting through old files and discovered Geoffrey's handwritten drafts of two projects. Both had been taken from Kara's own notes, duplicated down to the exact captions and quotes. As Kara touched the file, she'd used the sensitivity she had been blocking for weeks, a sensitivity she had been too ashamed to reveal.

Instantly images tumbled through her in a flood: Geoffrey and his assistant sharing an intimate afternoon rendezvous. "Client interviews" that turned out to be steamy encounters with a European reporter. Most painful of all had been her glimpse into Geoffrey's own mind. There was no mistaking his ruthless ambition or his contempt for her.

She had stumbled to the floor with the pain of her visions.

Geoffrey had merely laughed at this sign of her increasing "stress." He had stopped laughing when Kara rattled off days, dates, and details.

She had seen the fear grow in him then, churning around him like a gray cloud. Most of what he had said that afternoon Kara hoped she had blocked from her mind forever. She wasn't terribly surprised when Geoffrey resigned from *New Bride* the next day.

He resurfaced a week later at a competing magazine. His first major scoop was an interview with a reclusive French wedding gown designer. Every word was Kara's.

Kara had healed herself through work—long, unbroken weeks of work. Weeks later, she had finally rediscovered her balance and joy, using the creativity and skill that Geoffrey had sneered at her for lacking.

Two years had brought two promotions, and in five years the magazine's circulation had doubled. Soon Kara had become associate publisher.

During that painful time she had made a firm vow. Her singular gift of sight would forever remain her secret.

But Kara had never planned on meeting a man with eyes like a highland loch and a very rare kind of honor.

She frowned, determined to be ruthlessly honest. "Using people was Geoffrey's greatest skill. He used me. He made me consider it an honor to be used."

Duncan's fingers slid over her palm. "How did he use you, Kara? In work—or in bed?"

Kara looked down, watching a butterfly on the table, wings spread, uncertain whether to stay or go. "Both."

"Tell me." Duncan's fingers tightened.

"He ... twisted things. Made me doubt my own ability. Pleasing him became the only important thing in the world to me. Even when he was stealing my contacts and copying my notes."

"Bastard. There's nothing you can't tell me, Kara." His voice was fierce. "Nothing you can't want from me. In bed or any other way."

Kara looked down at their locked fingers. "I don't know if I can. Hiding my feelings has become a habit."

The contact of their hands was unleashing a flood of impressions. "Do you trust me, Kara?"

Did she? Had her body known the truth from the start, reaching out to him with no limitations? "Yes."

"Do you know that I would never hurt you?"

She nodded. The certainty was in their locked fingers, in the heat of his touch.

"Then show me, Kara. I want to be so close that I can feel your pulse in my veins. I want to know what your eyes look like when I'm all the way inside you. We can go upstairs right now and I'll make you forget Geoffrey Hampton and every other man you've ever known. But the choice has to be yours, because once we start, there won't be any stopping."

His voice was soft. Somewhere a bird cried shrilly.

"I'm ... frightened." Kara swallowed. "Frightened of feeling so much, of wanting so much."

"So am I. Sometimes it's good to be frightened."

She made a soft, uncertain sound in her throat.

"Give me two days. Somehow I'll think of a way to fit a lifetime inside them."

Lifetime. Kara shivered. For a moment images curled around her like mist—an ancient past, a trackless wood. Two lovers caught by betrayal.

Danger in the seeing.

It should have been so easy. All she had to do was stand up and follow him inside. All she had to do was trust him.

Kara frowned. It would never work. She would be left with nothing but regret.

And yet. And yet ...

"This is a rotten idea, MacKinnon. What would Daniella say?"

"We were never even close. After I met you, all I wanted was your mouth on mine, your legs wrapped around me."

Kara swallowed. Slowly, link by link, she pulled the burnished coin from inside his shirt. It was very old and very beautiful, worn smooth from centuries of use. She felt its weight, its smooth heat against her hand. The touch brought her Duncan—a man with scars he was too proud to show. A man of unwavering honor.

A man who had lived life in shadows for too long.

"Maybe ..." She cleared her throat. "Maybe you should get us that room."

Twenty-two ❧

Duncan's eyes went very dark. "Are you certain?" His hand found hers. "Everything, Kara. Deep and hard and all night long. You have to want that."

Something began doing flip-flops inside Kara's chest. "As much as you do." Her voice had a warm, husky rasp.

The sound made Duncan's mouth tighten. "Touch me now. Look all the way inside my head."

Her fingers on his coin linked them instantly. What Kara saw left her heart lurching. "I'm not . . . *beautiful* like that, Duncan. Not sexy."

"No? Then why have I been in a state of acute physical pain since the first time I saw you?"

Kara's lips curved. "Maybe I should ask you the same question."

Duncan coughed. "Let's get out of here, Fitzgerald. I have a few things I mean to discuss with you."

"Like security systems? Your personal fêng-shui chart?" Kara's lips curved wider. "I'd love to study *your* energy flow," she purred.

"Upstairs." Duncan's jaw was tense as he struggled for control. "*In private.*"

"Where are we—"

Kara's voice fell away as Duncan tugged her along a stone corridor into the cool, perfumed heart of Sedge's greenhouse. Behind them a group of noisy tourists spilled from a very large bus.

Duncan's eyes blazed as he pulled Kara between

a topiary rose and two potted orange trees. The air was heavy with perfume.

Energy charged through every vein and nerve of Kara's body. "Duncan?" Her chest felt tight, filled with a need that would never end. "Will you please—"

"Anything, *mo cridhe*. Tell me what you want."

Rose petals scattered over Kara's cheek. "Kiss me."

"I thought you'd never ask."

Her back was against the cool, smooth glass and her hair was strewn with petals when he moved their locked fingers beside her head. "Like this? Like it could last forever?"

She was just beginning to nod when his lips opened over hers, slow and hot and searching.

Forever became a sound. Perfect became a taste. Kara's restless fingers shoved at his shirt, wanting skin and heat and the link everywhere between them.

Cotton pulled free. She sighed to feel smooth muscle beneath her palms.

"Kara," he growled, looking down at her sweater, where the hardened tips of her nipples were clearly visible. "I want you. The sight of you is killing me."

"Why is it like nothing I've known before, Duncan?" Closing her eyes, Kara savored each exquisite point where their bodies met, wooed, clung. "I'm going to die any second."

"Not die." His big hands worked inside the band of her jeans and cupped her hips. He eased her against his thighs, where the awesome heat of him rode hard against her. "Something much better."

His mouth moved over her neck, stroking her skin until Kara made soft, choked sounds of pleasure. "Duncan, please. I want—I can't—"

"Yes, that way, love." His voice was low, hoarse, as erotic as every silken stroke of his tongue. "Want me. Want this. Right here."

Kara moaned as his fingers found her tangled curls and slid deep in search of heat. She arched, moving against his hand, blind with the pleasure he was building. Her sweater rose. Her nipple spilled into his mouth as he coaxed her to exquisite passion.

"God, you're tight. So hot against me. Open, Kara. Open for me."

In a daze Kara felt him inch deep and then withdraw. Need overwhelmed her, left her body clenching and her fingers digging into his back. "Duncan—oh, God—"

"Say my name, *mo chridhe.* Shiver when I touch you." He filled her, eased deep, then teased the sleek folds trapped beneath his palm. "Do you want me to hold you here? Or do you want my mouth instead, tasting every slick inch?"

Kara shivered at the hot love words Duncan poured against her skin. He sucked her pebbled nipples softly. Kara felt her body stiffen, her blood pounding in a drunken race. "Duncan, please, it's too much. It's too—"

"*Now*, Kara. Let me see your body sing for me. Let me watch you come apart in my hands. You're safe. No one will see but me. No one else will know how beautiful you feel."

Pleasure tormented her, forced higher by his relentless fingers. She couldn't. He shouldn't—

He eased back, filling his hand with her. Gently he flicked the exquisitely sensitive nub with one calloused thumb.

Kara arched in restless abandon. Her skin was on fire, her knees buckling. She was dying, dying.

And she felt his hands anchor her, drive her even higher, until she wanted and wanted. Until her teeth found his chest and pulled the skin taut to leave her mark upon him.

Just as he was leaving his mark upon her.

"Take it, Kara. Take me inside. God, let me feel you tight, riding against my finger." His words caught the erotic rhythm of his strokes, every thrust driving her higher. "Now, love. Here. I'm right with you."

Pleasure hit her like a wall. She cried out in shock as sensation caught her high and slammed her spinning into space. Time twisted off into thousands of corridors of endless opportunity, and down each one Kara saw Duncan's hard, beloved face. Her Scotsman. Her dark, honorable warrior.

Shuddering, she fell against him, watching colors without names flash before her eyes, feeling her soul being gathered up carefully and tucked right next to his.

Duncan said her name hoarsely just before her legs gave way and she collapsed against his chest.

Cool air played over Kara's cheeks when she opened her eyes. She was half against the glass windows, half sprawled against Duncan's chest, and his smile was as hot and smooth as fine Scotch whiskey.

"How are you feeling, Fitzgerald?"

Kara ran her hands over his beautiful chest and smiled to see a button hanging by a thread. Victim of her reckless fingers, she thought. "I'm rather ... overwhelmed."

"Don't be. Not yet. It gets much better."

"You're not afraid of me? Of what I'll see?" Kara touched his cheek uncertainly. "I don't mean to dig into your thoughts, but with the link this strong—" She gave a helpless laugh. "I'll be able to tell you the last thing you thought about before you went to sleep and the first thought you had when you awoke."

His smile was dark with challenge. "You already know. It was you, *mo cridhe*. In fact, I've been able to think of very little else."

"Duncan, you don't understand."

"I'm not Geoffrey Hampton," he said harshly. "I don't know the future and I can't read tea leaves, but I know this very well: I want you. I want what we will become together. You're not going to frighten me off with your warnings." His hand moved over the warm curve of her breast. "Not when touching you feels like the most sane thing I've ever done." His eyes narrowed, glittering. "I want to go upstairs,

Kara. That means giving everything, and no turning back.''

Kara's fingers tightened on his jaw. *Because you think it can't last. It's for me, not for you. The last gift you can make in the face of a death you expect within days.*

She couldn't tell him she knew. Her gift was to pretend she didn't understand.

Kara nodded.

With a soft curse, Duncan tugged her from the conservatory and up the stone steps.

Had other lovers through the centuries fled this way? She hoped so. She hoped there had been a world of laughter in their eyes and that they had found forever waiting at their journey's end. Somehow the thought filled her with a strange peace as she pulled Duncan to a halt, anxious to feel his skin again, anxious to plant hot, quick kisses over his chest.

"I know what you like. I know how you want me to touch you. I can feel every thought." She gently bit his neck as proof.

Duncan cursed, driving her back against the wall. Their lips hovered, meshed. Their tongues met in a hot, sweet exploration.

Kara felt her body go liquid and yielding. Then it was she who pulled free and set off for the quiet room Sedge had promised them.

Their progress was anything but smooth. They got up the stairs in jerky stages, stopping every other step to share urgent, wordless kisses. They were both out of breath when Duncan pushed open the door to a room nestled high under the eaves.

Roses spilled out of old Staffordshire pitchers. Roses filled fine silver vases. Roses of every hue floated in crystal bowls. The scent was intoxicating.

Kara shook her head and laughed unsteadily. "You knew I would say yes?"

"Hoped, Fitzgerald. Only hoped."

She took a deep breath. "They're beautiful."

"Passable. I would have preferred orchids," he said huskily.

Kara's cheeks flamed as she remembered his outrageous stories about Borneo. "Orchids? I don't know if—"

"Be quiet for once, Fitzgerald. Be quiet so I can love you."

He took his time over the zipper on her jeans. His fingers savored every curve, teasing, flirting, until her pulse was loud in her own ears. Finally, Kara shoved Duncan's hands away and attacked his shirt. Four buttons went zinging over the floor like an artillery barrage, and Duncan cursed as the soft cotton worked free of his waistband.

"Damn it, Fitzgerald, I'm trying to take some time here. I'm trying to do this the right way."

"This *is* the right way," Kara muttered, tugging at his sleeves until the denim shirt hung wildly askew on his shoulders. When one cuff clung obstinately, she made a ragged sound of frustration and went to work on his belt.

Half laughing, half groaning, Duncan caught her hands. "Stop. I want to see you. I want to feel you spill all over me like rain." The zipper came free with a hiss. Denim went skimming to her ankles, shoved low by his ruthless fingers.

"God ..." His eyes took in the length of her, her legs bare beneath a wisp of peach silk. "I like your taste in lingerie."

"They were ... a gift." Kara flushed.

"If they were from a man, I don't want to hear about it."

"From my assistant. She thought it was time for me to live dangerously."

Duncan studied the fragile lace flower appliqued in a most strategic spot. "They're just about guaranteed to accomplish that." He snagged the bottom of her sweater and eased it slowly upward. "Dangerous is going to be very easy."

One tight coral nipple peaked beneath the soft cashmere. Duncan's breath caught. "Incredible."

"I didn't have ... I didn't wear ..." Kara's voice caught in a breathy rasp as Duncan's mouth fitted sleekly around her. His lips were demanding, his wet heat triggering a desire that left her shaken.

The sweater slid higher. Duncan nudged it across her shoulders and tugged it impatiently over her head.

Then he froze. Tight Gaelic words filled the air. He just looked at her, a muscle pounding at his jaw.

"Duncan?"

Kara saw the image in his mind. She shook her head, confused. "I'm not like that. You can't really think that's *me*."

The images grew sharper.

"Gorgeous." Duncan's voice was hoarse. "Just when I thought it couldn't get any better." He gently cupped the weight of one breast. His thumb toyed with the sensitive crest that peaked at his touch.

Kara shuddered, her hands twisting, buried in his hair.

"Can you see it too, Kara? Your legs wrapped around me? Deep and hard. Do you still want that?"

The only answer she could make was an urgent shove at his shoulders, followed by a restless wriggle of her hips. Smiling darkly, Duncan eased to one knee before her. "Good." His tongue found the silken concave of her stomach and moved lower. His breath teased her skin.

Kara went very still. "Duncan, what are you—" She froze as he pulled her against him and nuzzled the edge of the wisp of peach silk. "You can't."

His laugh was husky as he hooked the sheer satin and drew her to him. His moist breath dampened fabric and skin. Kara felt her knees begin to tremble. She reached out and found the bedpost at her back, hard, cool, an exquisite counterpoint to his wet heat.

She wanted him. She wanted this.

Her fingers clenched in his hair as old memories snapped at her mind. Suddenly she felt a flush of uncertainty. Geoffrey had said—Geoffrey had always told her—

Her breath caught as Duncan molded the satin wetly until every copper curl lay clearly outlined beneath it. Her fingers dug at the polished wood. His name was a cry on her lips.

"Sweet holy God," Duncan whispered, fingers tight.

Kara froze, suddenly vulnerable. When she felt Duncan stiffen, she shoved wildly at his shoulders, desperate to push away.

But the bedpost blocked her, holding her captive against his fingers. Tears of frustration slipped over her cheeks.

"Kara?" With a curse Duncan surged to his feet. "Damn him. Damn him to complete and eternal agony. Look at me, Kara."

Her head turned wildly as she flinched. "No."

"Stop fighting me, damn it!" His hands anchored her cheeks, holding her still. "Now," he said softly, while his thumbs traced circles on her jaw. "Please."

Kara shivered and then stopped struggling.

"Look at me, Kara."

She swallowed.

Her eyes finally opened.

"He hurt you, didn't he? He laid down all the rules and told you anything else was wrong."

Tension filled her body. She didn't want to think, to remember any of this. He didn't have the right to ask it of her. Finally, after long moments, she nodded stiffly.

Duncan's breath hissed out in a rush. His thumbs moved to the outer corners of her lips. "He knew nothing, Kara. He was clever, but he knew nothing."

"I told myself that."

"You were right."

She gave a shaky laugh. "This is so damned stupid of me."

"Not stupid. Brave and incredibly honest. I'll never forget the sight of you in that showroom, muttering as you swept those jewelry cases for sound. You worked like a pro, Kara."

That won a smile.

"You're smart enough to understand how sick Geoffrey was, aren't you?"

She nodded.

"But the message hasn't gone far enough, has it? Not here." He kissed her mouth gently. "Or here." The next kiss fell on her neck. His hands skimmed her taut stomach. "Especially here . . ." He brushed the warm satin, then withdrew. "Feel it, Kara. Look inside my head and you'll see it's true."

Kara's eyes widened. She started to shake her head.

"I can't lie in my head. What I did was purely selfish. It was exactly what I wanted to do. Touching you like this gives me pleasure—as much pleasure as it will give you."

Kara closed her mind, battered by memories. Her body was stretched taut, her nerves raw. It was a terrible mistake. She wasn't meant for this. He deserved a woman who had no shadows, a woman who was beautiful.

"No, Kara, don't block me out. Say no because you don't like or want it. Say no if it doesn't give you pleasure. But anything else let *me* worry about, because you can be damned certain I'll be liking whatever I'm doing."

"I'm afraid, Duncan."

His gaze was unflinching. "So am I."

He was. And he didn't care if she saw it. His hands on her hair were not quite steady. "I want to please you. I want to make you forget any other man but me and any other. touch but mine. I want to be the first and the best and the very last." He gave her a familiar, lopsided smile that almost broke her heart. "I don't ask for much, as you can see."

"Only what I'd like to give you." Kara swallowed. "He—he told me you had had the most beautiful women in the world." Her fingers cupped his face lovingly. "I'm glad if you have, Duncan. I think they must have been very, very lucky to have known your touch."

Duncan's eyes closed. A sharp tremor went through him. "Fitzgerald, what am I going to do with you? You're too nice to have survived puberty."

"I'm not nice at all. I cheat at poker. I hate to lose at anything and I'm crabby before I have my morning coffee."

"I can see I have a serious degenerate on my hands." Duncan's hands slid over her hips, easing her against him. Slowly, his smile faded. "I want you, Kara. In every possible way. Believe that or nothing else."

She managed a ragged smile. "I'm starting to. You can be very convincing when you want to, Lord Dunraven."

"Hell, I haven't even *started* being convincing, Ms. Fitzgerald." His fingers moved along her hips and trailed back up the insides of her thighs. He watched her face from eyes that were sharp and impossibly blue. "Say no. Stop me whenever you want."

Kara's eyes were hazy. "I don't want to stop you."

Duncan's eyes narrowed. He traced the edge of that impudent little flower on peach satin and waited for her tension to return.

It didn't. Her breath grew low, ragged. She moved restlessly beneath his touch. When his mouth feathered over her stomach, she swayed and called his name.

He teased her through silk that was nearly nonexistent, through a wisp of sheerest lace. Her hands dug at his shoulders and her back arched.

And Duncan watched in calm triumph as she came apart in his hands, just as he'd wanted her to. He didn't stop, edging away the last scrap of silk while the tremors still ran through her.

Time, he told himself. *Give her time.*

This time when he found her silken folds, she didn't stiffen or draw away. Her body rippled, moving in a languid, sensual flow that left his pulse lurching. He hadn't thought his pain could grow any worse, but he found it could.

And still he waited, loving the sight of her, loving each wet touch of her as she came apart against him yet again.

Her eyes dazed, she slumped against him. "Duncan," she whispered, the word touched with awe.

"Right here."

Kara bit her lip. "I didn't—that is, you haven't—"

"We've got plenty of time." He smiled, feeling her utter pliancy as he eased her back onto the bed. In the process his coin slid down onto the curve of her naked breast.

The contact was instant, electric. Her body lurched. "Duncan, no. The coin. Your feelings, I can't—" Her eyes closed, and a shudder tore through her. The coin rose and fell with each wild breath she took.

And then her back arched. In shock, Duncan watched pleasure tear through her again. All from the contact with him, triggered by his coin.

He pulled away. He was watching when her eyes opened. Color raced furiously over her face.

"Talk to me, Kara."

She swallowed. "It was the coin. When it t-touched me, I saw you. I felt what you wanted. Every last incredible thing."

"This adds a whole new dimension to things." Duncan smiled darkly. "I can't begin to describe what you're doing to my weak male ego. Hell, how many men can drive a woman wild with just one look?"

"You." Kara's voice was husky. "It was ... extraordinary. Do you really want to do all those things to me?"

"*With* you. Very soon." Flecks of silver glinted in his blue-gray eyes. "But first, I just can't help wondering." He bent before her, lips sleek to hers. And as he did, the coin fell against her neck and shivered with the race of her pulse.

Kara's fingers tensed on the linen sheets. Her gaze blurred. "Duncan, no, I—"

His hands slid into her hair, and he closed his eyes, painting with sharp images exactly what she meant to him and all the ways he wanted to touch her. And just as before, he watched in awe as her toes curled and she dug into the sheets, back arched in pleasure.

He was there to catch her, whispering loving words in an old tongue shaped when language still held its greatest magic and power.

When Kara's eyes opened, she was frowning. "That wasn't fair."

"But it was beautiful. Amazing."

"This will be too." Kara sat up, her eyes fierce. Her fingers shoved at his belt, then attacked his zipper. Muttering, she worked the soft, faded corduroy down his hard thighs.

Her eyes widened when she saw the awesome thrust of him. "Lord, you're so . . ." Her hair spilled forward in a riot of copper as she eased him free and took him in her hands.

"Kara—" His voice was a slash of sound.

"*My* turn, Scotsman."

His eyes closed in exquisite agony as she brushed the velvet, pulsing tip of him with her tongue. Her gentle touch was paradise and torment. He was seconds away from explosive pleasure when he caught her face and wrenched her away. "No. Inside you, damn it."

He shoved her to the bed and followed her down, his face taut as he fought for control. She wasn't helping, her restless thighs urging him closer. Duncan grimaced, balanced between agony and exhilaration as he found her silken gate.

She was panting now, her fingers digging into his shoulders. "Duncan, *now*. I want to feel you against me."

The words burned through the ragged edges of his control. Like a circuit closing, he felt an electric lurch as he thrust home. Wildly, he rode its crest, driving deep, scattering the blankets and forcing her over the bed with each powerful stroke.

Kara cried out. Her back arched and her muscles clenched around him.

Duncan groaned as he felt her silken tremors. For now, the cold gray certainty of his death could be forgotten in the fire and beauty of her body.

His blood pounded savagely, the pulse of ancient

warriors who streaked their faces with woad and ran joyous into battle.

"Take me deep, Kara. God, I didn't think that touching a woman could be so—" His voice slammed into a groan as she clenched, shuddering over and over in tight, erotic tremors where she sheathed him. Duncan was swept along with her, rigid in the same dark pleasure.

Hands locked and bodies taut, they swam through an endless sea where time was only a word and happiness was a blinding color.

And all the while, trapped and forgotten between their bodies, the old coin danced like a golden, living thing.

Twenty-three ~

Afternoon light splintered off the crystal bowls and touched Kara's hair, spread gold and russet and copper against Duncan's chest. Her body was still, replete, her hand curled in the hollow beneath his chin.

Duncan was floating, exquisitely aware of every movement of her ribs and hands and perfect breasts. It had been extraordinary. Hard and breathless and—extraordinary. Even as he had been swallowed up in shattering passion, some part of his brain had registered that she knew, she *knew* exactly what he wanted and how he wanted it.

And she gave it to him, breathless and graceful. She made her body a gift to him, shaped to his pleasure, nothing held back.

Her gift stunned him. A woman like Kara Fitzgerald did not let down her defenses easily. What would happen to her if fate brought the death Duncan expected?

She'll cry, he told himself. But she'll cry in private and put on a smile in public while she goes about her work with her usual perfect competence. No one will know.

Face it, MacKinnon, the only honorable thing to do is break it off right now. He should tug on his clothes and walk out that door without turning back, he thought.

His hands speared gently through her hair, sparkling a dozen shades of red and gold.

He couldn't. Honor be damned and the future be

damned. He wanted today. He wanted all the pleasure she could bring him as she shuddered breathlessly beneath him.

He slid the sheet away from her body, marveling at the sun playing over her warm skin. He smiled darkly at the proof that she was most definitely a natural redhead. As he toyed with the auburn curls clustered at her thighs, desire left him stiff and painfully erect.

Ignoring his need, he kissed a path toward those welcoming curls. She sighed at his touch, sighed but did not waken, and Duncan found her heat and gently tongued an entrance. That was how she woke, her hips restless, her eyes already dim with passion.

When she moved against him, her body sleek to his touch, he muttered darkly, and in one shuddering stroke he filled her as man and warrior and lover.

For it was love that made his hands gentle. It was love that left his heart slamming as she rose in breathless passion beneath him.

Love. He loved Kara Fitzgerald. The knowledge throbbed in Duncan's veins as his hunger crested and sent his hot seed coursing deep inside her.

Love. Bodies locked, fingers entwined, with the MacKinnon seed spilling as hot and potent as the laird himself.

In his claiming Duncan was aware of stirrings of dim memory, images of another place and time when a stern warrior had committed his future to the life he hoped would grow within his lover's warm body.

Kara's hands were in his hair when his final passion was spent.

When his head fell and his eyes closed, he did not see the tears that burned like cut glass on her cheeks.

An insistent knocking woke them.

Only an hour in this lovely, quiet room, Kara thought, but it felt like years. Lifetimes even . . .

She brushed Duncan's chest, her fingers snagging in the soft, dark hair. She smiled at the sight of his shirt dangling crazily from the headboard. His belt was shoved around his ankle.

Eyes of silver-flecked blue studied her intently. "I hope you're going to tell me that pounding is your heart, Fitzgerald."

"You mean it's not yours?" Kara eased against him until their bodies met from thigh to thigh. Instantly he began to harden.

The knocking grew louder.

Duncan cursed softly, looking over every inch of her. "Just a minute." He tugged a plaid blanket from the floor and draped it around his waist.

"I like your kilt, Scotsman. Maybe I'll use it in the next issue of *New Bride*."

Duncan gave her a look that promised serious retribution for that comment. Then he opened the door.

"Sorry, Duncan. I waited as long as I could, when I saw that you two had—" Snow Sedgwick swayed from foot to foot, embarrassed. "You've had six calls from London already. The last one was frantic."

The two men's eyes met.

"Should I tell them you've gone?"

"I wish you could, but it wouldn't change anything. Who was it?"

"Someone named Lieutenant Sinclair. You can take it in my office. You'll be able to hear better in there, without the din from the pub. It will also be safer."

"What do you mean?"

"There were two journalists asking about you in the pub. I'm afraid news about Kyle has already begun to leak out."

Duncan's hands tensed on the bright plaid. "What did you tell them?"

"The usual. No Scotsman here, never even heard of Lord Dunraven. I stowed your motorcycle in the old stables, in case they might recognize it. But they'll probably be back, snooping around again soon."

A muscle moved in Duncan's jaw. "Thanks, Sedge. I'll be down shortly." Slowly he closed the door. When he turned, Kara moved into his arms.

"Duncan?"

"No, don't say anything." He kissed her fiercely, then stood away. "I'll be back as soon as I can. Ten minutes at the most, I promise."

Ten minutes came and went. Finally Kara dressed, worked her tangled hair back into some semblance of order, and went downstairs in search of Duncan.

Sedge was waiting on a balcony overlooking the mill pond. "Duncan's still inside," he explained, handing her a cup of steaming coffee, then returning to his scrutiny of the pond. "Do you know that there was a mill here six hundred years ago? We found written accounts of this area describing how smugglers used it even then. There was some far-fetched tale of a band of outlaws who lived in the Royal Forest, preying on the rich. This old mill was said to be one of their meeting places." He sighed. When he looked at Kara, his eyes were very tired. "I hope you like the coffee, Ms. Fitzgerald."

Kara savored the rich, intense blend. "It's wonderful. Any more and I'll never sleep tonight."

Duncan's friend looked at her measuringly. "If you're with Duncan I doubt you'll get much sleep anyway."

Kara flushed. She looked down at the cup, rolling it between her fingers.

"He's always been a creature of habit, you know. Up until now."

"I break that habit?"

He laughed softly. "You break *all* his rules. He has come riding in here dozens of times, brooding and silent on that motorcycle, his way of escaping bad memories. But always alone. Until you."

"What are you trying to tell me, Sedge?"

"Just this. Duncan and I go back a long way. We've watched each other's backs in some pretty nasty places, and I know him very well. He doesn't do this kind of thing lightly."

Kara clutched the cup blindly in her fingers. "Maybe this is just his way of . . . unwinding," she suggested.

The older man chuckled. "Unwinding? My dear, Duncan's idea of unwinding is to go off and scale an unmapped peak or swim the Great Barrier Reef. Whatever happened between you up in that attic room was special. Don't start doubting him—or yourself."

Kara felt heat fill her cheeks.

"I know Duncan damned well after all these years. I think I know you fairly well too, young woman. I also know what happened in London. Duncan and I used to be in the same line of work, and not much goes on in security circles that I don't hear about."

"There are ... things he's not telling me." Kara's fingers tensed on the polished wooden rail along the patio. "I'm not sure I can handle that."

"There are things Duncan can't tell *anyone*. But you can trust him with your life."

What about his life? Kara wanted to ask. *How can I bear knowing he expects every moment to be our last?*

She watched the petals of a rose flutter gently past Sedge's hand. Dread was building in her throat. "What will happen now?"

He shook his head. "There are a lot of people who can use a man with Kyle's skills. The only problem is that most of them think spilling English blood is cause for rejoicing." He looked up at the beautiful old inn. "Duncan helped me buy this place. After I lost my leg I wasn't worth very much for a while. Duncan came down every week, cursing and shouting and generally making my life miserable until I got on with renovating this old place. Until I got on with my life." He shoved one hand through his unruly red hair. "He's one damned fine man, but I sometimes suspect he feels responsible for what happened to Kyle. Rubbish, of course, but try convincing Duncan of that."

"Do you think Kyle will come after Duncan?"

Sedge frowned. "Kyle MacKinnon will do whatever suits him at the moment. He's a man with a lifetime full of hate, in spite of the love he got from those around him. And right now, I don't like the fact that Duncan still hasn't come out of my office."

"He's been on the telephone all this time?" Heaviness gathered in Kara's chest. At her feet petals spilled from the roses, scattering over the flagstones with a dry hiss.

"I'm afraid so. Which means something has gone wrong."

Duncan stood tensely, phone gripped to his ear. "I see."

Bad news.

Always bad news when Kyle was involved.

"How did he get away?"

"Damn it, we *had* him." Lieutenant Sinclair's voice was even more clipped than usual. "But there was a mother with a pram, and we couldn't take a chance on hitting her."

"Where is he now, Sinclair?"

"He was sighted heading toward Cornwall. We think he'll have a boat ready to put to sea. Where he goes from there is anyone's guess. Our job is to see he doesn't get that far."

You can't do it. He won't be found until he's ready to be found. Duncan felt his hands dig into the receiver. "He'll come after me, Sinclair. I'm the one he wants."

James Sinclair made a curt, snorting sound. "I have every confidence that my men can track a lone renegade, Dunraven. I hand-picked them, and each man has been thoroughly briefed on your brother's background."

"You don't know Kyle."

"But I damned well know *my* men! No, you're out of this. Go on to Draycott Abbey. We'll reach you when it's time to identify the body."

"You're very certain of yourself."

"I have to be, don't I? If my lads fail, then it's my failure, and failure simply isn't an option." Sinclair cleared his throat. "There is one thing you could do, however. We've found two bodies in a car trunk in

Norwich. They answer your description of the officers who stopped you and Ms. Fitzgerald in Sussex."

"Is there anything you can use to track Kyle?"

"I'm afraid not. That's why I hoped you might speak to Ms. Fitzgerald."

Duncan frowned. "Kara? I don't understand."

"Don't play the fool, Dunraven. I saw what she did in London. I don't know how she works, but she gets results. For that reason, I'm sending a car to collect her. The bodies are being held for her arrival."

Duncan tensed. "You want her to *read* them? You want her to touch them and open her mind?" Duncan's hands began to shake. "Do you have *any* bloody idea what you're asking?"

"I'm asking for a woman's assistance in a matter of government security," Sinclair said coldly. "I might also remind you that you swore an oath before you went into that showroom in London."

"I don't require a bloody oath to know what my responsibilities are, Sinclair. They don't include asking Kara to open her mind to that kind of horror."

"She's done it before, back in New York."

Duncan recalled her eyes, exquisitely sensitive as she'd touched his golden coin. He remembered the tremors that had racked her with just one touch. If she opened her mind with that same intensity, how could she bear the contact with a body shattered by violent death?

"No, damn you. I won't ask her to endure that. Even if she agreed, I wouldn't let her. You'll have to find another way, Sinclair. Use those perfectly trained lads of yours."

Sinclair's voice hardened. "Oh, I'll use them. I can count on them. I only wonder if I can count on *you*, Dunraven. After all, this man is your brother."

"Is that an accusation? Because if it is, there won't be enough of your 'lads' around to keep my hands away from your throat." Duncan swallowed hard, fighting his anger.

"It's not an accusation. Not yet. But I'll be watching you both. And I won't be the only one. My man at Ms. Fitzgerald's hotel tells me someone was nosing around the kitchen asking questions."

"Did you hold him?"

"He was gone by the time my people got there."

"Your people seem to be missing a lot of things, Sinclair." Duncan felt fury burn through his chest at the thought of Kara's becoming a target of his brother's mindless violence. "If you want to help, Sinclair, then seal off the source of the news leak," Duncan said grimly. "Two journalists have already been here asking questions."

"I'll take care of the leak," Sinclair said grimly. "Meanwhile, you keep Ms. Fitzgerald with you at the abbey, where I can reach you when it becomes necessary."

The line went dead.

Duncan looked down at his hand and realized it was shaking. His forehead was beaded with sweat.

He couldn't go to Kara like this. She would read his anger before he came within two feet of her.

He pulled back the curtains, frowning down at the quiet pond, willing himself to forget the conversation he had just had and pretend that this was a day like any other day.

"A problem, Duncan?" Sedge stood in the doorway.

"Just some bureaucratic details that needed to be cleared up in London. You know how these government types delight in last-minute delays. It makes them feel important."

But his friend wasn't buying it. "I don't suppose Kyle is part of those bureaucratic details, is he?"

Duncan turned back to the window. "Everything's fine, Sedge." He frowned. "Where's Kara?"

"Downstairs finishing her coffee and trying not to show how worried she is about you." Sedge's eyes narrowed. "Did she really do those things you told me? Touch things and read their energy?"

"She has a true and real gift of sight, so my old grandmother would have said."

"What about Kyle?"

"He's in their net."

Sedge snorted. "So they still don't have him. What the hell are they doing?"

Trust Sedge to hit the heart of the matter. "It's just a matter of hours, I'm told."

Sedge laughed grimly. "I seem to recall hearing that right before Kyle blew up a barracks and skipped the country. In Indonesia, as I recall."

"This time they're close, Sedge. He was monitoring us via video transmitter. Our people were able to trace him."

"And what about that young woman downstairs? We both know that no one's safe when Kyle is involved."

"I know that," Duncan said grimly. "Better than anyone. But it's done, understand? Let it alone, Sedge. Kara will be safe at Draycott Abbey." For a moment Duncan's fingers tightened on the curtains. "And now we'd better push off if we're going to make the abbey before nightfall."

Twenty-four ~

Kara studied Duncan's face as he strode over the moss-covered cobblestones. There were new lines of tension at his mouth and there was a hard set to his jaw. She didn't need to ask what had put them there.

Kyle. The word burned in his mind, along with something else he was shielding from her.

Duncan pointed toward the motorcycle waiting outside the ivy-covered stables. "We're leaving. We've got at least three more hours of traveling ahead of us, and I'm not foolhardy enough to take those narrow lanes in the dark. Nicholas Draycott will murder us if we aren't at the abbey by seven."

"Why?"

"He and Kacey have had a charity event planned for weeks now. It had entirely slipped my mind."

"But I *can't* go, Duncan. I haven't brought any clothes."

"That's all been taken care of."

Kara crossed her arms and stood staring at him. "What's *wrong*, Duncan? You're locked up so tight that you're not even here." Frowning, she reached toward his chest.

Duncan sidestepped neatly. Their eyes met for a moment, and then he looked away. "We'd better go."

Kara stiffened. Locking her fingers, she reached out with her senses, trying to understand what he had just heard in Sedge's office.

Duncan saw exactly what she was doing. "Don't try reading me, Kara. Not now."

"Has something gone wrong in London?"

"It's better if you stay out of it now," Duncan said flatly.

"What about the trust, Duncan? What about the sharing?" She reached out for the coin at his chest.

Duncan blocked her hand. "No. Not now."

"When?"

"When my brother is dead."

Kara sat stiffly behind Duncan as they sped east through sun-dappled hills filled with black-faced Sussex sheep. His shoulders were tense where she touched him, and Kara sensed his struggle to stay aloof.

He was blocking her out completely.

But it wasn't going to work. Their link was already forged. Now even the casual touch of Kara's hands at his waist brought blurred waves of emotion into her mind.

Anger, uncertainty, and fear—all of this Kara read in Duncan's mind. And there was something else hidden deep, something that Duncan was fighting to conceal from her.

Every time she reached for it, Kara touched shadows, along with the haunting sense that she had faced these shadows once before.

Long, long ago.

Twilight was inching up the valley when Duncan turned into the winding gravel drive that led to Draycott Abbey's rose-covered walls. When he turned off the engine, silence seemed to leap up around them.

"Are you going to tell me what has happened, Duncan?"

Kara felt his body stiffen.

"I see." Very carefully she slid from the motorcycle. "Then it's over right now." She shoved back her hair, tossed by the wind. "It has to be over. I'm not brave enough to take the pain again. Especially now ..."

He turned at that. His eyes held a darkness that might have been anger or pain. "Why?"

Kara felt the rose-fragrant breeze play through her hair. Down the hill the soft waters of the moat lapped gently against the abbey's granite walls. "Because I'm very afraid that I'm falling in love with you."

Duncan didn't move. A strange hammering filled his head, and his knees locked.

Because I'm falling in love with you.

Dear God, why now?

He looked down. His fingers were clenched white on the handlebars. In his mind he heard Kyle's chill laughter above the relentless ticking of a clock.

He didn't turn as he heard Kara move over the gravel. If he said one word to her now, the walls would fall, and she knew more than was safe for her already.

Duncan's jaw hardened as he watched darkness blanket the valley. He thought about trust and passion, about how much of her she'd given back in that rose-filled room at the inn.

What about the trust, Duncan? What about the sharing?

The coin lay cold on his skin as he cursed to the silence, to the night, to his brother somewhere in the shadows, foiling his happiness yet again.

Kara paced the moat house, oblivious to the fine satin chairs, the elegant roses in cut-glass bowls, and the moonlight filtering through the open French doors. She was restless, filled with nervous energy. She told herself it was the normal anxiety she felt when tackling a new issue.

Good try, Fitzgerald.

Idly, she thumbed through a tiny book covered in sheets of beaten silver. Beautiful and very rare, it had intrigued her since she'd first seen it.

Beside her on the bed lay a shimmering sweep of deep purple silk next to a magazine opened to an aerial photo of Draycott Abbey. For the tenth time Kara read the text that followed.

The Royal Flower Show will conclude with its most glamourous event at Draycotte Abbey, where patrons who have paid two thousand pounds apiece will dance until dawn und sample the abbey's extraordinary collection of vintage champagnes. Among the guests expected to attend are four royal patrons, exhibitors, and sponsors, and the reclusive Lord Dunraven, cousin to Lord Draycotte. The evening's hosts, Lord and Lady Draycotte, are devoted patrons of horticulture and the owners of what is held to be one of the finest rose gardens in Europe. A legend that the old moated abbey is haunted only appears to have added to the popularity of the event.

Frowning, Kara turned away to the window. Moonlight spilled over the moat, and the air was thick with the scent of roses in a landscape tailor-made for lovers. She had an hour before Lord and Lady Draycott's party was to begin.

Time to forget the tension in Duncan's jaw. Time to forget a pair of blue-gray eyes that held a pain that was decades old.

Maybe a lifetime old.

Kara shivered.

Forget Duncan MacKinnon.

Grimly she snatched up the telephone and punched out a number, pausing only for a quick glance at her watch.

"Megan? I'm glad I caught you. Oh, I'm just fine. No, I'm not in Scotland yet." Kara cleared her throat. "We need to check on the jewelry article we commissioned from Tiffany's. Keep an eye on the deadline, will you? Hidoshi has already finished the photographs, so you can start laying things out. Maybe you should fax me the draft of that celebrity piece on honeymoon memories. Most of the contributors won't be married to the same people now, and we'll have to be careful about legalities. The last thing we need is a lawsuit by an irate ex-spouse. Run everything past Martin just to be sure, will you? And for heaven's sake don't let him forget that tomorrow is the printer's birthday. In fact, why don't you just send an arrangement of flowers with Martin's name on it. Marielle will be crushed if she thinks he forgot."

Kara ran her hand gently along the gown's satin hem. "If there's anything very important, you can reach me at the number I left you in Kent. Scotland?" Her eyes filled with pain. "I plan to leave tomorrow. What? No, everything is fine, Megan."

Church bells chimed out in the darkness. Kara felt a prickling along her neck as the low tones echoed through the night. The smell of roses was intense, carried by the wind that spilled through the open French doors.

Kara had a sudden urge to watch the moonlight glistening over the moat. There was a sense of restless energy to the house that perfectly matched her own mood this night. "Yes, Megan, I'll be in touch. Tell Hidoshi—well, you know what to tell him. Just be sure he's ready to leave."

After hanging up, Kara slipped on the silk dress, pulled on a fragile silk scarf, then stepped into high-heeled gold sandals.

She wouldn't think about their burnished gold color or how it matched the medallion Duncan wore around his neck. She wouldn't think about the laird of Dunraven Castle at all, Kara swore.

She studied her face in the mirror and sighed, knowing she would think about Dunraven's laird every day for the rest of her life.

Over the hill, light spilled from hundreds of lanterns scattered throughout the abbey's woods.

Kara took a slow breath as she moved outside. Draycott Abbey was haunting tonight, caught in a dance of light and shadow that heightened its air of mystery. The old walls emanated power, and Kara felt keenly the force of love left by generations of owners.

In her pocket, forgotten, lay the tiny book from the moat-house mantel.

Some instinct made Kara step back into the shadows as a motor droned overhead. The noise grew deafening as a shadow covered the grass down the hill. The motors cut abruptly, and a man stepped from the helicopter, elegant in formal black attire. Goosebumps rose on Kara's shoulders as she recognized the blue-gray eyes and sun-bronzed skin.

Duncan would always do the unexpected.

Fog drifted up the valley. The Scotsman turned, searching the darkness near the abbey. Kara pulled back as the abbey's great oak door opened, casting a bar of light over the flagstones.

"There you are, Duncan. As usual, not a hair out of place." Nicholas Draycott moved toward his cousin. "Don't just stand there, man. We have two hundred guests arriving in half an hour, and despite my dear wife's unshatterable calm, I am about to experience total meltdown. You *have* brought the roses, I hope."

"Right in the back of *Mary*, over there."

"I'll never understand why you give your helicopters names."

"Each of those little beauties is dangerous. I like to establish a personal relationship with them." Again MacKinnon turned, studying the hillside.

"Any more news from Sinclair?"

Duncan plucked a rose from the granite wall beside the moat. "Only that the usual net of silence is in force. Everyone's working overtime to prove there was simply an electrical malfunction in Calendish's new security system."

"They can't keep this secret for long. And while we're at it, what's wrong with you? You've barely said a word to Ms. Fitzgerald all evening."

Duncan frowned down at the rose as if it reminded him of something. "Nothing's wrong. Why should there be?"

"Because you're too bloody quiet, MacKinnon. I

know when you're getting yourself in the frame of mind for work. *Dangerous* work. Don't tell me that electrical equipment you brought was for my sound system. And don't tell me that those four bull-necked fellows who came down with you from London are here to serve as a string quartet."

Duncan laughed grimly and tossed the creamy petals into the moat. "Your imagination is running away with you, Nicky. It must be your abbey weaving its dark spells. The new arrivals were Sinclair's idea, just a precaution in case you have uninvited guests tonight." He hefted pots of flowers from the helicopter onto each shoulder. "And now I'd better take these inside for Kacey and see what I can do to help."

"You can help by telling me what's bothering you, you great bloody Scotsman," Nicholas Draycott muttered. Then he shouldered his quota of exquisite centifolia roses and followed his cousin inside.

Kara didn't move.

The wind played with the scarf at her shoulders. Once again she heard the low, sad peal of church bells.

Something was wrong in London. Very wrong. Why hadn't Duncan told her at the inn, instead of blocking his fear from her? Didn't he understand that without trust there could be nothing between them, that each day of lies was a living hell for a person with her sensitivity?

Sighing, Kara tilted her face to the wind.

Forget Duncan MacKinnon. Forget how he made you laugh in a room full of roses.

Around her the petals trembled, rustling in the wind, and Kara felt an instant of foreboding so keen it was painful. And then a man in black broadcloth and crisp white linen moved out of the shadows.

Her breath caught. "Lord, but you frightened me."

"It was not my intention. You are . . . Miss Fitzgerald, I think." His eyes were gray, as gray as the weathered stones of the abbey. His face was a riddle, cast now in moonlight, now in shadow. His keen eyes burned over her face. "You are the editor of *New Bride* magazine."

"You know me?" Kara frowned. "I don't think we've met."

"We haven't." The eyes narrowed. "To my great sorrow. For you are a woman of beauty as well as singular skills." His brow rose. "You do not believe yourself beautiful?"

Kara blinked, hardly knowing how to answer.

"He was a great fool." A faint smile. "He regrets losing you already."

"Who?" Goose bumps rose over Kara's skin. Why were the man's eyes so knowing?

He neatly ignored her question. "Your past pains you still, my dear. You must learn to let it go."

To let *what* go? Her past was her own secret. How could this stranger know anything about that? "Who *are* you?"

His hand moved restlessly. Kara saw lace sweep over his cuff. An odd sort of costume, she supposed, but then many English aristocrats were confirmed eccentrics.

"Eccentric, you think me?" His full lips curved. "How amusing. As for my identity, I am Lord Draycott's assistant," he explained, bowing slightly. Even with his face half hidden in shadow, power seemed to shimmer about him.

"Something makes me think you're very good at what you do," she said.

"I am tolerably efficient. I suspect the same is true of you, Miss Fitzgerald. You have special skills for one so young."

Again Kara felt the burn of his keen eyes. "Skills? I don't know what you mean."

"Do you not?" The hard face turned chiding. "I'm accounted to be a good judge of character, Miss Fitzgerald, and perhaps of things more subtle than character." He laughed softly. "It is one of the reasons I am useful to Lord Draycott. Even more than he knows."

Something about his husky laugh made Kara unbend to this strange man. "My skills may be good," she said, "but I suspect that yours are nothing short of spectacular. Surprising, considering you aren't much older than I am."

"You think not?" Again the soft laughter. Around him the roses seemed to bow and sway, as if to his command. Kara blinked, struck by the sudden impression of light and shadow swirling about his tall form. "You are very wrong, my dear. I am far older than you know."

Kara felt her skin tingle. She sensed power all around him. She narrowed her focus, intent on reaching out to him.

Her hand rose. And then she gasped as her energy was thrown right back at her. The force of the contact left her white-faced.

Her companion was beside her in a second. "I'm afraid you had better sit down, Miss Fitzgerald. You do not look well."

Blinking, Kara sank onto the granite wall flanking the moat. When her vision cleared, she saw that he was frowning. He raised his hand, then lowered it quickly.

The uneasiness at her neck became a stab of warning. "Who *are* you?"

"No one you need fear." He turned away, gazing at the blooms growing riotously over the base of the granite wall. "But there are others about this night, people with far darker intent."

He stood stiffly. Kara couldn't pull her eyes away from the hard, brooding face that had too many angles to be handsome.

"How do you know that? Are you one of those men from London sent by Lieutenant Sinclair?"

A cloud ran before the moon. "I have not been to London for many, many years now," he said gravely. "I know these things because it is my responsibility to know everything about this abbey." His hands tightened. "It is also my curse."

Down the hill a pair of dark limousines glided into the quiet courtyard before the moat house.

Kara's companion watched the headlights cut through the darkness. "So it begins, despite us all." His eyes hardened. "I must go," he said abruptly. "Be careful what wishes you make tonight, Miss Fitzgerald. There is shadow as well as light around you, and a danger that draws close. For both you and the MacKinnon."

As he spoke, moonlight threaded a fairy path across the moat. He smiled faintly. Sadly, Kara thought. "Stay," she said impulsively. "Tell me about this house you love so well."

"You noticed that, did you?" He nodded as a dark shape appeared at his leg, purring softly. "Yes, Gideon, I quite agree. Her skill is unique." The cat's tail arched, and for a moment Kara had the unsettling sense that the two were communicating. "Alas, I cannot stay. Our paths do not cross the same wood this night, Kara Fitzgerald. On another night, perhaps. Or even in another time, or another place."

The great cat circled gracefully about his feet.

Something about the cat nagged at Kara's mind. "Must you go?"

The proud head bent. "You honor me, my dear, but I may not stay longer. There is too much to be done. Still, a word of advice, from one you may take as a friend. A very *old* friend."

Kara watched the long, aristocratic fingers slide over the cat's gray fur. She frowned, thinking of another cat, a cat that had leaped onto her bed as she tossed in angry dreams.

That cat had been gray. With burning amber eyes.

Something pressed at the edges of her mind. Nagging again, then suddenly gone.

She felt the exquisite old book through her silk pocket. Its sharp edges seemed to burn with a cold fire. Some instinct made Kara pull it out. Moonlight danced over the beaten silver images and made them seem to move.

"You found the book, I see. There are legends there, old tales you might find interesting. It was *her* favorite book, you know."

"Her? Lady Draycott, you mean?"

"Not the one you speak of. Another—long ago." Wind riffled the pages as he spoke, and again Kara had the strange sense that the movement was somehow at his command. "It is my abbey, as it once was. Before the shadows came."

"*Your* abbey?" Kara went very still. The energy hummed all around her now. *Danger in the touch.* "What was the advice you meant to give me?"

His long fingers moved over the cat's gray fur. "Use your gift as it was meant to be used. See with heart and mind and deepest soul, for this skill is yours by right and prior choice, won of old wounds and old faith. Use this skill again, Kara Fitzgerald. But watch always for the shadow. Even here you and your warrior are not safe. Nor were you then."

Kara did not move as the whispered words broke chantlike directly through her mind, almost as if they had bypassed her ears.

The moon slid from behind the clouds. Somewhere a car growled on the darkened drive, the sound noisy in the cool, still air. And even before she could turn, Kara knew he would be gone.

So it was.

Only a hint of lace flashed silver in the distance, then faded back into the unbroken shadows of the woods.

Kara did not move.

Not toward the brightly lit abbey. Not toward the open door, from which the strains of a waltz drifted out. She only stood, letting the power of the abbey play over her in a delicate web of impressions.

Roses.

Moonlight.

Laughter. A love as old as forever. Beneath it, barely felt, a current of danger, glimpsed with the skill that Kara now reached out to test.

Even then it held to the shadows, never clearer despite all her probing.

She stepped into the doorway. Hung beside the

door was a luminous painting of a river scene by moonlight. One of Whistler's early *nocturnes*, she thought.

Gently she ran one finger over the scrawled signature in the lower corner. Instantly power rocked through her, cold with the clinging mist of the Thames in winter. Opening her senses, Kara slid deeper into the flood of images until she caught an American accent.

There was no mistake. The painting was from Whistler's hand. But more curious still, the painting's power was enhanced by years of reverent attention, faintly luminous, like the energy that Kara sensed everywhere girding the abbey. Subtle but unmistakable, energy clung to the potted roses outside the ballroom and shimmered about the fine French furniture and antique Chinese porcelains.

Touching that energy made Kara think of the gray eyes of the man she had met outside by the moat. But already his features seemed blurred, and no matter how she concentrated she could not summon them clearly.

Probably she had called upon her gift too often during the last week. For her safety she must begin to close off her senses.

At that moment Kara turned. The little silver book shook in her fingers. "Are you spying on me now?" she asked.

Duncan was a slash of black against the shadows. "Not spying. I thought I heard voices."

"I was talking with Lord Draycott's assistant."

Duncan frowned. "Assistant?"

"Stop seeing monsters behind every tree. He was a perfectly nice man, even if he was rather eccentric. Now, I think I'll go in. It's growing *cold* all of a sudden."

Duncan blocked her way. "Stop running, Fitzgerald."

"I wasn't the one who ran this afternoon." Kara looked past him, her face grim.

"We made a deal. You get to spread Dunraven all

over that magazine of yours, and I get two full days. The time isn't up yet."

"Maybe I'm canceling the deal."

"I don't think so. You want Dunraven too much to back out now."

Kara turned away, finding it hard to think when he stood so close. Abruptly the words of Lord Draycott's mysterious assistant went through her head. *And a danger that draws close.*

"You're shivering, Fitzgerald. Remembering how I taste? How we felt together?"

Kara shoved past him. "You made your point at the inn, MacKinnon. Leave things as they are."

"Leaving things alone has never been one of my strong points."

"Then answer my question. What happened in London?"

Duncan shrugged. "More of the same. I'm not going to discuss it." His eyes glittered. "There are other things I want to do right now." He caught her waist. His hands were warm, all velvet strength.

Kara shivered. "No."

His hands tightened, tracing the bones of her spine through the thin silk. "You can't have forgotten, Kara. How it feels when you wrap your legs around me. How it feels when you cry out against my lips."

Damn him, she *hadn't* forgotten. She never could. She felt his desire then, and with it the tension in his broad shoulders.

"I want you, Kara. Right here in the long grass beside the moat. I want your hands in my hair and your body arching beneath me. I could have you that way, too, but I won't. Not until you want it the same way. Maybe all your talk of trust and sharing is just a way to deny yourself something that frightens you to death. I've been there, too, but this time was different. Kyle, London—that stays separate, for your safety as much as mine. But the rest of what is between us has no walls and no limits. That's the only way it will work."

Kara felt pressure build in her chest. The power of it shocked her. White-faced, she stumbled back as desire slammed through her body. She wanted this man. She wanted his hands on her naked skin, his mouth hot and demanding against her in his passion.

But she couldn't have him. The bond between them was already too strong. Without utter truthfulness, the clarity of her link would destroy her.

"You don't want me to come out here again, do you?" Her voice was like ice. "You've put up some kind of security beams, but he's out there somewhere right now, isn't he?"

Duncan cursed softly. "Leave Kyle out of this."

"I can't, don't you see? I'm part of it now. Even if you can't see it, your brother's shadow falls on everything you do."

"Damn it, Kara, I just want to protect you."

"You still don't understand, do you? Protecting me will destroy me. There can't *be* anything separate, not now. I've told you all along, but you didn't listen." Her hands locked, trembling, at her chest. "So it's over, MacKinnon. Don't touch me. Don't think about me. It's business now, nothing but business."

Duncan's jaws hardened. "It will *never* be just business between us, and you know it."

"Then God help us both, because I won't settle for half, Duncan. I've worked too long and hard to accept what I am. Geoffrey was part of that painful lesson. It's got to be everything—all of me with all of you until there won't be giving enough to satisfy either of us. It's that or nothing, Duncan. Anything less will tear me apart. This afternoon taught me that. *You* taught me that." She turned away, her eyes caverns of pain. "Every secret you hide, every wall you throw up hits me right *here*." Her palm opened over her heart. "*You* can separate, Duncan, but I can't. It's part of the miracle—and the curse—of this sight of mine. So don't try to touch me or hold me again unless that changes."

Duncan didn't move.

Kara's face was pale and cold in the moonlight. "I thought not." When she walked past him, her footsteps echoed hollowly on the flagstones, like scattered coins.

Twenty-five ~

Duncan didn't move.

His fingers dug against the granite wall. He breathed and ached, and he didn't move.

Because Duncan Douglas Wynters MacLeod MacKinnon, fourteenth earl of Dunraven, finally understood that the woman he loved was right. It had to be all or nothing.

Anything less would tear them *both* apart.

This painful realization haunted Duncan for the next hour as he watched Kara drift among the abbey's jeweled guests. She laughed at all the right moments, smiled and shook her head as required. And Duncan knew exactly how much the act cost her.

Love had left them linked. With every moment he wanted her more. He *ached* with wanting her, until there was no safety in his feelings.

But even more than he wanted her, Duncan meant to see Kara safe from the shadow that Kyle cast over them all.

"She's very lovely, isn't she?" Nicholas's wife was following his intent gaze.

"Very."

"She's also very good at what she does. She gives her readers a touch of magic, reminding them exactly what it feels like to fall in love."

Yes, Kara Fitzgerald would be very good at creating magic, Duncan thought. "Do you read the bloody magazine too, Kacey?"

"Of course. So does Nicholas. It's beautiful, elegant, and in unerring good taste. Times have changed. Weddings have changed, and *New Bride* reflects that change. All Kara Fitzgerald's doing, so I understand."

Duncan watched a man bend close and whisper something in Kara's ear. Even from across the room he caught the lilt of her laughter.

He scowled. "Why do I sense a sermon coming on, Kacey?"

"Not a sermon, just some good sisterly advice. Or should I say cousinly?"

"Either will do." His fingers tightened on the fragile stem of his wineglass. "Nicholas is the closest thing I have to a brother. Kyle doesn't exactly qualify, you understand, so go ahead. I'm listening."

"I don't know what happened in London, but I know Nicholas is worried. I also know those men you brought back with you aren't part of the catering staff."

"You always could spot a lie, Kacey." He gave her a lopsided grin. "Even a white one."

"*Especially* a white one. You do it because you care for people and want to keep them safe, but it's not the Middle Ages anymore, Duncan. You can't always protect people."

"I can damned well try," he said grimly.

"You're such a throwback, MacKinnon."

"A throwback to what?"

"I haven't decided yet." Kacey shook her head, and her long blond hair glinted beneath the chandelier. "You're too much like Nicholas, you see. You work too hard, laugh too little, and keep too many secrets."

"That transparent, am I?"

"Only to someone who cares for you very much." Kacey sighed. "I'm being inexcusably rude, I know. You can throw me in the moat if you like. I'm told you wild MacKinnons used to do that to the Draycotts all the time."

Duncan flashed her a faint smile. "I wouldn't dream of it, my dear. I like you far too much for that."

"Then maybe you won't mind if I finish my sermon. Take some time off, Duncan. Smell the lovely roses growing at Dunraven. Walk barefoot in the sand by that beach of yours. It will be good for you." Her lips curved. "So will Kara Fitzgerald, unless you let some ridiculous argument come between you."

Duncan only wished it were so easy. "Does that distinguished husband of yours know you are busy matchmaking, Lady Draycott?"

"Nicholas? *He* sent me over here, of course." And with that terse remark the viscountess moved on to her next guest.

Smell the roses, Duncan thought grimly. *Walk barefoot in the sand.*

Unbidden, his eyes drifted toward a slender figure in purple satin. Her hair was a red-gold halo, and her shoulders were erotically, *damnably bare.* A distinguished man with very carefully groomed silver hair slid a business card into her hand. Duncan knew the man was the owner of one of England's largest newspaper chains, but that didn't make him feel any better.

Scowling, he placed his glass on a nearby table and turned away. Even then Kara's soft laughter continued to torment him.

"What was that all about?" Nicholas Draycott, looking most distinguished in formal evening attire, eased an arm around his wife. He frowned as he watched Duncan stride off through the crowded ballroom.

"I believe your cousin has a burr under his saddle about our American guest."

"Which American guest, the ambassador or the senator?"

"Neither. The editor with the amber eyes. As you *well* know."

Nicholas frowned faintly. "I'd stay out of that, my

love. At least until this business with Duncan's brother is settled."

"I thought it *was* settled. Nearly settled, anyway."

"It won't be settled until Kyle is under lock and key, where he belongs," Nicholas said flatly.

"Then why didn't you cancel this wretched event?" Kacey said impatiently. "I noticed Duncan laying his black boxes all about the grounds. And don't think I didn't notice that you asked those two brawny friends of yours to arrive early tonight."

"You mean Dominic and Michael? I thought you enjoyed their company as much as I do."

"I *love* their company, you idiotic man. But they're not here for simply social reasons tonight. If there was real danger, you should have canceled."

Nicholas shook his head. "Simply isn't done, my love. Not without a specific threat. As far as we know, Kyle MacKinnon may be halfway to Timbuktu right now."

His wife snorted. "You and that damnable stiff upper lip." But there was a warm gleam in Kacey's eyes as she leaned against her husband's chest. "Sometimes, Nicholas, you really are so irritatingly—well, *English*."

"What a delightful compliment." The viscount smiled. " 'Burr under his saddle?' I'd say that describes Duncan's expression perfectly."

"He's unhappy, Nicholas. Both of them are."

The Englishman ran his hand over his wife's cheek, his eyes warm with tenderness. "You can't solve everyone's problems, my love, try though you might. When are you going to accept that?"

"Never, probably."

Nicholas chuckled. "Have I told you lately how very much I love you, Kacey Mallory Draycott?"

"Not in the last twenty-two minutes, you haven't." Kacey twined her arm through her husband's. "I wonder, Nicky . . ."

"Wonder what?"

"Whether anyone would notice."

"Notice what?"

"If we slipped away to the study." The viscountess reached up and straightened her husband's collar. In the process she managed to slide her body quite arrestingly against his. She whispered something in his ear.

"To hell with them if they do notice," Nicholas said thickly. Grabbing his wife's hand, he strode off toward the polished mahogany door at the far end of the room.

"But Northford House is the *perfect* showcase estate for *New Bride* magazine. Our tradition, breeding, and furnishings are impeccable." The man beside Kara bent closer, smiling down at her with very white teeth. "I'd be thrilled to discuss our plans with you in detail, Ms. Fitzgerald. Perhaps over dinner?"

Kara inched away. The Northford art collection had been sold years before, and the remaining pieces were all fakes. These days the roof at Northford House leaked, the stables were empty, and the present earl, the man who had just slid his hand along her backside, was desperate to launch a new hotel venture at Northford House. He was also up to his ears in debt to a very unforgiving set of lenders.

She certainly wasn't going to use *New Bride* to fuel his relentless real estate schemes. "I'll keep your card in case we have any future interest, Lord Northford."

"Simon, please." Cool fingers brushed Kara's bare shoulders. "I insist that you let me show you about Northford. Perhaps we could leave tonight. The evening seems to be winding down anyway."

Kara bit back a gasp of shock as his hand moved lower, fondling her thigh. "I'm sure your house is fascinating, but I doubt it has the style our readers have come to expect." Kara took an angry breath. "So bug off, bucko," she muttered as she strode away, her hands twitching with the urge to hurl the contents of her champagne glass in the earl's perfectly tanned face.

Kara breathed deeply, wanting desperately to be alone. The strain of her act was taking its toll, and her neck was knotted with tension. When she found a pair of French doors at the end of the long gallery, she lifted the heavy curtains and slipped outside.

Moonlight streamed onto the balcony as she tugged off her sandals and padded down the petal-covered staircase. The lawn was deserted, and her bare feet sank into the dewy grass. The conservatory glinted silver in the moonlight, catching her eye.

She fingered her gold evening bag. After three hours her makeup was probably a disaster. At the very least she could remedy that while she cooled off from the shock of Lord Northford's advances.

When she pushed open the glass door a dense perfume of roses, peonies, and potted lavender closed around her, and with a sigh she moved through a bar of moonlight and set her evening bag down on a long pine work table. Fortunately, the evening bag had been included in a box that had just come down from London. Kara didn't remember which advertiser had sent it, but it had come in very handy.

Sighing, she tossed her high-heeled sandals down beside a set of garden trowels and opened her bag. The moonlight would be adequate for a few quick repairs. But as she searched the cool satin interior, Kara's body tensed. Mist seemed to coil around her, and cold stabbed at her fingers.

She gasped as the bag fell. Something slid out of the purse. Square and white, it lay gleaming in the moonlight.

Kara didn't move. Danger coiled around her, and cold lapped at her hands. Trembling, she knelt on the flagstones.

The paper was part of a photograph torn from a larger scene, captured in grainy black and white. The main subject was Kara, her face pale and tense as she fled from the Calendish showrooms by the rear door.

Whoever had taken this photo had been nearby, watching her every move.

And Kara knew without a second contact that the person was Kyle. Even now she could feel the cold fury that emanated from the torn photo. Like a gray cloud it twisted in restless, angry shapes. She had felt that energy pattern before, around the photograph of Duncan left in the showcase in London.

Kara crossed her arms as fear pressed at her chest. Kyle's mark was everywhere about her. He had touched the bag in London, and he had left the trail of hatred over the torn photo.

He *knew*. He knew her gift and her sensitivity. He was toying with her, amusing himself yet again by giving pain.

And as Kara looked into the moonlight where angry visions twisted like trapped mist, she saw Duncan's death, awaiting him at the castle he loved.

She bit back a sob as the vision grew sharper. Cold washed over her, and she began to shiver.

First would come the wind, shrill from the north. Then a flame that cut through the night, ripping away the darkness.

"*No.*" She wanted to scream, but no sound came. She was trapped by her vision, a helpless captive to the certainty of a future she was desperate to deny.

At her feet the photograph blurred. She saw Kyle's evil imprint like a dim cloud of smoke that clung to her own features, a visible expression of all his hate.

The sight left her frozen.

Behind Kara the door grated open. Shivering, she seized a gardening trowel and raised it protectively before her chest.

Duncan stepped out of the shadows, a bottle of Dom Pérignon in one hand and two Murano flutes in the other. He frowned at the trowel she was holding. "What happened?"

"He won't stop. He won't go away, not ever." Kara's hands were trembling. "He's close even now."

Duncan set down the bottle and the glasses with a clatter. "You've *seen* him? Out here?"

A choked sound escaped Kara's throat as she shook her head.

"Then what is it?" Duncan pulled her against him as tremors worked their way through her. His strong hands were very gentle in her hair.

Kara let herself sink into his strength, drawing warmth from his powerful body. She was so cold. . . .

Danger in the touch.

"He—he knows, Duncan. About me. About what I did in London. He . . . left something in my bag."

Duncan cursed. His fingers tightened in her hair. "Are you hurt, *mo ghaol?* If it was a bomb, we have to—"

Kara shook her head numbly. "Not a bomb, a picture. A picture he took in London. While he was watching us. He left it to warn me."

Frowning, Duncan bent and studied Kara's pale features in the torn photo. "Damn him. He was so close that night." His jaw hardened as he shoved the photo in his pocket. Then he pulled Kara against him. "You're safe, Kara. He can't get anywhere inside the abbey, not with the surveillance I've set up. And I and those men of Sinclair's have personally vouched for every person we've let in tonight."

"He's out there. I can *feel* him."

A cold wind played through the open door, making her shiver. Without warning another image surfaced. Smoke against darkness and the roar of a motor. Kara clutched at Duncan as noise filled her head.

Death was what he wanted. Death was what he had always planned.

You first, Kara Fitzgerald. Kara could almost hear his voice, and the words he had said while he tore her photo in two. *Then comes my beloved brother.*

Shuddering, she closed her eyes, trying to blot out the images. "At . . . Dunraven. He'll wait for you there, Duncan. You're a sickness in his mind—like a hole with no bottom."

Duncan pressed her body against him. "He *won't* win, Kara. The rest are just threats. It's good strategy to frighten and confuse an adversary any way you can."

"But Dunraven—"

"Since he knows of your gift, then he knows you

can pick up his thoughts. He planted those images to frighten us away from Dunraven."

"Why, Duncan?"

His voice was hard. "So he can toy with us. So he can draw out the tension as long as possible. That's always been my brother's way."

His words came low and blurred, as if from a great distance. Kara felt a jacket slide over her bare shoulders. In an instant she was enveloped in Duncan's heat and his leather-and-citrus scent. Other impressions poured in too—his granite control, which warred with his rising fury. Even the fear for her safety that he had been trying to block from her all day.

She closed her eyes tightly. They were safe, she told herself. Kyle was trying to frighten her in order to get at Duncan. The abbey's granite walls rose around them, tall and impenetrable.

Suddenly Kara shivered as a new vision filled her head. Once, long ago, the abbey walls had not saved her. Terror had stalked her then too. Her throat tightened, burning. She felt cold waves rise up, choking her.

On the glass wall, shadows moved restlessly in the moonlight. Somewhere she heard the slap of waves and the creak of a wooden hull.

"Kara, talk to me."

Her fingers dug into Duncan's shoulders. Her lips opened, struggling to form words. Like a bag of bright gems, images spilled through her head, their sharp facets burning, cutting, always changing.

"Duncan, h-hold me."

"I'm here, *mo cridhe*. Right beside you."

But this time the words didn't help. Even the heat of Duncan's arms began to fade as another world closed in, trapping her with savage clarity.

Danger in the touch. Danger in the seeing.

No sound came as she cried out. No sound *could* come from her numbed throat as she fell into visions—memories—five centuries old.

And then the darkness exploded around her as she fell. . . .

The horses were winded as the ragged band wound over brooding hills and down into a cove that faced the setting sun. Wind lashed the waves into white foam beside the narrow pier, where the knight secured them passage on a boat that looked barely seaworthy. While the wind filled the sails, they watched the land of England grow small behind them and gave silent thanks as they put the sea between themselves and the sheriff's men.

At dawn a week later, the boat hove in between two pillars of rock that twisted up from the sea. Beyond, high on the brow of the hill, stood the walls of a castle.

"Home," the warrior said to the woman before him. His hands slid into her long hair, blown back by the wind. "It is not much, but its stone walls still stand. It will be our beginning."

Their fingers twined. For a moment Rowan de Beauclair looked as if he would say more. Then his eyes darkened as he felt Tamsyn's fingers circle his shoulders. The war-weary knight knew an ease then, a completeness that he had never felt before, and he vowed that this woman would never regret following him to these lonely, storm-lashed shores.

After days at sea, the boys were only too happy to climb the narrow path that led to the cliffs. Around them, the sea lay like blue glass frothed with foam, and the cries of sea birds welcomed them. With the specter of the sheriff gone, their good humor returned, and they were as wild as puppies, spilling into every corner of their new home.

"The walls are broad, my lord. The door is stout. It will be a fine demesne!"

"Will we have a room? A room of our own?"

Rowan nodded. "And land of your own to go with it." Shocked silence gave way to ragged cheers. A moment later they were gone, kicking up a cloud of dust as they raced off to survey this new domain ringed by heather-covered hills and sparkling seas.

The knight pulled his longbow from across his shoulders and slid it to the ground before him. His fingers idly smoothed the polished yew, and satisfaction filled him. He watched the boys race up the hill, kicking, tumbling, and laughing in the brilliant sunlight.

It was good, he thought. The gray walls were strong and would shelter his little band well.

It was then Rowan de Beauclair knew he had finally come home.

Tamsyn waited for him in the great hall. Moonlight streamed past her shoulder, and the pale light caught in her eyes and clung, filling her face with perfect beauty. She turned, her hair a fall of silver and gold over her simple dark kirtle. One day he would give her silks and satins, Rowan swore. For now he could give her only his love.

Her hand rose. Her fingers touched her heart, then moved to touch his.

I love you. He knew the gesture well by now.

"And I love you too, my little warrior. There is no joy you shall not know, no pleasure we shall not share; this I vow."

He pulled her to him. Her hands were as ungentle as his at their disrobing.

Beneath them rose the scent of pine needles, sage, and sweet spring grass, gathered within a cover of linen embroidered by Tamsyn's hand. He held her there, took her there, loved her well, as was his promise. Her back arched like a bow to his hand, and her long hair cascaded through his fingers as she rose against him, blind in her desire. When her tremors stilled, Rowan touched his heart, then moved his hand to rest between her breasts.

I love you.

Tamsyn sat up suddenly. It was the coldness that woke her, the stillness after the steady rhythm of his breath. Blinking, she saw he was gone. She stumbled to her feet, only to see a shadow moving over the stone floor.

De Beauclair stood before the window. His long arms were braced on both sides of the vaulted arch, and his head was bent low.

Darkness and light blended before her. She could feel

his warrior's pain, taste it, touch it where it lodged, deep in his scarred heart. So much pain he carried, so much need. Her only thought was how to heal him.

She moved over the cold stone in silence. Her arms slid about his hard waist and her lips touched his back.

She felt him stiffen and knew the force of his iron control. But she was wise. She fought him with the tools of a seasoned strategist, her lips to his rib, her hand at his tense shoulder.·

He sighed, a long, ragged sound. One calloused hand moved, gripping her wrist. "Whatever happens, I love you. Mark it well, Tamsyn, for I shall love no other, not now or ever again."

She slid against him, her answer in the flow of her body, endless warmth and utter giving.

When next they came, Rowan de Beauclair's words were all the more shocking for their brevity. "That is why you must go back. Now, before it is too late."

She trembled. She must have trembled. Her heart turned to glass as she felt the cold of the granite floor seep up into her veins. Go? He would send her away now, after all they had shared?

He answered, for their hearts were linked, and he could read the question in her soul. "I could never have let you go before, my little warrior." He knelt slowly, and his face was lost in pain. His hand rose and found the odd silver mark beneath her breast. He traced it gently, with infinite tenderness. "But now I have seen this, mignonne. And now I know who you are."

She shook her head, suddenly fierce. I will not go, the gesture said.

"You will." Again he knew her meaning, wordless though it was. "And you will go because of this mark, the mark of titled blood. I saw how it came to you."

She shook her head, her shoulders sharp with protest, hands fisted to drive away this new menace. But de Beauclair only smiled sadly and caught her fists, then pulled her close to receive a gentle kiss. "Barely ten you were, a bundle of dusty skirts and flying hair. Already wise beyond your years," he added gravely. "The Holy Land did that to many pilgrims."

Pallor touched Tamsyn's cheek; cold touched her heart. Did he know the secret of her past, locked up in her mind so long ago?

She pulled away, frightened. Images teased her eyes, never clear enough to understand or remember.

"You were enthralled by a singing bird of great beauty. In the chaos of the marketplace you were like an oasis of peace. When an assassin burst from behind me, sword raised, you saw him first. I remember your cry even now, as angry as it was afraid. It roused our brethren and sent me to one side, so that the blow missed me. But it struck you, my little love, when you threw yourself forward against me." He moved closer. His fingers traced the scar beneath her breast with gentle reverence. *"And there in the dusty marketplace you took a blow meant for me. Even then I loved you. Though you have changed much from that wide-eyed child, deep down I think I never forgot your face."* His hands moved gently over her cheeks, her lips, her throat.

"That blow was but the beginning, alas, and soon the streets rang to the clash of our swords. But we were taken unaware and outnumbered, and soon blood filled the streets. In the destruction that followed, brother was set from brother and mother from child. Beyond the smoke we could see the sultan's tents high on the hills, as red as blood. Women and children were put to sea in ships that rocked in a racing wind, and all too soon the end was upon us. I saw you last that day, torn from the gentle lord who was your father, lost from your loving mother. There was time for nothing else. The drum had sounded, and the infidels were upon us everywhere. There was no hope of winning, and the order for retreat was called. We lived to fight again, to cheer our victories again, but though your father scoured the earth for you, offering the highest reward, he never found you. Your father, the lord of Draycotte, never found you."

She trembled, her hands pressed to her ears. She did not want to hear, to know.

But Rowan de Beauclair, who loved her, pulled her hands away. *"You must hear me. The hardest is told, Tamsyn. Before your father left me to travel north, he gave* a last command. 'Find her,' he ordered. 'When I am gone, see that my fortune and lands go to her and to none other.' "

She was trembling, great, jerky movements that would not stop. He touched her hair, her eyes, her cheeks, his voice a caress. "And that is why you must go back. I had thought at first only to use you for revenge against my half brother, since William desired you so blindly. Now, knowing who you are, I cannot. Perhaps the old abbot is right, and my revenge should be left to God." He forced her to meet his eyes. "Come back with me. I will help you claim the name and honor that are yours."

She pulled away, her face furious. She crossed her arms, glared, and stamped her foot.

"So you will not go?" He chuckled, but the sound was sad. "You must. You'll have vast lands. Gowns of silk and enough ladies to satisfy every whim."

She tugged at her finger as if to pull off a ring. She clutched at her head as if to toss away a crown of gold. And then she reached down to the ashes in the long-dead fire.

The dark soot flowed between her fingers.

"Ashes—that is what they mean to you, rings and titles and gowns of silk?"

She nodded fiercely.

"But you must listen. Yours is a Draycotte's blood. I have the proof of it."

She smashed her hand upon a polished table, her cheeks red with fury. From her kirtle she drew a knife, its blade she dealt a cut to her thumb, which swelled with blood. The same she did to his, then pushed their flesh together until their blood flowed as one.

Her eyes were defiant as she pointed.

He laughed, a low, admiring sound. "Yes, our blood now runs together, mine made noble from yours. But the world is not so easily convinced." He turned away to the window, and his shoulders were very hard.

When he looked at her again, his face was as blank as the granite they stood upon. "Our intimacy changes nothing. Your birthright cannot be denied. What can this bleak castle have to compare with the pleasures you will find back home?"

A knowing look came into her eyes. Her lips curved as she caught his hand and pressed it to her breast.

"What pleasures," he murmured, understanding her answer even as she pulled him down to their pallet of pine needles and lavender. Her skin was warm and smooth against him.

"What pleasures indeed," he murmured. And then he gave himself up to the sharp, sweet pleasure of their joining.

It would be his very last, Rowan swore.

At dawn, the stranger arrived. His tunic was streaked with mud, his body weary from the road. His keen eyes narrowed as he took in the band of ragged boys who lounged at ease about the fire that burned in the great hall.

"Where is the laird?" he demanded harshly.

The tallest of the boys, a scar on his cheek, stood warily. "Who is it that asks?"

"A wanderer of the road, no more."

"I'll have a name to go with your face, or you will leave as quick as you come." The other boys rose, bristling like wary dogs.

The traveler fingered the cloak that rimmed his face. "No name will I give. What you need is to learn some manners, whelp." Before the boy could move, the traveler's bow was drawn, his arrow nocked, and the shaft sent whizzing to nail the boy's ragged tunic to the wooden shutter behind him.

Silence. Tense fear.

"What do you want, traveler?" The voice boomed from the far stairway, where Rowan stood.

"I seek the laird. But first I claim your name."

De Beauclair moved forward, a frown about his brow. "My name is not given easily, traveler. Only in friendship is it bought. And I don't believe I know you."

"Are you not Rowan de Beauclair, late of Acre?"

"Perhaps."

"The same de Beauclair who was son of Thomas, who was son of Gilbert?" The traveler threw back his cloak.

His great bow rested lightly in his strong fingers. "And do you not recognize the warrior who fought beside you on dusty hill and in desert sand?"

"Huw, is it truly you?" Rowan swept forward with a harsh cry.

"As truly as this old castle of yours still stands." The traveler's voice dropped grimly as their hands clasped. "Which it will not do for long, if your enemies have their wish."

Rowan brought his old friend hard against his chest. "Chaos to our enemies. May it be the long, clean road for us."

The Welshman nodded. Memories held them both for a moment, but there was too much joy in the reunion for the past to occupy them long. Laughing, Rowan shoved him toward the bench before the fire. "Sit, my friend. Tell me where you have fared. While we talk, I will see you well fed and with all the wine you can swallow." Rowan's eyes darkened. "Then I have someone for you to meet."

The Welshman's eyes narrowed, keen with knowledge. "The woman who rides with you. She who has no voice."

Rowan stiffened. Shadows crept to the edge of his mind. "Have they found us so soon?"

Outside, a fox barked in the night. The wind caught the sound and carried it high and shrill, until it echoed like wild laughter.

"They came by the score with William at their head, may hell claim his soul." The Welshman sat hunched, hands held out to the fire. On his hard face danced light and shadow, just as Rowan had seen before many a battle.

"But how did William discover we were headed here?"

"The information did not come lightly, I assure you." The Welshman's face was grim. "At tournament and market he searched for any who claimed friendship with you. That friendship was their betraying, for they were thrown into his dungeon until he plucked the truth out of them with his sweet mercy."

"I'll kill him."

"You cannot," Huw said grimly. "He sleeps in fear now, guarded by more men than even you can subdue."

The traveler stared into the fire, his fingers brushing the polished bow that lay across his lap. "And there's more to be told, I fear."

Rowan's body tensed. "More? Even William could not do more than this."

His old friend laughed darkly. "Far worse. Once he knew your route, he sent his men galloping to the north. Any family whose dwelling lay on your path was brought back in irons. A fortnight hence, he will drive them all to the square and watch them burn."

"All this because of me." De Beauclair's voice was tortured. "I can't have this, Huw. I must go back."

"He'll kill them just the same and add you to their lot," the Welshman said bitterly. "A wolf's heart does not change, only grows blacker by the day." He spit into the fire, which fizzled and hissed as if the very devil stood among them. Around them the boys watched in anxious silence, worried for loved ones and friends left behind, for innocents who would pay the price of their friendship.

In one sharp movement Rowan sprang to his feet. "We go, Huw. Tomorrow at dawn. If you are still with me, we'll have a chance."

The Welshman sighed. "I go. At your right hand or your left, as long as I am whole, though my blood tells me it will not be much longer with the trap that William has laid." He looked at his old friend and something slipped into his eyes. "What about the woman?"

"She stays." It was a harsh order that brooked no protest. "She is highborn, and I had thought to bring her back to claim her birthright. But I see now that she must stay here, safe, until William has been conquered." Rowan stared into the fire. "You see, my old friend, she is Lord Draycotte's daughter."

"Arduaine?" The Welshman made a sound of surprise. "The little girl who saved your life in the marketplace?"

"Just so." Around him the boys moved uneasily, shocked by this revelation. The woman in tattered clothes who had ridden with them, strong and uncomplaining through the long days of travel, was in truth the daughter of Draycotte's lord?

"William would like nothing more than to bind her to

him through marriage. Aye, there would be no safety in her return." The Welshman rubbed his jaw awkwardly. "When do you mean to tell her?"

Behind them came a rustling on the stone staircase. Slowly the boys moved aside to make way for the silent figure in a flowing cloak and tattered gown, her unbound hair falling almost to her feet.

"Arduaine." Rowan fell to one knee before her, head bowed. "My lady."

She lifted him up, her eyes as clear and sharp as glass.

Only then did he realize she was wearing her traveling cloak and the soft leather boots he had given her the day before. His brow furrowed. "You do not go, my lady. You stay, just as I ordered."

There was such fury on her face that the room seemed to fill with her protests. She stamped her foot.

When he did not move, her palm rose, and she slapped him full across the cheek.

A muscle flashed at his jaw, but still he did not move. "I am yours to obey, my lady. In all things but in this," he said tightly.

She moved close. Slowly she raised his fingers to her lips.

But he did not yield. "You stay. My answer will not change."

Her face turned red in the firelight. She spun about, her cloak tossed high. A coin, very old and very worn, went flying from her fingers across the cold floor. And then she flung herself outside into the night.

The Welshman shook his head. "A woman such as that is hard to lose."

De Beauclair did not answer, bending to the floor to pick up the old coin that had become his good-luck piece. "Aye, a remarkable woman. All the more reason that William must never have her."

He found her in the darkness, pacing the walls that overlooked the valley. Her shoulders were stiff with cold when he moved behind her and pulled her close.

She fought. Like a cornered fox, she fought with angry fists and hard, shuddering breath. But no sound came from *her throat, not even then, when she felt her heart so near to breaking.*

"I'll be back," he said, even as he struggled to hold her still.

She shook her head wildly.

"Once William is gone, you'll go home again and claim the title that is yours, as Arduaine of Draycotte."

Her only answer was to grip his hand, where a heavy, unfaceted sapphire lay embedded in gold. With tears burning down her cheeks, she fell to her knees before him, as he had done to her. Her head sank. She pressed her cheek against his leg.

"No." It was a harsh sound. He pulled her up with savage fingers and locked her to him. "It is your name. If you do not claim it, then I must claim it for you."

She looked up, and her eyes carried a universe of words that she could not speak. Slowly her hand fell. She cupped her stomach protectively, then took his hand and placed it over hers.

"A child. Dear God, a child! I would give my very life to see it done." With a great shuddering that rocked his powerful form, de Beauclair moved away from her. His face grew grave as he spoke. "But it changes nothing. You must stay and I must go. If you think to fight, I will lock you in the castle storeroom until I'm gone."

She watched him, a hundred angry words flashing in her eyes. When she saw he would not yield, all the fight drained from her. Her shoulders sagged and she swayed, her hands reaching out blindly.

With a curse Rowan caught her to his chest. His face was harsh with need and pain as he carried her through the dancing torchlight and up the stone steps to the room that faced the sea.

One night.

It was all they had. But love taught them strength and yielding and endless grace beneath the moonlight. He bared her, worshipped her, claimed her, and she did the same to him. Their love and need knew no bounds, and their passion no restraint. Her hands became her voice, pressed to every rib and muscle, each movement a haunting dialogue of desire.

They raced the rising of the sun, as if their fevered touch could hold back time. In the clouded darkness it almost seemed as if they had succeeded. -

When the first glow of dawn brushed the sandy cove, Rowan's dark head lay unmoving on the pallet, his hand locked across his lady's waist. He had given her his seed again and again that night and knew that she would bear his child. That thought brought him peace when nothing else could, and his dreams, as he slept, were not of death and vengeance but of a laughing child with her mother's keen violet eyes.

The cooing woke him.

The sound fell in the deep stillness. Slowly Rowan opened his eyes, yawning pleasurably and stretching weary muscles. A dove perched on the stone sill as he threw out one arm, searching for the warmth he had felt beside him throughout the long night.

But he found emptiness. He sprang to his feet, grabbing his tunic, his heart filled with dread. Only then did he look down to see sunlight glinting off an object left carefully before the door.

It was his gold coin, retrieved after Arduaine had flung it the night before, and returned with passionate kisses during their last bout of love. He had sworn her to carry it always, as long as she was by his side.

Now she had left it for him.

Rowan ran for the door, his desperate shouts ringing sad and hollow through the empty rooms.

In his heart he knew he was already too late.

Arduaine of Draycotte heard the shouts echo down the valley and drift over the water to the ship that headed south toward all she hated and feared. Her face paled, but she did not flinch. Her fingers tightened on the wooden rail.

Beside her Huw frowned. "I do this against all instinct and honor," he said flatly. "I do this because I know it is the one way to save him. If he returns and William gets *hold of him, Rowan de Beauclair will never see the light of day again." The old bowman sighed. "With your lineage you will be safe, my lady. I will see that it is so. Once your name is restored and the sheriff's power is checked, I will guide you back to Dunraven."*

But the Welshman's face was hard, and he crossed himself as he spoke.

Kara heard the shouts echo through her head, ringing down through the centuries. She sat up sharply, fighting waves of fear and confusion. Her throat was blocked, and not a sound would come from it.

So much loss. So much joy that had run through her fingers like sand . . .

She felt tears stream down her face, the tears of another woman in another time as she stood resolute and unflinching, her face to the wind while the man she loved cried out behind her. Then her own cry came, choked and desperate.

Twenty-six ～

Duncan MacKinnon's face was wet with sweat as he caught Kara in his arms. Nothing seemed to penetrate her unfocused, frightened eyes. All because of that damned note in her evening bag, more of Kyle's bloody work.

He muttered a curse. "Don't fold on me now, Fitzgerald."

He rubbed her cheek tensely, watching the pallor of her face. Damn it, why didn't she answer?

"Now, Kara. *Talk* to me."

Muted and blurred, the words trickled down into the deep waters where Kara rocked. She remembered the creak of sails. She remembered a hoarse cry.

"Can you hear me?"

There was something about that voice. Something familiar. Recognition prickled, making her sigh and ease closer, lips parted and searching.

She saw eyes like water, bluer than anything she had ever known. She saw hands, calloused hands. She saw a face with power.

Kara traced the proud Celtic cheekbones outlined beneath sun-bronzed skin. Familiar. So familiar.

So beloved.

Like the lover she had never met, except in the still, dark hours of night when she summoned up fantasies to mend a broken heart. Her body rose, fingers threading through the dark silk of his hair, as she pulled him down to meet her kiss.

Heat in his touch. Heat in his groan. Heat in the fingers that circled her waist and pulled her closer.

". . . finally awake."

This time Kara made the heat, and it was her fingers that circled Duncan's waist in a desperate search for his naked skin.

Their breaths mingled. Cloth pulled free, and she found muscled flesh. Touching him felt like forever, like the time before the dreams when the world had been young and whole.

She heard a hard curse. Felt hands buried in her hair, lips on her burning skin.

"Kara. *Mo cridhe* . . ."

Suddenly she remembered. The slap of waves carrying her away from the man she loved. The pain of that loss was like a fresh wound. Something had triggered the dark memories. She closed her eyes, feeling Duncan's hard arms around her.

"What *happened*, Kara?"

She swallowed. "I'll answer when you tell me about Kyle."

"Damn it, don't play games with me."

"The truth is no game. I need to *know*, Duncan." Otherwise history would be repeated and she would lose this hard, stubborn, honorable man again.

"Forget about Kyle." Duncan's voice was harsh. "I'm interested in *you* right now."

Carefully Kara sat up and pushed to her feet.

"What in God's name are you doing?"

"Standing up. Cleaning myself off." Kara took a deep breath, watching moonlight glint off the champagne bottle and crystal flutes on the nearby table. "I'm . . . fine."

"Like hell you are. I was here when you touched that piece of paper, remember? I saw how your face went white and you fell to the floor."

Kara swallowed. "He wanted to frighten me, and he succeeded. Your refusal to tell me what's been going on doesn't help."

Kara stood for a long time playing with a fragile glass goblet, unaware of how the moonlight turned her hair silver.

But Duncan was aware. Painfully aware. Certain parts of him ached in ways that would once have seemed unimaginable. "You want me to tell you? Lieutenant Sinclair wanted your help. Andrew Calendish has been found—his body, that is. Two other bodies have also been found. Sinclair wanted you to use your gift of touch to see what clues you could pick up about the other bodies. I told him no."

"Why?"

"Because I'm not about to let them send you into a morgue to touch a couple of corpses. Damn it, I've seen how sensitive you are. I know what that would do to you."

Kara shook her head in denial. "Andrew Calendish is dead?"

Duncan nodded grimly. "I won't apologize for keeping it from you. I hoped my brother was finally in Sinclair's net and that we could put this horror behind us." He laughed harshly. "I'm afraid I was wrong. Again."

"Is that why you're telling me now?"

"I'm telling you because you have a right to know this nightmare isn't finished—maybe not even close to being finished. If I had any sense, I'd send you back to the States on the next plane out. Only you wouldn't be safe there either. And until Kyle is caught, I want you where I can keep an eye on you." He moved toward her, a column of shadow in the moonlight. "Now, tell me what happened out here and why you were totally beyond reach."

"Just leave it alone, MacKinnon. Leave it buried." Kara's voice was taut.

"What if I can't? What if it's gone too far, Kara? Damn it, I need to know everything about you or I can't keep you safe. And the thought of failing is scaring the *hell* out of me."

"You're good at taking on other people's responsibilities, aren't you?" Kara frowned. "Four years at the London School of Economics, flouting a family tradition that called for Oxford. Then off to the Sorbonne, followed by a stint in the Royal Marines. After that a few pleasure trips to Asia and the Mediterranean." Her eyes narrowed. "But that was work, wasn't it? A cover for the kind of work you do with Snow Sedgwick."

"Did," Duncan corrected.

Kara's eyes shimmered, lit by moonlight. "You *can't* stop taking on other people's problems. It won't heal the wound inside you, the guilt that you carry because of what your brother has done."

Duncan's jaw hardened. "I asked my questions first."

"Too bad."

He slid through the moonlight, one hand rising to her hair. Tingles raced along her spine.

"What are you doing?'

"Testing vulnerability and defense perimeters. Exploring the terrain for friendly shelter." His fingers circled her waist and drew her against him. Kara felt an unbearable sense of safety enfold her.

"Damn you, Duncan, I—" His mouth cut her off, hot and persuasive. She shivered at the sharp sweetness of his tongue on hers. She felt the jutting outline of his arousal, and her own body responded in a rush of liquid yielding.

"Now tell me what happened out here," he demanded.

Kara stiffened. "You have no right."

"I have *every* right. Your safety's in question, or hadn't you noticed."

"Then our deal is off, MacKinnon. There will be no photography at Dunraven Castle. I am no longer your concern."

Duncan's jaw was hard. "Until Kyle is caught, you eat, sleep, and breathe within my sight. He's targeted you too, Kara. That's what that torn photo meant."

"Let me go," Kara said hoarsely. "Let us *both* go. It's too intense. Touching you is going to tear me apart."

"Then it will tear us both apart. I'm not letting you go. Kyle can't win, not this time. I know how he thinks, and together we'll keep one step ahead of him. We'll start by going to Dunraven, since that's the one place where I'll have an edge. It's *my* home turf, and I've made a few changes that are going to surprise him."

Kara looked away, her face silver in the moonlight. "I don't know if I can help you anymore, Duncan. I'm seeing too much. Every time you touch me, I lose a little more of myself. And all the time I feel the danger around us. Maybe I *should* go back to London." She took a deep breath. "What if there's something there that Sinclair's people missed?"

Duncan stood before her. His body was rigid, but his touch on her cheeks was very gentle. "You're *not* going to open yourself to that, Kara. Not now, when you've just told me how much more sensitive you've become." He took a harsh breath. "Sometimes I feel I've lived my whole life just waiting to meet you. You say that taking responsibility for others is a habit with me, and maybe you're right. I know it's true concerning you. Almost as if I *didn't* once before and ..." He shook his head. "Forget it. None of this makes any sense. Let's go back. I shouldn't have stayed away so long."

In case Kyle's watching.

In case he's making a move right now.

Kara heard the unsaid words as she studied Duncan's handsome face.

"But when this bloody party is finished, I'm going to take you in my arms and make you shiver."

Kara caught a ragged breath at his erotic promise. She felt heat twist through her while desire pooled sweet and dark between her thighs.

"There's no part of you I won't touch, no pleasure we won't taste tonight." Duncan pulled her close, and she felt the throb of his pulse, the hot stab of his manhood at her belly. "I'll go crazy if I don't have you tonight, *mo ghaol*." There was an edge of desperation in his voice as he bit the tender lobe of her ear with exquisite savagery. "And my damned brother will be the *last* thing on your mind when I drive you high and send you shuddering over the edge." His hands hardened as he heard a breathy little sigh escape her lips. "Now, come on, damn it. Before I forget all my promises and take you right here on that damned bag of peat."

Rough Gaelic phrases rippled off his tongue as he caught her hand and hauled her back into the crowded abbey.

"And this is Michael Burke and his wife, Kelly."

Candlelight and gleaming chandeliers shed a golden glow around the small group gathered outside the abbey's great hall. The celebration continued in full force as Nicholas Draycott turned to introduce Kara to a dark-haired man with penetrating eyes. His wife was luminous and very pregnant in a gown of imperial Chinese silk. "Michael Burke lives just to the north of Draycott. He's been a querulous neighbor for years, but the truth is, I only put up with him because of his lovely wife."

"That's Lord Sefton to you, Nicholas. And as for being querulous, I might say the same of you," Nicholas's old friend said easily. "It's only your phenomenal wine selection that brings me over here at all." As if by magic Marston appeared with a bottle of perfectly chilled Krug. "See what I mean?"

Impassive as always, Marston refilled their glasses. Lady Sefton declined, patting her stomach, and took a mineral water instead.

"And this is Lord Ashton, owner of La Trouvaille vineyards. His wife, Cathlin, is a wine expert."

Kara had heard of the up-and-coming vineyard in France. She smiled at the darkly tanned man standing beside Nicholas. "A pleasure, Lord Ashton."

"Call me Dominic."

Kara took the strong, calloused hand that enveloped hers in a welcoming grip. "I know your wines well. They have remarkable complexity. A team effort, I take it?"

Dominic Montserrat, Lord Ashton, smiled. "*She* does the grumbling and I do the worrying. We make a perfect pair."

His wife laughed softly. "We make a terrible pair, Dominic, and you know it. Marston claims that our wines have no *choice* but to be complex."

"Your wine is extraordinary," Kacey Draycott interrupted. And you can't be worrying all the time. You both look far too happy."

She was right, Kara thought. Lord Ashton and his wife were tanned and fit, and their fingers seemed to find any excuse to brush and entwine. Their obvious happiness left a hollowness in her chest.

"A good thing, too," Cathlin said with a ripple of laughter. "Our baby is due four months after yours, Kelly."

Once again Marston appeared, this time proffering a glass of mineral water with a slice of lime to the beaming Lady Ashton. "What a dream you are, Marston. Are you *certain* you wouldn't consider relocating to the south of France?"

"You are most kind, my lady, but I am quite content here at the abbey." For a moment a smile played around his lips. "I have every intention of keeping your offer in mind, however. No doubt it will prove useful in future negotiations when his lordship is being his usual stubborn self."

Nicholas smiled ruefully as the old retainer melted back into the crowd. That night Marston's immaculate dark jacket was coupled with a pair of neon purple jogging shoes. "He manages us all, that man. I haven't the slightest idea what we would do without him."

"You do seem to have a knack for acquiring extraordinary helpers," Kara said. "I met your assistant earlier."

"Assistant?" Nicholas studied her blankly.

"He was standing down by the moat. A very shrewd man, I think. Even that cat he had with him seemed shrewd. Do you know, I actually had the feeling the two of them could see right inside my head."

"Did you indeed?" The viscount's eyes narrowed. "By the moat, you say. And there was a cat?" He rubbed his jaws. "When exactly did you—"

He was interrupted by his wife, who calmly raised her glass. "The night would not be complete without a toast, Nicky." She smiled mistily. "To the reunion of old friends and the making of new ones."

With a clinking of glasses, the toast was drunk, and Marston reappeared as if by magic with another bottle of Krug.

"By the way, Ms. Fitzgerald, remember to have Duncan show you the longbow at Dunraven when you visit," Nicholas advised. "It is an incredible family relic, made of polished yew, six feet long and probably six hundred years old. Ask Duncan about the legend that goes with it, too, since those wild MacKinnons have legends for everything."

Kara glanced across the room. A red-haired woman in a dress that looked as if it had been painted on had just laid her hand on Duncan's sleeve. At the same instant, as if aware of Kara's glance, Duncan looked up.

Even ten feet away Kara felt the heat of his eyes, the restless hunger barely contained in his rigid body.

To her embarrassment, Kara found she had to clear her throat before she could speak. "Duncan hasn't told me much about his family. Although I've done a great deal of research on Dunraven Castle and Rose Cottage, I've never heard about the longbow."

Nicholas Draycott laughed. "Duncan claims that belief in family legends is a recessive Celtic gene. You already know about the legend of first night at Rose Cottage, I take it?"

"Whoever spends the first night of their honeymoon at Dunraven's Rose Cottage will never be split asunder." Kara nodded, intensely aware of Duncan's gaze upon her. "Yes, I've heard the legend. It's one of the reasons why I chose Dunraven for our honey-moon issue. Who can resist that kind of magic?"

"It's an extraordinary place," Nicholas agreed. "All mist and water and the most amazing roses. Some even predate those here at the abbey. I really must look into that some day, along with what the old abbey records have to say about the longbow." He smiled ruefully. "The thing of it is, my medieval Latin is not exactly up to snuff."

His comment produced all the interest he had hoped for, and soon he was retelling the favorite story of his boyhood. "The Draycotts—spelled with an *e* then—had been going through rather a difficult time. In a revolt against the crown they had taken the losing side, and as a result their lands were turned over to the church. The current Lord Draycott decided to repair to France rather than suffer the sight of his beloved keep converted into a cloister."

The viscount's eyes took on a faraway gleam as he fell into the familiar rhythms of the old tale. "Many of his men were let go at that time, scattered to the four winds. Among them was a wandering knight of exceptional skill with the bow. No one ever knew the man's name or lineage, only that he had returned with Draycott after saving him from an infidel's blade during one of the later Crusades. Some claimed the warrior was the natural-born son of a king, while others argued with equal force that he was just a schemer. The only truth we may ever know is this: wherever he went, this knight gathered strays about him like a shepherd his lambs. Orphaned children they were, tattered and hungry, some under sentence as outlaws. It was even said that he took to the green-wood himself, after a disagreement with the local sheriff."

Kara's breath caught. "Sheriff? As in—"

Nicholas laughed. "Oh, not Nottingham and his Robin of Locksley, though as boys Duncan and I spent many a happy hour convincing ourselves that it was so. No, this was a different man—a real man, not a legend. Even today the abbey contains receipts written by his own hand for things like damask cloth, wines, and spices. But the sheriff harried him without end, and fate finally carried him to the far north, where even the sheriff's men could not follow. It is said he and his ragged band finally found a home in the great, brooding halls of a Norman keep by the sea. Dunraven, of course, or what we know today as Dunraven. The only gift he took from his lord when he left with a great longbow made of fine Draycott yew. The MacKinnons say that he broke it by his own hand, refusing to let it serve any other lord but Draycott." Nicholas shook his head. "The Draycotts have always held that there was a woman—a Draycott woman—who was somehow involved, but we have never found any records to support the idea."

Nicholas looked at the circle of enthralled faces and shrugged, suddenly self-conscious to be telling a story so rich in boyhood fantasy. "Duncan can tell it better than I, no doubt. It has something to do with that dashing brogue he affects when it suits him."

Kara felt goosebumps play up her spine. Bits of a vision danced before her, keen images of singing arrows and the rich green shadows of a vast wood.

And of a knight without name or honor.

At that moment someone took her elbow. She frowned when she saw the pale, sweating face of Lord Northford beside her. Lost in her romantic revery, she had missed his question. "I beg your pardon?"

"I said, Ms. Fitzgerald, that you shouldn't be so shy among friends. After all, your American friend, Geoffrey Hampton, has already told the tale all over London. You can't hope to deny it."

Kara blinked. "What tale?"

Northford stopped Marston as he passed and swept up a glass of champagne, ignoring Kara's question. "By the way, this is an extraordinary evening, Draycott. Once again you manage to outdo us all. The roses are especially fine, I believe." He sipped the Krug appreciatively, aware of the curiosity building around him.

"*What* tale?" Kara demanded unsteadily. "What has Geoffrey Hampton been saying?"

Lord Draycott frowned at Northford. "I think you had better be more specific, Northford."

There was an unpleasant gleam in Northford's pale eyes as he lifted his glass in mock celebration. "Why, that Ms. Fitzgerald and Lord Dunraven have entered into a, shall we say, intimate business arrangement. Fabulously romantic, don't you agree?" he said icily.

"I doubt we're interested in hearing any more gossip, Northford." Nicholas's voice was decidedly cool.

Northford's eyes glittered with malicious triumph. "It's far from gossip. Hampton heard it himself. It seems that our prim Ms. Fitzgerald has offered to set her honeymoon issue at Dunraven in exchange for comprehensive services rendered. Entirely comprehensive, you understand. Rather desperate of her, wouldn't you say?"

Scowling, Nicholas Draycott moved toward Northford. "We've heard enough, Northford. It's time that you—"

"It's time to set the record straight, I see," a deep voice growled.

Kara felt a strong arm slide around her waist.

"Do excuse me, Northford." Calmly Duncan shouldered the man aside. "Kara and I were waiting until the end of the evening to make our announcement." He looked down and brushed Kara's cheek, his expression patently intimate. "You see, everything has happened so fast that we've barely had time to catch our breath. But I'm very happy to announce that Kara has done me the infinite honor of agreeing to become my wife. We're planning to rush through the formalities so that the wedding can take place at Dunraven. You will all be invited, of course."

Silence struck the group. Someone cleared his throat. Northford muttered angrily and tossed down the rest of his champagne. As he did, Duncan slapped him hard on the back, causing him to sputter. "There, Northford. Now you have the truth." His voice hardened. "Of course, no one with eyes in his head could look at Kara and believe she needed to offer 'services' to gain whatever she wanted." Once again his hand fell hard on Northford's back. "I suggest it might be *healthy* if you were to remember that."

"That's not what Hampton told me," Northford snarled.

"Hardly surprising," Duncan said silkily. "Hampton is just as great a fool as you are."

"Damn you, Dunraven, I—"

Nicholas's two friends moved discreetly to Northford's side. Without a word each took an arm and began ushering him toward the door.

Kara's face was sheet-white in the wake of Northford's viciousness. Duncan's arm around her waist tightened as her knees began to shake.

Like a ghost, Marston reappeared, two filled glasses on his tray. "For you, Lord Dunraven. And for Ms. Fitzgerald. With my warmest congratulations."

Duncan smiled slowly. "Thank you, Marston." He handed one glass to Kara, then took the other. "My toast to you, my love," he said huskily, bringing his hand under hers, so that their arms were linked. *"B'i sin reul ó an oidhche dhoilleir."* He brought his glass slowly to her mouth. "You are a star on a dark night."

The room, the guests, all were forgotten. Blindly, Kara tilted her glass and drank.

Around her the delighted congratulations began. She felt her hand being pumped and her shoulder being patted, but all she could think of was, *why?* Why had Duncan made such a rash statement before his friends? There could be only one answer, of course. Once again he was taking responsibility for other people's problems. Kara was shocked by the pain in the realization—and even more shocked by how much she had wanted Duncan's proposal to be real.

She cleared her throat. "Excuse me. I need some air," she said unsteadily.

Duncan's fingers tightened as he studied her face. "We'll go outside together. I'll show you the old roses."

"Don't fall for *that* line," Lord Ashton said, grinning.

But Kara pulled her hand from Duncan's fingers. "You stay with your friends. I need some time outside. By myself," she finished, turning away.

"Kara, you don't—"

Beside Duncan, Marston bent close and cleared his throat. "I'm very sorry to bother you, Lord Dunraven, but you have a call."

Duncan frowned at Kara's retreating figure. "A call?"

"From London." Marston's voice fell. "Most important, I believe."

Duncan ran his hand irritably through his hair. "From Lieutenant Sinclair?"

"Yes."

After another black look at Kara's back, Duncan turned to Nicholas. "Keep an eye on her, will you, Nicky?"

"My pleasure. Anything else I can do?"

Duncan slanted a last look at Kara. "I'll let you know after I speak with Sinclair," he said flatly.

"What do you mean, you haven't *caught* him yet?"

Duncan stood in the abbey's study, telephone gripped in his hand. His black tie was loosened, his jacket slung over a nearby chair, and his face rigid. "What's gone wrong, Sinclair? You said it was just a matter of *hours*."

"Calm down, MacKinnon. We were alerted to a man attempting to purchase receiving devices in Reading. We've narrowed the location. Now we have to go in flat by flat, and that could take some time."

"You don't have time," Duncan said grimly. "Kyle will be no more than a speck in the crowd by the time you move in."

"We can handle our own business," the officer said icily. "All *you* need to worry about is alerting us if Kyle tries to contact you."

"He already has. He sent a picture snapped at Calendish's showroom in London. It was left inside Ms.
Fitzgerald's evening bag."

"I'll send someone over to collect it. It may be
something we can use."

"Don't bother. Kara has already picked up everything of value. Kyle gets nasty when he's cornered,
and he's trying to frighten her, damn him. He also
wants to keep us away from Dunraven for as long
as possible."

"How do you know that?"

"Just accept it, Sinclair. Kara doesn't make
mistakes."

The security officer was quiet for a moment. "Have
you finished your preparations at Dunraven?"

"Yes. We leave tomorrow."

"You're not actually planning to go ahead with this
ridiculous idea of a photo session at Dunraven, are you?"

"I see no reason to cancel it. Not until *your* people
get something definite on Kyle."

Sinclair's voice hardened. "You and Ms. Fitzgerald
will do whatever we tell you to do."

"Until you make some headway in finding my
brother, I'll behave *exactly* as I think fit." With that,
Duncan slammed down the phone.

A light tap sounded at the door. "Sorry to intrude,
Duncan," Nicholas said dryly, "but I was turning off
the lights after showing Kara upstairs. I couldn't help
hearing you on the telephone. In fact, the whole
house probably heard you."

"Sorry." Duncan jammed a hand through his hair.
"That was Sinclair. More problems."

"Good God, not another bomb threat."

"No, Kyle is on the run. Sinclair tracked him to
Reading, but Kyle will be gone by the time the police
move in. Every move of the game has been Kyle's
so far, damn him." Duncan looked out at the moat.
"He wants to see me sweat, Nicholas. It's one of his
great pleasures."

Draycott sat down slowly. "Why? Why does he
hate you so much?"

"Because I killed our mother."

"Rubbish, man. That's *not* the way it happened!"

"No?" Duncan's eyes darkened. "It was my fault we were out in that boat. It was my fault she went over. In a very real sense, Kyle is right to hate me as he does."

"Your mother went into the water trying to save you, Duncan. She knew the risks and accepted them. If Kyle has turned into a bitter, cold-blooded killer with a score of brutal deaths to his name, it's no fault of *yours*, damn it!"

"No? Maybe not. But I'll never know for certain, will I? It's almost funny, you know. When Kyle and I were young, we were fascinated by that story of the old longbow at Dunraven. We were going to be heroes when we grew up and redress all the world's wrongs." Duncan turned away, jamming his hands into his pockets. "Guilt is a habit that's hard to break, Nicholas. Guilt about Kyle. An older one, too."

"What do you mean, an older one? You're not making a lot of sense, Duncan."

"Hardly surprising, since I can't make much sense of it myself. It's a feeling more than anything else. It's waking up shuddering, gripped by a cold fear that I've overlooked something very important." He slapped the cold marble of the fireplace.

"We all have nightmares, Duncan. After Thailand, I wasn't sure I could ever believe in anything again. But I did it—with Kacey's help."

"He might have been different if our mother had lived," Duncan said harshly.

"Her death didn't turn *you* into a killer. He chose, Duncan. He made himself what he is."

Duncan muttered something in Gaelic. "The long clean road or the short dirty one," he translated grimly. "How, Nicholas? How could a brother of my blood, a MacKinnon, do such things as Kyle has done?"

There was no answer.

But Duncan had never expected one.

Twenty-seven ⌒

Kara was inside the moat house, close enough to hear his step on the balcony. She turned slowly, her face pale in the light of the single candle beside the bed. Duncan's body hardened instantly at the sight of her. She wore a long silk sheath that shone the color of the heather that bloomed by Dunraven's south wall. Her shoulders were bare, devastatingly bare. Every movement sent silk rippling, clinging to the fullness of breast and thigh.

He wanted to tear the silk into tiny pieces.

He wanted her panting and desperate beneath him.

Duncan's hand tightened on the brass door handle. He shouldn't be there, he thought, not with the fury that burned in his blood. He would hurt Kara if he stayed—if not physically, then in the angry chaos of his uncontrolled thoughts.

Tonight there was no way for him to be a gentleman, not when he needed to be clenched in her heat.

Candlelight shimmered. Shadows clung lovingly to her satin skin.

Duncan cursed. "I'm going back inside. This—" He raised a hand. It swept over her, the room, then became a fist. "*This* is a mistake," he finished harshly.

She moved closer, all moonlight and dreams, wrapped in a fragrance of orange petals, sandalwood, and summer woods. "Why?"

Duncan's jaw was granite in the candlelight. "Be-

313

cause, feeling what I do, needing what I need, I'll hurt you," he said bluntly.

Kara studied him gravely, and again the light became his enemy, challenging his restraint by painting her throat and cheek and lip an earthy gold. His body strained, hard beyond enduring, and the helplessness that had goaded him all evening sent his temper ten degrees higher.

Kara looked at the cool white linen of his shirt, but he did not move. Memories of the afternoon tormented him. The low hiss of silk as she approached him made his fingers ache.

And still he did not move.

Her hand rose and hovered just in front of his chest. Focused inward, her eyes began to darken.

She was reading him.

"*Don't*, Kara."

Her hand moved, searching the heat and energy that swirled around him. "You're angry."

"I'm angry."

"You're tense, worried."

"Bloody tense." Duncan took a step back. A tufted leather ottoman blocked his retreat.

Kara moved closer. "You're taking on other people's problems again. I'm going to have to do something about that, MacKinnon."

Her hand sank against the crisp white linen. Her breath caught sharply.

"Feel it, Kara? You can see how I want you, all the things I'll do. Not gentle," he said hoarsely. "Not slow or careful." He muttered in Gaelic.

Kara moved another inch. He was trapped between the heavy ottoman and a hot vision of silk and naked skin. She found a silver stud, her eyes never leaving his.

The stud came free. Duncan felt her hands tremble.

"It will solve nothing." His voice was a stranger's.

"It will solve everything that can be solved. Maybe that's all there is."

Another fastening slid free.

Kara's hand eased onto his naked chest. Cursing,

Duncan captured her palm, wanting to pull it to his mouth, wanting to bite the soft flesh beneath her thumb and hear her moan.

Her eyes were smoke and amber, the color of the polished bow he had loved ever since he was big enough to walk to the glass case where it was stored at Dunraven.

"Touch me, Duncan. Now."

Touch me.

She knew what it meant. Damn it, she knew what just one minute of intimate contact would do to them both.

Touch me. His hands clenched at the thought, his breath turning harsh. She would be a stormy sea at dawn, all light and rippling color. She would slide around him, rock against him, feed fantasies too dark to have a name.

Touch me.

"No." He gripped her wrist. Anger sheened his eyes. "Before, it was different. Before, I wasn't afraid I could keep you safe. Before, I was in control."

"And now . . . you're not?"

"And now I'm not."

Heat clung to her skin. Challenge glinted in her eyes. "I'm not afraid of you, Duncan."

"You *should* be. Damn it, nobody's ever made me feel so hot. So . . . needy." He scowled at her wrist, wrapped inside his fingers. Too much, he thought. Too much silk and breathless lips. Too much wanting.

"No," Kara said raggedly. "Not enough." She found his lean waist and pulled his shirt free. "Now. Hard, Duncan. Until the heat is too much and there is only my breath to touch you, my mouth to cool you."

"It wouldn't cool me. It would be hell." He eased her one rigid inch closer. "And unspeakable heaven." His hand covered a flimsy strap of silk. The fabric pulled taut, molding the full breast, outlining the hard, erect nipple. With a hiss the silk began to tear.

Duncan's eyes closed, his face a mask of torment. "Kara," he said hoarsely.

Her finger worshipped his cheek. *"Touch* me."

The satin tore. He felt her before he saw her, breasts goading, thighs warm and searching.

Touch her? How could he do anything else?

He crushed her to him. Open-mouthed, he tasted the heat drifting from her hammering chest.

One tight peak nudged his mouth. He took and took, dimly aware of how she shuddered against him. Old words, harsh promises in a harsher tongue, filled the restless silence. With calloused fingers he shoved away the shredded silk and sank against finer silk.

Lower. Now.

Touch me.

Auburn curls parted to his hands, and he felt her liquid yielding. His hands were too big, too hard against her skin.

He didn't care, couldn't care.

With a curse he pulled free and wrapped her arms around his shoulders. "Hold on, Kara."

She did. As if he were her only link to life and joy.

He lifted her and kicked aside the ottoman. Soon he would take her right there on the cool wood, unless he blocked the feel of her hands, her breasts.

"Damn it, don't touch me."

She blinked, her eyes trembling between shock and pain. "No?"

He sank against the damask covers and moved her hands to the rails of the headboard. "No. Not now. Or I can't keep sane." Then his mouth was burning, twisting over her restless body until he tasted her hot, liquid desire.

Her fingers curled around the rails. Her back arched.

Duncan smoothed and tormented and worshipped until she was breathless, moaning.

He shoved at his shirt, then tore away the exquisitely tailored evening slacks.

And with his pulse hammering he spread her and sank home inside her. He closed his eyes, drowning in a chaos of texture and perfume.

He heard her cry out, felt her body shudder. And then her teeth sank hard against his ear.

"Touch me. All the way. Where I can't see, only feel."

His hands found hers. They wrapped, tensed, resisted.

Then the heat poured through him, filling her, marking them both. With darkness screaming in his head, he found her mouth and ground out her name as he drove down, slamming inside her while her husky cry rang through the air.

Down. Again. Deeper than memories, deeper than anger. Down where this was right, where his fierce need finally had a hope of being quenched.

And there he found to his amazement that the brush and tug of their bodies *did* solve something. It solved everything that could be solved this night. And just as Kara had said, he closed his eyes and poured himself inside her and found that for now touching was all that mattered.

Two counties away.

Night streets. Hollow darkness.

A man scowled, studying the room around him.

He wrapped the cloth tight and hit her again. This time the whimpers stopped and the woman did not move.

Meticulously he wiped his hands and looked in distaste at the small room with no furnishings.

Tangled black wool met his eye, and he nodded. It would work. Like a flame he fed on the power of his hands and the pain he had just dealt. It was the only time he forgot, when he saw the pain and shock jump into someone else's eyes.

He flexed his hands, letting the rough black wool slide through his fingers. Andrew Calendish had been useful. Together they had stolen over a half million pounds, neatly repaid by insurance funds. Then Duncan had come sniffing around and Calendish had gotten frightened.

He'd been weak, like all the others. For that he'd had to die.

They had taken his home, cut away his identity, but he was strong now, gorged on the sounds of weakness and fear.

The severe habit settled around his tall body and covered his gaunt cheeks. The wimple came last, smoothed with loving fingers.

There was no sound from the woman in the corner. Kyle MacKinnon barely noticed, his mouth twisted in a cold smile.

Tonight he had miles to cover and a sinful, restive flock who must learn the price of disobeying him.

"A nun?"

"Yes, sir. Over there. At least she was a moment ago." The young officer shook his head, looking rather dazed as lights cut back and forth through the narrow, noisy streets. Somewhere a car braked to a halt and a door slammed. "Now she's gone."

Lieutenant Marcus Sinclair held the radio away from his ear and cursed fluently. "Why in the hell should I care about a bloody nun?"

"You said to question everyone, sir. I asked her for the name of her church and where she was bound. Everything seemed in order. But—"

"I don't have time for intuition, Harris. I've got a bloody madman to find. Damn it, how did the man escape us?" Sinclair strode off through the darkness.

The young officer turned and looked at the alley's end, where a crumpled newspaper fluttered in the wind.

Just a nun. The lieutenant was right.

But there was a strange coldness at his neck as he moved off to join his fellow officers.

Twenty-eight

"*Mo cridhe.*" Kara's voice was as much a caress as his fingers, trailing along her hip. "What does it mean?"

"My beloved." His voice was dark, rich like fine whisky.

"And *mo ghuol?*"

"My heart. As you are." He frowned at the faint red marks that covered her chest. "I've hurt you. Why didn't you tell me?"

"Because you didn't hurt me. It was like coming alive, only from the inside out this time." Her hand anchored his jaw, her eyes fierce. "But never, *never* was it hurting."

He grumbled. He ran his tongue along the fragile skin at her collarbone. "Stubborn woman." He muttered again.

"Stop grumbling and—"

His fingers eased into a satin hollow warm with their mingled heat. "And what?"

"And kiss me."

His smile was just a bit lopsided, the kind that left her heart lopped cleanly in two. "Kiss you." He cupped her skin. "Like this?"

Velvet over velvet, slow and probing. Mingled tongues and silky heat, exquisitely paralleled by his clever fingers sheathed inside a sweeter heat.

"No, it won't matter," Kara said, her smile like the

Cheshire cat's. "It's not too soon. In fact, I can't wait."

"Stop reading my mind, witch." He eased against her, fully erect, driven by need once more. "How do you *do* this to me again?"

"This is the mere start of my magic, Lord Dunraven." Her hands fisted around his hot, swollen shaft. "See, here's another miracle."

Duncan closed his eyes. "No, the miracle will be if I can hold back long enough to do even half the things I plan to do to you."

Kara woke at dawn.

The quilt was twisted around her waist, and her legs were dangling off the bed. Duncan was jammed against her side. One arm was locked to her waist; the other cupped her breast.

She did not move, savoring the silence, savoring the strange aches in her body after a long and reckless night. Duncan's lovemaking had been desperate, uninhibited. Her own had been no gentler. She had shocked herself—and pleased him infinitely.

She brushed a dark curve of hair from Duncan's cheek, smiling faintly as he stirred and nuzzled her neck. He was thinking of leaving, of preparing that helicopter of his. She focused, reaching deeper.

Now he was thinking of that soft sound she made when he—

"I do *not*."

"What?" His smile was perfect sin.

"Sound like that." She frowned. "At least, only once. Twice at most." She started to roll sideways, only to find Duncan's hand locked over her hip.

He bent his head and nuzzled her stomach. His fingers slowly spread.

Kara's voice caught. Heat seared her.

"See, you do. That makes five." He smiled. "Maybe I'll go for six." He tugged the sheet away. "Just as soon as I've taken care of one or two other things. And this time I don't mean to be rushed, *mo ghaol*."

Kara moved beneath his teasing fingers. Her hips rose impatiently.

"Stop grumbling," Duncan whispered as he pulled her down against him, "and kiss me." His fit was perfect, hot and supple.

Kara complied.

But only after she'd made him do a little mindless muttering too.

Kara's eyes were shining and her cheeks were rosy from being scraped by Duncan's beard when the two walked through the courtyard to the abbey an hour later.

Duncan's hand was on her waist. "I'll fly us. It will be faster. Even with two or three stops to refuel, we'll make better time."

Kara nodded dreamily. Weddings were on her mind. She saw trails of lace and organdy, lengths of satin and peau de soie.

Maybe she should devote a whole page to antique lace gloves in the upcoming issue. Vintage clothes were exquisite to wear—and even more exquisite to remove.

Maybe she could incorporate tartans.

"Then again, we could always travel a shorter way."

Kara smiled, not listening. Authentic old tartans, soft with age and loving use.

"Via Kenya."

Kara nodded. Gloves would be perfect with the tartans. And maybe a small insert on eighteenth-century cameos.

Duncan pulled her to a halt. "Fitzgerald, you're not listening."

"I am," Kara protested. She flushed slightly. "Well, maybe not to every word. I've been thinking about weddings." Her flush grew.

With a harsh oath Duncan angled her back against the spiral staircase and kissed her until her blood sang. When he pulled away his voice was hoarse. "We'll take the shortest bloody route I can find."

They said their good-byes to the beaming viscount and his wife while their bags were stowed aboard the helicopter.

Kara stood frowning at the open door. "First motorcycles, now this. I'm afraid to ask what you've got in mind for me to ride next, MacKinnon."

His lips curved wickedly. "It will be one hell of a ride, I can promise you that."

Nicholas Draycott joined them at the door. "Keep in touch, you two. And try to stay out of trouble, will you?"

As they lifted high over the trees, Kara had an unforgettable view of the green lawns and gray walls. Her breath caught at the abbey's extraordinary beauty. The whole valley looked as if it had been untouched by time. Only the power lines and the red repair van parked just inside the abbey's gates looked out of place.

Kara gestured downward.

"The twentieth century intrudes," Duncan said, his voice sounding deeper through the headphones they both wore. "Nicholas has been having some trouble with the auxiliary power lines into the abbey. I hope this will end his problems once and for all." He scanned a row of dials, then looked over at Kara. "Why don't you get some rest. It's not as if either of us had much sleep last night, after all."

She was already scribbling in her note pad. "I can't. I've got an issue to plan, remember? I don't suppose you happen to have any old swords lying around Dunraven." Kara gnawed on her lip.

"What did you have in mind, Fitzgerald? Bloodshed before tea?"

"I want to do a period arrangement, something that recreates the atmosphere of a traditional Highland wedding. I was thinking of some old tartan fabric, a sword, and perhaps several pieces of old jewelry. I want Dunraven to look real, Duncan, not like a resort facade."

"I'll see what I can round up." Duncan's eyes darkened. "I needn't have worried about your playing fast and loose with Dunraven and forgetting its highland history."

"I should hope *not*. The history is part of Dunraven's unique appeal. Who else can boast an ancient longbow—"

"Broken," Duncan corrected.

"And a dashing outlaw who championed the poor."

"Never proved, I'm afraid."

"History doesn't only come in books and documents." Kara studied the vast and rolling fields beneath them. "Clothes show history. Jewelry does too. Maybe we should try something very modern next to something very old. That would catch the wonderful variety of the Highlands today. I hear there's some exquisite modern silverwork being done in the north. . . ."

Duncan shot a pleading look skyward and then bent back to the controls.

"How much farther?"

"About twenty minutes." Duncan pointed out the window to a line of mountains.

"Maybe we should include an old wedding invitation—something in Gaelic." Kara frowned. "Were invitations written in Gaelic in the past?"

"Probably. I'll see what I can dig up." Duncan adjusted a dial as the helicopter chattered north over pristine lochs and dark peat streams. Here and there herds of red-tailed deer grazed among the pines.

But it was a modern picture too, Kara saw. Sleek ships bristling with radar equipment rocked in secluded harbors, and several villages had billboards screaming the latest commercial craze.

Kara's eyes were drawn west, along an endless line of loch and firth and coast. Above everything trembled a lighter blue, soft and sheer, flung by a Seurat brush, where sea blurred into sky.

They went low, skimming a small airstrip where a row of helicopters nestled in the curve of a hill. "Yours, MacKinnon?"

Duncan nodded. "MacKinnon land begins just beyond that valley, but it will be twenty more minutes until we get to Dunraven Castle."

"Exactly how big *are* your estates?"

Duncan shrugged. "Somewhere between sixty and eighty thousand acres."

Kara whistled softly. "I had no idea. Heavens, that means you must be one of those potentates with your own salmon stream and trout fishing in the loch. Do you rent out fishing rights? I've heard Arab sheiks will pay through the teeth for a week's salmon fishing."

"No, I do *not* rent out fishing rights. MacKinnon waters have been fished by local residents for three hundred years, and I see no reason to change that."

"Even though there's all that money to be made by selling water rights?"

"They're called 'beats,'" Duncan said irritably. "And yes, a week's time share on a salmon run can sell for upwards of forty thousand pounds."

Kara's eyes widened. "For one *week*? That would be—"

"I know how much it is," Duncan said impatiently. "Too many of our best rivers have been sold to absentee landlords, Swiss financiers, or Arab oil kings. It might be lucrative, but I'm not changing the old ways. Besides, I'm not keen to have noisy strangers tramping across my moors with expensive guns that they don't know how to use."

Kara smiled faintly. "So what about the grouse hunting?"

Duncan gave her a wicked smile and banked the helicopter. "Hang on and you'll find out."

There was a glitter of gray just beyond the sweep of bright green meadowlands. Kara looked down to see a herd of horses charging over the hillside. Beyond them lay Dunraven Castle.

Her breath caught. The walls were pink, and light danced from dozens of windows. A roof of black slate rippled with gables and turrets.

"It's . . . magic," Kara breathed, following the narrow gravel road as far as her eyes could see, past neat rows of basil and staked tomatoes, past a maze of clipped shrubs. At the edge of the sea, green lawn led subtly into twenty shades of blue.

In that moment Kara knew there could be no more wondrous spot on earth for two people to share the start of their life together. Twenty-two kings had slept beneath its fantastic turreted roof, and three major wars had been planned there. It was rumored that more than one powerful foreign head of state had slipped away to Dunraven's rose-covered walls to meet the woman of his heart for a few stolen moments away from the public eye. Kara could understand the desire to escape to such a magical place.

"It's haunted, you know." There was something muffled in MacKinnon's voice. "Some say the ghost is the same one who haunts Draycott Abbey." He turned, smiling. "You didn't know the abbey was haunted, did you? You must be slipping, Fitzgerald. I thought all you Americans found ghost stories incredibly romantic."

For some reason Kara thought of the brooding figure in severest black and white lace. "Right, MacKinnon. *Every* English estate claims to have a resident ghost."

"Most of them do," MacKinnon said soberly. "With the history that we've had, a constant round of wars, revolution, and local uprisings, it's a wonder there aren't ghosts everywhere."

Kara frowned. "Are you telling me that Dunraven Castle is actually haunted?"

Duncan's lips curved. "I'm saying that legend holds it to be so. Let's just say that I've seen my share of unusual things while growing up in that wonderful, exasperating heap of stone down there."

"But surely—" The rest of Kara's words were lost in a whoosh of air as Duncan banked the helicopter and swept down to a flat cement circle at the edge of the woods. Down the hill Kara could make out the curving outline of a thatched roof, sprinkled here and there with red roses. Rose Cottage.

Duncan switched off the motor. He pulled off their earphones, then deftly unhooked her seat harness and lifted her into his arms. "Welcome to Dunraven Castle, Ms. Fitzgerald. It's been our custom to welcome visitors like this ever since one of my courtly ancestors carried a queen of Scotland over the muddy paths next to the pigsty."

Kara looked down at the pristine green lawn. "There's not a pig in sight, MacKinnon."

The laird of Dunraven Castle shrugged. "Ritual is ritual. Stop struggling and let yourself be welcomed properly. This is Scotland, after all."

The wind rushed through Kara's hair, rich with the tang of sea salt and pine needles. Duncan's hands were warm where they cupped her hips. "All right, Sir Galahad. Lead on."

At that moment a tall man with wiry white hair strode over the lawn, his kilt swinging above bare calves. He shouted something in Gaelic to Duncan, who chuckled.

"There you are, Mctavish. I began to think you'd given up on Dunraven and gone off to work on the North Sea rigs, as you've been threatening to do these last ten years and more."

"Oh, aye, that I would, except my ancestors would come to haunt me in the night." The old man looked measuringly at Kara. "It's a pleasure to welcome such a lovely visitor to Dunraven." He smiled at Duncan. "The usual ritual?"

"The usual."

Kara watched warily as Mctavish strode to a twisted tangle of branches, where a pear tree grew flush against the castle wall. Mctavish bent and plucked a twig of flowers, then fit it above Kara's ear. "*Ceud mille failte,* Ms. Fitzgerald," the old man said warmly. "Ten thousand welcomes. Legend has it that Charles II himself planted that pear tree when he stayed the night here, barely managing to escape five minutes ahead of his pursuers. As you know, the monarch had a great liking for the ladies, and he insisted that any woman arriving at Dunraven should receive a twig of flowering pear in his memory."

Kara looked questioningly at Duncan.

"Oh, the tale is true, I assure you. Angus Mctavish never lies." Duncan chuckled. "Not to strangers, anyway. Have you any salmon left, Angus? I'm fair famished, and I think Ms. Fitzgerald must be too."

"Take the lass upstairs and let her rest," the old man said curtly. "While she does, I'll find a bit of something for the two of you." He laughed as Kara's eyes widened. "You were expecting the medieval laird and the groveling peasant? Nay, not here at Dunraven. I'm as like to give the orders as himself." Mctavish's pale green eyes twinkled as the surprise grew on Kara's face.

Duncan pulled a travel bag over his shoulder. "Mctavish orders everyone about." But Kara wasn't really listening. Her eyes were locked on the soft green slopes and the fairy-tale castle.

Suddenly music spilled over the hillside, delicate and elusive, carried on the wind. It teased Kara's senses—there and then gone. There was something infinitely sad in its slow cadences. "Don't tell me you hire a piper to welcome your guests."

"Piper? The only people on staff are Mctavish and his wife."

"Don't you hear that? Those are pipes playing on the roof."

Kara felt Duncan stiffen. He turned slowly, his eyes following the direction of her finger pointing to the castle roof. "Up there?"

"Of course. Why are you two grinning like guilty schoolboys?"

Mctavish cleared his throat.

"Well?"

Duncan answered. "It would seem, Kara Fitzgerald, that you are one of the select few granted the rare privilege of hearing the pipes of Geordie MacKinnon, who died in the '45 rising. It is rare that he is heard—not since my mother's day, I believe." Duncan's eyes drifted over her face, and a smile pulled at one corner of his mouth.

"A ghost? You're telling me I'm listening to a *ghost* play that music?" As Kara spoke, the music swelled, then faded. "I suppose you expect me to put *that* in my story. I can see it now: 'Visitors are by tradition welcomed to the castle by a dead piper, killed in an early Highland rising.'"

Duncan's smile grew broader. "Oh, no, I don't expect you'll be mentioning that in your article." There was something positively challenging in his eyes now.

"Why?" Kara demanded.

Beside her, Mctavish cleared his throat again. "I'll be going to tend to that salmon now." Kara could have sworn she heard him chuckle as he moved up the path to the castle.

"Well?"

"You're certain you want to hear?"

"Of course I'm certain." The pipe music drifted away, and for a moment Kara thought it had disappeared. Then one fragment of song, light and clear, trilled on the air.

"It is said, my dear, that the Phantom Piper welcomes only a few to Dunraven Castle, and all of them are women. There's a reason for that, of course, but I'm not sure you're going to want to hear it."

"Try me."

Duncan set Kara on a weathered stone bench and looked out over the sea. "Legend has it that my ancestor was sadly tricked by his betrothed, who was to marry him when he returned from war. After pledging him her heart, she ran off with his best friend, who had known her intimately already. Poor Geordie never forgave her. He went into battle like a madman and died in the thick of the fighting, at his king's side. They say he always makes a point of coming out and passing judgment on any woman who enters Dunraven." His eyes narrowed on Kara's face. "Legend says he can only be heard by a woman who is destined to marry a MacKinnon." His voice fell. "A woman whose heart, once given, will never be untrue."

Blood surged to Kara's face.

"Is it true? Is your heart to be given only once, to me, *mo cridhe*?" There was a rough tug in his voice.

Kara looked down, flushing. "You and Mctavish could charm the grin off a shark with a house like this and all your legends."

"Not a shark," the laird said, grinning. "All I mean to charm is one fractious, frustrating woman with hair the color of a highland dawn."

You've already done that, Kara wanted to say. But for some reason, today, the realization left her uneasy.

Angus Mctavish was sturdy and sixtyish, with the whitest hair Kara had ever seen. When she came downstairs, he beckoned her through silent halls to a drawing room that faced the sea.

"I'm that sorry my Moira isn't here to meet you, Ms. Fitzgerald, but she's off visiting her sister in Glasgow. Greatly missed she is, too."

Against one wall a row of grandfather clocks chimed two o'clock. Kara cocked her head. "Why so many?"

The old man chuckled. "You'd best ask the laird about that. He's right outside, I think."

Duncan was wearing a woolen kilt in bold shades of red, green, and black; the MacKinnon plaid, Kara saw. The garment made him look profoundly different, as if he'd stepped out of an older age. As he cut wood on the terrace, his arms fell in smooth, powerful arcs. No movement was wasted. Every log split apart precisely.

He turned at the sound of her steps. "I'll be finished here shortly. Then Mctavish will bring us tea and whatever he's been able to round up on such short notice. I thought we might eat out here, since it's so clear and fine."

Kara nodded, strangely tongue-tied by the sight of the taut muscles beneath his open shirt. "Very nice, MacKinnon. Can I photograph you like that for my article?"

"Native Scot at home, dancing to the skirl of the pipes while he consumes home-brewed whiskey? Scotland is more than a *Brigadoon* fantasy, you know."

"I'll see that my readers get more. You have to start with what people know."

Duncan stared out at the water. Sea birds cried as they winged down toward the ocean. Slowly he put down the ax and rested one leg on an upturned log. "I'll let you in on a secret, Fitzgerald." He laughed dryly. "A Scotsman's pride is his greatest weakness."

"What have I done to attack your pride?"

He looked around him at the beautiful hills and flashing water. "Nothing. Maybe I'm seeing ghosts where none exist."

"You're talking in riddles."

"Scotsmen are good at that too." He smiled faintly as he turned to study the row of grandfather clocks through the window. "I heard you asking Mctavish about our timepieces."

"He refused to tell me a word." Kara pulled a notebook from the pocket of her flowered shirt and a pencil from her copper curls. "Another charming MacKinnon legend?"

"I don't think you're going to need that notebook."

Kara's chin rose stubbornly. "Cooperate, Duncan. I want the *real* Dunraven Castle, not some fluffy fantasy creation."

Duncan's smile widened. He moved past her into the sunny room and ran his hand over the polished base of the nearest clock. At its crown a wooden moon rocked against a background of painted silver stars. "These were gifts to my grandfather. It was my grandmother's way of thanking him."

"Thanking him for what? Are Scotsmen *always* so obscure?"

His eyes glittered, very blue. "Family legend says it was because of his traditional MacKinnon skill."

"Skill?"

"In her bed. Every time he satisfied her completely, she presented him with another clock."

Twenty-nine

Heat skittered over Kara's cheeks.

Around her the expensive clocks clicked, whirred, and banged expressively. "There must be over a hundred clocks here."

"One hundred and twenty-nine, to be exact. The MacKinnon men are known to be remarkably hot blooded." There was an edge of husky intimacy in Duncan's voice. "Something you well know."

Kara cleared her throat. *Work, Fitzgerald. You've got a magazine to finish, remember?* "May I see the rest of the house?"

Duncan held out his arm with grave formality. Kara took it, avoiding his eyes, trying to ignore the heated images he was projecting.

"You can delay, Kara, but not for long. You owe me one more day, and I'm going to collect." But Duncan frowned as he studied her face. "Let's wait on the tour. You need some rest."

"I'll be fine."

"Damn it, Kara—"

"I've got to finish, Duncan. Now, do you give me the tour or does Mctavish?"

"Bloody stubborn female."

First came the front hall. Polished walls gleamed golden in the afternoon sunlight, their grain so fine that the wood looked alive. Thick carpets of crimson and blue sent color spilling into the room.

Perfect, Kara thought as they walked beneath a stone arch into the great hall. She noted and approved the placement of the windows.

"Want to tell me what the joke is?" he asked.

Kara saw that Duncan was studying her. "You won't like it."

"Try me."

"Whoever laid out this room studied with a fêng shui master in the Orient." She smiled as Duncan's brow rose. "You see how those windows soften that line of columns? That's a very powerful use of light. There's also the placement of that mirror over the main entrance to the hall. See how it brings light into the heart of the house?"

Duncan nodded slowly. "Without that mirror, the whole foyer would be gloomy and uninviting. And without those windows, the columns would be stark." He looked at Kara. "My great-great-grandfather was part Manchu and spent many years in the Orient. Perhaps this was his doing."

Kara scribbled notes as they moved through rooms bright with tartan throws, English and Chinese porcelains, and embroidered pillows. Everywhere flowers added warmth, softening the formal arrangement of priceless old furniture.

But it was at the top of the stairs that Kara felt herself fall in love with the castle. Here, thick vaulted ceilings curved over a row of snug rooms, which Duncan now used for his office, study, and bedroom. Between the double-paned windows ran stone walls brightened by old paisley shawls and scores of framed watercolors of the Western Isles.

"Nice landscapes." Kara examined a misty scene of moon and silver water. "I don't recognize the artist."

Duncan cleared his throat and pulled her toward the door. "There are better things down the hall."

"MacKinnon?"

"We have a collection of old lanterns and a set of eighteenth-century champagne bottles."

Kara crossed her arms. "I'm waiting."

Duncan scratched his jaw. "They're mine. Are you satisfied?"

Eyes wide, Kara turned back to the row of framed pictures. Here was the castle pear tree and beside it a maze. The next painting caught the sea in full storm, slashed by fingers of lightning. "These are good, Duncan. *Very* good. You should show them."

"Absolutely not." Frowning, he tugged her out into the hall. "If I see one *hint* about this in that magazine of yours, you'll be sorry." His mouth curved. "But I think you'll find this room more interesting by far."

"Don't tell me. The laird does crewel work on stormy winter nights for relaxation."

"I have a better way to relax." Duncan opened a door. "Have a look. You're going to see a lot of this room."

"I am? Why would I—" The words died in Kara's throat.

His bedroom.

"I don't see what relevance this has." Kara's voice was not steady. "After all, we won't be using it in our article."

The laird's dark brow arched. "Perhaps I want a professional opinion about the fêng shui of my bedroom."

Kara cast a cursory glance about her. The bed was mahogany, draped with a thick tartan. Just beyond it wide windows overlooked a view of land and sea. Lying in that bed, a woman would feel warm and infinitely safe.

"I trust that my supporting beams and shafts are well placed."

Kara ignored the challenge in his voice, frowning as she trailed her fingers over the rich old plaids. "The placement of your bed has some major weaknesses."

"What kind of weaknesses?"

"First of all, your head is facing the door."

Dunraven sat down beside her on the bed. Their shoulders bumped. "So?"

Kara cleared her throat. "A bed should always be positioned so you have a clear view of anyone entering. It's detrimental to a relationship if you are nervous and jumpy, don't you agree?"

The Scotsman's eyes went a shade darker. "Oh, I'm never nervous and jumpy, Fitzgerald. Not in *this* room."

"I doubt you're here very much, in that case. You must have very strong *ch'i*, or you would have noticed the problem already."

His lips curved slightly. "My *ch'i* is wonderful. Or so I have been told."

Kara wasn't going to be sidetracked. "It's a serious error in placement and not to be taken lightly."

"So what do you suggest?" Duncan brushed a stray curl from her cheek.

Kara slid from the bed and paced the floor. "I suggest a mirror on the opposite wall. That would reflect energy to the bed and give you a view of anyone coming in."

"A mirror." His grin widened. "I like it."

"I also suggest a wind chime at the left side of the bed." As she spoke, Kara straightened a pillow and lined up a row of crystal figures on the windowsill, bringing them into the best possible alignment. Without conscious thought she rotated a pot of white camellias.

"Do you always fiddle with other people's things while you're assessing their rooms?" Duncan asked wryly.

Kara jammed her hands into her pockets. "Sometimes. It's a habit. When I can sense the flow so clearly, I can't help moving things."

"So this problem with my room is serious?" He lay back on the bed, hands crossed behind his head. "Are you expensive?"

"Expensive?" Kara caught a quick breath. The blasted man was enjoying every minute of this. She crossed her arms over her chest. "*Extremely.*"

"Too bad." A smile flickered on his lips. He eased open a button at his chest and ran his hands idly over the bronze skin. "Maybe you could make a few more suggestions."

As she sat on the bed again, Kara straightened her shoulders, refusing to look at him. "You should definitely add a mirror over your bed. It will draw in views of the loch. Since water symbolizes money, that will enrich your life."

"But will it enrich my love life?" he murmured.

"I suppose that follows." Energy shimmered between them. The words yin and yang took on a whole new meaning.

"How about if I become your guinea pig?" Duncan whispered as his fingers slid around her waist. He eased her back against him, and Kara felt the hot jut of his manhood.

"Guinea pig for what?"

"An experiment." His hand teased the warm recess behind her ear. Against every inclination Kara bent closer.

The next moment his lips brushed her hair.

She caught a husky breath and found herself turning into his embrace.

He smelled like sea salt and old leather. He smelled like mist and pine and the Scottish hills she'd seen outside the window. Kara made a low sound of protest as his lips ran over her forehead. "Duncan, we can't." Her voice was ragged. "I've got ... to finish."

"I've got a better finish in mind."

"No. Not—this. Like ... we are." *Great, Fitzgerald. Now you can't even talk.*

"Why not?" he murmured. "I like doing this. I *love* doing this."

"Because—" Kara held back a moan as his hand eased over the nipple mounded tightly against her cashmere sweater.

"God, you're sweet." Duncan groaned as he rolled the aching tip between his thumb and forefinger. "I've been wanting to touch you like this all day, ever since I noticed you weren't wearing anything beneath that sweater." He turned her face up and nibbled on her bottom lip. "You must be a miracle worker, Fitzgerald. My *ch'i* feels pretty spectacular right now."

Kara had to agree. He was hard and hot against her thighs, and she knew exactly how he'd feel inside her. "Duncan, I—" She swallowed hard. "I've got too much work to do." Her voice was plaintive. "I have to finish six layouts before my staff arrives tomorrow. It's going to be nearly impossible as it is. . . ."

"You mean it, don't you? You really do want this issue to be perfect."

Kara nodded, unable to speak, overwhelmed by him, by his beautiful room and his magnificent castle. "I don't have time." Even then, her hands were nuzzling the soft hair covering his chest and her eyes were hazy with desire.

Duncan gave a sharp curse and released her. "Then we can wait. I want this article to be perfect, and I want everything else between us to be perfect too. Ten minutes of hot, hard sex is not about to satisfy me," he said harshly. He looked at Kara, his eyes unflinching. "I want all night in this bed. I want to make you moan my name while you squeeze me dry." He planted a hard kiss on her swollen mouth, then gave her a shove. "Get going, Fitzgerald, while I can still let you. I'll be down in a few minutes."

After the pain goes down, he thought grimly.

If it ever would.

When Kara wandered into the kitchen twenty minutes later, notebook in hand, she surveyed the long pine tables and porcelain bowls filled with vegetables from the castle's gardens. She came to an abrupt halt when she saw Duncan at a counter preparing freshly caught salmon.

"I'll have this ready shortly. It will give me something else to hold in my hands besides you," he said darkly.

"*You* are going to cook?"

"Of course."

Kara watched in amazement as he launched a campaign against a pile of potatoes, two fish, and a mound of fresh vegetables. Celery flew into tiny slices and onions piled up in neat rows.

"Go out and work, Fitzgerald. You make me nervous. I'll call you when it's ready."

Kara fingered her notebook. Now was as good a time as any to make her preliminary layouts. The sun was high, and the light would be good.

When she was seated on a warm stone bench with the loch and sea spread before her, she made quick, sharp strokes that captured the proud stone of the castle, its windows glittering golden in the light of the western sun.

She sat back and studied the design critically. Not bad. Not bad at all.

Overhead a bird cried shrilly. Some impulse made her look east, toward the thatched roof jutting above a wooded slope.

The cottage took her breath away, half in sun and half in shadow. Kara walked closer. Roses clambered over the oak door, and honeybees droned in the wildflowers along the flagstone walk. In the narrow second-floor windows, Kara saw a blur of red tartan. Angus cleaning up, no doubt.

She knocked on the front door. When no one answered, she walked inside to a room of mellow wood and rich old stone, its low ceiling crossed by wooden beams. Here and there were scattered bright bowls filled with roses, and models of fishing ships covered the handmade oak tables.

Enchantment. The word came to Kara as she stood motionless in the shadows. All noise and movement seemed to be blocked, all time halted.

Enchanted. No other word described the feeling of this place so well. Perfect energy drifted through every inch of the room, captured in years of laughter and joy that spilled over the broad fireplace and shimmered along the twisting stairs.

Kara heard the faint skirl of bagpipes from somewhere high above. No doubt Angus Mctavish was playacting as the resident ghost in another MacKinnon ritual for arriving guests.

As Kara moved upstairs, the melody ebbed and flowed. She entered room after room, small and snug, every window shining, every chair in place.

But there was no piper to be seen, though the music teased her with every step she took.

Slowly she made her way back down to find Duncan at the bottom of the stairs. "Very funny. Where did you hide the recording?" she asked.

"What recording?"

"The one with the bagpipes."

Duncan stiffened. "You heard the piper?"

"Of course. I was on the bench, sketching happily, and then I saw a flash of tartan in one of the cottage windows. I decided to come inside. That's when I heard the piper." Her eyes narrowed. "Is this another Dunraven ritual?"

Duncan's fingers wrapped around her wrist. "You heard the pipes in *here*?" He stared deep into her eyes, as if denying what she had just told him. "Answer me, damn it."

Kara nodded. "What's wrong, Duncan?"

"Show me where the sound came from."

"I can't. It came from everywhere at once, climbing and fading like a mirage that retreats when you try to follow. It was no place—and everywhere."

"Then it's begun."

"What in heaven's name are you talking about? You make this sound like some kind of obituary notice."

He turned away, his eyes grim. "In a way it is. You see, Geordie MacKinnon only invades the sanctity of Rose Cottage under one condition—when the laird of Dunraven is about to die."

Thirty ~

Kara blinked. "You're joking. You can't possibly believe such a superstition."

"Superstition, as in energy flow and fêng shui placement?" Duncan said flatly.

Through room after room Kara followed him, watching with growing uneasiness as he flung open closets, examined empty drawers, and checked beneath every bed. There was no tape recorder, no phonograph, nor any other source for the music she had heard.

Kara felt a heaviness settling over him and knew he was thinking of Kyle's threat.

Duncan latched the front door and turned in silence, studying the purple hills above the loch.

"Duncan, you can't really *believe* this."

He started up the hill, but Kara wrenched him around to face her. "Talk to me, damn it."

"What's there to say? It's just an old superstition."

"But you believe it."

Duncan jammed his hands in his pockets. "Come back to the house. Dinner is ready."

They crossed the meadow and forest in silence. There was something mocking about the chime and whir of the clocks as they entered the dining room.

"Dinner was delicious, Duncan."

"How do you know? You hardly touched any of it."

It was true. Kara had tasted nothing. Her thoughts were too intensely focused on the phantom music in the cottage and Duncan's reaction to it. "I'm tired. I think I'll do some work and then go to sleep," she lied smoothly.

Duncan tossed down his napkin. "I'll show you to the ballroom. Your cartons have arrived and are stacked in one corner. Angus and I carried in a work-table for you to use."

She followed him to the castle's south side, where mirrored walls reflected a gigantic crystal chandelier. "It's beautiful," Kara whispered.

"We used it often when I was young. At one time my mother and father entertained a great deal." He reached up and gently tapped one of the crystals, which swirled beneath his touch. Abruptly he turned away. "The cartons are over here. Angus found some frames from which to hang your dresses."

"Thank you," Kara said stiffly. There were a hundred things she wanted to say to him, a hundred questions she wanted to ask.

Somehow they all stuck in her throat.

"If you need something, just ring the bell by the door. Angus will see to what you require. There's a telephone in the room next door." He stood stiffly for a moment, his eyes unreadable. In the light of the chandelier, his hair was the color of rich peat. "Get some sleep."

"Of course." Kara cleared her throat. "Sleep." She wanted to brush back the dark comma of hair from his brow. She wanted to touch his cheek and sweep the sadness from his eyes. "Duncan, about the piper . . ."

He didn't move.

"It's just a superstition."

"Like *your* vision, Kara? Like the wrenching images that brought you in search of me?" He laughed hollowly. "It seems that once again your sight is true."

"But—"

"I have heard the piper at Rose Cottage twice. Both times occurred just before the current laird died."

Then his jaw hardened and he was gone.

"You want me to do *what?*"

"You heard me, Megan." With one hand Kara held the phone, and with the other she pleated and re-pleated a lace glove. "Pull out anything remotely connected with Scotland. I want an advertising list on this issue that will keep Martin grinning for a month."

"That expensive, is it?" Kara's assistant said knowingly.

"Bigger than anything we've done. That means a backup photographer, extra film, and two extra models."

"Martin is going to have a heart attack."

"Not if he sees that advertising list first. I'm relying on you to put something together before you leave."

"In six hours?"

"Believe me, I'd do it myself, but I'm in the middle of sketching a pile of lingerie and bridal accessories. I can't seem to concentrate here, maybe because any minute I expect a band of angry highlanders to come riding over the hill, claymores in hand." Kara heard her assistant's pencil tap on the desk. "What?"

"I don't suppose this attention lapse has anything to do with the reclusive lord of the castle."

"Not a bit," Kara said sharply.

"How did he like that lingerie I made you pack?"

"What makes you think Lord Dunraven has had any chance to inspect my lingerie?"

"Fitzgerald, I can hear your biological clock ticking all the way from here. A brooding Scotsman would be the perfect thing to fill some of those leisure hours in your day."

"*What* leisure hours? By the way, I hope you were able to accomplish all the items on that *long* list I left on your machine yesterday."

"All taken care of," Megan said briskly. "Right

down to a tear-out reply coupon for all the major advertisers."

"Megan, you're a dream. I hope you don't ask for half of what you're worth, because Martin wouldn't let me keep you."

"Don't worry, I'm not going anywhere. By the way, Martin has been in a fabulous mood lately. It seems he's turned up some lingerie advertisers who really bought your Scotland angle. Believe me, you can do no wrong in his eyes." She laughed. "Just keep the ideas flowing and we'll squeak by."

Ideas, Kara thought after she hung up. She had too many ideas. She stared around her at the exquisite bridal gowns unpacked from tissue-lined cartons. She had found a museum-quality antique of silk douppioni with a dramatic bustle and ten-foot train. She cocked her head, expertly draping a length of tulle and a sash of Battenburg lace over the old dress form Angus had found in the castle storeroom.

She was trying to choose between elbow-length gloves or an ornate pearl choker when something brushed against the window. She looked up with a gasp, but there was no one there.

Only a tree branch shaking in the wind, Fitzgerald. Cut out the nerves. Anyone would think you were the one getting married tomorrow.

Rubbing a knot of tension at her neck, she moved to the full-length glass windows. A hint of silver was visible where moonlight crisscrossed the loch. In the curve of the coast, she could just make out a scattering of lights in the village.

Ideas. She needed ideas that didn't revolve around a man with wary eyes and hauntingly gentle hands.

Sighing, she turned back to the worktable overflowing with lingerie.

Lingerie was hot, Martin had insisted. Lingerie would give this issue wings. Kara looked down at a tangle of silk charmeuse and transparent lace confections that ranged from virginal to blatantly vampish. The problem, she decided, as one particularly erotic bit of nothing slid through her fingers, was how to keep the sizzle without losing the authentic atmosphere.

Kara frowned as the ache in her neck grew worse. She wasn't going to get any more answers tonight. She switched off the chandelier and stood for a moment. From down the hall came the chime and whir of the grandfather clocks.

"I hope I'm not disturbing you." Duncan had come, as always, with the silence of a cat.

Kara's breath caught. "No, not at all. I was just finishing up."

"I came by before, but you were glaring at a defenseless pair of silk gloves, so I decided not to bother you." He lifted a fragile negligee and watched it pool over his fingers. "This is the stuff of dreams, all right. Even a few X-rated dreams."

Kara watched the soft satin slip through his fingers. The faint, erotic hiss reminded her of a room full of roses. "Duncan . . ." She swallowed. "About the piper . . ."

"Forget it, Kara." The negligee landed with a soft swoosh back on the table. "I'll take care of Dunraven Castle and its protection." He turned, his jaw hard. "Go upstairs and get some sleep. I'll close up down here."

She moved toward him, but he raised his hand. "Don't. I'm trying to keep my hands off you. I'm also trying to remember that I'm a man who doesn't have much of a future. From now on, I've got to keep my head, Kara, and that's something I don't do well when you're around. I heard that music in Rose Cottage today too, and it was a wake-up call reminding me how careless I've become."

"You're treating me like another one of your responsibilities."

"Protecting you has always been at the top of my list," Duncan said grimly.

"Fine," Kara said. "I can use the rest." She walked through the shadowed ballroom, careful not to look back.

Duncan would never know how much it cost her.

*   *   *

The laird of Dunraven stared at Kara's retreating back. He told himself he was totally numb, utterly unconcerned.

It was a lie, of course.

Ever since he'd laid eyes on this woman, she had touched him in ways beyond imagining, opening doors where none had existed and summoning up emotions he had thought long dead. But what future could they have? In a week she would go back to her hectic office, and he . . .

Duncan frowned. If legend was to be believed, he had no future. The ghostly piper at Rose Cottage was an unshakable part of Dunraven's history. Every time the piper had been heard at the cottage, a laird had died—the last one barely five years before, when Duncan's father had died of complications from a heart attack upon hearing of Kyle's death.

A death that had never really occurred, Duncan thought grimly as he pushed open the terrace door.

He took a long, uneven breath, feeling the night's stillness. He had loved Dunraven Castle for as long as he could remember, loved its legends, its inconveniences, even the mysteries he sensed in its remote corners.

And he loved Kara Fitzgerald.

Duncan accepted that now, just as he accepted the ache in his groin when he looked up and saw her slender form silhouetted against the light beneath a high turret.

Was she slipping off her sweater and tossing aside that frothy skirt? Was she easing her golden body beneath linen sheets?

He turned away, thrusting his hands deep in his pockets. In the last week he had discovered fear, treachery, and betrayal that he had not known existed. In spite of that, he wanted Kara in his life and their wedding vows to be real.

A low whistling came from rocks beyond the cove. The seals were singing tonight, as they often did in warm, misty weather. As the strange, haunting music drifted around him, Duncan realized how much he had missed this beautiful old place.

Frowning, he checked the sensors installed around the castle. Everything appeared to be in good shape. Duncan only wished he would hear something from Lieutenant Sinclair in London. It was a vain hope, however. Kyle would strike without warning, when he was least wanted or expected. Duncan knew that, accepted that. And even then he couldn't summon the control he needed to keep his mind off a woman with amber eyes.

Beneath the stone arch at the entrance to the south wall he looked up at the capstone, where a single exquisite rose lay carved in granite. Legend decreed that the laird of Dunraven was always to touch that capstone when he entered the castle and whisper a complex Gaelic rhyme. If the custom was neglected, ruin would come to all within Dunraven's walls.

Duncan now whispered the familiar words:

> *"When summer and winter meet as one*
> *And music fills the stone,*
> *Broken shall be mended then*
> *When the shadow stands alone."*

As the old phrases rumbled from his throat, the wind rose, hissing under the arch and spitting into the courtyard. Duncan stared out at the dark woods, the rising moon, the crescent cove.

Something cold was in his throat and he knew it was fear. Of the darkness, the shadows.

Of a love he could not bear to lose.

Down the hill, leaves rustled against the faint, high chime of bells. With a sharp hiss, a dark shape spun through the air, plummeted off a rose bush, and thumped down on a dark flagstone.

The hiss became a shrill meow.

Well, did we manage it? Are you arrived safe and sound, Gideon?

The cat stretched slowly, licking sore paws. After

a moment he flicked his tail and looked around him in the darkness. There were smells here and a thousand fascinating noises to be tracked.

No hunting, Gideon. No stalking or sniffing out the salmon that you love. You are here for a purpose, and the time grows very close.

The cat's back arched. He studied the sea and the dark blotch that could have been an island—or could have been a ship. His great amber eyes glowed as the wind flowed past him, rustling the roses.

And he waited. As he had waited before by a quiet moat, feeling the certainty of danger slip around him.

Thirty-one ~

Kara woke often that night. She dreamed she heard footsteps in the corridor, the hiss of a cat, and the skirl of phantom pipes. One part of her mind prayed that her work would soon be done, while another part prayed that her time there would never end. Her eyes were ringed with shadows when she made her way down to the sunlit breakfast room the next morning.

Angus Mctavish was there before her, dapper in a kilt and black velvet jacket. "Come in, lass. Here's water on the boil, and it's a bonny cup of tea I'll have for you in just a moment."

Kara sat down at the old pine table beside windows that looked out on endless glistening water. Gratefully, she accepted the steaming mug Angus set before her.

"Himself is not astir yet. Sleeps poorly, does the laird." Mctavish shook his head, frowning. "Carries the weight of this grand old place too heavy, if you ask me. But then, no one does ask me, so I'll say na more." His keen eyes observed her. "Not to be rude, but it appears you had some nasty dreams of your own last night, miss."

Kara toyed with one of Angus's scones, hot from the oven. "It was the wind tapping on my window."

"Funny, and I thought the night had been a still one."

"Perhaps it was the bed. I'm not used to such a soft mattress."

"Most guests swear that your bed is the most comfortable they've ever slept in," the old man said shrewdly.

Kara didn't meet his eyes. She took a sip of tea, then pushed her chair back from the table, her scone uneaten. "Thank you, Angus, but I'd better get to work. Hidoshi, my photographer, will be here in several hours. I've got a thousand things to finish before then."

"You'll have the strength to finish none of them without eating, miss. You've touched nothing of that scone and drunk barely half of your tea." Mctavish crossed his arms and fixed her with a militant glare. "Eat you will, or you'll na leave my kitchen."

Kara's eyes crinkled. "It's a dreadful bully you are, Angus Mctavish." A dimple peaked from one cheek. "And I can see why Duncan rates your services so highly." She looked down at the scone and frowned. "Did Duncan tell you that I heard the piper—at Rose Cottage?"

"Yes." The old man seemed to stand very still. "And did you truly?"

"As clear as I hear your voice now. Duncan told me what it meant. Do you believe that too, Angus?"

Mctavish looked out over the green slopes and shining water, his eyes filled with regret. "Yes, I do believe and no, I do not. The two sides war inside me. Any highlander feels the same, for we're an odd tangle of old and new. Did the laird ask you to keep what you heard to yourself?"

Kara shook her head.

"Aye, I did not think he would. Proud as a cliff of Hebrides granite is the MacKinnon. But if he will not ask it, I am not so proud." The old man looked at Kara. "Keep this to yourself, lassie. Tell no one that you've heard the piper at Rose Cottage. It will distress many in the village." He was about to say more when he heard a noise coming from down the hill. "That will be old Graham Ramsay, come to deliver

our milk in that rattling wreck. I'll be off to speak
with him, if you'll excuse me."

"Of course. I'll stay here and make headway on
this scone." But Kara's smile soon faded. She sat
back, pain settling in her chest. She refused to believe
that Duncan would die. There had to be some way
she could help.

She smiled thoughtfully. A mirror in the upper corridor would deflect blocked energy from the low ceilings. After that she was definitely going to make
some changes in Duncan's bedroom.

So intent was she in her plans, she didn't hear
Angus come back inside.

" 'Tis not Ramsay at all, but a man to see *you*,
miss." Angus shook his head. " 'Tis a man with purple hair."

"Hidoshi!" Kara flung herself to her feet, smiling
broadly at the slender figure standing behind Angus.

"Here's the list of gowns I've chosen." Kara sat in
the ballroom, hunched over a table packed high with
gowns of every variety.

Hidoshi studied her sketches and nodded thoughtfully. "Interesting. The blend of modern and period
pieces will be striking. Add some kilts and period
lace and it will be beautiful, Kara." He sat back, his
eyes thoughtful. "Martin is going nuts for this issue.
Megan told me to tell you that she might never speak
to you again."

Kara sighed. "It's turning into more work than I
realized."

"Something tells me it isn't just the work that's
getting to you. Maybe it has something to do with
that brooding Scotsman I passed as I was driving in."

Kara sat up a little straighter. "Scotsman?"

"Long black hair. Dressed in a kilt, plain as day."
Hidoshi rubbed his jaw. "I thought that stuff was
just legend."

"Don't talk that way to Angus or you'll have a
fight on your hands." She ran a hand through her
tousled hair. "What do you think of our deadline?"

"We'll manage. You've got a great concept. All I have to do is plug into it. Of course, that still leaves one problem." Hidoshi cleared his throat. "The fact is, I happened to misplace my film."

Kara stared at him. "You? The man who packs for a three-month trip with a toothbrush and three suitcases full of cameras and film? The man whose idea of a celebration is a closeout sale at a film store? What's happened to you, Hidoshi?"

The photographer flushed. "Actually, I was busy tying up some loose ends last night. With Megan. I ended up staying rather late. At her apartment." He dug his hands in his pockets. "*Very* late," he said. "I—we—" He cleared his throat. "Damn it, Kara, you know what I'm trying to say."

"Oh, Hidoshi, I'm so happy! I'd just about given up on you two ever seeing the light!" She wrapped her friend in a warm hug. She had been watching the two of them move from awkwardness to friendship and finally to intense attraction. Everyone around them had noticed; only they had seemed oblivious. "I'm going to worm all the details out of Megan, I warn you."

Hidoshi flushed faintly. Kara kissed his cheek.

At that moment the laird of Dunraven Castle strode into the ballroom. There were lines on his forehead, and his mouth was grim. "It appears as if I'm disturbing something."

Kara spun around. "Duncan, this is Hidoshi Sato. He's our photographer and resident miracle worker."

Duncan didn't smile. "Welcome to Dunraven, Mr. Sato. I'll see that Angus brings in your baggage."

Hidoshi shrugged cheerfully. "I haven't got any. I always travel light."

Duncan looked at Kara. "I'll be in the village. Angus will help with whatever you need." Without waiting for an answer, he strode off down the corridor.

Kara's eyes snapped with anger. "Excuse me for a moment, Hidoshi."

"Don't mind me."

Kara caught up with Duncan and grabbed his arm. "That wasn't what you think, Duncan."

"And just what do I think it was? The kiss of a lover after a week of enforced celibacy? Do you make those soft little sounds for him too, Kara?"

She took a step backward, shocked by the cold cruelty of his words. Her face drained of color.

Duncan stood stiffly. "I'm sorry," he said finally. "I had no right to say that. In fact, it's better this way."

He didn't look as if it was better. He *looked* absolutely furious. "But Hidoshi and I, we're not that sort of friends."

Duncan stared past her. "It doesn't matter, Kara. What you do with him—well, it's not my business. I accept that." His voice was harsh. His words were like a blade sliding into her heart.

Kara's eyes took on a furious glitter. "I'm *so* glad you understand," she purred. "I was afraid you might be difficult about it." She gave a high, very false laugh. "Now I can get back to work. Hidoshi and I are going to be very busy for the rest of the day, and I think it would be best if no one disturbed us."

Let him make what he liked of *that*, she thought furiously.

Hidoshi turned as Kara returned. "What was that all about? Lord Dunraven looked furious."

"He *always* looks furious," Kara snapped. "In fact, he's the most hateful, high-handed, and unpredictable person I have ever met."

"Like that, is it?"

"Like what?" Kara glared at him.

"Don't ask me. I'm simply here to take some photographs." He was careful to hide his smile as Kara angrily flung down a pile of silk gloves.

By the time lunchtime rolled around, they had argued over lighting, scene composition, and layouts. Kara was exhausted, and her head was pounding. As she stood up and stretched stiffly, she heard footsteps out on the terrace, then the slam of a door, followed by Angus's knock.

"Will you be wishing to have luncheon served, Miss Fitzgerald? The laird has said you are not to wait for him but to eat whenever you like."

Kara sat up straighter. "I see."

"He's had a call from his factory, you see. Some problem with one of the prototype diving units. He will be gone the rest of the day."

"What Lord Dunraven does and where he goes is no business of mine," Kara said stiffly.

Angus was far too clever to say anything.

"Since we're nearly done here, perhaps we could eat out on the terrace. The light is splendid today." She looked at Hidoshi. "There won't be much else to do until Megan arrives this afternoon. We might as well enjoy the view. The film I ordered from Glasgow won't arrive much before that, anyway."

"There is one more thing I forgot to mention." Hidoshi cleared his throat. "It has to do with the models, I'm afraid."

"Don't tell me there were last-minute substitutions."

"Not exactly."

"They'd better not be *late*, Hidoshi. You know we only have a few days to finish here."

Hidoshi squirmed. "No, they won't be late. Actually, they won't be coming at all."

Kara's eyes took on an unnatural glitter. "Hidoshi Sato, what do you mean, there are no models? I thought we had that all arranged."

Hidoshi smoothed his purple hair irritably. "So did I. Someone intervened. Enticed them over to a competing magazine."

"*Who?*"

"Geoffrey."

Kara sank into a chair. "Geoffrey again. The man is twisted and will stop at nothing to hurt me. What are we going to do now? We have no film and no models."

"Luncheon is served, Miss Fitzgerald. On the terrace, as you wished." Angus looked bemused. "And

I thought you would wish to know that an auto has just arrived from the village. I believe it holds one of your staff."

"I don't suppose it's carrying three long-legged creatures with perfect skin and three striking males as escorts."

"Just one woman. She looks quite likable. I believe she told me her name is Megan." Mctavish smiled faintly. "Right before she tripped over a chair, dropped her suitcase, and spilled the contents of her handbag all over my kitchen," he added blandly.

"That *has* to be Megan." Kara looked accusingly at Hidoshi. *"You're* to blame. She was the most efficient person in the world until she fell in love with you. If I didn't like both of you so much, I'd be furious." She looked at Angus. "Would you mind setting another place, Angus? And if you happen to see any fashion models wandering about by the loch, do show them up."

The salmon was perfect and Angus cheerfully confided that Duncan had prepared their venison stew that morning and the rest of the dishes had come from the castle's freezer. The confession did nothing to dim anyone's appetite, and the superb venison stew garnished with fresh thyme disappeared in record time.

Kara bit into a fresh strawberry. "What about the two Romanian models we used last year? Didn't they move back to England?"

Megan shook her head. "They moved to Australia. The last I heard, they had opened a bed and breakfast and were doing extraordinarily well."

"Blast," Kara said tightly. "Maybe there's someone in the village."

"No luck," Megan answered. "I asked on the way up. They looked at me as if I'd suggested one of their children take poison."

"Then what are we going to do?"

Hidoshi looked at Megan. Megan looked at Hidoshi.

The photographer rubbed his purple hair. "There might be a solution close at hand."

"You know someone?" Kara sat forward eagerly. "I'm desperate, Hidoshi. Name your price."

"I don't think money is going to be a factor this time."

Kara frowned. She saw Hidoshi studying her thoughtfully. Megan was looking at her the same way.

The realization hit her. "Oh, no, you don't!" She jumped to her feet. "I refuse, do you hear?"

"Refuse what?" Dunraven's laird strode in through the terrace door and dropped a box onto the table. "More packages for you." His hair was tousled from the wind, and he smelled like the sea. His white linen shirt was open to a very bronze chest, and the sight of him made Kara's heart lurch.

"I refuse to model any lingerie, that's what. Not that it matters, since we don't have a man, either."

Hidoshi looked at Megan. Megan looked at Hidoshi, who cleared his throat. "Not exactly."

Kara frowned. The two were looking at Duncan.

"No," she said stiffly. "Absolutely, positively *no.*"

"This whole idea is *ridiculous!*" Kara glowered at Hidoshi. "I still don't understand why this blasted photo shoot has to be done today."

"The advertisers are worried. Geoffrey made certain word got out that our usual models aren't available. The lingerie firms want finished proofs in their hands by tomorrow at the close of work or they're pulling out of the issue."

Twelve cartons of photographic film packed in special lead-lined hampers were carried past, shepherded by two men who had flown in from Glasgow.

Kara paid no attention. "That means they'll pull out of any exclusive advertising sections too."

Megan nodded. "Martin said I wasn't supposed to remind you how much money we have riding on this."

"He would." Kara looked at Hidoshi. "How much time do we have?"

"I think our time ran out yesterday."

Kara sighed.

"You've seen a hundred shoots, Kara." Hidoshi studied Duncan, who was frowning from an armchair near the door. "I have no doubt that Lord Duncan will catch on equally fast."

Megan nodded eagerly. "I know you can do it, Kara. Don't you remember last year when that young French designer was so taken with you? He wanted you to model his whole spring line."

"Etienne was interested in my doing many things, Megan, but modeling his couture creations wasn't very high on the list," Kara said tightly. "No, it's just not going to work."

A chair squeaked. "Are you going to give up without a fight, Fitzgerald?" Dunraven stood looking at her, arms crossed. "I'm willing to give it a try. After all, how difficult can it be?"

Beneath the table Megan kicked Hidoshi.

"It's not as easy as you think," the photographer said. "You have to forget everything but the camera and focus on bringing the clothes alive. And you have to do it over and over again, until we get it exactly right."

Duncan muttered something in Gaelic. Hidoshi knew better than to ask what he'd said.

"How long will it take?"

"Three hours. Maybe four."

"I'm in."

Hidoshi kicked Megan.

Duncan's hair was mussed, his shirt sleeves were rolled up crooked over his forearms, and he had an oil smudge just above one cheekbone. Kara thought he was the most handsome man she had ever seen.

She glared at him. "Just don't say I didn't warn you."

"What do you mean, I moved?" Kara said to Hidoshi. "It was *him*. He jammed my elbow just as you snapped the picture."

"What about *you*?" Duncan jerked angrily at the black silk robe he was wearing over black silk pajama bottoms. He caught a look at himself in one of the mirrored panels and winced. "Hidoshi told you how to stand, so do it."

"I *can't*. You keep jabbing me in the ribs and making this damned lace thing fall off my arm." Kara tugged on the gown of silk organza under antique Battenburg lace. It clung to her body with revealing intimacy.

The effect was probably worth its $15,000 price tag, Duncan decided. "That damned thing falls off because it doesn't fit."

Kara's chin rose. "Are you saying something is *wrong* with my *shoulders*?"

Duncan jammed his fists on his hips, sending his black robe flapping like a cornered bird. "I'm saying the bloody thing doesn't *fit*, that's all!" He looked down, furious at the perfect shoulders so lovingly revealed by the antique lace. Furious, too, at the fine flush that made Kara look healthy and vibrant.

Furious most of all because his body had been in serious physical torment since Kara had eased out of a tartan robe to reveal the slide of lace that was to be the focal point of the lingerie session.

"Clothes to keep the hearth fires burning," Kara's assistant had called them. She seemed to know a great deal about the subject.

Not so her boss. Usually competent and utterly efficient, Kara had suddenly become all thumbs. Her smile was wooden, her body stiff, and even her breathing was jerky.

Any other time Duncan would have felt sorry for her.

But not today. Today he was sharing this nightmare with her, and the pain was burning him up.

He wrenched off the ridiculous silk robe that kept sliding from his shoulders. Muttering, he tossed it into a heap beside the lights assembled in the ballroom. What kind of man wore a silk robe, for God's sake? Scowling, he looked up, ready to blister Kara's ears if she offered the slightest provocation.

And then Duncan MacKinnon went entirely still. A small, hard knot began to form in his stomach.

Kara was turned toward the window, one shoulder slumped against the paneled wall. Only from where Duncan stood could anyone have seen the single tear sliding down her cheek.

"Are you having trouble with that sleeve again?" Megan looked up. "I can try tape, if you want."

Duncan saw Kara brush at her cheek. "No, it will be fine." Her chin rose. "I guess I'm just not built for this."

Proud. Damnably stupid. Totally unforgettable.

Duncan sighed.

She wanted this to work. She had planned for this layout, dreamed of it, and now nothing was going as she'd hoped.

He squared his shoulders. If Kara wanted perfection, he would give it to her on a silver platter. "Hidoshi, I think you and I had better have a talk outside. Man to man."

Thirty-two

"The robe looks ridiculous."

Hidoshi rubbed his jaw.

"Any suggestions?"

Hidoshi looked at Duncan. "Other than canceling the shoot, I'm not sure. Kara's desperate for this to succeed. She's been dreaming about this castle for weeks now. She wanted every detail to be perfect, and now she's totally frustrated with herself."

He was right, Duncan knew. Kara imagined every problem was a sign of her own failure. All the more reason to see that this damned photo shoot succeeded.

His eyes narrowed as he studied Hidoshi. "You two must be very close. Working together. Planning. Traveling. All sorts of late hours ..." His jaw was hard as he said the words.

Hidoshi just looked at him. After a moment he began to smile. "You think Kara and I are *lovers?*"

Duncan glared at him. "Aren't you?"

"Kara? Me?" His purple hair shook as he sank into a chair, laughing.

"I fail to see what's so funny," Duncan said stiffly.

"It's just—she's beautiful, she's talented, and she's fun to be with, but she's like an older sister." He smiled ruefully. "Besides, Megan would rip off my fingers joint by joint if she thought there was anything between us."

Duncan's lips thinned. "You mean that you and Megan ..."

"Megan and I."

"Bloody hell. What about that French designer you mentioned? Were he and Kara—"

"No," Hidoshi said flatly. "There's been no one for Kara since that damned Geoffrey Hampton. He hurt her. Sometimes I think none of us knows exactly how much." Hidoshi stabbed at the air. "And if you have the slightest idea of hurting her too, I'll cut your throat myself, Dunraven."

A slow smile began to play over Duncan's lips. "Hurt her? I want to see these photographs make fashion history. I'm no expert, but I think she's nervous about her face being splashed across the pages." He frowned down at a pile of extra lighting equipment. "Why not shoot in shadow, with our faces blurred? After all, the clothing is the main emphasis here. That way your readers can project themselves into the scenes."

Hidoshi sat up straighter. "Shadow," he murmured, scratching at his jaw. "No faces . . ." His eyes began to gleam. "MacKinnon, I think you've just had the idea of the century. But we're going to need a smaller room where I can set up some elaborate lighting effects. We are also going to need period furniture—pillows, crystal, and authentic accessories. Can you manage that?"

"My mother's old sitting room will be perfect. Nothing has been changed in there for years. How much time do we have?"

"Three hours tops. That leaves barely enough time for my developing."

"I can buy you some time by having one of my people shuttle the proofs by helicopter to Glasgow."

"A miracle worker." Hidoshi grinned. "I can see why Kara fell in love with you."

Duncan smiled crookedly. "Who said I—"

"Don't bother denying it." Hidoshi patted the Scotsman on the back. "Welcome to the club."

"That obvious, is it?"

"Only to another victim."

A man in a gray uniform walked past, carrying a canister of film.

"That goes in the storeroom at the end of the hall," Hidoshi called out.

The man shrugged. "First the workroom, then the kitchen, now the storeroom." Muttering, he strode away.

Duncan began to finger a handful of lace. His eyes took on a gleam. "Give me some time, Hidoshi." The lace spilled between his fingers. "Some time alone with Kara, to set the mood."

A look passed between the two men. After a moment Hidoshi nodded. "Get going, MacKinnon. I just remembered that we have to reset our filters. I can't imagine why I didn't think of it sooner."

Kara was standing before the open French doors. Duncan saw the tension in her shoulders. As he dropped a pile of pillows and gauzy fabric, she spun around.

"Are they ready?"

There were lines of strain in her face. They made Duncan angry. "Not yet." He moved to the window, where a world of silver and blue stretched to the ocean's end. "Seals gather down there at the headlands. When it's warm and humid, they sing, and the sound is like nothing else you've ever heard. World's End I always called it as a boy."

Kara clasped her arms. Duncan saw her shiver. "Cold?"

She shook her head. "It's just . . . so different here. The house, the legends, the sea. Everything calls to me, making me feel I've just come home from a long journey."

"You're trembling." Duncan slid a lace shawl gently around her shoulders. Very carefully he moved behind her and eased her back until she was resting against his chest. "Better?"

She nodded. He felt the tension slip out of her body. His hands moved up her shoulders, his thumbs tracing gentle circles. "You didn't sleep well, did you?"

She shrugged.

"Some whiskey will do the trick. Tonight you'll take a healthy drink before you go up."

Kara didn't turn. Her eyes were locked on the distant waters, restless and unpredictable as they washed against the curve of the cove. "I saw something in my room, some sort of a poem. It was in Gaelic."

Duncan bent his head and spoke softly, repeating the old phrases he'd learned at his nanny's knee. Lulled by the strange words, Kara's eyes half closed and he heard her breathing grow calm.

"What do they mean?"

"I'll translate them for you, though it won't do much good. Like any good poem, they raise far more questions than they answer." Duncan searched for the words to shape those ancient anonymous lines.

> "When summer and winter meet as one
> And music fills the stone,
> Broken shall be mended then
> When the shadow stands alone."

His lips were against her ear by the time he finished. Gently, he nuzzled her satin skin.

Kara gave a small sigh and eased closer. "I don't understand."

"It's said that the words prophesy the fall of Dunraven Castle. I'm not worrying terribly much, you understand, since summer and winter are not likely to meet as one anytime in the near future."

His hand was just below her breast, warm and solid. There was no tension or resistance in her body as she leaned against him. "You're very beautiful in this gown, do you know that?"

Kara shook her head. Her hair brushed his cheek, teasing him with a soft, elusive perfume.

"Ah, but you should, Kara Fitzgerald. You are a

sight to fire a man's dreams. Hidoshi wasn't lying when he told you these pictures will be wonderful."

Kara turned. She burrowed slightly against his chest. "How much did Hidoshi pay you to come in here and brainwash me?"

"Nothing," Duncan said gruffly. "He didn't have to." His hands rose slowly until they trapped her breasts. "I'm beyond hiding the effect you have on me."

He felt a shudder go through her as she recognized the hard muscle pressing at her hip. "I want to make love with you right now, Kara. Any man would, seeing you in that gown." His lips nuzzled her neck, planting hot, unhurried kisses all the way to her shoulder. He found the first of the small buttons at her thigh and eased it open.

"Duncan?" Her body stiffened.

"Hush," he murmured. "May your heart hold fire, Kara Fitzgerald. May the seals sing for you at midnight." Another tiny pearl slid free. Kara's breath was coming soft and uneven now. "May you find the world's end."

Duncan was not about to be hurried. He kissed the hungry skin that pressed against his fingers, barely contained by fragile lace.

He wanted her. His body was hard and heavy with wanting her. Cursing, he put the thought out of his mind. "I've discussed the photo shoot with Hidoshi. He's going to go with a shadowed image. No one will see your face, only the gown. The look will be lush, full of period objects, and very romantic. Hidoshi says it will probably be the very best work he's ever done."

He smiled when he heard the breathless sound escape from Kara's lips. She was beautiful, and he wanted to give her incontrovertible proof of that fact. He knew that if she saw herself now, eyes heavy with passion, body fluid and supple, she would see it too. And if several million other people did too, when they thumbed through the pages of *New Bride* magazine, then so be it.

She wanted her perfect article, and she was going to get it.

Two more buttons slid free beneath his careful touch. He felt the silk of her thigh beneath his calloused palm and the sharp throb of her pulse beneath his fingers. Her head turned. Her lips moved over his ear. Duncan grimaced with an instant stab of desire. The weight of her filled his hands, and her proud nipples nearly escaped the pristine lace.

The combination could have driven a man to his knees and left him howling. It certainly had every indication of doing that to him.

Duncan turned her slowly and slid soft kisses over her eyelids, smiling as she sighed and slid her hands around his neck.

Beautiful. Any more beautiful and he couldn't stand to look at her. Quickly he caught her up into his arms and strode upstairs to the sitting room, praying that Hidoshi had done his work.

He had. Silk walls reflected the gently muted light that Hidoshi had arranged with a master's eye. Flowers spilled over the fine old furniture. Here and there lay a lace blouse, an overturned silk slipper, a heavy pearl choker, as if left where they had fallen, removed in the slow, heady prelude to love.

Yes, it would be the best thing Hidoshi had ever done. It would quite likely be the most beautiful photograph that *New Bride* magazine had ever published, and that thought filled Duncan with unspeakable pride.

He set Kara down before him, nodded silently to Hidoshi, then spoke softly to Kara. "Turn to me, love. That's it. Put your hand on my shoulder." He eased her cheek back against his chest and murmured Gaelic phrases as the camera whirred gently, capturing a moment of pure enchantment.

Yes, he would give her this. Even if their paths led them apart, she would always have this, Duncan vowed.

This time when the frothy lace sleeve eased lower

on her shoulder, it lent an ineffable sense of seduction, hinting at an unveiling only moments away.

Duncan's heart was pounding with his fight for control when Hidoshi finally nodded and stood up, his camera caught at his chest. As if from a great distance Duncan heard him move outside.

The door closed softly.

"It's over?"

"All over."

"I'm . . . afraid, Duncan."

His eyes were hard as he locked the door, then pulled Kara close. "You don't have to be. Not here at Dunraven. What I miss, Angus won't."

"Not that. It's—it's the dreams. They're always in my thoughts. Dear God, I can't help thinking I've brought the danger here, back to *our* time."

He cut her off with his lips, open and slow and hungry against hers. At any other time he would have felt a stab of pride at how little it took to still her protests. Now it only made him angry at the cruel dreams that tormented her.

He didn't *believe* in past lives. He didn't believe in unfinished debts, at least not the kind that reached beyond death. The only thing that Duncan MacKinnon believed in at that moment was a woman with haunted eyes and racing pulse, a woman he loved beyond imagining. "Nothing's going to happen to me. How can it, when touching you leaves me invincible?"

"I'm frightened, Duncan. The piper. Kyle. Most of all you, and the power of what I'm feeling right now. You . . . *overwhelm* me. And I damned well hate to be overwhelmed."

He smiled at the anger in her voice. "The only thing I'm afraid of is waking up and finding this is just another fantasy."

She cleared her throat, her hair a copper cloud on her pale shoulders. "Thank you for what you did. I . . . was stupid and stiff. I would have ruined everything."

"The timing was wrong, that's all. This gown was

meant for your body, meant for you to shatter male hearts with."

"Don't lie. I'm not a woman who makes heads turn. It has to be honest between us, remember? There was desperation in her voice. "I'm not going to make the mistakes I made with Geoffrey. You deserve more than that."

"We both do." Duncan's voice hardened. "Marry me, Kara. Tomorrow, right after we finish that bloody wedding-gown shoot with Hidoshi."

Her face filled with color. "I . . . I don't know what to say."

"Say yes, damn it."

She laughed shakily. "I want to. I can't get you out of my mind. And as for my body . . ." She ran her hands over his tense shoulders. "That doesn't seem to be mine anymore. I'm changed, shaped for your touch. I can never go back to being what I was."

Duncan's fingers tightened in her hair. "I can't promise you forever, Kara. The piper has never lied before. You need to know that."

"You're *not* going to die. I'll take charge of your fêng shui. I'll change every mirror and chair and take these ceilings apart joint by joint, if I have to." Her fingers eased over his chest. "Now, about that energy flow I mentioned, Lord Dunraven."

His breath caught as she eased her hand beneath his shirt. "I'm listening." Dying while he did it, but listening.

"Maybe some realignments are in order. I have a few moves that might stimulate your *ch'i* flow."

"My *ch'i* is flowing bloody fine right now, Fitzgerald."

"Are you absolutely certain?" Her voice was all whispered innocence. "Maybe I should have another look at your bedroom to be sure."

"Forget the bedroom," Duncan said harshly. "We'll never make it there."

"Then what are we going to do about—"

"*This*." Impatiently his hand moved down the row

of tiny buttons, sending them flying as he freed the costly folds of old lace and seed pearls.

And then he simply stood, drinking in the sight of her, long legs, high, full breasts, and the flush of passion already blooming over her skin.

"God, Kara." His voice was strained. "It hurts to look at you. You have the beauty that counts, the kind I can see with my heart."

When he saw something slide from her eyes, he cursed. But before he could move, her fingers hooked the waistband of his pajamas and tugged the black silk down over his hard flanks. He felt himself swell painfully beneath her scrutiny.

"So do you, Duncan MacKinnon." And then, very gently, her hand closed around him.

He shut his eyes and ground his teeth with the pleasure she was giving him. When her gown whispered, forgotten, to the floor, Kara shoved it aside with a callousness that would have brought its high-strung designer instant cardiac arrest.

Her eyes were on his face as she traced his granite length. "I love your castle, Lord Dunraven. I love this beautiful land and your lush pear tree. I love your beams and shafts. But most of all . . ."

She planted soft kisses over his chest, stopping only to nuzzle the tight nubs of flesh nestled in the soft dark hair. "Most of all, I love the castle's intractable laird."

MacKinnon swallowed. "Is that a yes to my proposal?"

"It's a definite . . . maybe."

"Damn it, Kara, I don't want a *maybe*."

Lightning raced out over the sea. The first gusts of rising wind tapped against the shutters. Neither noticed, caught in their own flaring storm.

Duncan's fingers clenched at the pleasure her hands gave him. All she wore was a necklace of freshwater pearls, gleaming softly against her skin. She flowed against him like silver water, her body infinitely generous, made only for him.

"Say yes, Kara. Tell me now." His hands opened

on her hips, locking her against his rigid flesh. "I want to fill you and know it's forever."

She made a little choked sound as he eased her down upon him, his big hands wrapped around her hips. She was warm and yielding, already urgently in need of their joining.

But the blood of ancient warriors flowed in his MacKinnon veins, and Duncan would not forgo his exquisite torment until he heard the words he wanted. "Tell me, Kara." He held her above him, teasing an entrance but not completing it. "Now."

"Please, Duncan. You've already got my heart."

"Give me more. Give me the words. Say you trust me."

Her nails dug into his shoulders as he found her, then pulled away. "I do."

"Say you'll marry me."

A husky sigh. "Yes. Tomorrow. I only hope you don't regret it."

Slowly he impaled her on his hot length. "Like I'm regretting this?"

"Oh, God, Duncan, this feels—you feel . . ." Kara's eyes closed as pleasure ran through her in driving waves. "Perfect. Perfect inside me. Like the World's End."

He rocked against her and felt her exquisite tremors begin. Time melted around him, and his control frayed to nothing. Her climax came, and he groaned beneath the sweet, milking squeeze of her pleasure, then caught her ankle and pulled it around his waist until their bodies were locked. Duncan took her fiercely then, bone to bone, no longer calculating her pleasure. He was thrown far beyond that, blinded by the soft, erotic tightenings where she sheathed him.

"Dear God, don't let it stop. Hold me, Kara. Don't let this be another fantasy," he growled.

Kara gave him a crooked smile. Her body opened, rippling and soft, to receive him. "Does this feel like a dream, Duncan?"

He prayed for strength, wanting to shout with his

pleasure. "No dream. Even my best fantasies never felt *this* bloody good."

"Does this?" Kara's hand eased between them, cupping the exquisitely sensitive spheres where their bodies met. Battered with pleasure he had never known, Duncan muttered hoarsely and gave way to a slamming wave of desire. Again and again he drove into her, flooding her with his hot seed, claiming the very deepest part of her.

His smile was dark, ancient, a warrior's smile, as he felt her cry out and tighten against him one last time.

Thirty-three ～

Time passed.

Finally his blood began to slow its frantic race. He touched her mouth gently. "Still with me?"

"With you? I think." Her laughter was husky.

Duncan felt her legs begin to wobble, and somehow he managed to lock her against him before sinking back against the cut-velvet sofa. Outside, angry arcs of lightning tore at the night. Blindly, too tired even to open his eyes, he found her face with his lips.

Then he said the words he'd never said before, in rough Gaelic and in low, broken English. He said them for the mother he had loved and lost, for the boyhood innocence he'd forfeited too young. Most of all, he said them to the woman who had turned him inside out and touched his soul.

The woman he swore would tomorrow be his wife.

Duncan smiled at the thought. "Shouldn't we be looking for some things borrowed and blue?"

"I don't think I could manage it right now. I doubt I'll ever move again," came Kara's husky answer.

"Some kind of bridal expert you are." Duncan teased the silky skin where she held him. "Maybe some *ch'i* flow is in order."

"Duncan, I *can't*." But amazingly, she could.

Her body arched. "But you—you couldn't possibly. I mean, not yet."

His smile was whiskey-smooth. He began to harden, moving inside her again. "Can't I? You must have worked miracles with that bedroom rearrangement, Ms. Fitzgerald. Allow me to demonstrate."

"Show-off," she said.

And then they closed their eyes, beyond the need for words.

Duncan awoke two hours later to the sound of the shutters banging in the wind. Kara was curled against him, her fingers buried in his hair. He smiled gently, eased off the couch, and looked around for his clothes. Damned if he was going to put those *silk* things on again.

As quietly as possible, he tugged on his navy trousers and a dark sweater, then padded barefoot to the corridor. Outside, darkness covered the sky, and he could hear the distant growl of surf slamming against the rocks beyond the cove.

"Bad weather coming, Duncan." Mctavish emerged from the kitchen, frowning. "The radio says we've a gale-force storm moving in from the Faroes, and we'll be lashed with rain before morning." The old man's lips curved. "Not that being out of touch with the outside world is going to bother *you*."

Duncan smiled crookedly. "You can be the first to congratulate me, Angus. That stubborn woman in there has agreed to marry me. If she doesn't drive me mad, I'm going to be the happiest man on earth."

Mctavish pounded him on the back, smiling broadly. "I knew the piper never lied. As for that nonsense about Rose Cottage, it's nought but empty legend." He cocked his head. "You'll be hungry, I wager. There's cold ham in the refrigerator and oatmeal bread that my wife just put in. Those two friends of Miss Fitzgerald's are down in the ballroom, arguing over f-stops." Mctavish rubbed his jaw. "At least I think that's what they were arguing about."

Duncan chuckled. "Let them argue, Angus. They're two people in love. Now, take yourself off to bed. I'll see to whatever we need from the kitchen."

A smile lurked around Mctavish's mouth. "I un-

derstand congratulations are in order for the successful photographic shoot today. Black silk pajamas, was
it? I'll have to ask my Moira for a pair of my own."

The pounding of the surf woke Kara. Hard and
erratic, it slammed against Dunraven's rocky cove.

Kara blinked, brushing away tendrils of sleep and
squinting at the clock. Eight P. M. and the sky pitch
black. A storm brewing.

Slowly she eased up against the arm of the couch.
As she did a velvet smile curved her lips.

World's End. She had found it with Duncan. She
had raced the storm and heard the seals sing. For
tonight, that was enough.

She felt something brush at her shoulder. The lacy
remains of her gown, the gown that Duncan had removed with such single-minded haste. Heat filled her
at the memory. She stared out at the darkness.

She had told him yes.

She was going to be his wife.

After all the years of wariness and evasion, she had
finally found a man to trust, a man strong enough to
bear the weight of her singular gift.

A tear slid down Kara's cheek, but she shoved it
away.

Now was no time for tears. Now was a time to
sing and laugh and plan for a house filled with
scraped knees and grubby hands and dark curls.

Exactly the color of Duncan's hair.

Duncan . . .

Kara jumped to her feet. He must have gone to
explain their odd disappearance to Hidoshi. Her
cheeks burned at the thought, but she couldn't keep
a smile from filling her eyes. She was in love, and
she wanted *everyone* to know it.

In the darkness she bumped against a chair leg.
Wincing, she made her way to the switch on a Tiffany lamp nearby. Muted light spilled from beneath
the glass shade depicting a rose-covered cottage that
bore a striking resemblance to the cottage down the
hill.

Shivering, Kara pulled on her skirt and sweater, then turned to look for her long-forgotten shoes. Rain skittered over the windowpanes, but inside all was quiet, glowing in the mellow rose and gold of the exquisite stained-glass lampshade.

Then Kara saw the tall glass case that filled the far wall. Inside the case, on a pedestal of carved mahogany, lay two polished shafts of English yew, each three feet in length. A stout string was twisted around each nock and then draped loosely over the broken grip where the two shafts should have joined.

Kara felt a drumming in her chest.

The Dunraven bow, the one Nicholas Draycott had so lovingly described. There was beauty here, beauty and dreams and a wild, savage past. Who had shaped those shafts and carved their grooves? Who had slid bowstring to yew and then pulled the great string taut?

Drawn by the ancient weapon, Kara leaned forward and stretched out her hands. The glass case was cool, smooth. She closed her eyes and let her senses drift and climb.

Drumming. Horses at the gallop.

Outside, the wind hammered at Dunraven's walls. As Kara listened the sound changed, swallowed up by the neigh of horses and the shouts of angry riders.

Huw led her to an old mill on the banks of a quiet pond. The Valley of Draycotte was only a league away, and the dust of the road filled their throats.

The miller's ale was smooth, his attentions pronounced. At Huw's urging, Tamsyn—or Arduaine—donned the cloak that Rowan had given her.

"Most fine, my lady. A Draycotte you look, in truth."

But her looks would not protect them, Tamsyn thought. Only Huw's stout arm and the truth of her birth as witnessed by Draycotte's abbot could shield them from the sheriff's wrath.

She turned to look for the miller, only to find him gone. In truth the whole mill yard was suddenly empty of man and beast.

Cold filled her heart. She looked for Huw, who was already reaching for his bow.

"Make haste," he cried.

Horses thundered into the yard, flecks of foam on their heaving flanks. Shouts filled the air, and above them rang the sheriff's shrill cry.

"The outlaws! There, just as I swore."

Tamsyn stared at Huw in terror. He cursed in an unknown tongue, then pulled Tamsyn toward the kitchens. "Damn the miller for betraying us. We must confront William in the abbey, where his villainy can be witnessed. Not here, with no one to check his fury. Make haste, my lady. By the Savior, make haste!"

Through the narrow hall they ran, scattering chickens and dogs. Huw pushed her through the door and down into a stone tunnel musty with age.

"Faster," he growled as footsteps echoed behind them. "It's only a few steps until—"

Before them stretched the tunnel mouth, bright with afternoon sun and a border of overhanging roses.

Then a shadow filled the light, and another and another, until no more light was left.

Tamsyn's hands began to tremble.

The knife point glittered in the firelight. Honed and lethal, it rose and toyed with Tamsyn's hair.

"Where is he, fool?" William hissed at Huw, held captive by four brawny guards. "Speak, or the outlaw's whore will find her useless throat slit by my blade."

"He stayed behind," Huw answered.

"You mean to convince me that Rowan de Beauclair let you ride back into my hands unescorted?"

"We tricked him. While he lay sleeping, we slipped away."

The blade caressed Tamsyn's cheek and neck and then her breast. "Sleeping, was he? Worn out from riding his whore's milk-white thighs, no doubt."

"Be careful of your tongue." Huw struggled wildly, his face red with fury. "I serve a noble lady, a lady of highest blood."

William laughed shrilly. Spittle slid down his jaw. "Then your eyes are weak."

"She is Arduaine, the daughter of Draycotte. She wears the scar of proof on her chest."

A hush filled the hall. William's eyes narrowed. "You lie," he hissed.

"Ask the abbot," Huw thundered. "You cannot hope to hide this evil. Even if you slay me now, Draycotte will learn of your treachery toward his daughter. His wrath will be even worse than de Beauclair's."

"This is much talk for a bound and captive man," William sneered. "As for Arduaine, I would see your proof."

His blade slit the loop of her cloak. The fine wool pooled over the floor like blood. Again the blade fell, glinting in the taper's light, and this time Tamsyn's worn linen gown parted cleanly.

In the dancing light her skin was molten gold. On the curve of her left breast there was a single crescent scar.

William cursed beneath his breath, then jerked his blade back to her throat. "A trick," he cried. "A mark most easily copied by a clever outlaw and his whore."

But his men were restless, uncertainty filling their eyes. Mutters of surprise turning to certainty rose from their lips.

"Silence!" the sheriff cried, his breath hot at Tamsyn's neck. "No outlaw's whore shall mock me and live. We shall wait until de Beauclair returns. Then he will join these two, and all three will feel the stretching of my noose!"

She paced the cold stone of her darkened prison, praying Rowan would return—and praying he would never come. William had made her climb over stairs covered with thorns, and now her bare feet left a trail of blood over the cold floor.

But Tamsyn did not notice the throbbing in her soles or the cold that racked her body. She was numb.

Her lips moved, framing prayers for her lover's safety.

Incense rose in billows. Candles blazed from every wall. Each monk had taken his proper place. All except the abbot, whose duties were being carried out by another.

William the sheriff watched with barely contained impatience as the chapel filled. His eyes ran over every face, but nowhere did he find the one he sought.

His fists closed. He thought of the woman hidden in the curtained alcove to his left. Tonight she would speak. Tonight she would plead to do his bidding, once de Beauclair was in his grasp.

Sweat sheened his upper lip. Heat stabbed at his swollen manhood. Tonight . . .

Someone jostled his arm. Down the aisle stumbled a cripple. His pockmarked face was streaked with dust, his arms covered with sores.

William drew back in disgust.

The acolytes filed in, incense drifting around them. On the altar dais, William's own priest raised his hand in a curt order.

Tamsyn moved down the aisle, guided by two of William's strongest men. Her long hair fell unbound, spilling almost to her bare feet, and a single garland of blood-red roses covered her brow.

Abbey roses.

Blood-red for the outlaw's whore.

Her eyes found his. Her contempt was like a blow.

William cursed softly as he came to his feet beside her. Soon she would learn a wife's proper respect.

His fingers gripped her wrist, tightening cruelly. His other hand dug into her waist. But she would make no move to escape him, William knew. Not with the Welshman laid out upon the rack in William's keep.

His eyes glowed in a haze of madness and lust. Around him pure young voices rose in song. Meanwhile, threescore men circled the abbey, and twice that many scoured the neighboring hills.

Today, he thought, his half brother would die, and tonight Draycotte's daughter would be his.

Tamsyn's face was a mask, her step unflinching.

On she walked, past priest and beggar, hauberks and surcoats a blur. Then she felt a prickle at her neck. A heaviness in her chest. She blinked, looking to her left.

And saw a familiar face, and then another.

Rowan's band, cleanly scrubbed and garbed as acolytes. Which meant that Rowan, too . . .

Her breath caught. Rowan!

"Hold, wolf spawn!" The lone voice thundered through the great room.

William's fingers tensed. He turned slowly, his blade hidden beneath his long cloak.

"Well met, de Beauclair," William hissed. "But you calculate most poorly."

Tamsyn froze as a man stepped from the shadows and shoved back his hood. No cripple now, his back was tall, and his staff was revealed to be a great bow made of yew wood.

No, she screamed in vain silence as a dozen of William's men inched up the aisle toward the man she loved. Silently, at William's prearranged nod, the archers hidden in a side niche nocked their arrows and stepped forward.

Fear slammed down her chest. Anger tore at her throat. Muscles clenched in searing pain.

Archers leveled at Rowan's back as he stood there, unaware.

She gave a cry—hoarse, unformed, almost that of a woodland creature. It rang down the aisles, spilled to the high vaulted arches, and sent William stumbling backward.

"For that, you'll die," he screamed, blade to her neck.

Tamsyn fought wildly, kicking her bare feet. Her throat burned as she struggled with her demons of fear, desperate to force out the words that would warn Rowan of his danger. Somehow she could do it. She had to manage, before it was too late . . .

Kara shuddered, blinded by the scent of incense, the taste of fear. Unconsciously, she twisted, and with that sharp movement sent the glass case falling, shattering on the floor. Trancelike, she was drawn to the ancient bow resting among the shards of broken glass. Mellow wood filled her fingers.

In a searing burst of sight, she knew.

Danger in the touch.

Duncan had to see. Duncan had to understand before it was too late.

Outside, the wind hurled itself at the windows and clawed at the slate roofs. A shadow moved and Kara's eyes widened.

Her scream was swallowed up in the fury of the storm.

When Duncan emerged from the kitchen, he was carrying a tray stacked high with buttered bread, ham, and Mrs. Mctavish's handmade fudge. He was grinning hugely when he shoved open the door to the quiet sitting room with his foot.

Inside all was in shadow. Raindrops rattled against the windows.

"Kara?" he asked softly. There was a rustling in the darkness to his right. "Are you awake, *mo cridhe?*"

With shocking force light slashed into his eyes. He blinked, nearly dropping the tray. "What the devil—"

The hard, low laughter that filled the room made him go rigid.

"Dear, dear Duncan, how thoughtful of you to bring me food after my long journey."

Smiling coldly, Kyle MacKinnon stepped from the shadows.

Thirty-four ~

$H$is eyes were pale, not as blue as Duncan's, and his face was thinner, but the resemblance between them was still shocking.

Duncan's fingers tightened on the silver tray. "Kyle." It was an oath.

"You remember my name. Odd, I thought you had forgotten, after you left me in that wretched jail."

"That was your friends' doing, not mine," Duncan said grimly. He stared into the shadows, his eyes glittering. "Where is she?"

"Do you mean the American woman with that extraordinary skill?" As he spoke, he shone his flashlight across the room. Its beam picked out Kara's motionless figure, seated on the sofa. Her hands were tied before her, and a silk gag covered her mouth.

"Damn you, Kyle, if you've laid a finger on her, I'll—"

His brother's cold laughter cut him off. "She's very beautiful, but no, I haven't touched her. Not yet."

As Duncan started forward, Kyle slid a revolver from his pocket. "Not so fast, brother. We have a bit of unfinished business first."

"Let her go, Kyle. She has nothing to do with us."

"She saved your life in London, old man. That makes her part of it." The revolver rose as Duncan's hands tightened to fists. "Don't tempt me," Kyle hissed. "Otherwise she'll get a bullet between the eyes." The words were as cold as the rain that lashed the windows.

"What do you want, Kyle?"

"First I want all the English pound notes in that safe in your study. And don't bother to tell me you've got nothing there because I watched you put them in just two hours ago."

"What else?"

"The keys to that helicopter out by the woods."

Duncan gave an explosive laugh. "In this weather? Even *you* aren't fool enough to try that, Kyle."

"The keys are to ensure that you don't follow me, brother dear." He moved closer.

Duncan saw that hardness had lined his mouth and dissipation already etched his face. "What else?"

Kyle smiled faintly and looked across the room at the woman on the sofa. "Then I fancy that Ms. Fitzgerald and I will go for a little trip."

"*No, damn you!*" The words were an explosive roar.

Kyle raised the muzzle of the revolver. "Oh, yes. Just to ensure that you don't do anything stupid, like try to follow me. Not that you will, of course. You're going to be too busy here at Dunraven trying to locate all the little surprises I've left for you."

"Lies, Kyle. You haven't had time to rig explosives here. Angus would have noticed something out of place."

His brother laughed softly. "Oh, but the preparation was done long ago. All I had to do was bring my playthings here and put them in place. You *do* remember the workmen carrying all those cans of film today, don't you? Damnably easy to slip my things in among them."

Duncan didn't betray his anger by a single gesture. "You're bluffing, Kyle."

His brother's eyes narrowed. "Three, Duncan. Two here and one in Rose Cottage." His eyes glittered, driven by an anger that edged toward madness. "And this time you won't have the woman's skill to help you find them."

The wind cracked against the windows and sent a

shutter slamming free. With a scream of protesting metal, it shattered the glass and hurtled inside.

It was just the distraction Duncan had been waiting for. In the split second that Kyle turned away, Duncan hoisted the tray, threw it at his brother, then dived toward Kara.

The slam of contact made Kyle drop his flashlight, and the room was thrown into darkness. Frantically, Duncan groped for Kara's feet. There would be no time to find the revolver in the darkness. At most, he hoped to see Kara to safety before Kyle recovered.

Duncan felt the outline of one bare ankle and squeezed reassuringly. As he pulled Kara to her feet, his mind raced. Two meters to the door. No other way out. Tugging Kara close, he spun to the left while Kyle cursed and scrambled across the carpet in search of his light.

Kara swayed against Duncan in the darkness. He could feel her trembling. Only two more steps, then through the door, down the hall, and into the kitchen to the phone.

Light flashed through the room. "One more bloody inch and I'll shoot you," Kyle hissed. "But before I do it, I'll shatter *her* spine."

Duncan's hands tightened on Kara's shoulders. For a moment anger blinded him. Slowly he shoved it aside. He couldn't afford any emotion now. "I'll fly you out," he said expressionlessly. "In the helicopter you can get farther than you could in any craft at sea. Wait until morning, when the wind has died down."

"Not possible, old boy. I've some nasty friends at my heels, people who didn't look kindly on me when they found out their money had vanished. I plan to be long gone before they come marching into the castle at dawn. They've been one step behind me for weeks now."

"There's no end to your callousness, is there? Is it part of you, Kyle, a disease you were born with? Or was it because of what happened out on the loch?"

Duncan was stalling, groping for any possibility of escape. The odds weren't very promising.

"Don't think to waste time so Angus Mctavish can come to your rescue. The old fool is lying in the storeroom. I hit him rather hard, I'm afraid. He was bleeding badly when I locked him in. A pity if he never comes 'round."

Duncan's fists tightened. "You never change, do you, Kyle?"

"Why should I? Everything has worked out just as I wanted. First Calendish goes, then those two inept fools I hired to arrest you. Oh, yes, I mustn't forget the nun. Taking her habit was rather a stroke of genius. No one ever really looks at a nun, after all." He laughed. "Now, go get the money and those keys, and don't try anything clever." He eased the muzzle of his squat revolver beneath Kara's chin. "Go, damn it."

Grimly, Duncan started for the door.

"And you can forget about trying the telephone." Kyle's mouth curved. "You'll find that the line's been cut."

Nicholas Draycott frowned as he punched in a quick series of numbers on his telephone.

"Sinclair? Draycott here. I'm worried. I've had no answer at Dunraven Castle."

"Only to be expected." Sinclair's voice was casual. "There's been a storm driving out of the Faroes for the last hour. I've been listening on the radio. The lines are probably down."

Nicholas knotted the phone cord restlessly. "Look, I know you said that Kyle was intercepted just off Portugal, but something doesn't feel right, Sinclair."

There was an explosive sound from the other end of the line. "I didn't say anything of the sort."

Nicholas sat up straighter. "But I had a message from your office."

"When?"

"Yesterday evening."

"Not from *my* office, you didn't." Sinclair cursed. "Get yourself to Hastings, Draycott. I'll have a plane pick you up there in twenty minutes. We're going to Scotland."

Duncan's face was harsh in the glare of Kyle's powerful flashlight. "Here's the money and the keys to the chopper. Leave her here, Kyle."

"Impossible, brother dear. That would spoil all the fun, you see. And I've been waiting for this moment for a very long time." He pulled away Kara's gag, untied her hands, and tossed her a coat. "Put it on," he ordered. "And I suggest you be careful about it. Any tricks and I'll see your lover's blood splattered all over the carpet."

Fury filled Duncan as he looked at Kara's white face. Her hands were unsteady, slipping awkwardly as she pulled on the dark wool coat. "Where are you going, Kyle? You'll never get far, not in this weather."

"I don't need to get far. Only far enough so that certain former associates lose my trail." Without taking his eyes off Duncan, Kyle caught up the precious old longbow from the table at his side. "A pity if this were lost. It has so much family history, after all."

He took a step back and glanced at Kara. "Hurry up, damn it." There was a pinched look on his face. "Haven't you ever wondered why I hate you so, Duncan?"

Duncan shrugged. "Because you're a coldblooded bastard, I guess."

Kyle MacKinnon's pale eyes glittered. "Look at the Bible in the attic someday, brother dear. Read the entries. Read them carefully."

"What do you mean?"

"Twins, born minutes apart. All rested on so much."

"So?"

"So, *you* were the younger son. It was all supposed to be mine, but one day our dear father decided it would be better if he switched the entries. He meant to cut me out of any chance of having Dunraven."

Duncan's face paled. "You're mad, Kyle."

"The old bastard never could stand me, of course. Once, I heard him tell Angus that I wasn't fit to inherit."

"He couldn't have done such a thing. And our mother—"

"You always were a gullible fool," Kyle said contemptuously. "They did it together. They made *you* the laird of Dunraven."

Duncan's head was reeling. "But what about the birth records? The official documents?"

"A few judicious phone calls took care of that. We were born here at the castle, after all. Only Mrs. Mctavish was present, and it was an easy matter to buy her silence. He simply said there had been a mistake with the times and saw to it that you became his bloody, beloved firstborn." Kyle's eyes glittered. "I'd suspected it after I'd gone through his desk several times. I confronted our sweet, weak mother. Oh, she never admitted it, but I saw the truth in her eyes. Then I found the old Bible. They didn't dare lie there." Kyle laughed coldly. "That summer I tried to murder you on the loch. I would have done it, too, except that *she* came along. She knew what I was planning and hoped to stop me. That oar was meant to knock you under, not rescue you."

"You killed her, damn it. You would have killed me too, if the other boats hadn't come out when they did."

Kyle shrugged. "She never should have tried to interfere. She was weak—for that she deserved to die."

Thunder cracked overhead, rattling the shutters. The sound seemed to shake Kyle from his dark reverie. With a curse, he grabbed Kara, shoving her before him. "Good-bye, Duncan. One move outside, and you can be certain I'll kill her. You'll be too busy in here anyway." Laughing, he tossed his watch down on the table. "You now have exactly two hours until detonation."

"Unless you trigger them by remote control first."

Kyle's eyes glittered. "Always an intriguing possibility, isn't it?" He moved toward the door, only to find his way blocked by Hidoshi and Megan.

"What's wrong?" Hidoshi said. "We heard noises—" He stopped when he saw the gun at Kara's throat. "Let her go, damn you!"

Duncan stilled him with a sharp gesture.

"Very good of you, brother dear. And bloody wise. At least this way she'll have a sporting chance. Just like the good old days, isn't it?"

"The old days were never good. Not with you, Kyle."

The last thing Duncan saw was Kara's white face, her eyes full of terror. And then he realized that she had picked up Kyle's watch. It would be full of his energy, heavy with his emotions.

Her jaw tensed as she shoved it into her pocket.

She was reading it, Duncan knew. She would use it against her captor when she got the chance.

If she got the chance.

He waited ten minutes, giving Megan and Hidoshi terse instructions all the while. "Then get Nicholas Draycott on the shortwave. You'll find it up in my study. Tell him to get up here with Sinclair and some men." He turned to Megan. "Megan, my damned brother left Angus somewhere in the storeroom. Can you find him and take care of him? I'm afraid he may be hurt badly."

Megan nodded briskly, though her face was pale. "But what about Kara?"

"I'll take care of Kara," Duncan said grimly. "Once you have Angus, you three get out of here. Take the Land Rover down to the village. Stay to the main road and go slowly. You should make it in twenty minutes." He pulled a canvas bag over his shoulder and moved toward the door. "Whatever you do, touch nothing in here and be sure that you go out *only* through the broken window."

"But why?" Hidoshi was frowning.

"Because my cursed brother has wired the castle to blow up in a little less than two hours."

Thirty-five ~

It seemed as if Kara had been hunched against the storm forever. Her heart was slamming against her ribs and she could barely see with the wind gusting around her, lashing her with rain.

Behind her, Kyle rammed the revolver into her back. "Hurry up, damn you. We don't have much time."

The storm growled and pounded around them and they moved on in the darkness, the seconds crawling past.

Kara heard scuffling, and then a dark shape hurtled through the air, a compact body that landed deftly on four feet.

Kyle cursed. His gun rang out in a rapid spatter of sound. As it did, Kara threw herself sideways in a desperate effort to escape.

Kyle hunched against the slanting rain. "If you run, I'll trigger the explosives here and now, bitch. They'll all go up—your friends, Angus, and my brother along with them." He pulled a small box of dark metal from his pocket as he spoke.

Kara had no doubt he was telling the truth. Biting back a sob, she stumbled to her feet. "I'm here, damn you."

He sent a blow across her jaw that left her reeling, but Kara didn't make a sound. In truth, she had wanted the rough contact, for in that instant she had seen deep into Kyle's cold mind.

He was frightened. He knew he was being tracked. His enemies were close now, and it was only a matter of minutes before they would find him.

"What, no tears? Proud little bitch, aren't you? But we'll see how proud you are in the middle of the ocean in a gale-force wind." As he shoved her forward, Kara felt the outline of a wild plan taking shape in her mind.

The instant ten minutes had passed, Duncan jumped through the broken window and bolted for the helicopter.

Hidoshi and Megan had already roused Angus, his head bloody from a blow by Kyle's revolver. Together the two helped the old man down to the car, and Duncan watched the vehicle lumber through sheets of rain toward the village.

Frowning, he fingered the radio, praying that Kyle had not had time to destroy it before his departure.

Static filled the air, then the crisp voice of a military operator.

Duncan barked out the code words Sinclair had given him in the event that Kyle surfaced. "London, this is Mad Dog-1, calling for the Piper. Do you read me?"

There was a slam of indrawn breath, followed by an instant of static. Then he heard Sinclair's voice.

"Dunraven, is that you? Good God, we've been trying to raise you for hours. Where *are* you?"

"At the castle. Kyle's just been here."

"I'm en route right now with Nicholas Draycott. We should be there inside the hour."

"Not soon enough, I'm afraid. Listen, Sinclair, stay away from the castle. Kyle has been here. The whole thing is rigged to blow up in two hours."

"At 2300 hours?"

"Close enough. Kyle's got Kara. I'm going after them."

"Dunraven, what can we do to help?"

"You can pray, Sinclair. Pray loud and long and hard. It's a gale up here and zero visibility."

"But how will you—"

Duncan dropped the receiver and started to run. He was at the edge of the terrace when he saw a flash of light, followed by the muffled snarl of three fast shots.

He cursed.

Some instinct made him slam his hand into the ancient carved capstone while he prayed desperately that Kara was still alive.

Kara could hear waves crashing against unseen rocks. Spray pelted her face, mixed with pounding rain.

Kyle cursed as he tripped, then righted himself. His powerful flashlight sent a beam of light down into the snarling waters. "There's the boat. You're coming with me as insurance, in case my bloody brother tries anything heroic."

"You'll never get away. Friends and enemies— they're all after you now." Kara let her fingers slip over the watch Kyle had thrown onto the sitting-room table. Even now the cold metal burned at her touch, heavy with his anger. "If your nasty friends don't get you, your own government will." The contact was excruciating, bringing her a terrible awareness of Kyle's sordid past. Images of violence choked her, but Kara couldn't let go. The information from the contact was too valuable.

"It's not *my* government, Ms. Fitzgerald. I'm a Scotsman, remember?"

"Don't pretend this is for politics or honor. You don't have any honor, or any politics beyond yourself." Kara swallowed, trying to focus the flood of images. "There are three of them, aren't there? You know exactly what they're capable of. They don't let anyone who has betrayed them get away."

He slammed the gun against her chin. "What the hell do you know about them?"

"I can see the future, Kyle. All of it. It was I who found your bomb in London, don't you know? They're out there right now, Kyle."

He stiffened, looking sharply around him into the darkness. Then he slapped her once, very hard, directly across the mouth. "No more talking, damn you."

And in that instant Kara knew her plan was the right one.

Kyle cursed, muttering in harsh Gaelic. A powerful tri-level speedboat rocked before them now, the lines creaking in protest before the ten-foot waves.

"Get in, damn you." He shoved her onto the boat, and her knee slammed against the metal rail. As she fell, something slid against her ankle, something soft but with tremendous power.

Kyle jumped down after her and shoved her to one side, his fingers busy at the controls. If she bolted now, she might just make it. In the dark, his shot would probably miss her.

"Forget it," Kyle said, without bothering to look back. "I can detonate that castle any time I want, and my brother with it. But maybe I won't need to. If they try to tamper with any of my handiwork, they'll blow themselves to Antarctica."

Kara sank back against the seat. Her fingers clutched at the wave-swept sides of the boat as the motor growled to life.

They were easing away from the cove when a sound came from the boat's shadowed companionway. "How very nice to see you again, Señor MacKinnon. We have waited many days for the pleasure." A man emerged. His eyes were flat and hard.

There was a revolver in his hand.

Duncan could have sworn he'd heard a cat.

There had been a burst of gunfire, then a shrill cry that sounded feline. Kyle must be heading down to the cove, probably to a boat moored there. But why a cat, out here in the storm?

Duncan glanced down at his watch, hoping that Sinclair knew enough to stay away. There was no doubt that the castle would go up like clockwork, just as Kyle had promised. He forced down a wrenching wave of pain at the thought of the proud old stones shattered by a MacKinnon's mad rage.

And then he forgot about everything except Kara.

"There it is, just ahead," Sinclair shouted to the pilot hunched grimly at the controls. The wind was a howling fury now, and even the huge military helicopter was struggling to stay airborne. "Thank God you SAS fellows are used to this kind of muck."

"Bit of a blow, Lieutenant, but we'll have you down in the village in a few minutes."

"Be careful. Under no circumstances do I want to be seen."

The pilot nodded, and Sinclair looked gravely at his watch.

"And now, Señor MacKinnon, you will come away from the motor and throw away your weapon." The man with the dead eyes moved forward, flanked by two companions. Both were armed.

Kyle didn't move. "And if I don't?"

"You will die now. In a far more unpleasant way than you need to."

"Bullshit, Santiago. No matter what I do, you're going to make it long and painful."

The man smiled slowly.

Kara watched Kyle reach into his pocket. She gently brushed his arm, too lightly for him to notice. Focusing, she picked up shapes and outlines.

Three bombs. One triggered by mercury, one using some sort of magnet as a trigger, the third a simple timed device hidden in a lamp in Duncan's bedroom.

Anger washed through her, swift and sharp, tangled with fear.

"You will come with us now, Señor MacKinnon. Our boat is moored close by. First we will talk about our money that you stole. Then we will talk about other things."

Kyle yanked Kara in front of him, using her as a shield. "I think not, Santiago."

Thunder rumbled through the sky.

"Do not think you can escape us, Señor MacKinnon."

Kara felt the sharp point of the bow wedged under Kyle's arm. She could hardly believe he'd retained his hold on it. Desperately, she jerked to one side, pulling the bow with her, then jammed it into his back with all her might. Cursing, he arched in pain.

Suddenly the night exploded into furious color. Kara gasped at the burst of noise and fury that had nothing to do with the storm and everything to do with the bomb that had just gone off at the castle.

Dunraven Castle, she thought in horror. Too late, too late. Kyle had won.

In that blind moment of shock, Kyle slammed past her, knocking her to her knees and scrambling over the deck toward the starboard rail.

But he had not seen the big sailboat thrusting toward them, its moorings torn free in the gale. Nor had he seen the shattered boom that pitched wildly with each swell. Had he been standing, the jagged edge would only have struck his knees and sent him hurtling overboard. But he was crouching, lurching forward as he searched blindly for his gun.

The splintered boom slammed upward and caught him straight on, impaling him through the throat.

Kara gasped as she heard his gurgling curse of pain. Then there was only an abrupt silence while he hung, grotesquely suspended on the pitching boom.

The man in the companionway said something angry in Spanish, then spit onto the deck. With a sharp nod he summoned the others. Together their footsteps pounded over the deck; then they melted over the boat's side, into the night.

Behind Kara came the cough of a motor. She barely heard, staring blindly at the grisly sight before her.

Then she felt the touch of strong, familiar hands on her shoulders.

"Duncan!" Her throat tightened convulsively. "He didn't hurt you."

"No, *mo ghaol*, he didn't."

Smoke drifted on the wind. Kara shuddered,

locked against Duncan's chest. Behind them came the din of voices and the rumble of motors.

"The castle, Duncan."

"It doesn't matter. Only that you're safe. My God, when I thought of what Kyle might do to you." He said no more, his hands clenched harshly on her back as the smell of gunpowder filled the air.

A moment later Nicholas Draycott and the tight-lipped Lieutenant James Sinclair jogged over the hill. "Lord Dunraven, are you there?"

"Right here, Sinclair."

"And Ms. Fitzgerald?"

"Right beside me, safe and sound."

"Thank God. What about your brother?"

"Over there." Duncan pulled Kara against him so she couldn't see. "I'm afraid his unpleasant friends escaped."

"Don't worry, we'll find them. When we do, there are quite a few questions we'll be asking them."

The wind howled as they started up the hill, squinting against the rain. "I'm glad you got my message about the castle, Sinclair. It would have been suicide for you to try to go anywhere near it."

"Ah, now, there you're wrong, my lord." Sinclair looked at Nicholas Draycott, smiling broadly.

"What do you mean?"

"I mean, Lord Dunraven, that that explosion was one of *ours*. Set off a safe distance away, on the great lawn, I might add. That way Kyle assumed his nasty work was all done."

Duncan stared. "You mean, he didn't trigger his bombs? The castle—"

"—still stands, as strong and beautiful as ever," Nicholas broke in. "However," he added, "there's one essential chore yet to finish. Kyle's bombs are still timed to go off in just about an hour—unless we find and defuse them first."

"I can help with that." Kara looked at Duncan. "I know exactly where they are and how they're triggered."

Duncan reached for her hand and squeezed it

tightly. "You read it when you touched Kyle's watch."

She nodded, her eyes not wavering from his.

"What would I do without you?"

"And you can thank those three we left in the village," Sinclair added. "Your man Mctavish insisted on guiding us up here, even though he could barely walk, and those two young people were most courageous as well."

Something brushed Kara's foot, something soft and furry. "Duncan, did you feel a cat just now?"

"Cat? No, I don't think so."

The movement came at Kara's legs once again. She bent down, but felt only gravel and windblown sand. "I suppose I was mistaken."

"As soon as we deal with those bombs at the castle, we have a vehicle waiting to take you into the village." Sinclair motioned to a driver.

But Kara was staring at her skirt. "Duncan, shine that flashlight over here." As the light struck the damp wool, she gasped. "There. It's a clump of gray hair. *Cat* hair!"

Duncan lifted the pale strands, frowning. "More likely it's milkweed fiber, carried here from the mainland by the storm."

"But I felt a cat; I know it. Once beneath the arch by the castle and again on the boat."

"Lord Dunraven, the vehicle . . ."

"Forget the cat, Kara." Duncan dropped the wet strands and hauled her against him. "Let's go home."

"But Lord Dunraven, the vehicle is waiting to . . ." Sinclair frowned as he watched the two slip into a long and very passionate kiss. After a moment he shook his head. "Well, now, Draycott, I think we'd better set off by ourselves. Our bomb people can get things set up. It looks as if those two might be down here a few minutes longer . . ."

Epilogue ～

Beneath the thatched roof and behind the old blue shutters, darkness lapped around the edges of the small room. The light of a dying fire flickered over the oak floor, while the wind sighed and hissed, tossing rose petals against the mullioned windows.

Without a sound a figure separated from the shadows by the door. Black-clothed, features hidden by a black woolen cap, he moved with absolute stealth.

The woman in the bed lay unaware of the intrusion, her eyes closed in sleep. In one hand she clutched a golden coin.

The man's eyes narrowed as he picked up a magazine lying open on the bed. On its pages stood a man and woman wreathed in shadows, caught in an achingly erotic prelude to love.

He cursed softly.

Her cloud-soft peignoir slid through his gloved fingers. There was no expression in his eyes as he tugged the golden coin from her grip and dropped it into his pocket.

And then his hand slid toward her throat.

Her eyes flew open and she gasped. "Who—"

Black leather sealed her mouth. Some nameless emotion filled her eyes as he caught the coverlet and shoved it to the floor.

Her body was gold in the firelight, lush curves barely veiled by a fine silk chemise. Black leather eased over white silk. Her eyes went dark with surprise.

The silk slid lower, then went flying.

She bit down hard on the glove clamped over her mouth.

"Damn it, Kara, you *bit* me!"

"Of course I did, Duncan MacKinnon! Look at your wrist. You've *hurt* yourself."

The laird of Dunraven pulled the woolen cap from his head and stared down at his wrist, where blood lay drying over a jagged cut. He shrugged. "Apparently so."

"Twenty-four hours out of my sight, and you come back full of holes. What am I going to do with you?"

The Scotsman's eyes went dark. "I can think of quite a few possibilities right now, wife."

"Behave yourself, MacKinnon." Kara pulled a box of medical supplies from beneath the bed and began cleaning his wrist.

"Oh, bloody hell, I'll admit it. If *you* had been with me, I wouldn't have missed that last trip wire outside the outer gate. As it was, I barely managed to avoid breaking my leg when I jumped it."

Kara looked up, her face tense. "And you ended up cutting your hand in the process. I hope there weren't any other unexpected problems."

The wind hissed up the hill and rattled the shutters. "The expected ones were bad enough. First came the climb up a sheer cliff in complete darkness, then a silent trek past eight armed Royal Marine bodyguards. How I managed it with barely two weeks of preparation is beyond me. Thankfully, all the Corgis were safe in their quarters," Duncan said darkly. "I waited until one of the officers disguised as a gillie led them away, and then I went in. She was most impressed, by the way." He reached into his pocket and pulled out a beautiful filigree ring bearing a large E in ornate Celtic design. "She asked me to bring you this."

"It's beautiful, Duncan, but I couldn't possibly accept it."

"I'm afraid you'll have to, my sweet. No one *ever* says no to the Queen Mum." Duncan's lips quirked slightly. "I was very good, you see. None of the officers patrolling the grounds spotted me; nor did the patrol dogs. That, of course, is *exactly* what Sinclair had suspected, but he needed the proof to convince those cloth brains down in London to beef up security."

"So you really did it." Kara shook her head in awe. "You made your way inside the Queen Mother's summer residence."

Duncan dropped his rucksack onto the floor. "In fourteen minutes flat. There are going to be some very unhappy people in London tomorrow."

"I'm *very* impressed, MacKinnon." Kara finished bandaging his wrist, then sat back on the bed. "You're sure you're not hurt anywhere else?"

"Not a scratch. Everything went exactly as we'd planned. The Queen Mother said she wants to thank you personally for your assistance, by the way. Not that it can ever be publicly acknowledged."

Kara looked down at the filigree ring and smiled. "It's enough just to know. It will make a wonderful story to tell our children." Her hand opened gently over her stomach.

Duncan frowned. "No problems with the baby, are there?"

"I've never felt better. Nicholas's wife told me I'm a disgrace to my sex. She said I should be lying around demanding herbal tea and soda crackers, the way she was."

Duncan snorted. "You might be healthy as a horse, but I'm taking no chances with your safety until after the baby is born. Your only training climbs will be here in the castle, where I can watch you. And where *you* can watch *me*. The truth is, my love, you're the best training partner I've ever had."

"You've never *had* a training partner before."

"Only Kyle." Duncan's voice was very low.

"Duncan, are you—"

"It's done," he said firmly. "His ghost is finally

laid to rest, Kara, just as it should be. It's all your doing, *mo cridhe*."

Their hands met, fingers entwined. Duncan sighed and pulled her against him. As he studied the quiet room his gaze came to rest on a glass-and-mahogany cabinet of exquisite simplicity. "You had the case repaired?"

Kara nodded. "I asked an artist friend of Hidoshi to make a new design. The bow looks much better displayed upright, don't you think?"

"Absolutely. It looks almost Japanese, with a beautiful simplicity of line. I can almost feel the power of it from here."

For a moment Kara couldn't speak. "I . . . felt that too. They knew exactly what they were doing when they broke it, Duncan."

"Who did? And just how would you know—" Duncan's eyes narrowed. "I see. When you touched the bow that night with Kyle, you saw its past, didn't you?"

Kara nodded. "After their marriage, they wanted nothing more to do with fighting. They also knew that someday this bow would save the life of one of their descendants. I couldn't have escaped Kyle on the boat without it."

Duncan's hands curved over her silk-clad stomach. "And in doing so, the bow saved the life of our child."

Kara closed her eyes and nodded.

As Duncan looked around the room, he noticed a silk panel embroidered with English and Gaelic writing. "You've been busy, my love."

"Mrs. Mctavish helped me with the Gaelic. She said I have a very good ear." Kara frowned for a moment. "I've been thinking about that poem. I think I understand it now." She looked at the textile, softly reading the old phrases. "When summer and winter meet as one." Kara frowned, gnawing at her lower lip. "That one stumped me for a while, but now I have it."

Duncan sat back smiling, loving the sight of her mind at work. "Go on. Don't torture me."

"Summer refers to *me*."

"Hot?" her husband said huskily. "If so, your husband would be only too happy to do something about that."

Kara shot him a quelling look. "Kara Elizabeth *Summers* Fitzgerald. And winter is—"

"Me." Duncan studied her over steepled fingers. "Duncan Douglas *Wynters* MacKinnon," he said softly. "Bloody hell, I think you're onto something. What about the next line?"

Kara's eyes momentarily dimmed. She looked out the window, remembering a night filled with rain and fear, a night when she was certain she had lost this man she loved. "When Kyle shoved me outside, we walked beneath the rose capstone on the old arch and I heard a noise. It was the music of the phantom piper."

"Music fills the stone," Duncan mused. He gripped her fingers tightly. "Death came too bloody close for both of us that night. Without your help, Kyle would have won."

"You were meant to be the laird here," Kara said firmly. "Both your parents knew that. And on the day I arrived, the piper at Rose Cottage was announcing Kyle's death, not yours. He was actually the next laird."

Duncan slid a finger through his wife's copper hair. "What about broken becoming mended? The bow certainly isn't mended. Father always said it was left that way for a reason and should stay that way so long as a MacKinnon lives as laird at Dunraven."

Kara took a deep breath. "It was your family honor that was made whole that night. The scars Kyle left upon it were finally removed. He was the shadow on your family name. But at the end he was alone, with no friends, only enemies." An ember hissed and popped in the fire. "By the way, there *was* a woman involved in that ancient time, just as your father always said." Kara's eyes misted. "A very beautiful woman willing to give her life for the man she loved. Thank heavens, it wasn't necessary. Not that the sheriff knew that."

Duncan walked to the handmade cabinet, carefully lifted out the old bow, and carried it to the bed. "They must have been very special people."

Kara nodded, gently cupping the fine grained wood. Her eyes closed. "Before they came, this was Draycott land."

"Nicholas will never let me live this down!" Duncan's smile faded as he turned to Kara. "Kara?"

His wife's eyes were closed, her breathing steady. As she stroked the old bow, voices rose around her— old voices, gentle and rich with love.

Clear and high, a woman's voice rang through the abbey.

Villagers shivered and crossed themselves. William's men muttered as they studied the shadows. Only William did not move, his face hard with fury.

Again Arduaine's voice rang out, spilling beneath the high arches, through the crowded rows.

And the beggar who was truly Rowan de Beauclair raised his hand.

Two and twenty monks moved from the back of the church. Their eyes were filled with determination. And before them strode the abbot himself.

"Let the woman go, William," he ordered. "She is Lord Draycotte's own daughter. Do not desecrate the sanctity of this holy place in your lust for power."

William laughed wildly, his fingers tightening on his captive's arm. "But neither you nor anyone else can prove it, abbot." His blade played over the lady Arduaine's neck. "And if you make one move to free her, she will die by my hand."

Rowan strode up the aisle, the crowd parting in silence before him. "Her death will give you nothing, William. Release her."

His half brother's laughter was high and mocking. "Never. Tonight she will be mine. And then I will watch both of you hang, along with your friend." He gestured tightly. Hidden in an alcove, a bowman leveled his arrow and took final aim at Rowan's back.

Arduaine's face filled with terror. She wrenched to one side, feeling the sharp blade slide against her neck.

At the sight of her desperate movement, Rowan cried in fury and flung himself at his half brother.

And the lone arrow, whizzing through the incense-filled air found its mark in William's chest instead of Rowan's back. For a moment the two men stood in shocked silence. William's face was locked in ugly surprise as he looked down at the arrow that sent blood oozing over his fine silk tunic. "You've won, my brother. All is yours. For that—I curse you. May you remember this moment and how my blood covers your hand. May you carry the guilt of my death forever."

His eyes widened. His voice caught with a wet gurgle. And then he toppled forward into Rowan's arms.

Grimly, Rowan lifted William's body and carried him past the rows of pale, tense faces. Only when the dead man was settled on the marble steps, his eyes finally closed, did Rowan raise his eyes to the abbot, his old friend.

"It had to come to this, my son. The curse can not bind you—except as you allow its power to weigh against you. It was William's own evil that killed him."

Rowan bowed his head. "Perhaps. How can I ever know?"

Behind him came the stamp of feet and Rowan looked up into a leathery face, dark with years of campaigning under a desert sun. Into steely eyes that had known dangers to try a man's deepest soul.

Into the face of the lord of Draycotte.

Rowan fell to one knee. "My lord! But how—"

"With God's grace, de Beauclair. Only God's grace could have saved me. Truly, I have been well blessed." He turned and smiled at the woman who took his arm. "A daughter found. And soon a son acquired by her marriage. Yes, it is not often that a man finds such happiness in one day." He raised Rowan and nodded. "But tales of my adventures can wait. Call the abbot, so that prayers can be said for William's cursed soul." He caught Rowan's

hand and laid his daughter's atop it. "And after that I believe we have a wedding to plan."

Two weeks later, sunlight fell in golden waves through the high abbey windows. Amid the drifting incense a crowd of villagers pressed close, their laughter hanging in the air. Behind them moved a line of boys, well fed now, their faces clean and smiling.

The abbot of Draycotte nodded and turned to the lord of Draycotte beside him, who said, "By God's grace I have returned at a happy moment to find my lands restored, my abbey in good hands, and my daughter yet alive." His hard, wind-burned face surveyed the two people before him. His daughter, with bare feet and red roses in her hair, stood beside Rowan de Beauclair. "What say you, knight? I offer you my daughter's hand."

"Beggar, cripple, or knight, I would have your daughter in marriage, to cherish and protect," Rowan de Beauclair thundered.

Draycotte took his daughter's hand, and his features softened. "What say you, Arduaine?"

Her fingers trembled. She struggled with the words. "I agree. Beggar, cripple, or knight, Rowan de Beauclair will be my lord."

After a moment, Draycotte nodded. "Rowan de Beauclair, my loyal right arm, do you take my daughter, Arduaine of Draycotte, to be your wife, with your vow witnessed here in the eyes of God and church and your sovereign lord?"

The knight nodded, his eyes very dark. "I do this willingly, my liege."

"And you, my beloved daughter, returned to me at last by fate, do you take Rowan de Beauclair as your lord and love, with your vow witnessed in the eyes of God and church and your sovereign lord?"

Arduaine smiled, her eyes very bright. Slowly her lips curved. "I—"she swallowed, every nerve focused on her task—"do," she finished fiercely.

The villagers gasped and crossed themselves in response to this second miracle. Surely the defeat of the scurrilous, wolf-hearted sheriff was the first miracle, which would be *whispered through the town's streets and alleys for years to come. This healing would be the second.*

"Then so do I witness this holy bond. With the consent of our king, I charge you to love and honor and set not aside your vows in life."

"Neither in life nor in death," Rowan said softly.

The bow fell from his back. Behind him Huw's laughter rang out loudly as Rowan drew his wife into his arms. "Kiss her, Rowan. Now's no time for a great warrior like you to stand shy!"

They drew close. Rowan's hands slid into her hair and pulled her against his chest. "I love you. As the lady Arduaine or as Tamsyn. Until the very last breath I draw—and perhaps long after that."

The abbey rang with cheers as his lips came down over hers.

"Kara?"

Kara's eyes flickered open, and she slid back against Duncan's chest with a husky sigh. "They were very happy, Duncan. This old castle rang with their laughter."

"And the old verses? Were they theirs?"

"No, they came from the hand of the abbot, a man with a very rare gift of sight." She smiled unsteadily. "I'll tell you all about it some day, my love. But right now ..." Her hands eased over his chest and she saw him wince. "Not *another* wound!"

"Just a bruise," Duncan lied. His rib was burning where he had slammed into an iron rail while skirting an unexpected guard dog. The Queen Mother had wrapped up the wound herself, after he'd made his way successfully to her private sitting room.

But Duncan wasn't about to mention any of this to Kara. He had far more important things on his mind that night. "Lord and Lady Ashton sent a case of that fantastic new wine of theirs. They want our opinion, since this is a different style for them. They're going to name it for Draycott Abbey, I believe." Smiling, Duncan reached into his pocket. "And I found this for you in London." He held out a Roman coin on a golden chain, a perfect match to his own. "Now you can stop filching mine."

Kara slid the chain around her neck, smiling wistfully. "I like the feel of you around me when you're gone." Her eyes closed as the cool links played over her skin. "Duncan, you were thinking about me when you bought this. You were planning what you would do after you gave it to me. How we would—" Her cheeks filled with color.

"Correct, Lady Dunraven." He eased her back against the damask sheets. "And *this* is what I was planning."

"Duncan, I—" Kara's lips parted to meet his searching tongue.

Duncan groaned as her fingers tugged at his belt. In a moment, they were hungry, urgent, shoving clumsily at each other's clothing. His boots hit the floor with a *thump.*

"Hidoshi and Megan are coming to the cottage next week."

"Ummm."

Kara wrenched at the prong on his belt. "He has some wonderful ideas. He's going to do a book."

"Hummm."

"He already has the models picked out."

Duncan froze. "No, you don't, Fitzgerald."

"MacKinnon," his wife corrected. "Lady Dunraven."

"Either way, the answer's no. If Hidoshi has the faintest idea of getting me into another pair of silk pajamas, he's going to be bloody disappointed."

Kara's lips curved as she worked his pants down over his lean flanks. "Actually, he was thinking of using silk boxer shorts this time. Possibly something in a tartan design . . ." Her fingers closed around the hot length of him.

Duncan's breath hissed out in a hoarse groan of pleasure. "Much more of this and I'd probably agree to pose naked."

Kara cocked her head. "A thought. A definite thought. Except I refuse to share the sight of you with anyone else."

Duncan shoved the last button free on her chemise and sent it flying to the far wall, where it struck the glass cabinet and hung at a crazy slant. He stared in awe at his wife, whose lush breasts were gilded by the firelight. "God, you're beautiful." He frowned suddenly. "You're sure you're up to this? I mean, with the baby coming ..."

Kara laughed. "Not for another six months, you sweet idiot."

"A man can do a lot in six months," Duncan said darkly. "By the way, Geoffrey is now the laughing-stock of London. It seems he was tossed out of a royal garden party after brandishing a pass that turned out to be counterfeit."

Kara gasped. "Duncan, you didn't! It was only wishful thinking. I never dreamed you'd actually *do* it!"

"Actually, Nicholas did it. He and Lord Ashton arranged for a counterfeit pass to be substituted for Hampton's real one. They were on hand to see him being bodily removed from the event. It was most amusing, I understand. In fact, Kacey Draycott said that when the word gets out, Geoffrey won't be able to get a job selling ad space in supermarket circulars." He frowned. "What are supermarket circulars?"

"Never mind." Kara closed her eyes and fell back on the bed, laughing. "Poor Geoffrey. How his social aspirations must be dashed. I must ask Nicholas for all the gory details tomorrow. They arrived tonight just after dinner, and Genevieve has already claimed every corner of Dunraven as her own."

"A true Draycott, I see."

"She heard the piper, Duncan. Only at the castle, I might add."

Duncan smiled slowly. "So the youngest Draycott has a date with a MacKinnon, does she? What did the doctor in Edinburgh tell you about your test results?"

"Nothing," Kara said firmly. "I don't want to know anything except that our child is healthy." She frowned as her husband carefully placed a velvet box on her stomach. "What are you doing?"

"Giving you a gift. I'd planned to give you more, but I'm afraid they'd cover every inch of this castle."

As Kara opened the tissue-lined box, a smile touched her lips. "Duncan, it's lovely!" She held up a miniature grandfather clock, worked in diamonds and sapphires.

"To match the one you gave me."

"One?" Kara objected.

"Actually the dozen or two you've given me."

"And I'm certain there will be many more," Kara purred. Her eyes darkened as Duncan found her silken heat and made a slow, teasing penetration. "Sooner than you might imagine, Lord Dunraven . . ."

Duncan's eyes burned over the golden thighs and gentle curves spread beneath him. He felt love swell, filling him like warm mist on a highland hill. She had brought him so much, this woman.

Hope.

A future. Even an understanding of his past, now that the old shadows had finally been banished.

"I love you, Kara Elizabeth Summers Fitzgerald."

"MacKinnon," his wife corrected huskily, easing around him and taking him deep inside her. Then her body froze, for she saw the linen handkerchief drawn in a makeshift bandage atop his rib. "Duncan, you're hurt!"

His eyes were closed. "Sweet God, so I am."

"But you should have *told* me."

"I did tell you. I'm in *terrible* agony, lass. Death is definitely in store."

Her frown wobbled. She gasped as he moved powerfully inside her. "Duncan, you shouldn't. That is, we can't—" Her eyes closed as she rose to meet him, hands clenched on the damask coverlet. "Duncan, no, I—"

He moved. Deeply. Expertly.

Her soft, breathy cry filled the room.

Duncan smiled crookedly, his body tensed above

her. He whispered a phrase in Gaelic and kissed her forehead.

And then he drove home inside her while the wind hissed over the loch and the last glowing embers crackled in the grate.

Somewhere up the hill, where a rose lay carved against the weathered capstone on Dunraven's granite arch, the lilting strains of a phantom piper echoed through the night.

Author's Note ⁓

Dear Reader,

Men in kilts.

Big, brawny men in little skirts.

Remember Mel Gibson charging down the hill in *Braveheart*? Liam Neeson in *Rob Roy*?

Yes, there's definitely something about a man in a kilt. I hope you have enjoyed my own MacKinnon in a kilt. If you want to read more about Duncan's nineteenth-century ancestor, you'll find him in my Dell historicals *East of Forever*, *Come the Night*, and *Come the Dawn*. And if the descriptions of loch and highland sky intrigued you, you can find a wealth of additional information about these rugged, wave-swept isles. Two of my favorite books on Scotland are *Scottish Islands*, by Charlie Waite (London: Constable, 1989) and *Scottish Country*, by Charles Maclean and Christopher Simon Sykes (New York: Clarkson Potter, 1992).

To read more about the two hundred years of conflict that made up nine different crusades, you may enjoy *Chronicles of the Crusades*, edited by Elizabeth Hallam (New York: Weidenfeld and Nicolson, 1989), which records firsthand accounts translated from Armenian, Russian, Italian, French, and Persian. Great reading, fascinating times.

Like Kara, I was intrigued by the ancient Oriental theories of fêng shui. If you'd like to know more about energy patterns and room arragement, drop me a note, and I'll send you a newsletter from an expert practitioner who makes—yes, house calls!

Finally, if you would like to receive my next newsletter with current information about upcoming books set at magical Draycott Abbey, please send a self-addressed, stamped long envelope to me at:

111 East 14th Street, #277M
New York, New York 10003

I would love to hear from you and keep you up-to-date on all the happenings at the abbey!

Oh, yes, a final wish from Duncan. May you, too, hear the seals sing and find your own World's End.

With warmest wishes,

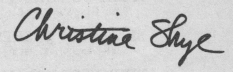

Christine Skye

Bestselling Author

CHRISTINA SKYE

"CHRISTINA SKYE IS SUPERB!"
Virginia Henley

BRIDE OF THE MIST
78278-2/$5.99US/$7.99Can
Urged by a psychic to visit England's Draycott Abbey,
magazine editor Kara Fitzgerald is thrown into a passionate
encounter with one Duncan McKinnon—an encounter laced
with fiery desire and ancient rivalry.

A KEY TO FOREVER
78280-4/$5.99US/$7.99Can

SEASON OF WISHES
78281-2/$5.99US/$7.99Can

BRIDGE OF DREAMS
77386-4/$5.99US/$7.99Can

HOUR OF THE ROSE
77385-6/$4.99US/$5.99Can